Nightscript

VOLUME FOUR

———◆———

EDITED BY C.M. Muller

CHTHONIC MATTER | St. Paul, Minnesota

NIGHTSCRIPT: *Volume Four*

Tales © 2018 by individual authors. All rights reserved.

FIRST EDITION

Cover: "Love and Pain, aka Vampire" (1893) by Edvard Munch

Additional proofreading by Chris Mashak

This anthology is a work of fiction. Any resemblance to actual events or persons, living or dead, is entirely coincidental.

Nightscript is published annually, during grand October.

CHTHONIC MATTER | St. Paul, Minnesota
www.chthonicmatter.wordpress.com

CONTENTS

Sugar Daddy | *V.H. Leslie* | 1

There Has Never Been Anyone Here | *J.T. Glover* | 6

The Thing in the Trees | *Joanna Parypinski* | 20

By the Sea | *Steve Rasnic Tem* | 29

A Harvest Fit for Monsters | *L.S. Johnson* | 35

The Monkey Coat | *Daniel Braum* | 47

Seams | *M. Lopes da Silva* | 61

A Gut Full of Coal | *Mathew Allan Garcia* | 78

Crow Woman | *April Steenburgh* | 90

The Dandelion Disorder | *Charles Wilkinson* | 99

Of Marble and Mud | *Farah Rose Smith* | 109

All Is There Already, Just Not Seen Yet | *Armel Dagorn* | 117

Half-Girls | *Cate Gardner* | 130

A Different Sunlight | *Jackson Kuhl* | 141

Cinnamon to Taste | *Christi Nogle* | 148

The Strigoaica | *Ross Smeltzer* | 160

Swim Failure | *Jennifer Loring* | 175

Visions of the Autumn Country | *Tim Jeffreys* | 182

Stella Maris | *Elana Gomel* | 194

Rainheads | *Mike Weitz* | 208

My House Is Out Where the Lights End | *Kirsty Logan* | 219

Preface

———◆———

WELCOME TO THE newest installment of what one reviewer recently called "an annual highlight of the genre." Sentiments such as this keep the enterprise afloat, amplify the passion I've always held for this book of strange wonders and the genre through which it was conceived.

Another highlight is in discovering new talent, and I am honored and delighted to include a "first" within this edition. Those wishing to rebel against the established ToC are encouraged to do so. Your entry-point: page 208.

While it's gratifying to publish new fiction from seasoned veterans, I'd like to continue the trend of profiling the work of those just beginning their journey. That said, I'd like to encourage newcomers to submit their tales during my next reading period, which opens this January.

I think you'll be well-pleased with Volume IV, and if you are, I'd like to ask a favor: spread the word, share the physical or e-edition of this anthology with friends and loved ones, and if their enthusiasm is aligned with your own, encourage them to repeat the process.

Finally, and as always, thank you to the Nth degree for including *Nightscript* in your reading queue. May your October be strange, darksome, and grand.

C.M. MULLER

Sugar Daddy

V. H. Leslie

———•———

AMIRA'S FATHER HAS arranged a neat spread on the coffee table. Her new boyfriend sits at her side, helping himself to a scone and topping it with dollops of her father's homemade jam. He has made this conciliatory effort, this modest banquet in goodwill, though he has already decided to hate David. She knew it would never be easy, bringing home a man who is only a few years shy of her father's age. There is something unsettling about a disparity in age, something that for some people is hard to stomach. Amira's father offers David a salmon sandwich and she can feel him chewing over the situation as he pours tea for everyone.

To the untrained eye, it is a simple fare, sandwiches and scones, cakes and cream, but she knows that this seemingly humble endeavor has probably taken her father days of planning and preparation. For one thing, the ingredients would all be locally sourced, the scones and cakes baked by her father's hand that morning. But the icing on the cake—so to speak—is her father's homemade jam. Jam-makers, she knows from experience, are a curious breed, the alchemists of the culinary world, and her father, after many years of practice and experimentation, is unsurpassable.

Perhaps it was her mother's early death that forced him into the kitchen, obliged to fill the domestic void she left. Amira has a vague recollection of her mother's improvised meals, the hotchpotch of flavors and spices she'd lump together: fenugreek, cardamom, turmeric. She didn't believe in lists and instructions. Whereas her father's cooking is based on exactitude and order, the kitchen more like a laboratory, filled with fancy gadgets and gizmos. Now Amira's father occupies what was once her mother's space and her mother is consigned to the living room, her urn perched high on the mantelpiece. Watching proceedings.

Would she have liked David? He isn't much to look at. Overweight, with crumbs on his shirtfront. But he has skipped lunch to be here, persevering with the dainty crockery that's too precarious in his big hands. And he isn't wolfing it all down, but weighing up whether to have another scone, whether to risk eating more under the scrutiny of her father. Amira wonders if her father has engineered it this way, to make it difficult for David, the low coffee table, the finger food. But afternoon tea is the logical choice for an encounter like this, a midway point between lunch and dinner, far less formal than a sit-down meal, though not without ritual. Amira herself is on middle ground, seated between these two men, her loyalty divided like the scone in front of her, cleft into two equal parts.

Amira hears the key in the front door and realizes with dismay that her sister Zahra is home. She hoped David would've escaped meeting the whole family in this one encounter.

"Well, what's this?" Zahra asks, eyeing the feast and David in one glance.

"This is David."

"David," she repeats, perching on an armrest. She reaches for a slice of almond cake, refusing the napkin her father offers. He withdraws to the kitchen, shaking his head.

"Cook much?" she asks with her mouth full.

"We prefer eating out," David replies. He does this a lot, speaking on behalf of them both.

"Don't say that in front of the Old Man," Zahra says, taking another bite, and Amira hopes David accepts it as an affectionate term for her father rather than a reference to his age, and by extension, David's own age. But in her father's absence David is happily loading another scone with cream.

"So, what's in it anyway?" Zahra asks holding up the jar.

"Pomegranate I think."

"And?"

Zahra is right of course. Her father passed the point of making perfect pomegranate jam years ago. Where do pioneering men like her father go after mastering a recipe, why, they push forward. What secret ingredient did this innocuous jar contain, what special process had been used to turn this seemingly regular jam into something extraordinary?

Zahra sniffs the jar and tentatively dips in her spoon.

"It tastes fine to me," David asserts, though Amira doubts his palate is refined enough to appreciate the subtleties within.

Some of her earliest memories are of her father making jam, wearing her mother's floral apron while stirring various bubbling concoctions, all the while waxing lyrical on the protean qualities of sugar. He'd talk her through the stages of boiling, drawing thread-like particles from the pan, the slivers enmeshing the spoon like a sticky nest. She'd watch him line the counter with sterilized jars, administering the sugar thermometer to the boiling pot with the same care he used when looking after her and Zahra when they had a fever. How she'd love to watch those bright mixtures strain through the muslin into the depths of the jars. The lucent gleam of their promised delights through the glass.

Once Amira and Zahra found a recipe for Nostradamus' love jam among their father's books. It is no surprise to her now that this notorious forward thinker—quite literally—was an avid jam-maker. Like her father, he marveled at the preservative virtues of sugar, which must have seemed to belong to the realms of magic all those years ago. She remembers abandoning the recipe when it called for the blood of seven male sparrows, though she and Zahra ran out into the garden anyway, to declare war on the birds, chasing them up into the air.

Her father returns from the kitchen with an extra cup and proceeds to pour Zahra tea.

"Lovely jam," David says, holding up the scone as if making a toast, "so what's your secret?"

Now Amira's father smiles; having sweetened David up, she realizes he has been waiting to answer this question all afternoon.

"Ambrosia," he whispers.

Zahra laughs, and David looks at Amira uncertainly.

"I'm quite in earnest," he continues. "After all these years, I've finally managed to make an anti-aging jam."

David doesn't have much of a sense of humor at the best of times. He places the half-eaten scone down and sits upright. "If this is about the age difference," he begins.

"Well, quite," Amira's father replies. He sips his tea with a satisfied grin. "You don't need to thank me. I've engineered it so that if you eat a spoonful of my jam each day, you will stay at this age forever. Perfectly preserved."

David looks at Amira again and back at her father. Then he slaps his knee and lets out a bellowing laugh.

"I'm being perfectly truthful," Amira's father continues, "in twenty years you'll be an old man, who knows how incapacitated or decrepit, and who will look after my daughter then?"

David stops laughing. "Listen, I'm trying to take this in good humor but…"

"But what?"

Amira notices Zahra smiling. Her father is prone to such eccentricities. Once when she'd brought a boyfriend home, his showstopper was octopus in aspic. It was a beastly specimen, a veritable kraken, floating within the savory jelly, its tentacles defying gravity.

The boyfriend never returned. It must be some kind of protective impulse, the use of these scare tactics. Her father's concoctions are designed to test a man's mettle and at the same time to protect his children from getting hurt. It is as if she and Zahra are preserved in aspic still, encased in a gelatinous bubble of their father's love.

"This is ridiculous," David says standing.

Amira can see how David would think so. But another part of her wonders if her father has actually managed to accomplish it. If Nostradamus, that great seer, who was able to forecast so much, believed in the power of jam, why shouldn't she? Made with the right ingredients, in the right way, he claimed that jam had the power to induce love and passion, to cure the plague. Who could say it couldn't stop the aging effects of time?

And if the elixir of life, the nectar of immortality was going to take any form, it is right that it should be jam. For what other substance enhances the sweetness of things and has such a long shelf life?

Amira eyes the jar cautiously, her father's panacea to be consumed on crumpets and toast. To restore the natural order David has upset.

"We won't stand for it," David continues, speaking for Amira again. "I love your daughter and I'm not going anywhere."

And suddenly Amira sees that this is true. David, who has jam at the corner of his lips, leading his simple, sedentary life, is already sealed in a glass jar. He doesn't need a spoonful of sugar each day; his character is already fixed, rigid as if he were set in jelly.

Whilst Amira is still growing, changing, becoming who she is meant to be.

"You should patent this," Zahra interrupts, spreading the jam generously over a scone. "Much easier than bathing in the blood of virgins, eh?"

No one says anything for a while. Then her father walks slowly to the mantelpiece.

"Cinnabar, jade, hematite, gold," he says, lightly touching her mother's urn. "Many ancient alchemists experimented with making life-prolonging potions. They thought these precious substances might somehow bestow their properties of longevity on those ingesting them. But my secret ingredient is closer to home."

Amira picks up the jar, looking for the tincture of vermilion, a dusting of gold but there is no trace. Part of her doesn't want to know what is in the jam. Forbidden knowledge always demands too high a price.

"What if you eat too much?" Zahra asks.

"I wouldn't do that," her father replies. "Theoretically, you would age backwards."

"Backwards?"

"You would grow younger."

Amira can sense this has David's attention as he sets his plate down. Perhaps he isn't immune to the temptation of going back to his prime. Amira can't imagine David ever having a heyday, though it rankles her that he would favor the past—his younger self—than the man he is now, with her at his side.

As for Amira, how far back would she go? How much pomegranate jam would she need to eat to be a girl of twelve again, to exist in that time before aspic and jam and death. When the house smelt of cinnamon and rose, their suburban English life spiced with her mother's exoticism. Could her father make enough for Amira to see her again?

She lets David take the jar out of her hand. He holds it to the light.

"Why don't you take that one," her father says. "I made a big batch."

David looks at Amira then screws the lid hesitantly in place. He stands up, beckoning her to follow. We are leaving now, is what she hears in her head, but she doesn't move.

Because she can feel herself surrounded by an invisible glutinous mass, a gummy weight around her feet and arms, a sticky, unbreakable bond David could never compete with.

She watches David pocket the jam and leave her behind.

Her father smiles as he pours himself another cup of tea whilst Zahra licks the jam from her fingers. And Amira can see her mother in her mind's eye, somewhere far away, whilst her urn, she imagines, overflows with pomegranate seeds.

There Has Never Been Anyone Here

J. T. Glover

———•———

[First posted April 26, 2018 to ListRVA, a Central Virginia classifieds site, not unlike Craigslist or WeiPoint Market, but with social media functionality. Revised July 28, 2018.]

$169960 / 3br - 1490ft^2 - **PRICE REDUCED** Motivated Seller! (Richmond, VA)

CHARMING and Well-Maintained Cape Cod w/ DETACHED GARAGE is a 1936 Chestnut Hill-Plateau MUST SEE. Beautiful 0.23 acre lot is landscaped, with mature oaks (treehouse-sized!). Classic Kitchen w/ New Upgrades & Appliances, Family Room (with retro SHAG) and Living Room, 4BR, 1.5 Baths. Some HARDWOOD FLOORS. Patio. Garden shed, 2-YEAR-OLD roof, virtually Pristine Siding on this piece of Richmond history. A catch at original list price, & a Northside STEAL now! Owner relocating, MUST SELL.

• seller does NOT wish to be contacted for services, offers, or opportunities

LRVID: 4.26.16.462   listed: three months ago   share online

July 30, 2018

The ropes vanish between sheetrock and cobwebbed studs, stretched from somewhere to someplace. Francesca can't see either end from where she crouches, peering into the spider-crusted dormer access space at the back of the closet where she once hung her letterman's jacket. Taut after however many years behind these walls, the ropes' bundled expanse makes her think of the synapses of a psychotic the night before the shopping mall, dreaming of screams and gun oil. She wipes sweat from her face, reaches out to run one finger along something that feels too sinewy and sticky for rope.

"How long's it been here?" she says.

Gray-green dust rises in the wake of her finger's passage. Up on the sweltering second floor of the old Cape Cod, her head already feels swimmy, and Francesca can practically see ripples radiating inward from the slanted ceiling. She blames the heat for the idea that the dust coalesces into something, a writhing mass that twitches and stretches toward her before it dissipates.

In the middle of the summer, she's decided that she can't take what the house is doing to her head during these marathon cleanup sessions. Just being inside is torment, to say nothing of the second floor—fans or no, window A/C or no. 10:00 a.m., and already she wants a Bud tall boy. No Arrogant Bastard or Pyramid—just ice-cold and watery, with the faintest bitter aftertaste.

"Fucking bullshit. So tired of this."

A woman's voice from somewhere over her shoulder, shrieking incomprehensible rage. It's loud as a tractor-trailer bearing down on a toddler, shaking the walls. Francesca's back spasms, even as she ducks her head. Her heart throbs, like being squeezed by a massive fist.

She turns to look, and—of course—no one is there. Not a blessed soul in her gently decaying former home, robbed since her mother's death of the good cheer that used to well from every board. Mama's bright, resolute joy always kept whatever else lives here at bay. Now the cat face doilies are just lace, the cross on the wall in the spare bedroom is no more than felted yarn and sticks, askew with no one left to straighten it every day.

"There—is—no—one—here," Francesca says, tapping her foot rhythmically.

No response.

She stands up, knees popping, and walks toward the stairs. The voice comes from the closet this time, now quiet as leaves riffled by a gentle breeze, but broken by something like static:

"There has never been anyone here. Not even you."

FIELD INTERVIEW 17
DATE: January 20, 2029
INTERVIEWEE: KIMBERLY WOODHALL
INTERVIEWER: JACOB SANTOS-RUIZ
PLACE: Woodhall residence, Phoenix, AZ
File 1 of 2

SR: Mrs. Woodhall, you said you moved to Arizona back in... 2019. But that wasn't when you left Richmond?

W: No.

SR: What caused you to leave?

W: It was time. What came out later, or, I guess, what didn't — nobody heard all of that. We compared notes with a few neighbors when things started to get weird, but nobody connected any dots, not really. After a while, we didn't know who was safe to talk to.

SR: The *Times-Dispatch* had some articles about gas leaks, a train derailment...

W: Young man, do you mind if I smoke? You really can't in public anymore, but I still hate to impose, even in my own house.

SR: No problem. My grandfather smokes all the time.

W: Gracias. [snap of a lighter] It was hard to know what was happening. When things started going haywire, I'd sometimes read things in the RTD or *Style Weekly*, and it wasn't. *Gas leak.* Ha ha. Ha ha ha. [pause] Look, you're — you're writing about this in grad school. Dan asked me once if I thought it was God. That was after the thing with the boys. They were sitting playing with their phones in the back yard. I told you before, but I'm telling you again: eyes *rolling*, nosebleed *at the same time*, and what came out of their mouths was — nothing. It was just this empty roaring. Like what you used to get between radio stations.

SR: It's OK. We don't have to cover that again. I'm wondering if you remember exactly what made you decide to move.

W: [silence]

SR: Mrs. Woodhall?

W: I'm thinking. The business with the kids had happened,

and that was almost enough. I mean, we went to the E.R.? What a joke. We think our kids are dying, I'm sobbing, we're worried about some fucking poison or gas, and that doctor — right out of med school, barely looked *twenty* — she tells us the kids got overheated. It wasn't just medical. No way in Hell. And I'd started to hear, well, sounds in the bushes. We didn't move fast enough, though. Whoever could do... Frodo took off one night when we let him out to do his business, and he never came back. My husband found his ears hanging from the doorknob one morning. They were strung together on a shoelace.

SR: [silence]

W: I can see that you don't get it. Don't worry, whoever listens to this will know you're doing a good job. It's really — you're too young to understand how hard it is. To abandon a place you've made for yourself. Just up and leave.

SR: Mrs. Woodhall, my parents brought us to the U.S. from Juárez right after I was born. They left with me and my sisters the same day my tía's corpse was found on a trash pile. The same day. Everyone knew what was happening in Juárez at the time. There were so many feminicidos, and I had three sisters, but still my parents didn't want to leave.

W: I'm so sorry. I didn't —

SR: It's okay, it's okay. [deep breath] Can you tell me more about what happened?

W: I couldn't sleep. It was the third night of a power outage. So humid. I don't miss that. We always put off getting a generator, so the windows were open. No one was living at the Kendall place just then, as far as I knew. I saw something, though. It was a full moon, and that house shone like black neon. Their siding was almost new, a light tan, and somehow it was the darkest thing I'd ever seen.

SR: It had changed colors?

W: I don't know. I thought maybe I was dreaming. Next morning it looked like normal. My fingers hurt, though, and I found a bunch of splinters in them. I examined the windowsill in our bedroom, and there were gouges where I'd gripped the frame. Gouges. We left the next day to stay with my sister in Baltimore, and a year later we were rolling up to a townhouse in Chandler.

SR: Some of your neighbors have talked about mass hysteria.

W: [laughter] Why am I not surprised. Did you talk to Mary? Mary Byrne?

SR: The anonymity clause...

W: Of course, of course. She's the only one I remember saying anything close to that is all. I wonder what happened to her. Sure, it could have been mass hysteria. I don't know. Can you have mass hysteria and mass hypnosis at the same time? I was completely freaked out at the time, but now it's just...something that happened.

SR: I've talked with Francesca Kendall. She doesn't think —

[Thumping sound. Recording stops, then clicks back on.]

SR: Let's talk about Baltimore. Why didn't you stay?

W: At first things were fine. The kids were OK? It was — I started checking the news. A lot. I took some drives down to see the old house. I'd park and just look at it, and I'd tell Dan and the kids that I'd been visiting Jenny from high school, in Harrisburg. Then one night Dan was helping Carter with a social studies report, and he stumbled into the "Research" folder on my desktop, thinking it was stuff for the kids. It was my file of weird photos and news stories out of RVA. *Weekly World News*-level stuff, if that means anything to you. We talked and decided it was time for a clean break. It had to be somewhere new. Somewhere with less history.

[Manuscripts Division, Colonial Virginia Research Center. "Letter to Jeremiah Williamson by Unknown Author" CVRC Digital Collections. Accessed September 1, 2028. http://collections.cvrctr.org/items/b3ex5a43-3qfbd-z913-o994-o001488274521]

> Virginia, June 17th, 1745
> To Jeremiah Williamson, Esq'r:
>
> SR:
>
> The enclosed Letter is for your eyes alone, God as my witness. I shall send it under the name of Temple, in the care of Capt. James Allingham of Boston. In these last years

I have oft undertaken commerce with him in what is now Richmond, and he is a man of no little Honor. Even with such secrecy, I am mindful of the need for Circumspection.

My dearest Mary is in Mortal Dread, for which I can offer her no reproach. I pretend that I can face this Threat with equanimity, but at heart I am afraid. The Disturbances I told you of last year have not dissipated. I did not say then what I say now: that our grandfathers would have blamed Witches or the Devil himself. Not a fortnight gone, I saw a Well of Shadow swallow a great oak in the woods of Henrico, not far from the place we have inhabited. The night brings voices not from the forest, but from so close as to surround our very ears. At first we feared rogue Iroquois, spurred east, perhaps, by the conflict that late inflamed the Shenandoah, but I have come to susp

[Text ends. Charring at the bottom, plus singeing over whole leaf suggest this may have been removed from a fire. Given by an anonymous donor, who stated that she found it in an armoire acquired at auction in Richmond in 1993.]

```
FIELD INTERVIEW 15
DATE: November 6, 2028
INTERVIEWEE: FRANCESCA KENDALL
INTERVIEWER: JACOB SANTOS-RUIZ
PLACE: Dominion Health Retreat, Staunton, VA
File 3 of 4

SR: Francesca, do you remember what you were wearing on
August 15, 2018?

K: You fucking kidding me? Do you remember what you were
wearing ten years ago?

SR: No. But that date didn't matter to me at the time.

K: [laughter]

SR: Is that funny?

K: It was just the end, my friend, the end of the world.
That's all.

SR: Do you believe the world has ended?
```

K: Bring me some Chick-fil-A next time and I'll believe anything you want.

SR: Last week you mentioned the disappearances. Do you trace them to your mother's house?

K: I trace. I grace a lace, ace.

SR: [silence]

K: I don't remember much about that night. It was scorching hot, so I was probably wearing a tank top and shorts. Sneakers.

SR: The one picture that I can find of you from that night, you're wearing a yellow house dress, covered with dirt and soot.

K: Isn't that funny.

SR: I don't th—

K: Look, it's not an accident I don't usually talk with people. My memory's shit — I'm genetically predisposed to dementia, which you probably already know. I'm only talking to you because I haven't had a visitor in a long time. Most of that night...it's like anyone's memory of an average day. I mean, obviously it wasn't, but.

SR: Do you know what happened to the property?

K: Not after the city eminent domained it. Haven't been back to Richmond in a long time, either. I've been locked up. In a "committed" relationship with Dr. Greene, ha ha.

SR: The building was really damaged —

K: Right, the fire.

SR: — and eventually they had to demo it. Something was wrong with the foundation, too, apparently, but I haven't been able to figure out what. The sinkholes on your block got so bad in the autumn of 2018 that people started to leave. Eight years ago the city closed the roads and fenced off five whole blocks. A lot of real estate, but they haven't done anything about it since then.

K: [whispering] Not sinkholes. Tunnel-wounds, fennel-boons.

SR: Made by?

K: [silence, followed by snuffling]

SR: Are you saying that something lived underneath your mother's house?

K: [silence]

SR: Okay, let's see here. Ah, do you blame...these things for what happened that day you were accidentally released? When they mixed you up with another patient?

K: What they do. I don't think it's intentional. It's like a tide. They wash in, part of you washes out. It doesn't come back.

SR: Do you feel that someone was controlling you that night?

K: I'm saying I didn't wave a wand and make the fucking staff at Taco Bell swallow their tongues. That day at the house, I didn't tell Mr. Itoh from across the street to come over and scoop his eyes out onto my mother's lawn! Put that in your fucking dissertation.

SR: So you don't accept any blame in —

K: If you want to blame anything, go jump the fence. Stay overnight where the house used to be. See what happens. You'll learn *real* fast.

SR: Okay, Francesca, I didn't mean to upset you. I can come back tom —

K: See what happens, see what you learn. Learn. Spurn. Churn-burn. Burned. Burrrrned. It burned. Burned. BURNED —

[From the Richmond Times-Dispatch, *p.9, May 15, 1919]*

HOUSE BURNS

Catastrophic Fire Destroys Chestnut Hill House Belonging to R. M. Benton

A beautiful Queen Anne house, the property of R. M. Benton, junior partner of Stratford, Benton, and Benton, was in the early hours of Tuesday morning destroyed by fire on Fourth

Avenue, a short distance from Hornbeam Street. Witnesses heard screams and observed the escape of Mr. and Mrs. Benton and their daughters from the fast-moving flames. The fire was extinguished after some hours by firemen from Engine Company No. 5.

Investigation the next morning by a mounted policeman uncovered no accounts by witnesses of suspicious persons in the area. One very aged resident of the neighborhood did recall another house that burned in the same place some seventy years gone. Evidence from within the wreckage, much damaged, suggests that the origin of the blaze may have been inside the building, as the base of the coal chute appeared much battered. Investigators have no suspects at this time, but are seeking further information from the Bentons, who have decamped to Raleigh, North Carolina, where Mrs. Benton's brother owns a dry good company.

August 15, 2018

The copper pipes run through the basement like they always have, the dull gleam visible through the grime if Francesca holds the flashlight just right. Apparently at some point since she left for college, her mother also cleaned out the liquor boxes that she remembers piled higgledy-piggledy from childhood. That much is still about the same.

Francesca walks over to a wall, runs one finger across the failing concrete. The cracking is bad. Looking at the variations in color, it seems likely that some of that's repairable, merely cosmetic.

The rest of it, baby, that's foundation. How much is that going to cost? Well, would it cost, if...

Would. So much implied down in the sweltering hole in the ground. It's quiet outside for a Monday afternoon, and not even a passing garbage truck interrupts the fall of dust. The *would*, that hypothetical-flavored bit, is on full display. The cracks in the walls are repeated on the floor, including something more like a crevasse than a crack. It stretches from the street side of the house to the opposite corner and widening at the middle, as if to accommodate the tendrils that run from it to the walls and up into the darkness, like a living spider web.

Francesca looks at the ropes, wonders if that's what you call these woven tendrils that grow and ooze, that rise from the earth like the roots of great plants whose leaves are subterranean nets that bind soil and rock. This is the part of the house she put off until last, dreading it since she looked into the access space up in the closet. Left the house on the market (for all the good *that* did), avoided the cracked door next to the stove, yellowed by years of greasy smoke, hoping somehow to avoid the slow, creaking walk into the earth.

"This is not your place," someone whispers from the far corner of the basement, where the shadows are too thick for daytime.

A digging in her chest, the second cousin of pain. Francesca barely jumps. She's been wondering about her heart, her blood pressure. She took off the Fitbit long ago, certain that its readings could not be accurate, not wanting to know if they were. And then—

Francesca's cheek is numb.

She sees stars, bouncing flashes.

Grit from the basement floor is digging into her cheek. The last time she remembers this upside-down flipping, this loss of breath, she was eighteen on a soccer field. Something has knocked her flat, and at three in the afternoon, the basement is darkening as if a storm is coming.

A sound like a sheet hung to dry caught in the wind, and she raises her head to look. Something slips from the crack and coils like a squid's tentacle, and she is the half-cracked vessel on the woodcut sea. Figures cluster now at the other end of the basement, silhouetted against the last light trickling in from the ground-level windows. The thing coiled in mid-air whips toward her, enwraps her ankle, and its rough and thorny protrusions puncture her skin.

The scream that rips out of her is a throat-shredding apocalypse. Surely she cannot make this much sound. Surely a jet engine is rushing toward her house. The pain fills up the world, but still she sees silhouetted mouths opening and closing. They are the crackle of a dying radio transmitting from a place where there is no meaning, and they cry nothing at her.

Body convulsing, Francesca flings her hand out, hard enough to crack her knuckles against the concrete. For an even-more-miserable moment, she wonders if she's shattered her own hand before she starts scrabbling for something—anything. The tendril rope tightens and caterpillars up her calf, clenching as it goes, cold and greasy like a worm right before the winter freeze.

Her fingers brush against splintered old wood. She wraps her hand tightly around it, swings toward the tendril. Her salvation is a rusted hoe that she uses to beat something impossible that has enwrapped her leg. Even as she swings the hoe, she's thinking gas cans, matches, purification.

Roaring all around her, and now Francesca's coughing out gouts of laughter. The rope around her leg is loosening at last. The laughs are starting to sound like something else. The tendrils along the walls are shaking.

They're laughing.
They are laughing back at me.

The Woods Are Lovely Dark and Deep

23:10 24 MARCH 2029 / ANTHROGRADMAN / LEAVE A COMMENT

Time to put up or shut up, my friends. I've scoured archives for The Great Project. I did legwork in Arizona, Georgia, Maryland, and here in Virginia. My advisor thinks that I've got enough, and he knows what he's talking about, but he's been at BigStateUniversity forever. Getting a job is not something he has to worry about.

We all wtf the system, and the NAAUP something something academic freedom...but I still want tenure, you hijoputas. If I want a shot, I've got to be rigorous and community-engaged, and without a book/media deal...well, I have to have something camera-ready if a network comes sniffing around.

For obvious reasons, I haven't talked details, but I've been looking at what appears to be a very long-lived haunting. The first time I heard about it? Complete accident, reading letters for a colonial U.S. history class. Since then, I've uncovered evidence that suggests—maybe, possibly—this story has *never* been collected. Not one article, no mention in any collection of tales, barely anything online. Residents in the area have done all kinds of things to propitiate or banish the presence(s), but people think it's still hanging around. You're going to hear "oral tradition" and laugh, but I think there's a chance. Occasionally things have bubbled into the media, but nobody's made the link.

The last couple days I've been putting together lists for my site visit. The obvious stuff: recorders, tablet, a real camera. I'm also taking ropes, pitons, and light sticks. (In a cavern, in a canyon, excavaaaaating for a Ph.D.) No holy water or stakes, but I'm going to be honest: it's unnerving how consistent eyewitness accounts have been about the behavior and appearance of the supposed presences. The last few weeks I've been sitting awake late, wondering what I'll find. So, you know, a solid pair of running shoes is *definitely* on the list.

Before I hit the road, gotta holler for mi pareja, MIGUELBB82015. Every post I write that you, my comrades and loyal readers, wait anxiously to read—they're written while he waits, supporting my profitable, profitable dream by working at LargeFinancialCorporation. Gracias, Miguel, te amo.

TAGS: fieldwork, tenure, gradschool, ghosts, spooky, ghosthunting, spouselove

1 LIKE / 3 ACADWRITING SHARES

POSTS FROM ANTHROGRADMAN YOU MIGHT ALSO ENJOY

Fieldwork for the Absolute Novice, or, I'm Not an Impostor, You Are!

Spirit-Hunters and Tarot-Readers: Postmortem of a Seminar Disaster

Mid-Atlantic Ghosts and Where to Find Them

8 COMMENTS

ETHNOGRAPHOMATIC 07:10 25 MARCH 2029
Good luck, buddy. And don't be afraid of no ghosts!

PINGBACK: Anthrogradman's big adventure / 09:02 25 MARCH 2029 / ethnographomatic.acadwritinglab.net

ANTHROGRADMAN 11:06 25 MARCH 2029
Thanks, man! On site soon, and armed with some *fierce* comebacks if I get any ghost-lip.

SONIASTUDIESSIRENS 18:10 25 MARCH 2029
Hey, anthrogradman! Que pasa? Inquiring minds want to know. Wish you were streaming!

SONIASTUDIESSIRENS 12:01 26 MARCH 2029
What up, buddy?

ETHNOGRAPHOMATIC 09:45 28 MARCH 2029
Hey man, I texted and mailed. People are getting worried. Holler at someone!

PINGBACK: Have You Seen Jacob Santos-Ruiz? / 09:02 16 APRIL 2029 / soniastudiessirens.acadwritinglab.net

PINGBACK: Student Researcher Missing / 01:02 27 APRIL 2029 / richmond.com

November 15, 1979
  Sunlight streams into Francesca's bedroom as Flopsy, Mopsy, and Cottontail dance merrily on the walls, happy like bunnies should be. Mama's arms are warm around her as she reads about Peter and Mr. McGregor. Francesca alternates between looking at her sweet friends and at the trees outside her window, waving in the wind. She remembers dimly when Mr. McGregor scared her, back when she was just a *baby*, but now she knows that Peter will escape, and so she watches leaves and branches flap and flutter.
  "...bread and milk and blackberries for supper. And there you are, darling."
  She turns from the window and looks up at her mother, who smiles indulgently at her. The soft, red-haired woman with the starring role in her

world is late "putting on her face" today, and Francesca thinks she looks tired. There are dark pockets under her eyes, like grocery bags.

"I love you, Mama."

"I love you, too, sweet pea. Are we ready to make dinner yet?"

"No!" Francesca says, hurling herself backward, head thumping into the pillow as she kicks her feet.

Her mother laughs and darts her fingers up and down Francesca's sides, and soon they're both laughing and rolling around on the bed. Thoughts of anything are far away, except for maybe a PB&J, until a creaking sound rises to slice through their giggles. Francesca looks up and sees that the closet door has swung open.

"Wow, baby," her mother says, "that's a little louder than usual."

"Uh-huh. Mostly when they push it open, it's slow and quiet."

Her mother looks down at her, watchfulness replacing laughter in her face.

"Sweet pea, you know I don't like it when you talk like that."

"Mama, the monsters are in there!"

"There *are* no monsters, darling. How often has Daddy come in here and shown you the closet, with the light on? And it's empty every time."

Francesca frowns and sits up, looking into the dim gulf, where her dresses and pants hang.

You're just a closet today. That's all you are.

"People tell stories about monsters, but they're make-believe."

Francesca looks up and sees the lines in Mama's face. They are like the not-enough-money lines, or the why-isn't-Daddy-home-yet lines, but deeper.

"Mama, is our house haunted? Like on *Scooby*?"

Her mother laughs, but somehow the sound makes Francesca feel no better. It's not a rib-counting laugh, not a silly story laugh.

The furnace comes on, and warm air starts to circulate around the room. It sends mobiles twirling and the edges of the sheets fluttering. The closet door stays right where it is.

"Mama, why do you always tell me to hush about the monsters?"

Her mother's face is drawn as she looks to the window, the ruddy light turning her to flat bits, rounded bits, corded bits. She says nothing. Francesca starts to wonder if she heard her.

"Sweet pea," she says at last, "I tell you to hush because we all face monsters. You're afraid of goblins, I'm afraid of bills. We all have to fight them, eventually, if they don't leave us alone, but usually they do."

"Sometimes they aren't goblins, Mama," she says softly. "Sometimes they're people, like the ones in the closet. They look like people in books from old times."

Mama looks at her, mouth pursed, opens it—and the radio comes on downstairs, stopped between stations where it just crackles. Mama looks toward the door, toward Francesca, toward the closet. In the November light, she no longer looks so young and pretty, with cracks in her lips and gray in her hair that Francesca's never noticed before. It makes her tummy hurt, like too much candy.

"The old times are gone, darling, and I won't let anyone hurt you. Anyone or anything."

Her voice is steady, but there are tears on her cheeks, and Francesca feels her chest start to hitch. Then her mother wipes away the tears, smiles, and gives her a quick hug. They get up together, the bed protesting, and Mama closes the closet door with a *thump*. Her mouth makes the ooo-shape, and Francesca imagines her doing ghost sounds. They both laugh as they head downstairs to make dinner. It's sloppy joe night, which is always a good night, and so Francesca doesn't think to look over her shoulder, as she sometimes does, to make sure that the room is empty.

The Thing in the Trees

Joanna Parypinski

———◆———

WE COME TO the park to make our new home, and it's just after dawn, a Monday, in the cold cruel beauty of early sunlight. The forest is all alive, like one great animal waiting to fully wake up, and when it does it will transcend the trappings of whatever we think it is now, and become something else. It's a season of becomings, isn't it, the fall? When the leaves turn and the trees shed their tired old souls, and the world becomes whatever cold distrustful thing it is in winter. But we're only just on the cusp of it, now. It's a hint on the breeze, on the tip of your tongue.

Here it is, the park, and here I am, its ranger. Good glory.

I brought Sandy with me, of course, and the dog, and they both seem happy enough with the little wooden structure that is to be our home. I hope Sandy is as taken as I am with the vista of undisturbed wilderness that surrounds us. And when it gets dark, at night, boy does it get dark, the like you just don't see anywhere else. It's a little too dark, I think, for her. She turns in her sleep and grasps around for me in bed with the desperation of someone who thinks she's gone blind. Owls hoot out the window and the trees rustle in long sad sighs. I feel her hand grasp mine in the unfamiliar dark and then let go suddenly, with a shock, like reaching out for your wife in the dark and feeling the hand of a stranger in bed with you. Her breathing shudders.

All these years she's reached out in bed and felt the small calloused hands and soft smooth face of a woman. What must it be to get so used to that and then reach out to your spouse and find there lying next to you a man?

"Rain's coming," she says in the morning over coffee.

She's right; a wet exhale hangs in the air like water suspended.

"Isn't it funny how different it looks?"

Yesterday, sunlight gladdened the warm yellows and reds of the maples and sourwood, made the creek sparkle with blue secrets; today, the trees are dull and the rivers gray. The yellows look sick and the reds look brown.

"I wonder what it will look like when I wake up tomorrow," she muses conspiratorially over the steaming mug. "Snow, perhaps?"

"Too early in the season yet," I say. "But I guess you never know. I'm sure this place is full of surprises."

"I guess I'll warm to it," she sighs. "It'll take some getting used to, I think." She laughs, as if she is being silly, and I wonder why. Do I make her nervous now? Does she feel like she has to make excuses for herself? "I'm such a city girl."

I reach across the table for her hand as if to remind her that it's still me. "Thanks for coming out here with me."

Her smile is a straight line. "I'm your wife," she says. "Where else would I go?"

Every time I looked in the mirror, during those first few months, I tried to imagine looking at myself through Sandy's eyes. For me, it was like I finally recognized my own face, like I had been living inside of a stranger's body my whole life.

It was harder to understand the look on her face when she reached out and touched my hard chiseled jaw, square and covered with stubble, with such wonderment and hesitation, with such strange fear.

"You look like a man now," she said.

"I *am* a man."

"I didn't marry a man."

"You married me, didn't you?"

"I'm sorry," she said, laughing uncomfortably, the way I had heard her laugh around other men, the men she worked with, the men who were taller than she, the men who intimidated her although she would never admit it. "It's just—strange."

"You don't have to act like that," I told her.

"Like what?"

I almost said, *like I'm a man,* but of course she had to act like that. I am a man. I have always been a man, even if she didn't know it.

THE MAJORITY OF a ranger's duties consist of patrolling the grounds, and since this is a vast park, it takes me most of the day to make it around to all of the designated areas.

I find a camping spot on the northwest side of the park, ensconced in a little thicket of trees. There are campers here today, two men cooking beans over a fire and drinking beer, and they wave to me as if they know me even though we have never met. Perhaps it is some other familiarity, something in me they recognize, my face or the uniform. They ask if I would like a beer, but I decline.

It is getting toward nightfall and the air has cooled significantly. I step closer to their fire just for a moment, just to warm myself a bit before heading back to my own cabin where Sandy must be waiting, bored out of her mind and long since done with her crossword puzzles.

The campers, Carl and Francisco, tell me that they come here every year. "For the last five years now," says Carl, and Francisco nods solemnly. As dusk settles around us, by some trick of the light the fire draws us in closer.

"In honor of Ames," says Carl, and they both raise their beers and take a drink.

"It used to be all three of us," Francisco adds. "As a way of getting back to nature, you know? Carl's in construction, I do data entry, and Ames, he was a computer guy. Then I got a promotion, Carl got married...you know how things go. Tough to find time to just be with the guys, yeah?"

I nod.

"We had been camping a few times, but with my new job and Carl's new wife, we just couldn't swing it that year. So Ames went by himself. He was into that kind of thing. Just doing things by himself, in his own way. Carl and me, we felt bad though, so we planned to meet him the second day of his camping trip, on Sunday, just for the day.

"When we got to the camp site, we found his tent and his bag and even his clothes hanging on some tree branches, but no sign of Ames."

What a surprise, how quickly dark falls in the forest. Five minutes ago, it was still plenty light out, the grayish light of early dusk. Now it is almost pitch black, and the crackling fire our only tether to the visible world.

"So what happened?" I ask, accepting the proffered beer this time.

Carl takes up the story now: "We searched. First just us, then we got a few friends to join in, and the park ranger at the time. We searched all around the area for weeks. Eventually, we had to give up. Winter was coming on, and it was too cold. No way he was still out there—not alive, at least.

"But we decided then that we were going to come back each year and keep looking, until we found him. So the next year we came back, and we set up camp and planned out where we were going to hike to see if we couldn't find his body. First day, no luck. But that night—"

Carl falls silent as the wood, staring contemplatively into the fire.

"That night what?"

Francisco answers, "We were sitting around the fire when we saw something in the tree above us. It was that one, wasn't it?" he asks, pointing. We all look up at the dark canopy enveloped in the spectral guise of moonlight. "It was Ames."

There is nothing in the trees.

"He was up there, crouching on the branch, staring down at us, and you could see the fire reflected in his eyes."

"I don't know why we didn't say anything. Surprised, I guess. We just sat there, and so did he. Eventually I had to go take a piss, so I walked out into the trees. As I was zipping up, that's when I saw a person standing there. And guess who it was?"

"I thought he was in the tree?"

Francisco shrugs. "That's what I thought too. So I called out, 'Ames?'"

"And the figure standing there echoed back, in *his* voice, or a perfect imitation, 'Ames?'"

"I bolted for the fire, but before I even got there I heard the thing still crouching in the tree echo back, too, 'Ames?' like a parrot. And then it was like the whole forest was echoing his name, like there were things in every tree calling out 'Ames? Ames?'"

Francisco takes a long drink from his beer, his eyes as wide as silver dollars.

"That was it," says Carl. "We waited 'til morning and they were gone. So we're still looking for him. Haven't seen him since, though."

I finish my beer uneasily. "Pretty wild story." It's late, and I know I need to head home, that Sandy must be wondering after me, that it's a long walk back through the dark, but a part of me doesn't want to leave the primeval safety of the fire. "You tell that to all the park rangers who happen by your campground?"

Francisco shrugs. "Just the ones who stop for a beer."

Feeling as if I've just drunk pomegranate juice in hell, I set down the empty bottle and take a step back from the fire. Who are these men? I suddenly have the feeling I've been talking with ghosts.

"PEOPLE GO MISSING in this forest?"

"People have gone missing in every forest."

"But this one was never found?"

I shrug, wishing I hadn't confided the story to Sandy. Her mind works in too many different directions that I sometimes can't keep up with her as she dashes from one awful possibility to the next. I suppose I've always just been more narrowly-focused than her, which is why I can walk through the forest for an hour in the dark to get back home thinking only quiet thoughts where if she did the same she might drive herself crazy with the noticing of every snapping twig or the rustling wings of an owl or the strange small lights you see sometimes which turn out to be animal eyes.

She gazes out the window at the cloudy gray sunlight with a look of both longing and apprehension. The way she looks at me, sometimes, when she thinks I'm not paying attention. She wants to go out there, can't be cooped up here any longer, but now there are dangers that lurk behind the trees.

"They can't come set up the internet until next week," she says. "I think I'll have to drive to town."

"Don't be ridiculous. Save the gas. Enjoy the week off, and you can start working when it's hooked up."

"I want to work *now*," she says. "I don't like just sitting around."

"You can come out with me and explore the forest."

She frowns, looking out the window again at a world that seems only half real. "It's not quite what I thought it would be."

When I go out, I find a pair of jeans hanging in a tree.

They are men's jeans, well-worn but stiff-legged now, as if they have been there through a good rain. The wind flaps the legs back and forth, and for a moment it's as if there are actual legs in there, swinging like a child might do. But the pant legs are flat, empty of all but an occasional breath of wind.

I look around me, but this is nowhere near a campsite. Whose pants are these, and how did they get here?

They seem ominous now, inexplicable, like a strange talisman hanging in the tree.

IT SEEMS IMPORTANT to me that they are men's pants, not women's. Women's clothing has always seemed foreign to me. Even when I had the shape of a woman, I never shopped in the women's section. Didn't Sandy ever notice? She knew I wore large tee shirts and shapeless jeans. "But some girls do that," she insisted once. "Things like that don't matter so much anymore. If I started dressing up like a clown, would that make me a clown?"

"Well, sure."

She waved me away. "Bad example."

I know I can't blame her for not having known. Hell, I hadn't really known, at least not in my conscious mind, until recently. It just wasn't something I had ever let myself think too much about. It's like Sandy told me once about having anxiety—she was always anxious, even as a kid, but she never had any clue she had anxiety until she was an adult. She just thought her experience of the world was normal, that everyone carried that terrible dread around with them every day, because she'd never known any other way to be.

Once you notice, though, you can't stop noticing.

Once I'd told her I was a man, she started noticing that all my clothes were men's clothes, as if she'd never seen them before. She didn't want to touch these foreign objects then. We used to throw our laundry together and pick it apart when it came out clean and tangled together, but then she bought a second hamper. What did it mean?

After my top surgery, she touched my chest gently, tentatively, and tried to hide the tears that came by turning away and looking out the window, as if she'd just noticed the blue jay calling on its branch. I told her not to be sad, that they never meant anything to me anyway. She said they meant something to her.

"I'm happy for you," she was sure to say, to make sure I knew. "It's just... different. It's like I don't recognize my own marriage. Like I'm living in someone else's life right now. I don't suppose you know what it's like, thinking of someone one way and finding out they're not what you thought."

I was angry. How could I not be?

"Come on, Sandy."

Maybe I shouldn't have been so angry, but I don't think she understood how terrified I was of other people's reactions to my very presence. Would I make people uncomfortable now? Would they find me abhorrent? Would I be mocked, shamed, lynched?

The one person whose reaction I had never worried about was hers.

"I'm not trying to be cruel," she said in that tone of voice that told me she was not about to start a fight. She hated fighting, even though she usually won. "It's just...you're *you*, but you're not *quite* you. It's uncanny."

"I'm the same exact me I've always been. I haven't changed."

"But you *have*."

As I GET deeper into the forest, I find a few more items of clothing. A plaid shirt tangled up in a tree, a single dirty sock draped delicately over a low branch, as if someone hung their clothes here deliberately and then just left them. And even though they seem like they've been there for a while, they weren't there before. They weren't there yesterday.

Eventually, as the day draws on, I make my way toward the camping area where I found the two men last night, thinking somehow that seeing them again will calm my unease. Perhaps I will have another beer with them and share another story, and the telling of another tale will prove to me that the first one was only a fiction all along, that there was no Ames in the trees, that there never had been. The act of telling, around the warm fire, will be a balm on my unquiet nerves.

When I get to the campsite, though, all I find is a cold heap of ash and burnt stones where the fire had been. The men are gone. In the gray dewy day that is again fast approaching night, I crouch down over the ash but it looks as if it has been out a long time. It looks like the fire is older than yesterday.

It looks like there hasn't been a fire here for days, or weeks.

There is no sign of the men. They have packed up their gear and taken it with them, and the campsite now is a haven for ghosts.

Rather than feeling calmed and assured by the warm bright fire against the cool dark night, I am left feeling cold and uneasy and alone. There is something about twilight that has this effect on me—about the change from light to dark, about being in-between, neither day nor night, but a purgatory of dim sad gray.

The forest creeps and creaks around me. I hear things that sound like footsteps, and, even knowing that these are just the typical sounds of the forest, of the animals and other creatures, still I call out half hopefully, "Carl?"

I turn around and peer through the gray trees. For a moment, I think I see a person peeking around the corner from a trunk, just the curved edge of a face only slightly visible, enough for one eye to peek out. The sight makes me jump, but when I move to the left to see if there is a person behind the tree, I realize there is nothing there. Perhaps it was just a shadow.

"Francisco?"

Only the wind calls back, and the trees bend back and forth, back and forth hypnotically.

I don't know what possesses me to call out again.

"Ames?"

From the distance, where I thought I saw the figure behind the tree, comes a low echo—"Ames? Ames?"

The echo grows and spreads, catching through the forest like fire. I hear it picked up all around me, and high above, something in the trees calling out.

Did the forest eat Ames? Is it still chewing on him, slowly, ponderously?

I run away, fleeing toward the sanctuary of home as the dark falls around me, making the park unfamiliar. Seeing a light ahead, I hurry toward it, thinking I have arrived, but the light vanishes when I get close and I realize I am only deeper in the unkind forest after all, that home is nowhere in sight, maybe nowhere at all.

When I turn in a circle, looking around me for signs of familiarity, I know that I am lost.

I switch on my flashlight and shine its harsh white specter on the trees around me, bleeding the color from them and making stark brutal shadows of their branches. I walk more slowly, assessing the path as I go, but nothing looks familiar, all is strange. I should know these trees, but I don't; I know similar trees, I know these kinds of trees, but I don't know *these* trees, and that unsettles me. I could be in a wood halfway around the world.

Here I am, the ranger, the master of this forest, and I am lost and afraid—the forest too large to be commanded, like a great living being that has swallowed me. I am only a visitor here, after all, a stranger.

After walking in what I am convinced is actually the wrong direction, I look up and see our little cabin ahead of me. The reason I had not seen it from a distance is because all the lights are off. It is a cold building, secreted in darkness.

I am hesitant in opening the door.

All the house is dark and quiet, but it is too early for Sandy to have gone to bed already. I check the bedroom anyway, but it is empty, the bed still made.

How strange, to go back home and expect to find someone there, whom you love, only to find it deserted. What a strange thing is a house abandoned, a place meant to be peopled.

She cannot be far, I tell myself, as I head back outside into the lonesome dark. But I see no one around, not even the car in the driveway, and I wonder briefly where it is.

I can only think to call out—"Sandy?"

And then the dark calls back.

Her name, a resonant echo brought in on the breeze. *Sandy? Sandy? Sandy?* In a voice unlike my own, in a voice like the movement of leaves or the creep of an animal, the stolid old voice of the trees. Once it starts, it picks up a little more each time, ringing around me like the voice has caught fire around the cabin, and in the woods all around are these inquisitive echoes, wondering, "Sandy? Sandy? Sandy?"

I start out into the trees, maddened, unable to shut out the voices, holding my hands over my ears and stumbling, staring about wildly for some sign of my wife, waiting for the trees to swallow me and engulf me and assimilate me into the forest where the jeans flap in the wind and the campgrounds enclose strange ashes, and I have just about had enough, have just about lost it with the echoing when suddenly it dies away and leaves me with profound, naked silence.

I have stumbled out into the trees, now, into the dark, where only the moon in its clever perch above lights up the way in white. And then I hear a solitary voice parroting back to me from up in the tree ahead—"Sandy? Sandy?"

The moon reveals to me the shape of my wife crouching in the branches, clinging to the bark. I can only just make out her face to know it is her, but the moon leaves her partially in darkness, as if it is only half-her and half-something else.

"What are you doing up there?" I call out, wishing I still had a hold of my flashlight to shine up at her. It seems to me that if only I could shine the light upon her, she would become real, and I would feel safe again.

"What am I doing up here?" she says.

A chill goes through me. "Sweetheart," I say. "Is it you?"

"Sweetheart," she repeats. "Is it *you*?"

"It's only me."

"It's only me."

I think, for a moment, that I will climb up the tree heroically and bring her down, but this seems melodramatic. Sandy does not need to be saved, and I have no saving to offer anyone. It is only me, after all, and it seems a thing I've said so many times these last few months—*it's only me*.

"Will you come down?" I ask, and a moment later, I regret it. I don't know why.

"I will come down," she says.

But now I am backing away, convinced that this, whatever it is, cannot be my wife. It is only using her shape, her voice.

Then I think, don't be ridiculous. She is clearly confused. She got lost, as I did, as it is so easy to do in the dark. She climbed the tree to see if she could spot the cabin, not having realized how close she was all this time to home, and then she got stuck up there, and it was dark, and she was too afraid to climb down. There is nothing in the world that can imitate this woman who you love, who you know so well, as well as you know yourself.

She begins slowly to climb down the tree in jerky, uneven movements, because she is a city girl who is not used to climbing trees, but it is a terrible kind of movement that seems to imply that she is not used to her own body.

Suddenly I do not want her to reach the ground.

I back away again, letting the moon from above cast her in near-darkness as she staggers down the rest of the way.

Suddenly I wonder, where is the car?

Then she approaches me and I cannot turn away because she is my wife, and when she steps closer she brings her terrible face to me and I see, then, what she really looks like, and her mouth throttles my scream.

BY THE SEA

Steve Rasnic Tem

———◆———

WHEN A VERY young and precocious Sarah Kingsley first learned the word "solvent" she thought of that vast sea beyond her home, *limitless* as far as she could determine, *incomprehensible, unforgiving*. These were all vocabulary words Mother gave her to keep her occupied.

The family lived on a small Carolina vegetable and apple farm near the Atlantic coast, along with a few cows and chickens, a goat and a goose or two. Despite the general smallness of her world there was a great deal of serious trouble a child could stumble into if insufficiently engaged. Farm animals weren't always the best-natured playmates, the fields nearby had snakes and foxes and the occasional sink hole, and further out were the high cliffs and caves along the shore.

Her father worked continuously sun up to sun down, but always began and ended each day with a joke and a hug. Because of the hard work of the farm Mother didn't always have time for Sarah. A *taciturn* woman by nature, she doled out her affections sparingly. So when Mother was busy in the gardens and orchards she delegated Sarah's supervision to her three older siblings: two brothers who had never had much to do with her, and her sister Peggy, who at least spared a kind word now and then and seemed to enjoy brushing Sarah's hair.

The farm was not far from an isolated stretch of beach where the four would play nearly every afternoon after morning chores were done. Her siblings insisted on it, and since they had been properly delegated the authority Sarah had no choice. Her brothers and sisters loved building sand castles and splashing around in the edges of the ocean. It's where they learned how to swim. It's where they escaped from the hard work of the farm.

Sarah, of course, had never learned how to swim. And when their father, trying to help, told her *Sweetheart, there's no reason to be afraid. Did you know that human beings are mostly water?*—she had been *appalled*.

For Sarah, the ocean was a very different experience. She hated the way the sand got in between her toes and stayed there. On the walk back to the farm the tiny bits of stubborn grit burned into her skin, and so the journey was almost always accompanied by tears. And her siblings, often sour about having to leave this favorite place, called her "crybaby," which at that point in her short life was the foulest insult.

There was always a certain repellant *persistence* about the sea, a quality which back then she had no words for—how it would invariably chase after her when she felt brave enough to approach it, the long distorted fingers of it relentless no matter how fast she ran. And how, when the others sculpted fine castles and farm houses, and even people out of sand the perfect degree of damp, the sea always returned and destroyed them, intolerant of anything humans attempted to build along its shores. What was even worse was how her siblings laughed at the destruction of what had taken them hours to create. It was left to little Sarah to mourn, to be devastated as all that hard work was washed away.

At least these daily trips to the beach only went on for a few years, and when Sarah was old enough to stay at home while the others went off to tease the ocean, she did, content to pick apples or plant flowers with Mother in the gardens around the house, or remain in her room and read of far off lands, some with a coast and some without, but at least when there was a coast it wasn't *her* coast, not the one she could hear at night in the midst of some fitful dream.

When there was a storm in her childhood, it seemed that storm almost always came out of the sea, the mountains of cloud rising somewhere out over the middle of the ocean, then rolling in with much darkness and the drama of lightning and torrential rain. The storms always left things worse off than they had been before—plants flattened, branches snapped, and trees down, sometimes shingles and even entire roofs blown away. She often heard that the destruction was more terrible the closer you got to shore, and along the shoreline itself. Sarah took their word for it, unwilling to venture close enough to see.

Her oldest brother went out before one such storm, on a small boat with friends. He never came back. A few weeks later some fishermen pulled his body out of the water, or so she was told. Because she did not witness these things herself she could always believe they weren't quite true, that facts had been exaggerated or misinterpreted. The last she saw of him was that long box in the church. Mother had laid out his good Sunday suit for the occasion but the undertaker told her sadly that because of the body's *engorgement* it would no longer fit. The casket would be closed. Sarah had understood very little of what was going on. She'd seen a dead cat once, and a few birds, and one of their cows had died giving birth to a stillborn calf. And how could she grieve when all she had was a box to stand over? And what was grief anyway but a sadness over the unseeable, the untouchable, when the one you knew now seemed someone only imagined? And her brother had been so much older they could hardly be called friends. He'd paid very little attention to her, from what she could remember, and never offered any particularly memorable kindness.

What had struck her most about the funeral was how the box had been so short, when he had always seemed so tall. Hadn't the undertaker talked about swelling? Something was obviously awry. Sarah eventually decided the casket must have been empty, and simply there so the preacher could say some words. In truth the ocean had taken her brother, and selfishly hadn't thrown back even a shoe for the family to take home.

After a year had passed she had almost forgotten what he looked like, and had completely forgotten the sound of his voice, which made her feel badly about herself. Certainly, she thought, she was the most heartless sister who had ever lived. Of course she told no one she had become this awful human being. It was a dark secret known only to her and the sea. People might not have believed her and she would have felt compelled to provide them with all the terrible details, having to confess the worst thoughts that had ever passed through her *corrupted* brain.

A few years later, at the end of high school, and before she was to board a train for the different life to come, Sarah walked down to that private stretch of beach for what she intended to be the last time. What bothered her most was discovering how very close it had been, much nearer than she had remembered. When she was a child it had been such an arduous journey, but the fact that this dangerous place was actually so *proximate* was almost too much to bear. No wonder the ocean had invaded her dreams. What had ever possessed her parents to raise a family in such a place?

Still, this was something she needed to face before leaving home, possibly forever. Her train wasn't leaving until late in the evening, but she wanted to get to the beach hours earlier, in the fullness of daylight, when she could see more and avoid its most unpleasant associations. But she'd been delayed, mostly because of entreaties from her father that she not go. Mother said nothing during her father's speech, but left the room from time to time to hide, returning a little more red-eyed and *haggard* each time.

She did not enjoy disappointing either of them, but even more she hated the emotional fuss, the secret tears and the attempts to make her feel as if she were doing them some terrible wrong. They'd lost one child—how could they afford to lose another? By the time Sarah was finally able to *extricate* herself the sun had set, and she required a lantern for most of the way to the shore.

She took the dark path down to the water. Years of coastal erosion had steepened the trail. Lowering the lamp was necessary to make sure she placed her feet safely. At the bottom she discovered a much wider band of sand than the one she remembered. It wasn't until she raised the lantern again that she fully appreciated the vastness of the fluid body stretched out before her. Because it *was* a body. It was impossible, staring out at that distant horizon, its edge softly illuminated by a fallen moon, to think of this as a collection of individual waves, of cells or bits or droplets of water. This was all one *ravenous* creature, moving sluggishly as if asleep, pushing its appendages here and there experimentally in response to some half-considered thought or hungry dream. There was a soft murmuring noise as its edges pushed up and nibbled on the beach, the sounds of some *thing* ingesting the world at its own lackadaisical pace, unconscious of all the damage it was doing, uncaring of the human lives it might destroy.

This was where the world ended, she thought. This was where, if you went too far, it was impossible to come back. Her brother had journeyed too far out over the skin of it, and like a great annoyed beast it had swatted him down. All that kept this from devouring the rest of the globe, she supposed, was an ancient inbred laziness, a lack of ambition. Wake it up too much and one day it would take away everything we knew.

She walked closer to the water, intent on staring it down. Tonight it seemed intent on keeping its distance. The tide was out further than she expected, and some tiny creatures moved and flapped about where it used to be, waving claws and segmented limbs, struggling for purchase on the *insubstantial* ground. There were also the usual bits of both ragged and smoothed wood, polished stones, twisted sodden bits of seaweed or some other plant, some other being, creatively destroyed.

She almost gagged from the reek of it. Out in the distant black the silver edges of the waves looked razor-sharp and eager.

"Come," she said softly. "Take me or leave me. I can't stand the waiting."

She paused as long as she could, but still with no answer she turned away.

When Sarah Kingsley next returned fifty years had passed. Not a good fifty years, but half a century just the same. She had had several careers, various love affairs, lost a husband, lost an only child. She had also travelled widely, roaming through Europe and Asia numerous times—although she never liked flying over the ocean, and always found ways to distract herself until that necessary passage was done. She liked to imagine what lay below as some vast, painted backdrop (or more accurately, drop cloth), covering the great *abyss* between what is and what is not.

She thought often about the deaths of others, both the ones she had loved and the ones she'd only encountered briefly. No one she'd ever known was a person of note. None of them were people you'd ever read about in the paper or see on the news. Like her parents, her siblings, and herself, they were people who lived their entire lives without notice, subject to the whims of the planet, of the weather and climate change, of the politicians and the governments and the armies which—as far as these insignificant people were concerned—were every bit as elemental as the weather, as *obstinate* as the ocean.

But rarely did she consider her own death. What was there to think about? You were there, and then you were snatched away into the *unfathomable*. Or perhaps "snatched" was the wrong word, because some people appeared to be inevitably drawn there, pulled by forces beyond their control. Sarah had long suspected that something in the sea—some parasite, some nearly extinct creature, some consciousness—knew all about what lay waiting in the worlds beyond, but she was quite sure this being was not someone she wanted to meet.

Decades before, her parents moved off the farm into a small town nearby. There they died—first her father and then Mother years later. She'd been there for her father's last illness. They talked and laughed and even now she still couldn't believe he wasn't somewhere in the world waiting for her to visit. She missed Mother's final years but hadn't been surprised when sister Peggy told her the dying woman had had very little to say.

The farm had remained in the family—Peggy owned the land and whatever was left. From her wheelchair she gave Sarah her blessing but declined to join her on this final journey back to that *insignificant* stretch of coast.

The last two Carolina hurricanes had transformed or *expunged* entirely most of the landmarks Sarah could recall. The orchards were gone except for the occasional twisted trunk, denuded branches bent in a desperate reach for the ground. The farmhouse itself had vanished except for scattered piles of stone tracing the pulverized foundation. The landscape beyond was runneled and carved into a network of gullies and washouts. She maneuvered through them as best she could, her old bones hardly up to the task. Overhead the screams of gulls followed her down to sea level, where the landscape ended in a series of low dunes and a broad expanse of beach. The water here was calm, the horizon line a blur of silver haze. She recognized nothing. With this final *dislocation* she sank to her knees in the sand.

She struggled to find the words, and then remembered. "Come," she whispered. And when nothing changed, she closed her eyes and said it louder, "come," seeing all that she had lost and what little she had left to lose. "I can no longer stand the waiting."

Then she felt that distant change in the world, that fundamental shift deep in the bowels underground, heard the telegraphed rumble, and opened her eyes to see that the ocean had finally stood up to speak.

A Harvest Fit for Monsters

L.S. Johnson

———◆———

ALENE SWUNG THE axe up and down, cursing her tiring arms. The blade slid a little further into the upright log. Sweat ran into her eyes and made her armpits slick. She could have gone to town to arrange for some kind of firewood—a day's walking, but easier than the axe. Instinctively, though, she knew that the day she could no longer cut her own wood would be a turning point, from which there was no coming back.

Besides, there was hardly anyone in town now; hardly anyone anywhere. It was a country of old women and little children. All their strength and vigor was rotting in the fields, in the swaths of land lapping at that single contested border, just a line on the maps of madmen.

Or so she thought when she reflected on her circumstances, which she hardly did anymore. She had buried self-reflection with her husband and children, along with a myriad of emotions: happiness, kindness, that particular sorrow that cleanses the spirit. Her husband had been mortally wounded in the volunteer corps of those too old to serve and too inflamed to know better; her daughter had fallen in the fields not five miles from where Alene stood; her son had been killed in a camp accident that she knew was no accident. Once she heard the news of her son's death she had waited for them to come for her, because of the things he had described in his letter. She had even put her house in order, packed a suitcase, chosen a dress to wear for her execution. But the only thing that had arrived was his battered trunk, appearing on her doorstep one morning like discarded refuse, and that had only angered her more: that the terrible things her son had described mattered so little, in the end it wasn't even worth the effort to kill her.

Until now.

She let the axe slip to the ground as she watched the figure walk towards her, erect and purposeful, the grey of his uniform stark against the brown fields. Only the one, though, and on foot. She waited long enough for any vehicles to appear, and then relaxed a little. It still happened from time to time that a soldier would pass through, searching for a way back to the world they remembered. So many landmarks had been razed, they were often stunned as she gently placed them: yes, these were the outskirts of town; yes, this road was the market road; yes, there used to be four great windmills.

Years ago, the windmills; years of war in-between, and nearly a year of peace now; and still they came. Alene caught up the axe and walked back to the house, wiping her hands on her shirttails. They would want water, and perhaps supper.

AT FIRST HE was just a shadow in the doorway, made looming and shapeless by the cloth rucksack he carried. She beckoned him inside, the glass of water in her hand; he stepped into the filtered sunlight and the glass fell, shattering between them.

"I'm not him," he gasped, holding up his hands. "I swear! I'm not him!"

Still Alene could not speak for gaping at him, her heart hammering in her chest. A face she had seen only in grainy print, now suddenly alive before her. The General; *her son's* general. The papers had called him Savior, then Butcher; her son had called him *the Monster*—

"I'm a cousin, nothing more! Just a distant cousin," the man cried, cringing much as she was. "I had nothing to do with him, I curse the day he was born! Please believe me. I have papers, I can prove it, you must believe me. I was merely a soldier, I had no part in his crimes. Please." He took a step backwards. "I just want to go home," he said in a smaller voice.

She felt behind herself, gripped the back of a chair to keep upright. Trying to understand. They had never found him; they had believed him killed in the last, terrible push to reclaim the capitol. A cousin? She tried to superimpose the news photos atop the face before her. Certainly he was more gaunt, older, but so was everyone.

"I'll go," he said. "I don't wish to upset you." He managed a lopsided smile. "This accursed face," he added.

"Wait." She shook herself. "Show me your papers."

He hesitated, wary, then reached carefully into his breast pocket and drew forth a worn booklet. He had to extend his arm fully to reach her, the papers pinched in his trembling fingertips. She took them with a decisive flick of her wrist that made him flinch. Now that the shock had worn off she could think more clearly. How could he have made it so far, if he was the monster? Ever since the treaty was signed they had scrutinized everyone, searching for the last of his conspirators. Impossible that he should have come so far, to find himself on her doorstep of all places, as abandoned as her son's trunk had been.

The name was different; the photo showed a healthier version of the man before her, one that looked nothing like her recollection of the Monster. She had seen many false papers over the years; these looked official.

"You must be thirsty," she said, handing the booklet back to him and gesturing to her little table. "I've had enough mistrust for this life. Haven't you?"

At that his shoulders sagged. "More than enough," he agreed. With an odd little bow he crossed the room to the table, sitting down with a sigh and letting his rucksack slide to the floor. The shape of him, how he nearly banged into things, it reminded her of her children's friends, awkward in their adult bodies even as they prepared to fight adult battles. Her throat closed for a moment, though she had thought herself done with crying over the past.

"Thank you," he said, and again when she set a fresh glass before him: "thank you."

With a nod she set about sweeping up, watching him surreptitiously as she tidied the mess away. He swallowed thirstily, his stubbled throat flexing. A large, ugly scar knotted the tissue beneath his left earlobe, running down his neck to disappear under his collar. A close call. She had seen worse, but she could well imagine the fear and pain from coming so close to dying.

"You have family nearby?" she asked.

"An old friend." He wiped his mouth on his sleeve, then flushed. "I apologize, my manners…"

"You've had more important things to worry about." But she laid a napkin before him and refilled his glass, then put the last of her loaf before him as well. He tore into it voraciously. Just another man; it could easily have been her son or husband before her.

"I didn't think there was grain, still," he said around mouthfuls.

"Very little." She sat across from him. "Everything is poisoned, but they don't know why. Some say it's chemicals, some say it's all the metal in the ground…but I think it's the blood." At his startled look she gestured to the window. "A battle was waged here. We buried so many, we were shoveling for days, and all that blood went into the dirt and isn't that a kind of poison? So much slaughter?" She heard her own voice, loud and shrill, and held up a hand. "I'm sorry. I've been alone too long."

He had paused in his eating. "It must be hard," he said. "To do everything by yourself, at your age."

"We've all learned to do," she replied. "Those of us that are left."

He was nodding even as he pushed more of her bread into his mouth. Still her gaze kept returning to his scar. There was something about it, something that tugged at her, but for the life of her she could not remember what.

HE WENT TO rest, though he kept insisting he would be on his way by sundown, and no matter what he would repay her for her kindness as soon as he reached his friend's farm. Despite his exhaustion, it was some time before she heard the creak of the narrow bed-frame, and she could not shake the sense that he too was listening to her movements—

oh, she had been alone too long.

She should have been starting their supper, should have been carving up her precious store of root vegetables and scouring the landscape for any last hints of green. Instead she found herself sitting on the bench at the back of the house, where she used to pluck fowl and clean vegetables. The scar bothered her, why did it bother her? There was something about it…

Alene had learned, in the last few years, that when she needed to think of something the trick was to think of something else, so she turned over in her mind the old problem of how to grow vegetables again. A raised bed, with some kind of barrier beneath? How small could it be and still sustain her? Who might have good soil that perhaps she could barter for, she still had a little gold—

and then she thought of her son's letter.

THE BOX HAD once contained her prayer book, a useless tome, for what had their prayers brought them save death? Only when Alene received the letter had she understood what prayer really was: the decision-making of the choiceless. A last pretense that you had any power in a mad world.

Slowly, reverently, she lifted the lid on the box and laid it aside, letting her fingers brush the yellowed papers within. Five dense, bristling pages. More than he had written in his life, she knew, for had she not taught him his letters? Leaning over him at the table, watching him struggle to trace the words she had painstakingly written over and over.

Five pages that she kept in the box, the prayer book discarded long ago.

Kept carefully flat and sealed away, for after the third reading she had felt something change in herself, as if the words had somehow written themselves into her very blood. All her boy's pain, all that he had done, first blindly, then with a terrible understanding. All the suffering caused for one man's madness.

She took the letter out and scanned it, phrases echoing with memory:

he told us to cut out their tongues lest they report us
afterwards I found her corpse and the basket only held a doll
gutting them would be the only message they understood
told me I had to, or he would kill her and her sister both

Until at last she found what she was looking for.

Last night he had a woman brought to us. He said she was a traitor and we had to know what she told them. She was barely grown. He brought out his tools and she started screaming…I tried to reason with him but he turned on me and the others seized me, and he said that even if the girl was innocent she could serve his purpose. She must have seized the knife while he spoke to me. When he turned back to her she tried to cut his throat, but though she caught him under the ear she could not finish the blow…oh Mother, when they were done with her you could not tell her from a butcher's scraps, and all I could do was watch—

Please understand that this is why I must stop him no matter the price. So many already mimic his behavior and speak his words. I must stop him before he makes Monsters of us all.

Alene read it through twice before putting it away. The scarring beneath his ear—oh, it was too similar to be coincidence. Not the clean line of a knife wound, but wouldn't he go to great lengths to mask such a distinguishing mark?

The house answered her with silence. She thought, *I should kill him now*; she thought, *I must be sure.*

And then she went outside once more, catching up her shovel as she strode out into the fields.

HE CAME INTO the main room just as she was dusting the pot with a last precious pinch of spice. Though he rubbed his face as if newly awakened, his uniform was barely wrinkled. "That smells magnificent," he said.

She made herself smile at him. "It's merely bone broth, but it will nourish."

Carefully she ladled out the steaming liquid, making sure to catch the small pieces of bone, the slivers of parsnips and onions. When she put his bowl before him he nearly dove in, his eyes focused on the steaming surface. She took her time filling her own bowl, took her time crossing the room, her every gesture that of a tired old woman.

At last she sat in her chair and said, "You don't have to wait for me."

For a time there was only the sound of his enthusiastic slurping, the vigor with which he sucked at the bones, piling them beside his bowl. She made as if to sip her own, watching him; at last he became aware of her scrutiny.

"You're not hungry?" he asked, his expression changing to wariness again.

"I have little appetite at my age," she demurred. Still his unease persisted; she made herself take a mouthful and visibly swallow. She had vowed never again, and never again after that, but there had been so little for so long…

before he makes Monsters of us all

He relaxed as he watched her drink and leaned back with a contented sigh. "That is the best soup I've had in some time," he said. "Could I possibly lure you to my friend's house? He's a good man, not much younger than you."

"I had a husband," she replied. "I don't want another."

"Children?"

"A son and daughter, both lost to the war."

He looked truly abashed, and her resolve wavered. "My apologies. That was thoughtless of me…it's just, sitting here feels so normal, as if nothing has happened."

"Some of us will never have such moments." She raised the bowl to her mouth, pretending to drink again.

this is why I must stop him no matter the price

"Well, we know who's to blame, eh?" He smiled at her. "But we showed them who is the greater. They'll never dare to assault us again."

"I'm not sure there's anyone left to assault us." She rose and carried the bowls to the sink. "So you enjoyed the broth?"

"As I said, one of the tastiest meals I've had in many days. Clever of you to keep the bones of your game." Was there a sly tone creeping into his voice? "Another thing you learned to do, or country wisdom?"

"There hasn't been game here in years." She stared into the sink, where the axe lay, and beside it the bullets she had removed from the pistol in his rucksack.

"From a butcher? I'm honored, it must have cost a fortune—"

"I was standing here when it started." She watched his reflection in the window glass, coiling and uncoiling her fingers around the axe handle. "The grain was waist high, it looked like they were floating in it. Thousands of soldiers, so dirty and ragged you could barely tell ours from theirs. They had run out of ammunition, it was knives, swords, even rocks. It was the most brutal sight I had ever beheld."

His reflection shrugged. "It's been terrible, especially this last year. But war is always terrible. We must put the past behind us now and focus on rebuilding."

"I learned my daughter was among them, somewhere, and I took an axe and ran out to find her." She realized she had stopped speaking to him; who was she speaking to? "It's easy to kill when you can't really see them, when they're just blurs, howling like animals. That was the first thing I learned to do, General. Perhaps you of all people can appreciate such a lesson?"

He straightened in his chair. "I told you I'm not him." His hands suddenly hidden.

"Afterwards there was nothing in the field but bodies. I told myself I would starve before I touched them, yet you cannot make a broth without bones." She laughed softly. "No more grain, no more animals, but we have plenty of bones, General. A harvest fit for Monsters."

The click of the pistol made her look over her shoulder. "I think we've had a misunderstanding," he said, taking steady aim at her. "You have been alone too long, grandmother. I am going to leave now; please don't make me use this."

"Is that what you tell yourself about the girl who cut you?" Alene touched the flesh below her own ear, mirroring his scarring. "It was a misunderstanding? What about the soldiers you ordered gutted after their surrender? The children you swore were carrying ammunition to the front line? My son was one of your lieutenants, General, and he told me *everything*."

He squeezed the trigger but there was only an empty click. Cursing, he lurched to his feet and reached for his rucksack. Alene turned completely, swinging the axe out and wide, crossing the room as fast as she could. She felt strong, as strong as she had in the fields that night, she could already feel the blade driving into his flesh—

stop him before

—her feet tangled, she twisted her ankle, and then she was hurtling against the table, the edge winding her as it drove into her belly. The axe caught him in the chest, knocking him backwards as the handle shot out of her grasp. Blood splashed her face.

For a moment she lay gasping atop the table, her hand burning. Every wet drop on her skin scalding hot. When she eased herself upright, jagged pain radiated from her shoulders and she tasted bile.

A hand seized her ankle and yanked it forward; her hip cracked against the table as she fell again. She kicked wildly until the hand released her and then scuttled out of reach, pressing her back against the wall as, wheezing, she tried to slow her racing heart.

The Monster was curled on his side, trying fruitlessly to grasp the blood-slicked handle. His hands and chest were drenched, half his face painted red. More blood pooled around him, soaking into her worn rag carpet.

A new thing learned: what it meant to kill a man at close quarters, and in daylight. Watching his mounting terror, smelling his failing body. That her children had each done this, had experienced this moment at such a young age…oh, her grief swelled as it had not done for months, tightening her throat and stinging her eyes. She clenched them shut, pummeling her sorrow back into the depths of her belly, and when she opened her eyes again the Monster was staring at her.

"Not…" he wheezed, more breath than sound. "Not him…"

"Some of us had no choice!" she cried, her voice loud and harsh. "Some of us could only be what you made us!" She crawled forward. "We learned to *do*, General. We learned to kill with our hands and eat corpse-meat like vultures! We did terrible things, my children did terrible things, you made us all Monsters…"

But she was shouting at a corpse.

SHE DRAGGED HIM into the fields step by ponderous step, struggling to hold armpits sticky with blood. By the time she dropped him into a weedy patch she was shaking with exhaustion. Every step a cacophony of pain. She could barely see her house for the gloom of twilight as she stumbled back, leaving both corpse and axe in the wilted grass. In the morning. Everything could wait until the morning.

Inside were the meaty odors of soup and blood. Flies hovered over the stained floorboards. His splattered rucksack had been kicked in a corner. The rug would have to be burned, the floor bleached and scrubbed. It was all she could do to latch the doors and windows and fall into bed.

ALENE WAS WADING through the darkened fields, the grass taller than her waist. Everywhere was movement, everywhere she could hear panicked breathing, smell a rank miasma of sweat and blood and urine that blew over her in gusts. The General rose up before her, his face photo-gray, robust in the moonlight and his jacket gleaming with medals. She swung the axe, cutting deep into the scar tissue but she couldn't complete the blow; when she pulled the blade back his head flopped to one side, revealing black, muddy soil beneath. Slowly he crumbled before her, and the axe in her hands was not wood and metal but a clay that cracked in her fist. *Everything's poisoned*, her husband rasped in her ear, the deathbed voice that she had learned not to cringe at. *Even us, we're sick inside now. Nothing good will ever grow here again, Alene. Best to raze it all.* She spooned up soup to silence him, she wasn't ready to listen to him, she would never be ready. Only the soup was heavy, sludgy, and she realized she was feeding him mud and it smelled delicious…

She awoke, cotton-mouthed and disoriented, inhaling over and over the smells of dirt and broth and blood, ears ringing with an incoherent cry; her arm reached for the side of the bed and she mewled aloud at its emptiness. Only then did she see the stains on her hands and arms. She sat up, sheets pooling around her waist, and saw that she had gone to bed without washing. Past the window cawing birds circled over the dried grasses; a crushed trail led back to her house as clearly as a line on a map. Still she felt the dream clinging to her. What were the odds that he would come here, to *this* house? Had she not once also believed, truly believed, that she had seen her daughter walk up the road and into the house, had run back from the field with racing heart and tears in her eyes only to find it empty?

Slowly, stiffly, Alene got out of bed, shaking and pinching herself. The chill in the air setting her skin alight. Outside the birds rose and dropped, jostling for access. As they had after the battle, clouds of birds swarming down upon the corpses. But they had drifted away as the land withered and died; where had these come from, these birds, how far had the smell of dead flesh carried? How starved were they, to cross acres of decay? She felt a strange pang, a mixture of grief and sympathy for these scrawny creatures with their jagged wings, creatures she had once despised.

Not him…

But it could only have been the Monster. The likeness, his weak denials—impossible that he could be anything but. Her renewed certainty made her first steps out of her bedroom bearable, kept her steady when she saw the great stain on the floor, the spray dotting the walls.

She dragged the blood-stiff rucksack onto the table and began pulling out its contents, all the things she had barely noticed when searching it for weapons. A change of clothes, an empty flask. Dried meat wrapped in a kerchief. A book of prayer, a fancier version of the one she had thrown away, with many phrases underlined:

May I never take the blessing of freedom for granted
I am enclosed by wickedness
Give me victory over the corrupt
It is better to trust in the gods than mortal leaders

She fanned the pages, searching for—what? Some phrase that would confirm it all, that would ease that small nagging doubt—when a photograph fell out.

Three figures in all: an older woman, flanked by two young men. All clearly related, and the men bore the mark of him. A family. Even Monsters, it seemed, had people who loved them, people who would perhaps do to her what she had done to him.

Did they miss him, were they waiting for him? Did they see him walking up to the door, full of life, only to find he was never there?

Alene waited to feel sympathy for this woman like herself, who had perhaps lost children as well as her husband now. But while she could feel something for the birds eating his corpse, she could feel nothing for the woman who had shared his bed.

And what did it matter? He was dead; it was done. Just another corpse among thousands.

As she put aside the rucksack, however, she heard the sound of a motor in the distance. Not the stuttering engines of one of the dilapidated vehicles from town; this was a steady, well-maintained purr.

Alene looked at the stained floor and walls, her own filthy body. So lost in her reverie and now there was no time. A swift, fleeting panic ran through her: she must concoct a plausible story, perhaps a third party who had followed him and attacked him in the night…

But as swiftly as it began, the panic faded, and she merely went to the sink. She washed her hands and face and combed her hair; she checked the buttons on her dress, that there were no unsightly gaps. A turning point, when you no longer cared enough to dissemble. A point from which there was no coming back.

Nothing good will ever grow here again, Alene.

The vehicle turned out to be an official-looking little truck. It stopped at her door; the two soldiers that came out had ribbons on their jackets and carried sidearms, but they flushed like schoolboys when she opened the door. So young! As young as her own had been when they first left, before they understood what they were giving themselves over to.

"Very sorry to intrude," one said, holding up a photo. "We're looking for this man."

The gaunt man from her table stared at her, clad only in a thin, sleeveless shirt. The scarring, she saw now, extended over his shoulder and down his chest, like it had been splashed onto him. In black and white the resemblance was even stronger, but now the tiniest differences leapt out at her. The thinness of his lips—hadn't the General's mouth been fuller, kinder? Was the anger in the staring eyes from being captured, or from being mistaken for another?

Was the scarring a poor attempt to mar the original cut, or a terrible coincidence?

"This man is wanted for questioning regarding his wartime activities," the other soldier continued, clearly reciting. "All participants will be held accountable. Every citizen is expected to help, or suffer the consequences of collaboration."

The taste of the broth came back to her, the familiarity of it. Were they speaking of the General, had they been ordered to vagueness? Her feet were still grimy with blood and dirt. Or perhaps they did not know who they hunted?

We're sick inside now. Nothing good will ever grow here again, Alene.

"He's in the back," she said.

They blinked in astonishment, hands dropping to their holsters. One gestured for her to come out, but she only smiled wearily at him. "He's in the field," she corrected. "He'll give you no trouble."

The soldiers exchanged a look; then they ran around the house, pistols drawn. She watched them run, the early morning light glinting off their helmets, and for a moment they were her son and his friends, wrestling and mock-fighting in the thick, waving wheat...

Best to raze it all.

She took a bowl of water and cloth into the bedroom and washed thoroughly, then put on her most handsome dress. Everything was poisoned, and perhaps it had been for longer than she had realized. How quickly had her daughter enlisted, with her husband's encouragement? How had Alene struggled to keep her son home for one last precious year, despite his anguish at being kept from the fighting? All of them so eager to kill, even her husband in his old age, even herself.

She had never unpacked the suitcase she had prepared after her son's letter came. Now she dusted it and placed it by the door. In the field she could hear the soldiers arguing, probably about what to do.

It could only be him. But to send two boys, to find the most fearsome of their leaders?

It could only be him.

When at last one came back inside he took off his helmet, but also kept his pistol half-raised, as if he wasn't sure whether to beg her pardon or shoot her. "Who else was here yesterday?" he asked, a hint of pleading in his voice.

"No one," she said, then, before he could reply, "it is *him*, isn't it? The Monster?"

He just looked at her blankly. The woman in the photograph, the grown sons. *You could not tell her from a butcher's scraps.* "It's just that everything is poisoned now," she said. "You, me, the very earth we stand on. And the things we've done—!" At his growing unease she leaned over and patted his arm. "Not you, of course," she amended.

The soldier glanced over his shoulder, at his fellow who had appeared in the doorway; the latter made a little *go on* gesture.

"Ma'am," he said carefully, turning back to her, "I'm very sorry to say I must arrest you—"

"Of course you must." She patted his arm again. "Only—could you bring me back here, after? To the fields. The birds will be so hungry…" She picked up the case and slipped her shoes on, then looked from one to the other. "It was him, wasn't it? Of course you cannot say. But it was him, I'm certain of it. I learned to do, after all. A Monster just like he was."

The Monkey Coat

Daniel Braum

———◆———

June watched her daughter lift the black fur coat from Grandma Estelle's old trunk and hold it up so they could see. Long strands of monkey hair hanging from its arms caught the light, raising a faint iridescence in their inky darkness.

Last week, there'd been a murder. One of their own. In their own suburban town. It made the news but the police weren't giving full details. That always meant it was something bad. June had known the guy. She'd been friendly—well, much more than friendly—with him during her wild time right after David had up and left. Though the storage facility had a security booth with a guard and a well-lit lot, June was uneasy and had waited for a morning when Ivy could come with her after getting off work, even though the divorce was final and she'd had the court order granting her access to the locker for over a week now.

"I'm selling it," June said.

"No, Mom," Ivy said. "*Listen* to your *dear* daughter for a change and go out and paint the town red."

"Sorry, love. I'm selling it," June said. "Hopefully for enough cash to cover your first semester of college."

"Enough, Mom."

"Sorry. I know. I'm glad you came, Love."

Besides Grandma's old trunk the locker had been empty. David had gotten away with everything. She shouldn't have allowed herself to have even hoped for otherwise. Ivy had it right. The jacket *was* beautiful. Vintage. Authentic. And so *chic*. Just like Grandma Estelle. A true original from a bygone time. On how many of her wild adventures had she worn this coat?

The waist-length jacket was tight around the bottom where the fur was shortest. Long strands of hair tapered down from the chest and shoulders and hung from the arms forming an elegant fringe. June loved the jet-black color and sheen that even decades of storage couldn't dull. Classic vintage fashion. But it still had that rebellious edge that personified June in her school days, back before working at the shop, marrying David, before Ivy and everything took her and spun her and spun her and never stopped.

June watched her daughter spin the coat around and inspect it.

She had just come from work and June didn't like the low cut of her blouse. Her pinstriped pants suit was nice but much too tight. She was striking, with her father's ivory complexion and green eyes and June's own dark hair and figure that she'd had when she was Ivy's age, but that didn't mean a mother had to like it. She did like that Ivy thought with her heart just like her mom and didn't listen to anyone who told her otherwise. Not that there was anyone who gave a shit anymore.

"It's so you, Mom," Ivy said.

"It's so a semester of college."

"Mom. Stop. I'm fine."

"I don't like you working there."

"I'm only the hostess. It's good money and I don't do any of the other stuff."

"I don't like that you work nights. That you have to."

Times were tough for a third-generation artisan. And things had been careening downhill long before David left. June's mom had died just as the printed word was transitioning to digital leaving the impossible responsibility of the business solely on her. She loved the big old printing presses but had to let them go when she tried downsizing the shop to stay afloat. Their bulky, pigment-stained hulls had felt like home. Letting them go had been letting go of an anchoring weight. Since then she felt that she, her family, everything, was drifting, drifting away. She should have kept them, somehow. She should have found a way, or made one. David always used to say that. June hated that she was thinking of him now. He was off somewhere in his new life, uncaring that Ivy was now a host at the Golden Stallion Sports Club and that she worked as a floral designer at Laine's where she used to buy their holiday arrangements back before her shop went under.

June let Ivy help her into the coat.

"There," Ivy said. "It fits perfectly. I wish we had a mirror."

"Does it? You don't want it?"

"No. It's yours. It's how I imagined you back when you were my age."

"Don't you wonder what your great-grandmother was like? She was a suffragette, in London. Tell me you remember what that is and don't say Bowie."

"I know, Mom. That's the song you made my ring tone."

June knew Ivy knew the Bowie song but doubted she knew much of the women's rights movement.

"Mom used to tell me all about crazy Grandma Estelle and the wild adventures in Europe she had before moving to New York with your great-grandfather."

Estelle had founded E Books. If only she had lived to know the terrible irony of the name. One of Estelle's more colorful adventures had been a stint as a showgirl in Paris but June didn't say for fear of giving Ivy any ideas.

Someone rapped on the roll-up metal door. It was a man in a Self-Storage uniform holding big red-handled bolt cutters.

"I'm here to let you in. But looks like you already are."

"Thanks, Captain Obvious."

"Ivy, be nice," June said.

"They said upstairs we got the court order and you're okay to go in."

"The court's lock was cut when we got here," June said. "I opened the padlock my husb—*ex*-husband and I left on it. Same combination."

"Good thing you remembered then," he said absently, his attention and ability to form words captured by the two female forms before him. "New coat?"

"Yeah, well new to me," June said.

The guy whistled playfully.

June gave a spin. Ivy loosed a cat call and they all laughed.

"Have a nice day, ladies. Holler if you need me."

"See, it looks great on you, Mom. Even that guy said. You think it's real fur?"

"There wasn't any other kind back then."

"Ooohhh, Dad would absolutely hate it."

The smile left June's face.

She wanted to say why do you have to bring him into everything but lately it seemed like all she did was harp on her.

"Sorry. It's just I was thinking of him," Ivy said. "You remember when I asked for a stole for my sixteenth? He asked me why I needed a hot enema death wrap around my neck to make me feel pretty."

"Priceless. He said that?"

"You don't remember?"

"He said a lot of shitty things. Mister Hypocrite in his leather boots and leather jacket."

June thought of the long ago day she and David skipped their afternoon classes and snuck onto the roof of the Fur Vault in the Cedar View Shopping Center. He took a steaming whiz into the fresh air intake of the ventilation system. Then they dropped water balloons full of red paint on all the trophy wives on their way out. They'd been so young. And still believed love conquered all.

"Sorry. I shouldn't have said that. Your dad loves you. At least he did when I knew him. He's got a fucked-up way about him. But he loved you."

"He loved you too, right?"

"Doesn't matter anymore if he did or didn't. I'm done. And done talking about him."

She put the coat back in the trunk.

"Yeah, Dad would have hated the coat."

"It's probably why he left it," June said.

"Maybe he forgot to throw it out or take it."

"No, it feels like one last fuck you."

"Enough," Ivy said. "I'm going home to get some sleep."

"It's almost seven-thirty. I have to be at work soon. Thanks for coming with, you."

They exchanged mock European kisses on both cheeks, then Ivy left for the elevator. June stood staring at the empty places where she had hoped to find treasures from her life that had been, or at least anything she could sell to get them through.

Ivy was right, June thought. David *had* loved her. Only at some point along the way she had stopped loving him. Now she didn't even miss him anymore. She missed the comfort and stability they'd once enjoyed. She just hadn't figured things would fall apart without him. At least not so quickly and completely.

Yeah, David would have hated the coat. Absolutely hated it. And that was exactly why she was going to go out and wear it.

JUNE WALKED INTO work at Laine's Floral of Five Towns just past eight, wearing her grandmother's fur.

"Oooh la, la," Laine said. "New coat?"

"You like?"

"I *do*. What's the occasion?"

"The occasion is I'm a happily divorced woman and *I'm* going on a date after work."

"You gonna get some?"

"Maybe. Don't need an occasion for that."

"Andrew or Randall?"

"Andrew."

"Oh, good for you. You deserve a nice guy. Andrew deserves to get lucky. I like him."

"And maybe he will."

Laine ran her finely manicured hand along the sleeve. A strand of long black fur snagged on the large diamond of her wedding ring and she yanked it free.

"It's not real," Laine said. "Is it? It looks so real."

"Yeah, it's real. Vintage Grandma Estelle."

Laine's expression changed to the one reserved for the male customers who routinely asked if there were any cheaper bouquets and the *goyum* who didn't know not to ask for deliveries on Saturdays.

"Oh, June. You know how they make those things."

She didn't say the rest. She didn't have to. June had heard her say the word "suffering" so many times before. June didn't live in the neighborhood, like Laine, where everyone kept Kosher. Eat no suffering, was the answer Laine gave time and time again whenever asked for the reason she followed the ancient laws. Bring no suffering into your body. June supposed this also included wearing no suffering, apparently.

"Yes, I know how they make them," June said.

What about my suffering, she thought. Who around here really gives a shit about me when push comes to shove? She's never worried over making it to her next paycheck. She goes home to her Jason and their big, paid-for house. Her only worries are making it on time for her pedicures and where the maid misplaced the laundry this time.

"Don't worry, Laine," June said. "Grandma Estelle said these were one hundred percent organic, fair trade, certified road-kill monkeys. No suffering here."

Except mine.

"Bless you," Laine said in Hebrew. "You are so strong. You are strong for all of us."

June hated when she spoke in Hebrew. It reminded her of everything she didn't have. Everything she didn't pass to her daughter. Plus Laine and the rest of her ex-customers used to always lay that phrase on her, usually right before pressuring her to complete their orders on impossible time tables for their convenience.

June took off the coat, put it in the back room, and got to work on the arrangements for the big wedding order. Laine turned on the TV that was mounted above the front counter. The crawl beneath the local news announced the name of the murder victim. Franklin Lamont. The man who was a man no more. Forever an empty space in his family where his life had been.

When David left, it wasn't like he disappeared and left an empty space, it was more like he shattered, June thought. There was no void where he had been, she didn't wait around or sit around feeling lonely waiting for it to come and swallow her. She went out and lived. So it felt like David, or more like what had been their life, had shattered into parts, all of them lesser, each of them a distinct piece of what they had and what he had been to her, and each of the parts residing in the different men she kept around.

Franklin Lamont, or Frankie, as June called him, had been one of those men. He hungered for her where David had grown complacent. He was eager to please her. Pleasured her when fleeting moments of pleasure was the only respite she had. He was reluctant to leave her bed when she told him Ivy would be home soon, sad when she stole away so his wife wouldn't catch them in his. Along with these somewhat endearing things came his refusal to take no for an answer when she decided it was time for her to move on. He repeatedly called at all hours. Showed up at the 7-11 where she got her morning coffee. Sometimes even waited in the lot or came into the flower shop. On her bad days his twisted attention was the only indication anyone gave a damn she was still alive, that she still mattered in some way, to someone. Even if that someone was broken and embodied everything that was broken about her.

Frankie's stalking was what sparked her epiphany. It had dawned on her that these men she numbed herself with were mere pieces of what she'd once had, approximations of the things she missed, the things she feared she'd never have again. And she was drawn to them because they each filled her emptiness in a different way. But it took a while to realize they were poison. Poison that tasted good going down but never, ever filled the void, only fed its insatiable burning with fuel.

After what felt like countless days doing everything she could to make ends meet she decided she didn't need men to preserve herself.

So she resolved to stop seeing them. All except for two. Andrew, the accountant from town with whom she had a date tonight. And Randall, mister big shot, who was walking through the door of the flower shop right now.

Laine giggled as Randall approached the counter. He was a retired cop. Laine claimed his week-long absences to "consult with certain law enforcement agencies," as he put it, were really because he had another life and another family in a different state. June never asked. She didn't care.

"Nice coat," Randall said. "Fur? A bit warm for it, no?"

She hadn't realized she'd put it on.

"Yeah," she said.

"You got yourself a fur coat after I just spotted you another month's rent, plus…"

"Plus what?"

"Plus you don't strike me as the type."

"And what type is that?"

"I mean…you know how they make them, right?"

Not you look good in it. Not what do I think. All about himself. Just like David.

Yet she wanted him. Just like she had still wanted David. Even in the end.

SEX WITH DAVID had been a lot of things. Transcendent at best, tender at times. Healing. And then a mediocre downward spiral to the way it was in the end. Dead. Just like their relationship apparently was, long before she knew it. She thought they would get better. Thought the sex would get better. If they would just stop fighting. What did he know about raising a daughter? Their headstrong daughter who failed in school. Took drugs but refused her prescription meds. All the time she had been hoping, hoping, hoping he had been methodically transferring their assets into his name alone. He had cleared out their bank accounts. A week before he left he had even told her he was taking her wedding ring to be cleaned and she had fallen for it.

Sex with Randall was nothing like it had been with David, even at its best. In the absence of the familiar she found rage. And pleasure. And a rage for that pleasure. For the depth of pleasure that could blot out all else. Where she could be lost in the heat and freedom of serving lust and only lust. No contemplation, no self. The rage only knew heat and skin and teeth and sweat and the pulsing from the inside, the rush of blood pushing faster and faster. That was being alive. That was being whole again, serving pleasure faster and harder until she disappeared and the sting and dullness of the world and remnants of the smoldering ashes of her life subsided for a few sweating, heart-pounding moments.

Laine and Randall were both standing there awkwardly. Had she missed something?

"Well, I just came in because I saw on the news about Franklin."

"Yeah, terrible," June said.

"Guess he's not going to give you trouble anymore."

"Really? You're sick. You came here to say *that*?"

Randall had been nowhere to be found on the nights she had needed him because Frankie had been waiting around.

"No, I came to tell you my wife is out holiday shopping tonight and is staying at her mother's in Jersey."

She decided just then that Laine was right. She deserved a nice guy.

"And why would that matter to me?" she said. "I'm done with you."

He slammed his hand down on the counter.

"You're not done with me, yet."

June decided she was going to jump over the counter, put her hands around his neck, and show him just how done with him she really was. But Laine interceded.

"Randall, I'm going to have to ask you to leave," she said.

When he didn't move, Laine picked up the telephone.

"Okay. I don't want any trouble," he said.

His tone sounded like he did want trouble and that he'd be back. But he left.

"You're sweating," Laine said. "I actually saw you gnash your teeth. I've never seen anyone do that."

"If he comes back I'm going to rip him a new asshole."

"If he comes back I'm calling the police. All right? Calm down. Take the jacket off. Go out back and have a smoke and just calm down. Please."

She went out back. Lit up and called Ivy, who was sleeping and did not pick up.

"I *am* listening to you, dear daughter. I'm not painting the town red but I am going out. Andrew's taking me to dinner and a movie. Don't wait up. Love you. Thanks for coming today."

Andrew picked her up at five. He brought flowers. Laine rolled her eyes at the sight but told them to have fun.

"Nice coat," Andrew said as he held the car door open for her. "You look lovely."

"Why thank you. This old thing? I just threw it on."

"Doesn't look like it. You look so, wow!"

"Okay, I lied. I wore it just for you, sailor."

JUNE WOKE TO a blinding light. The sun coming through windows? Morning already?

The bed was so warm. The man next to her, so warm. Still snoring, blissfully. Andrew?

No, Randall.

June sprung out of bed. Randall snored on.

How the fuck had that happened?

She got dressed and stole from the room, not bothering to wake him.

As she crossed the living room heading for the door, one of Randall's daughters, a teenaged girl whose name she didn't know, emerged from a doorway and crossed the hall to the bathroom, sleepy-eyed.

Oh shit, did she see me, June thought as she left the house.

"Fucking whore!" June heard the girl scream as she closed the front door behind her.

That settles that, June thought.

Thankfully her car was outside. On the short ride home she wondered what had happened. Had things gone that badly with Andrew? Had she had *that* much to drink and went to Randall's without remembering? She didn't feel hung over.

The door to her apartment was open when she arrived. Ivy had just gotten home too.

As June walked in Ivy gave a startled cry.

"It's just me, love," June said. "Just getting home too."

"Mom? You scared me. What the fuck? You're wearing the coat?"

"Indeed I am."

"Mom, where are your pants?"

June looked down at her bare legs and bare feet. She could have sworn she had gotten dressed. She felt the coat's silky lining on her breasts, the bare skin of her arms. She was naked except for the monkey coat.

"Take it off," Ivy said. "I don't like it one bit."

June didn't hesitate to comply.

"It's going back into the trunk. I'm putting it there myself tonight on my way to work."

"Fine. Good riddance. I wanted to sell it anyway."

"Mom, take it off. Now."

"I could have sworn I just—"

Ivy stomped over and helped her take one arm out, then the other. It looked like a deflated, dead thing was draped over her daughter's arms.

"Suffering," June said.

"What?"

"I said I'm freezing," June said.

"Get dressed. You have to be at work. What's wrong with you? I told you to go out and hit the town. But I didn't expect you to listen."

June went to the bathroom. Showered, got dressed, and went to work.

Her day added insult to injury. It seemed like only blissfully married couples came into the shop.

Who were these people? Were they real? Didn't they have real problems like her? Like she and David had had? Ivy wasn't David's biological child.

She was pregnant with her when she had met David. Ivy's real father, a man twice her age she had met while cocktail waitressing at the Limelight, had told her to get rid of it. She hadn't even been attracted to him. He was rich. And older. The glimmer of the fancy hotel he had taken her to didn't make him better in bed or keep her warm when he left at dawn. She had only wanted to try being someone's trophy on for size.

David told her to keep the child and to forget that guy. They put David's name on Ivy's birth certificate and raised her as if she were his own. But she wasn't his own. And what did he know about raising a daughter? What right did he think he had to try to force her to go to school or to take medication that dulled her down?

"How'd your night with Andrew go?" Laine said. "You have that glow, darling."

"It's the glow of embarrassment. Not so good."

"No? What happened?"

"Don't know."

"What do you mean don't know?"

"I mean I got into a fight with him and went to Randall's."

"Oh, dear."

"I know. I like Andrew. How do I fix it?"

"Flowers fix everything. I'll make you a bouquet. And your job today is to go deliver it."

Laine made her a wonderful bouquet and sent her to Andrew's office. Andrew's secretary up front was delighted and let her into his office unannounced and without an appointment.

"For me?" Andrew asked.

"You like them? I'm sorry."

"Get out of here," Andrew said. "And take your flowers too."

"What? What'd I do?"

"Are you kidding me?"

June burst into tears and ran with the flowers back to her car. She returned home. Ivy was already out doing something before work. June put the flowers into a vase and turned on the TV. She changed into sweats and went to 7-11 to get fuck-the-world ice cream.

She was halfway through the pint when she started thinking of David saying find a way or make one. She threw the ice cream away. Showered up and dolled up. She took the flowers out of the vase, wrapped them as best she could and headed for Andrew's. It was time to find a way or make one, fuck David and his phrase, it was her phrase too, her phrase now.

She rang Andrew's door and was pleasantly surprised that he answered even though she knew he had seen her through the peep hole.

"You're wearing that coat," he said.

June looked down to see the black monkey fur. Apparently she *was* wearing the coat. She hadn't given it a second thought and just assumed Ivy had taken it.

"Andrew, I don't know what I did. I honestly don't remember but I came here to tell you I'm sorry and I really like you—"

She noticed cat-sized shapes moving in the darkness of the tops of the tall oaks on Andrew's front lawn.

"June, you don't look so good," he said.

Andrew helping her inside was the last thing she remembered before blacking out.

A NAKED MAN laid face-down splayed on the bed. His arms and legs were tied, pillows under his mid-section propped his ass up. He struggled to get free.

Randall?

Randall mumbled muffled curses through a gag over a tinny sounding Suffragette City.

Bowie singing *Wham-Bam-Thank-You-Ma'am* played in a loop on her phone. It was on Randall's night stand. No, it wasn't Randall's night stand, it was the night stand of a fancy hotel. She realized it was the hotel where Ivy had been conceived. It had been redecorated but it was the same place all right; she recognized the layout and remembered bits and pieces of arriving with Randall.

Ivy was ringing again and again. June wondered what could be so important and contemplated the lamp from the night stand she held in her hand.

She wondered why she was holding it. Then she remembered, walked to the night stand, and silenced the phone.

She took the shade off the slender lamp and smashed it against the top of the night stand. The bulb shattered. The bound man on the bed screamed through his gag. She bashed the lamp on the table again and again until part of the metal cylinder broke away revealing twisted white and red wires. A lone spark arced from the jagged mess to the plush carpet, extinguishing as it fell.

June knew the way monkeys were farmed was with a stainless steel instrument much like a thermometer but with enough electric current to kill without marring precious fur. First they were restrained. That caused only a little discomfort but the whole process lacked dignity. When the juice flowed there was a blossom of pain, then it was over.

This she knew was going to be different. The broken lamp was not like the stainless steel instrument. It wasn't going to fit so smooth. She tried.

Randall struggled. The stink of burnt hair and skin along with Randall's shit and piss and flatulence filled the room. He kept struggling, so she leapt onto his back and choked him until he was still enough so she could get it done right.

THE LOCAL NEWS broadcast an interview with Franklin Lamont's mourning family. They claimed he had died of electrocution and expressed concern why full details had not been released. The police spokesperson denied protecting one of their own. They did not want specific information about the manner of death released while awaiting forensic testing so as not to compromise their investigation. Both sides asked anyone with any information to come forward. Which always meant that they had nothing of value to go in.

EVEN FROM THE hostess stand just inside the Golden Stallion, Ivy knew it was her mother's voice she heard in the lot arguing with the bouncers.

"I told you," June shouted. "I do not want her working here."

Ivy rushed outside.

"Mom? How'd you get the coat? You're not wearing pants again, aw Mom. Are you wearing anything at all under there?"

Two tall muscular bouncers each held one of June's arms as she strained against them, struggling to reach the entrance of the club. Patrons on their way in watched from a distance.

"You think you're hot stuff walking around with dead things on you, bitch," one of the patrons called, a young girl Ivy recognized as one of the newer dancers. "Don't let her touch you. Lady's got a cloud of bad juju on her I can see a mile away."

Ivy ignored her and the crowd snapping cell phone photos.

"Guys, it's okay. I'll take it from here," she said. "Just help me get her to my car."

"I said I don't want you working here."

"You got it, Mom. I'm done. I quit," Ivy said and winked at the bouncers. "I'm taking you home, Mom. Just come."

Mother and daughter sat in silence for the short drive home. Ivy opened the car door for June and June walked with her to the front door and rattled off the list of chores she needed Ivy to do, the bills that needed to be paid, and things that needed taking care of as if nothing had happened.

"Mom. Cut the shit. Are you okay? What's going on? Is that blood on your hands? Did you hurt yourself?"

"No."

"Did you hurt someone?"

June didn't answer. They went inside.

"Okay, just take the coat off. We'll get you cleaned up."

"No."

Ivy tried to take the coat off but June wouldn't let her.

"Fine, keep it on, let's get you into the shower."

"Fine," June said.

June let Ivy lead her into the shower. June went under the running water, coat and all. Dirt and sweat and monkey hair and a little blood ran down her body and pooled at the slow drain.

"Mom, whatever happened I know it was the coat. Not you. You have to take it off. It will be okay."

"Why does everyone always think things are going to be okay? Things are not going to be okay. I didn't raise my daughter to be an idiot."

"I'm not an idiot, Mom. I'm just saying I can come up with something. Please just get out of that thing."

"Nobody tells me what to do. Nobody forced me to put it on. I chose to."

After an hour of trying to get her mother out of the shower, Ivy went to the couch to wait her out but fell asleep to the sound of the water running and her mother talking to herself.

Ivy woke sometime during the night and checked on her mother. She was met with curses and a command to close the door and let her shower. At one point Ivy went outside to check the bathroom window to make sure she hadn't stolen away but she was still in there, cursing and showering. Ivy woke again before dawn and this time she knew her mother was gone. Just like the day she knew her father was gone. She just knew.

The bathroom was all clean. Spotless and shiny. Not a speck of dirt or water to be seen. The coat was hanging from the hook for robes behind the door all clean and dry; its black sheen out of place among the dingy, old blue tile.

Her mom hadn't left a note or taken anything.

It was terrible each day she was gone. Worse was each day that passed where no one noticed or seemed to care.

Weeks later the police came calling. They asked questions about her mom and some of the guys she had slept with. They asked if she knew where her dad was and she told them last she knew of it was Paris. They asked if they could look around. They did and that was it.

Over the years Ivy resisted the temptation to sell the monkey coat. It reminded her of her mother. Ivy wore it to work now and then on those days she was feeling spite or the rage that sometimes came, but mostly she just wore it because she knew it would piss off her mom. She still worked as a hostess only, never the other stuff. Eventually she became one of the managers of the place. She found she had a way with numbers. She listened to one of the regulars and enrolled in business school aware that it was what her mother always wanted. She told herself she didn't care at all what her mother, or father for that matter, thought. She never saw or heard from her mother again.

She sometimes daydreamed that her mother was working as a showgirl in Paris, like Great Grandma Estelle. She once woke from a nightmare that she had received a postcard, from Paris, with the words *sorry now you really will never see your father again* scrawled in her mother's handwriting along with bloody fingerprints.

Ivy took it that she imagined these things because some part of her wanted her mother to understand that she had left her the way Dad had left them both. Alone and with only the monkey coat to show for it. But eventually she even stopped caring about that and wondered if the coat would look good on her, on those times when she even thought about it at all.

SEAMS

M. Lopes da Silva

———•◆•———

LESLIE FIDGETED WITH the edges of her collar, her sleeves.

At one point, and not so long ago, Leslie had been "Lee," with hair cropped like her name, and a temp job and a cat. But after marrying Mark Hancock she'd become "Leslie Hancock," a person she'd never been before; a hybrid of her teenage self, still flirting in braids, and a stranger. Leslie Hancock grew her hair out. She quit her temp job and had to give the cat up for adoption because Mark was deathly allergic. Leslie Hancock left her Los Angeles family of benevolent misfits and bitter artists to move to the midwest, where people measured your worthiness in how many awful winters you'd survived. A native Californian, her starting value was obviously quite low.

Mark was wonderful; patient and kind, if often abstracted by his work. You could come up to him and ask him about the weather and end up getting a sort of diatribe about bureaucracy and shipping departments, with the influence of bad weather on cost as the main theme. But he liked having her around, and although they didn't talk about many deep or important things, there was a sort of Norman Rockwell coziness that oozed about the couple. Their mutual corniness was a point of pride and embarrassment for Leslie, who usually just flushed red when anyone touched on the subject.

Leslie loved Mark, but she had yet to feel anything for his hometown. They had moved there for reasons—very important reasons at the time—a new branch of Mark's company opening up in the city an hour away, Mark's mother and father getting older, starting a family in a "genuine hometown". But now these reasons seemed shockingly naive to Leslie. Mark's daily commute was so long that he tended to work late at the office, taking overtime and eating dinner in the city more often than not. Mark's parents made Leslie uncomfortable; she could not relax in their presence, especially if Mark wasn't around. And Leslie had not felt like starting a family since she'd arrived. The fancy four-poster bed with the brightly-patterned quilt thrown across it did not entice her. The ubiquitous flat green fields going brown in patches reminded her of mange she'd seen once on a stray dog. The bright blue sky, though dazzling, filled her with a strange fear she'd never known before. She shrank against the blueness, shuttering windows, even though she was certain that she'd seen skies that blue before back home.

She wondered if this fear of blueness was a kind of homesickness, and didn't mention it to Mark. He had enough to deal with at work. She tried to focus on homemaking; doing simple mechanical tasks kept her numb enough for a while. She called and messaged her friends in Los Angeles when she could, but already she was slipping into the purgatorial fog of "acquaintance" for many of them. Friendships were always easier to maintain in person.

Mark told her: "Why don't you go out more? Try making friends in town."

Leslie tried. She took sixty dollars to spend frivolously, but there wasn't much for her to spend it on. The town was about six square blocks that included a diner, a drug store, a movie theatre that wouldn't open until seven that evening, a hardware store, an antiques shop, and a sewing supplies shop wedged in between two competing liquor stores. She didn't even bother counting the gas station. Leslie went into the antiques shop and soon walked out with a cast iron paperweight of a sleeping cat and a paperback mystery. The woman in the shop had been impossible to talk to; a stern-faced monolith who furrowed her brow at Leslie's smile.

Leslie Hancock stood on the sidewalk, considering her options. She decided to try the diner. The windows were so yellowed with dust that it was impossible to see inside, but the view was really more of the same; yellowing counters with murky pies hidden beneath yellow translucent glass. Yellowed menus, unpeeling from their lamanations like paper bananas. Leslie sat at the counter, squinting through the stains to see if the daily special was a pork chop or pot roast, when a waitress approached.

"What'll you have?" she asked. Leslie looked at the woman—in her mid-twenties, but not a strand of her hair out of place. Her expression was flat, but it wasn't the flatness of exhaustion and bone-weariness, it was the disinterested glance of a prom queen. Leslie suddenly felt very frumpish and dull, and pulled her sweater more tightly over her shoulders.

"I'll have a chocolate milkshake, I guess," Leslie said. She smiled, even though she was abruptly conscious of how chapped her own lips were.

The waitress nodded and walked back to the kitchen. Leslie looked around the diner, curious to see if there were other patrons. An old man dozed in a corner booth by a cup of coffee. A pair of middle-aged women, buttoned up to their necks in stylish wool coats, sat along the wall by the window. They shot sharp looks at Leslie periodically and tended to pet the fabric of their own coats as they chatted with each other. Their eyes were perfectly groomed, their nails flashing. Leslie wondered where they'd gotten their nails done—she hadn't seen a shop in town. She decided to ask.

"Excuse me," she said, approaching them with a wave and smile, "I couldn't help noticing your beautiful nails—where did you get them done?"

The women stared at Leslie. They blinked at her languidly, letting the moment sink into the very pit of her gut, before one of them, a brunette, answered: "We do our own nails here."

Leslie nodded. "Well, you do gorgeous work! Thanks!"

She retreated, her neck burning, to sit back at the counter. She fought the desire to pick up her iron cast cat and go. The waitress returned with the milkshake, and Leslie forced herself to smile politely and sip. It was good—maybe the best milkshake she'd ever had—but all she could think about was that she'd have to invest in a better makeup kit if she wanted to survive around here. She'd never been around women so stuck on appearances—at least in a non-ironic way.

When the waitress came back with the check, Leslie asked, impulsively: "What do the locals do for fun around here? I'm new—just moved into town with my husband."

"Mark Hancock."

"Excuse me?" Leslie frowned.

"Your husband," the waitress said, her eyes suddenly heavy on Leslie.

"Yes, I know he's my husband," she replied snappishly.

"We used to date in high school. Tell him Donna says 'hi.'"

"Oh," Leslie said. She fidgeted with her napkin. "Sure, I will."

Donna went to the register with Leslie's money, ringing up the lone charge. When she returned, Leslie tried again.

"So, what *do* people do around here? I'm honestly going stir crazy at the house all day."

Donna's eyes flickered, taking in the diner and all its occupants. When she turned to Leslie she couldn't suppress a leer that crawled up the back of

Leslie's spine and transmuted into gooseflesh on her arms.

"Stick to your husband."

LESLIE LEFT THE diner and felt the dazzle of sunshine pierce straight through her retinas to the back of her skull, inspiring a throb of pain. She held her hand against the light, the awful blue spread of sky above. She shrank to the narrow line of shadows along the sidewalk, embarrassed at the sudden mental image she had of herself, flailing against the sun. Peripherally, she sensed the presence of townspeople, their judgement silent but inescapable. Just to her left, at her sweatered elbow, there was a needlepoint sampler displayed in the window, a precisely executed and yet impressionistic depiction of a galaxy in a night sky blushing with indigos and violets. The colors were arresting, promising kind things to her aching eyes. Next to the sampler, a paper flyer was posted in the window. It read: Sewing Circle, and listed a series of dates and times.

Leslie had never sewn before, had never had the inclination to sew before, but now she entered the sewing supplies shop with resolve, though her heart hammered miserably like a bird trapped in a house. She had interrupted three women—one behind a wooden counter and two before—in conversation. The air snapped with the sudden hush of sound. Six eyes, their lashes curled to coquettish perfection, stared at Leslie.

"Hi," Leslie began, her throat abruptly papery. "I saw the flyer outside and thought I would sign up for the sewing circle."

How old were these women? They floated in nebulous middle age, their skin uniformly pale and unblemished. Leslie took a hesitant step backwards, her ankle losing skin as she scraped it along the corner of a wooden display. The pain was sharp, and she could feel dots of blood dew up.

"You say you want to join the sewing circle?" One of the women asked—the one behind the counter. Leslie focused on her. Her hair was like a blonde clump of cotton, fixed in place by hairspray she could smell across the room.

"Yes?" Leslie hadn't meant it to come out as a question, but there it was.

"Aren't you Mark Hancock's new wife?" This question came from a redhead who stood in front of the counter, her eyes so pale they looked almost milky.

Leslie attempted a smile, but it sagged midway like a half-pitched tent. "His only wife, so far as I know."

The women across the room surprised Leslie by laughing at the meagre joke; their laughter was low, clucking. It reminded Leslie of the thunder that bowled across the fields at night.

"Didn't Ellen already give you an invitation?" the blonde asked.

Leslie frowned and performed a quick mental fumble. Ellen was…the name of her new mother-in-law, of course. She tried to remember, and a dim interaction—stiff, buttoned up—in the middle of her living room rose up in memory.

"If you ever consider applying yourself to anything, my sewing circle is accepting new members," Ellen had said. Leslie scowled inwardly—surely Ellen hadn't been that cruel, like a passive-aggressive cartoon mother-in-law printed in a newspaper strip. But that was where the words hid, buried in an insult.

Standing in the store, she sagged a bit. She felt so incredibly tired. Leslie didn't know how long she stood there, silent, her fingertips awkwardly dancing along the heavy paperweight she still held. She doubted the wisdom of her plan, of joining anything at all. Suddenly the blonde spoke up, smiling:

"Have you ever sewn before?"

"No," Leslie replied, her eyes drifting absently around the shop.

"Then you'll have a lot to study."

And the blonde woman, who was named "Maryanne," was suddenly among the racks plucking items and piling them up on the counter, explaining each object she set aside. One object in particular caught Leslie's attention, waking her up from her sudden inertia.

"Oh, I don't need scissors. I have scissors."

"Yes, but do you have *shears*?"

Leslie frowned. She had to end all this planning; she wasn't going to join the sewing circle after all. "No—but that's all right. Thanks for your time anyway!"

A hand encircled Leslie's wrist, firm and smooth. Leslie glanced up and saw the third woman, a brunette who hadn't said a word, smiling back at her. She was the one who held onto Leslie.

This woman was perhaps a bit younger than the other two—closer to Leslie's age. She had the kind of green eyes that broke hearts, like wet gems, and now they broadcast a wistfulness that quickened Leslie's heartbeat in recognition.

"Scissors are for paper, shears are for cloth," the brunette smiled conspiratorily, as if sharing a test answer.

Leslie laughed nervously. "Now I know I'll mix those two up at some point."

The brunette took the shears from Maryanne and placed them in Leslie's hands. Leslie glanced down, surprised at the weight and heft of the object. The metal of the shears chilled her palms, the cold thrilling up her fingertips.

"You won't mix them up," the brunette laughed, winking. Leslie was impressed with the wink—she had never been able to pull off a wink organically. The gesture looked ridiculous in her own face, but perfectly charming in the brunette's.

She was right, too; Leslie wouldn't mix up these shears with the flimsy plastic-handled scissors she had back home. Shears had a primeval weight to them; they were an antediluvian tool, a heavy object that could do the work around the farm and be plunged into the heart of wolf, if need be.

"I guess I won't," Leslie said.

"I'm Kathy, Kathy Winslowe," the brunette extended her right hand to shake Leslie's own, and Leslie had to bobble the shears around for a moment to free her hand for the gesture.

"Lee—Leslie Hancock," Leslie replied, smiling.

The hem of her pants, attracted to the blood on Leslie's ankle, kept clinging to the skin there. As she walked out of the shop, her arms loaded up with forty dollars worth of sewing supplies, Leslie could feel the newest scab attempting to form rip free.

"HAVE YOU EVER been married before?"

"What?" He sounded bemused.

Leslie tapped the edge of her tablet, closing an ebook she'd been skimming about introductory sewing. "I met some women in town today—they called me your 'new' wife."

Mark laughed. "You *are* my new wife."

"No." Leslie frowned. "It was how they said it." She wondered why she'd told Kathy that her name was "Lee." She thought she'd left Lee behind, but realized now that couldn't be true. She wanted to hear the word come from someone else's mouth. It was like a spell she'd been placed under, and she was waiting for her name to break it. She drew her knees closer to her chest.

"Mark," she asked, her voice small. "Will you—?"

He looked at her, raising the remote control to mute the television. "What is it, Leslie?"

Leslie couldn't say it. This was all so silly, anyway; she was a different person now. "Will you drive me to your mother's sewing circle before you take the car on Thursday?"

"Sure," he said, "I didn't know you were interested."

"I went to the sewing shop in town. It looked fun."

He smiled. "That's great. My mother always said that she wanted a daughter to take with her."

"Well." Leslie glanced at the television screen; the image was darkly lit, and a sharply dressed woman stood in front of an indifferent modern building. Cities always looked so cold in serious television shows. "I really want to get to know a woman named Kathy Winslowe—she seemed nice. Do you know her?"

"Sure I know Kathy. That's Donna's mom."

Leslie stared at Mark. "Donna? The waitress Donna?"

Mark's eyes went vague. "I don't know if she's a waitress. I went to high school with Donna, though."

Leslie gently chewed on the inside of her cheek. "That doesn't make sense. This Kathy Winslowe looked maybe thirty-five, tops. And you're forty-six."

He shrugged. "Maybe it's a cousin or something."

"I guess." But Leslie was thinking that Donna hadn't looked a day over twenty-five.

She would have to go to the drugstore and raid their makeup counter tomorrow.

LESLIE HANCOCK STOOD underneath flickering, unflattering fluorescent bulbs that lit the town drugstore like a halfhearted rave. The shelves were wooden, splintered constructions warping beneath the weight of their wares. Although the drugstore was well-stocked with manicure supplies, there wasn't a trace of any facial makeup—not even a dried-up lipstick or a campy pink blush. She frowned, chewing the inside of her cheek with consternation. Clearly the locals had another source—did they order their makeup online? Or did they still do door-to-door sales out here?

She would have to order her own supplies online and hope they arrived on time. She was still getting mail mix-ups and delays after the recent move. Leslie spotted a teenager sitting behind the counter, slumped over a magazine with her sweatered fists squashed into her cheeks.

"Excuse me?" Leslie called out. The teenager rotated her neck so that she faced Leslie, but still managed to keep her face mashed against her fists. She resembled a fish, her mouth slack.

"What?"

"I was wondering where I could go buy makeup—I only saw nail products on your shelves."

The teenager dropped her fists to the countertop. "The city."

"Right," Leslie laughed. It was only an hour away—of course that's what the women in town did. "Well, I'll buy these here." She approached the counter and handed her the manicure supplies. The teenager started ringing her up.

"Hey, I'm not going to say anything to anybody, but shouldn't you be in school?" Leslie asked.

The teenager froze mid-bagging. "I'm homeschooled."

"Oh, I'm sorry," Leslie laughed nervously, "I shouldn't have assumed anything."

She resumed bagging the items. "That's okay I left the high school."

"Why's that? If you don't mind me asking."

The teenager shrugged. "I just don't make friends around here. I'm not a joiner, my grandpa says."

Leslie smiled. "I'm not always good at making friends, either."

The teenager suddenly glared at Leslie, flat contempt stamped upon her face. "I can *make* friends just fine. I said I *don't* make them around here."

Leslie shrank beneath the teenager's scorn, her face blazing red. "I'm sorry," she murmured. She wanted to die. She hadn't felt the wrath of a kid burn her skin up for years. It was a cruel nostalgia. She paid the money she owed and left the drugstore and winced at the sky as tears streamed down her face. It was so goddamn blue.

AT NIGHT THE darkness swallowed up the land completely and the crickets sang in relief from the heat. The stars were brighter and more significant out here than they'd been back home in Los Angeles. That was the one thing that Leslie Hancock could say for certain was an improvement about Mark's hometown. She stood on the porch that looked out over the fields and heard the wind mutter low across the grass before it stung the naked skin along her arms. She shivered. Maybe getting to know Kathy would start to make things better. Or if that didn't work out, maybe Leslie would meet someone else who would befriend her.

It was so hard to exist without an echo; someone to listen and support, to be listened to and supported in turn. Without a friend every decision felt heavier and more intimidating. There were holes that opened up within, frightening questions she'd never wanted to face alone. She couldn't bear to look at the voids that pocked her; when she had a friend nearby, Leslie felt the voids diminish to pinpricks. Mark couldn't scare so much as a pothole away, for some reason. He always suggested therapy when she tried to describe the holes to him.

Charging a professional for what Leslie wanted felt essentially unsatisfying—like a dessert made without sweeteners. She wanted the sugar of friendship. She wanted to feel the buoyancy she'd felt back home, walking streets as familiar to her as her signature. She realized now that her friends had been like extensions of her own arms, helping her reach whatever she wanted; a night out on the town, tickets to a band she adored, trips they saved up for collectively and even freelance art jobs, from that period in her life when she'd wanted to be an artist.

But that woman with her web of electric arms had vanished, lost in transit along with a box of heavy metal T-shirts and porcelain dogs that the movers couldn't account for. Now Leslie Hancock remained, with memories of another woman's life gradually fading under the brightness of a damnably blue sky.

Leslie glanced down at her cell phone, pushing the button to light up the screen. Her friend Gwen was supposed to call, but she was already an hour late. It was possible that she'd gotten stuck in traffic, but even more likely that she'd forgotten about the phone call. Leslie had only wanted to chat because she'd remembered that Gwen was in a sewing circle back in L.A., and wondered if she had any advice. If Leslie were being honest, she just wanted to hear Gwen's voice again; the possibility of spellbreak was tempting.

The crickets made Leslie nervous—they sounded too similar to the ringtone of her cell phone. She fussed over the phone for a bit, settling on a loud pop song that didn't sound at all like crickets, and waited some more. She shivered again, wondering why she hadn't brought her sweater out to the porch but not moving to go grab it. Her cell phone reception worked best outside the house.

"Leslie? Are you coming to bed?"

She could hear Mark's voice groan out from the staircase. The words were from a dialogue frozen in the 1950s, now miraculously unthawed by their marriage. Her jaw started working slowly, nervously.

"Leslie?"

The fields were inky black, but the stars were startlingly dramatic. "I'm going to stay up a while longer. I'll come to bed soon."

There was a long moment filled by droning crickets, and then Leslie heard Mark shamble and creak up the stairs. She felt a mix of emotions assail her, an outdated certainty that she was a bad wife that didn't deserve her husband prickled among them. Where had that idea come from? Leslie frowned at the stars. After a while, she scratched a persistently itchy patch on her scalp, and felt a twig-like thing caught in her hair. Withdrawing the object and subjecting it to the scrutiny of her cell phone screen's glow, Leslie determined that it was probably a piece of hay or a weed and tossed it away. She idly wondered how long it had been stuck in her hair for, and if the teenager at the drugstore had noticed it. Her molars finally found the soft flesh of her inner cheek and went to work. When Gwen didn't call after another half hour of waiting, Leslie went to bed.

THE PACKAGE OF makeup arrived Thursday morning, sending Leslie into a flurry of video tutorial watching and muted shrieks of frustration as things kept going awry. Mark didn't have to go to the office until four that afternoon—there was an overseas video conference he was attending that evening. He avoided her manic grooming with the nervousness of someone made deeply uncomfortable by anything pragmatic involving a human body. He promptly isolated himself in the living room with a cup of coffee and his cell phone. His actions inflamed Leslie's frustration into a minor fury; he could escape from her suffering with ease, but she was stuck in.

She went it alone, battling mascara and blenders until she looked mildly airbrushed, but was unsatisfied with the result. The women in town didn't just look pretty, they were *polished*. They dwelt in the nebulous realm of models and actresses who knew how to seduce cameras, only mysteriously without the help of a sympathetic lens. The more Leslie tried to highlight and blend, the more convinced she was of their perfection and her own flaws.

She finally took a break to sip a weight loss smoothie carefully from a bendy straw, her silken matte lips barely parting. Mark ate a turkey sandwich in his undershirt, eyeing her from across the table.

"You look nice," he said through a mouthful of turkey.

"Thanks," Leslie replied. She glanced down at her phone; no missed messages from anyone.

"We should go out to eat in the city some time. There's a little Italian place I think you'd like a lot. They still put candles in wine bottles on the tables."

Leslie met Mark's gaze. He hadn't invited her out like that since they'd gotten married. Her upper matte lip curled. "Is it the makeup? Really? That does it for you?"

Mark's eyebrows twitched—up-down—a nervous tic Leslie hadn't seen before. She felt like a sort of domestic Cousteau, cataloguing a previously unknown creature from the sea. She laughed.

"I'll bet it does. Growing up in this town, all the ladies were painted. I bet your first blow job left a lipstick ring around your dick." Leslie was shocked at the abrupt cruelty winging free from herself so casually. Mark was turning red, his embarrassment boiling his skin. Immediately she regretted her words.

"Hey, I'm sorry—" she began.

"You're such a bitch sometimes," he said.

They sat, stunned, in the kitchen. The sunlight was high and bright and illuminated everything in cheery detail. A lovely room, a charming couple, but something imperturbably wrong with the scene. The impact of their words left the space hollow, uncertain; the scene of a crime seconds after the gun fired.

A few minutes more and the apologies gushed forth, eager to fill the room. Mark was effusive, and Leslie extracted a promise from him that he'd never insult her like that again. She was uncertain if a promise like this could be kept; once the first insult had been spoken it was always easier for more, and meaner words to follow. But Leslie took Mark at his word and refused to cry—she'd worked too hard on her makeup.

"Look, you're going to be great," he said. He put his hand on her left knee and smiled from behind the steering wheel. "Don't worry about a thing. At least you know my mom, right?"

Leslie tried to return his smile, but lost it along the way. "I'll be fine."

Mark squeezed her knee before he returned his hand to the steering wheel. "Do you have a ride home? Or should I pick you up at the diner later tonight?"

Leslie laughed meagrely—he was treating her like a perfect child, now. "We need to buy another car soon. I can't stand feeling like a kid with you."

"Sure," Mark agreed, "whenever you like. We can even go car shopping this weekend if you want."

His affability was woollen, heavy; Leslie rolled down the window on the passenger side of the car. The sky was fading from blue to indigo, the last of the sunset squashed on some other horizon. They pulled up in front of the high school; the sewing circle was held in the old gymnasium there. That fact had surprised her, but apparently the group was so popular that the sewing shop couldn't hold all the members comfortably. The parking lot was full of cars, not a single one with a banged-up bumper or a coat of dust on the paint. The consistent cleanliness had an artificial feel to it, reminding Leslie of a used car lot.

"Everyone's keeping up with everybody around here," she said.

"What do you mean?" Mark asked. He was checking his phone for messages.

"I don't know. Nothing. Mark?"

He looked up from his phone. "What is it?"

Leslie pinched a piece of her cheek between two canines, released it. "Sometimes...would you mind calling me 'Lee'? Not all the time. Just once in a while."

"Sure. What's this about...Lee?"

She blushed and turned away. It had sounded so awkward coming from him, so forced. "Forget it. It was a silly idea. Just—I love you."

"I love you, too. Don't worry so much! You're great. I'm sure you'll fit right in."

Leslie closed her eyes. She hadn't wanted all those extra words. They ruined it, somehow.

"I'll call if I get a ride, but plan to meet me at the diner." Leslie forced a smile, removing the cheap paperback she'd bought at the antique store from her purse. "Don't worry, I brought a book."

He laughed and they kissed—lightly, the skin barely making contact in an effort to preserve her lipstick—and then she was out the door, holding a wicker hamper full of odds and ends in the crook of her elbow while she tried not to sweat through her foundation.

To her surprise Leslie saw Donna leaning against a lamppost at the edge of the lot, smoking a cigarette under the cone of light. She hesitated, then approached the waitress, who now wore the kind of long, stylish coat that frequently appeared on opera-goers in old movies. Leslie marveled at it.

"That's a beautiful coat."

"Yeah?" Donna asked. "What's so beautiful about it?"

Leslie took a step backwards. "Look, we don't have to be enemies, Donna. I don't care if you dated my husband once. We're adults, right?"

Donna snorted, cigarette smoke huffing from her in a swirl. "I'm the best friend you've got in this town. And as a *friend*, I'm telling you this right now: you should leave."

Leslie's eyes went hot. "I deserve to make friends here as much as anybody else!"

Donna swore, throwing the cigarette to the ground and stubbing it out with her boot. She muttered to herself incoherently, her immaculate brows furrowed. When she looked up, Leslie was gone, her heels clattering a trail to the gymnasium. Donna followed gloomily. As she shook out her hair, a few pieces of straw fell free.

THE GYMNASIUM WALLS were covered with quilts and the old wooden ceiling beams were draped with quilted bunting. The quilts were startlingly vivid, each one depicting actors performing in some arcane scene; a young girl carried a string of dead hares, a man dangled upside-down from his ankles above a field of wheat, a stag stood in a field with several indeterminate woolly objects dangling from his antlers.

Women bustled among each other in long, stylish coats or opera capes, their faces flawlessly made up. Leslie stood at the doorway, holding her hand to her face protectively, desperate to keep her handiwork unsmudged by her own liquid emotions. She was in this state, overwhelmed and hardly able to make sense of a damned thing, when the blonde from the shop—Maryanne—spotted Leslie and approached.

"You're here! So glad you could make it." Maryanne said. "Kathy saved you a spot."

"She did?" Leslie asked, despairing at how pathetic she must sound. "That's so nice of her."

"Here she is!" Maryanne called out, spinning around with a wave. Leslie turned and saw Kathy approach in a long jade coat that matched the color of her eyes.

"I feel so underdressed," Leslie said meekly. "I didn't know there was a dress code."

The two women laughed. "You'll have something nice to wear for the next meeting. We make all our own clothing here."

"Really?" Leslie had assumed that the coats were store bought—there was nothing obviously homemade about them. Now her guts churned; they were presuming a lot of her ability if she was supposed to have a coat that nice ready by the next meeting.

Leslie felt a comforting squeeze encircle her wrist. Kathy held her hand, smiling brightly. "Come on, let's go sit down. Then you can meet everybody."

Leslie let Kathy lead her through a maze with suspended quilts for walls. The sewn images were beginning to catch Leslie's attention, seeping into her consciousness peripherally. She was starting to notice details, things that unsettled her though she couldn't articulate exactly why. A ring of mushrooms encircled a sparrow on its back. There was a horse with a laughing rooster face. One quilt was all cabbages and spiders.

The art was mesmerizing, gorgeous; Leslie was enraptured by the way the stitching could ramp up from pure abstraction into intense realism and back again. It reminded her of being Lee, doing art jobs on the side again, hunting the eternal, elusive stag in her private hours of making, and never returning home with her quarry. But the thrill of the hunt, the lifting brush, had lit the days when nothing else could.

There was a quilt of emerald green boas twining among butterflies and flowers, and Leslie felt her heart kick like a leg. This was beauty, and this was power, and Leslie wanted it. She wanted it very much.

She stopped and tugged on Kathy's arm. "How much is this? I mean, would the artist be willing to sell? I love this quilt so much."

Kathy smiled. "Oh, that's Donna's. She'd never sell. But soon you'll be able to make one just like this, if you want."

Leslie burned red. "No, I mean, that would take me years to even be half as good."

"Once you understand the materials you're working with, it's easy."

Leslie turned—Kathy hadn't said this. It was Ellen, Mark's mom, buttoned up to her chin in white.

"Hello, Ellen," Leslie said, forcing a smile. She could feel the sweat oozing down her scalp, and tilted her head back slightly to prevent streaking.

"Good to see you here, Leslie," Ellen replied. She did not smile.

"Well," Kathy said, "shall we sit down?"

She gestured at a circle of plastic folding chairs in a cleared space at the center of the quilt maze. The wood of the basketball court made peculiar shapes beneath them. About forty chairs were set out and soon filled by immaculate women in beautiful coats. Leslie sat among them, fidgeting in her dress, pulling at the edges of her collar, her sleeves. The chattering died down to utter silence at once. It was haunting, the sudden swoop into quiet. Leslie had not been expecting it.

After a long minute, unpunctuated by a cough or sigh, the redhead with the milky eyes that Leslie had seen in the sewing shop stood. She wore an opera cape of bright blue, the hue forcing a squirm from Leslie that sounded hideously loud in that quiet space. Eyes were drawn to the rustling of fabric and remained on her. She tried to smile through it, but felt certain they knew that she was only baring her teeth.

"Tonight we have a new member here. Let us welcome Leslie, wife of Mark Hancock, to our circle."

"Welcome, Leslie," the circle of women said.

"Hello," Leslie squeaked in a small voice, timidly raising her hand in a wave. The women laughed, and she began to work the back of her cheek between her molars.

"Look at her!" the redhead cried, grinning as she gestured at Leslie. "All alone in a new town! And yet here she is, among strangers, and why is that?"

Leslie felt fresh sweat needle her scalp. She didn't understand what was going on, exactly, and swallowed heavily.

"Because she seeks the circle," the redhead continued, "she was hungry, and sniffed our apple pie sitting right there on the window sill!" Knowing chuckles arose from the group.

"I have seen so many women who were empty shells, looking for something to fill them up," the redhead smiled, "we are allowed such meagre powers! What are we given? Beauty. Beauty is power, but we all know that beauty has a limited expiration date on it, don't we?"

Leslie frowned. She didn't agree with any of this at all. She had met beautiful old women. These words about beauty, sickeningly familiar, were the tired phrases she'd heard in college, bantered among young men as they went about rating women like restaurants. As if women were only sacks of skin, devoid of hearts or minds. She fidgeted and Kathy placed a reassuring hand along her arm, gave a squeeze and a smile. But a disquiet had unsettled Leslie and even Kathy's smile couldn't obscure it from view.

The redhead continued: "We've all been treated like objects. Isn't it better to approach this on our own terms? Isn't it better to become the object *you* want to be, rather than let them decide what you are?"

Murmurs of agreement, and a smattering of applause that soon grew deafening swelled up in the quilt-confined space. Leslie chewed on her cheek quickly, a mild panic thrilling her limbs. She looked across the room and saw Ellen sitting in her white coat, clapping passionately at this speech.

Suddenly the redhead raised a pair of shears above her head, the metal shining in the gymnasium lights. "Let the revelation of truth begin!"

Two women from the crowd approached to take the shears and help the redhead off with her coat. Without the coat, she was naked, her body contoured to the current popular sizes and weights of "beauty." In a moment she turned her back to Leslie, and that was when Leslie saw the seams.

They were barely noticeable at first glance, and could almost be mistaken for shadows or fading tattoos. Long, thin lines ran vertically down her neck, her back, her limbs. As Leslie was puzzling over these lines one of the women slipped the blade of the shears into the seam and firmly snipped.

Leslie smothered a scream, but no blood spurted out. Instead, the redhead's skin split apart like fabric, straw springing free and scattering on the floor.

The women gathered in the circle applauded. "All straw!" One of them cried out ecstatically. "All straw!"

Leslie tried to stand, to get up to run, but Kathy held her right arm firmly, and Maryanne held her left. "Please let me go!" she cried.

"The moment of revelation is painful!" The redhead thundered. "But the gift of beauty is eternal!"

Ellen abruptly stood up, holding out a long, flat fabric costume in her arms. Leslie was pinned to her seat, sobbing. Nothing made sense. The redheaded woman was stuffed with straw, but she was alive. As Leslie wept, she caught Donna's gaze from across the room. Donna was not applauding or cheering. She was watching Leslie, her eyes flat and sad.

Leslie's mother-in-law drew nearer, extending the costume forward with a flourish, showing it off. In growing horror Leslie realized that the fabric was not a costume, but a fully realized artificial skin.

It was a fascinating sight—so strange that Leslie's sobs died down and turned to hiccups. The skin was a material she'd never known before, perfectly pliant and soft. But it was the face that hypnotized her. Even empty of muscle and bone, the fabric face was beautiful. It was the face of a woman she'd never seen before, but familiar—a version of herself that had only existed in her most confident daydreams.

The fatigue Leslie had been feeling lately returned. Weariness settled in her limbs and the women on either side of her sensed that Leslie was no longer a danger, and withdrew their hands. As she sat there, staring at the skin, Kathy whispered into her ear about the "procedure."

"They slip you out of your old skin into your new skin, and over time the leftover meat inside turns to straw."

"Does it hurt?" Leslie whispered.

Kathy patted her arm lightly. "After the new skin is on, it doesn't hurt at all."

"No, I mean—"

Kathy laughed, the sound lilting and bright. "Honey, all beauty hurts. You ever have a waxing?"

Maryanne, who'd overheard the joke, joined in the merriment.

Leslie felt hot. The quilts seemed to suck away all the air currents in the gymnasium. She kept staring at the fabric of her face in Ellen's hands, eyeless and perfect.

She was asked by the redhead if she wanted to wear immortality, and Leslie said yes. The moments after that were long and muddled, smeared with quilted faces and real faces that were quilted. She was stripped free of her pantyhose and high-waisted elastic underwear. She was momentarily embarrassed, but the women around her cooed nothing but kindness. She waited, standing in the middle of them, naked and trembling, when the cold tips of the shears slid in from behind and made their first cut.

Leslie screamed throughout, blood puddling below in quickly increasing amounts, the pain relentless. Ellen held the shears, cutting with expert speed. In mere minutes Leslie was flayed, an exposed agony of muscle and bone that could no longer weep. But arms were there to guide her quivering raw foot into first one leg of her new skin, then the other.

When her flesh was completely encapsulated by the fabric skin, cool relief surged along her nerves. She felt sleepy, and giggling women guided her to lay face-down on a pile of quilts. Leslie lay there, her new eyelids closed, while busy hands stitched up her seams. She dozed amid their comfortable chatter, their confident hands sewing her flesh in place. Galaxies were stitched and unstitched within her dreams, a long, thin thread running through them all.

LESLIE SAT BENEATH the yellow light of the diner, quiet, bent over a cup of coffee. It turned out that she hadn't needed the mystery book after all. Donna worked behind the counter slowly, methodically taking the orders of a couple of elderly patrons haunting the booths. She had put the cup of coffee in front of Leslie without saying a word.

"We're friends, right?" Leslie asked suddenly.

"Best friends," Donna said, abruptly reaching over and giving Leslie's shoulder a light squeeze.

A car horn honked outside. Leslie looked over her shoulder and saw Mark's car waiting in the lot outside. "Well, I'll see you tomorrow, Donna."

"I'll see you then," Donna replied.

Leslie left a five dollar bill on the counter. When she got in the car Mark was all smiles, his tie half-pulled and pungent with expensive colognes and perfumes. She leaned over, pressing her lips close to his with sensual abandon. Delighted with the kiss, he drew her closer to his chest and extended it.

"I take it you made friends tonight." He grinned. "You look stunning, by the way—did you get some makeup tips from them?"

She laughed. "The best advice a girl could get."

They spoke of light, inconsequential things in the car. At one point Mark brought up car shopping again.

"I mean it—if you need your freedom, I want you to have it. We should get you a car soon."

Leslie shrugged, indifferent. "It doesn't matter. Why don't we hold off? Everything I need is in town, anyway."

That night they made love, clinging together as if they hung over the edge of a precipice. His passion and excitement were palpable, a thrill she could feel vibrating in her own body. When he drifted off to sleep and she could not, she stood, walking to the window.

The stars were still there, abundant and glowing, but they were not as beautiful as the galaxies she dreamed of, sewn raggedly through her thoughts. She held up an arm to the starlight and twisted it, looking for the seam there. She soon found the line and ran her fingers along it.

When she began to chew on the inside of her cheek, it tasted like wool.

A Gut Full of Coal

Mathew Allan Garcia

———◆———

"You back again, Señor Tomas?" Ignacio, the newest dead boy, whispers. His voice comes from everywhere at once, carried on the winds as they ricochet down the mouth of the mineshaft, tornado-like, dusting soot and coal into my red-veined, tired eyes. I tread slowly, feeling carefully with my sandals on the wet logs stitched into the crumbling wall. They glisten black from recent rains. The boy takes my hand, leading me down, promising me he has found my girl at last, my daughter—my little Anna.

Some of the other boys do not remember the events leading up to their deaths—some don't even remember that they've died. They work on, loading coal into sacks, the moonlight shimmering through their translucent bodies as they make their way up the shaft, shining brightly as though wanting so badly to be alive, to be noticed. Only *I* notice them now. Only I am left.

Ignacio seems to know he is dead, but his memories prior to that are questionable. He knows I work here, but that is all I've gathered. If he remembers more, I doubt he would be guiding me. None of the others do anymore.

Today, Ignacio seems genuinely happy to see me. There is a curiosity in his tone when he greets me. His cold fingers slip into my hand, squeezing every time I take a wrong step. The staircase winds down against the wall of the shaft like the spine of some long dead serpent. Its bones shift below me, groaning as I slowly make my way down, my flashlight and canteen of water hitched around my belt.

Touching the soft, pliable clay down at the bottom, I grip metal. The carts lay scattered and the pulley system hoisted on the mouth of the cave is deserving of suspicion. The rope is frayed and chewed by rats, and squeaks with the gentlest wind.

The metal screeches as I push the rope aside and follow Ignacio's pull as he guides me through a cavern towards a flickering light. Directly beneath the light there is a hole of about three feet wide, perfectly round, around which there appears to be a thousand tiny dusty fingerprints. The men not-so-lovingly called this tunnel entryway *El Ojo Del Diablo*, the eye of the devil. I crouch down to look inside, and a draft as cool as ice water caresses my cheek, makes the hair at the back of my neck stand. Within the hole there is only blackness. For a moment there is an irrational fear that whatever limb I stick in will never come out again.

"Show me where she is," I say to the boy, "before I change my mind."

"Yes, *jefe'*," Ignacio says. *Yes, boss.*

I should go back. I know I should go back.

Instead, I hear myself say: "Take me. I'm ready."

A split second later, Ignacio fits his tiny body inside *El Ojo*.

He beckons me to follow.

SHE WAS JUST staying with me a week. Linda, Anna's mother, sent her down to me on a bus from Guadalajara to my shithole of a town. She said if I had time for my whores, I had time to spend with my little girl. Truth was, I didn't have time for either.

In the morning we'd take a shuttle to a nameless settlement on the hills of the mountain known as *La Coronita*, or the little crown.

It was raining when Anna arrived. By two in the afternoon the sky was muddy gray. Lightning, looking like the bones of some ancient forgotten gods, branched out across the sky. My feet were submerged in a foot of reddish dirt, numb from the cold.

Back at the mines there were two dead already, countless others trapped. Impossible to know the real damage until the rain stopped. Until the bloated, swelling bodies rose like driftwood in a black river to be collected and thrown out.

These are the worries that plagued me every waking hour, so I hardly noticed Anna as she stepped off the bus, rolling her small white suitcase behind her as people filed out. As usual, I thought of the coal, the numbers.

My hand caressed the phone in my pocket, waiting for the call from my superiors. Anna settled her hand into mine and by some strange magic all those worries melted away. I jumped.

The white little shoes I had sent her were sopping wet by the time she reached me. "*Mi amor*," I said. "*Mi pequeñita*. Look at your shoes…"

I hugged her, pulled her up into my arms. Tears welled in my eyes. Too long, it had been much too long. I was cold, but holding her filled me with warmth. It was the happiest I had been in a long time.

Anna smiled, rested her small head on my shoulder, and hugged me. Her arms reached halfway across my back. How she'd grown. "Papa," was all she said. All she had to say to break my heart.

And I promised her *everything*. That I'd quit, that we'd go home together and be a family again. That I'd take what little money I'd saved and buy us a house by the river in Morroan, her mother's hometown, and be happy.

"I have so much planned for us," I said. And I meant it. "Let me just settle some things first."

A day later, little footprints in the mud were the only sign of her.

THE ODOR DOWN here is wet and metallic from long days and sweat. Stale smelling now that the men have abandoned the mine. When it was in operation, some of them, so tired and weak from lack of daylight and nourishment, didn't bother coming up for anything other than filling their jugs with more water, and the smell hits you when you come about halfway down the staircase. It doesn't bother me at all anymore, but I've been in or around these coal shafts all my life. It's all I know. The smell of shit is the least of my worries.

Another lifetime ago, when I was a boy, Rafa took me from a life in the streets. Gave me work in the coal mines.

Back in those days, when I'd follow him around, Rafa would stand at the entrance and inhale deeply, take in all that sweat, coal, and excrement, and proclaim, "Smell that, Tomas? That is the smell of money."

"It smells like shit to me, Don Rafa," I said.

Rafa just frowned, leaning back to lock his gray eyes onto mine, his slim body roped with muscles. He was a man who knew the worth of hard labor, who had lived it. It was all I could strive for. "Well, you'll have to learn to tell the difference."

I was eight years old when I began working in *La Coronita*, and I must have moved coal through hundreds of miles of tunnels such as the one Ignacio and I now enter.

I hold my breath as I sit down on the lip of the hole and begin lowering myself in, legs first. Upwards, towards the entrance, the generator thrums on and the light above flicks bright, bathing the walls a burnt sienna, revealing drawings on the stone.

I've seen them before. Shadow families, drawn by the children with bits of coal. The biggest is of a woman with her arms outstretched, a fresh crop of children settled down around her, the words *La Madre,* the mother, scrawled beneath her feet. Her eyes are on them, two blackened specks, downcast, as if in mourning. On the ground, a circle of wasted candles and matches lay scattered. The mere sight fills me with anger. Live flames in the shaft were strictly forbidden for obvious reasons.

I turn to tell Ignacio this, but I see him looking up at me as the light dims. He and the drawings fade into the dark, while his touch on the soles of my sandals push me up. "No, no, *Jefe,*" he says. "Head first. You'll need your arms to pull you through."

I turn my body around, swallowing my fear down, visibly shaking. Ignacio giggles from the shadows, and then stops himself abruptly. I paw at the darkness as I lower myself, trying to find the bottom. Ignacio grips me by my shoulders. His hot rancid breath is on me, teeth clicking together, putrid tongue lolling behind them.

I close my eyes and hold my breath.

IMAGINE ME A boy. A boy of five, slim for my age, long arms and legs, eyes the color of honey like my father's, or so my mother told me those first two years after he left to start a better life for us in America.

Imagine me a fatherless boy. My father's mistress wrote to my mother to tell her what my father did not have the guts to tell her himself. It was over; there would be no more money, no life in America for the two of us. We were alone.

Imagine us in a part of town where the sidewalks crumbled underfoot, where the beggars shit and died on the same street corner and returned to the soil without anyone giving them a second look until the smell of their flowering bodies got unbearable. Where everyone was "passing through" and anyone who wasn't might as well be dead.

Imagine my mother, a curly-haired, fair-skinned *Hondureña* whose parents, like my father, abandoned her on their way to better things, leaving her as she ate her tacos *de carnitas* at a stand just outside of Jalisco.

Imagine her scared and cold, calling out for her mama and papa in the middle of the night.

"The road is long, and you must unburden yourself with heavy things," I recalled her saying, whenever I caught her looking at old photos, or letters from my father, casually wiping the tears from her eyes so I wouldn't notice. She would look straight at me, her eyes of too many colors. Cheeks lightly dusted with a fine line of freckles just below her eyes. "Luckily, you do not weigh a thing, Tomas. I will not abandon you."

She said it like it was meant to be funny, but it looked like a painful, sardonic joke that hurt coming out, and tasted bad for hours afterwards.

When times got desperate, my mother would take me for a walk to a town over. The night market on La Purisima was like a tour of Central America, bursting with an optimistic life of tourists and *immigrantes* passing by on their way to better things. The Salvadorians slung hot *pupusas* filled with *quesillo* and mashed black beans, topped with *curtido*. They cooked them on baking sheets sitting on burners, and as we'd pass we'd get a whiff of the melting cheese and hear the sizzling juices, smell the fermented cabbage relish.

Across the street a vendor sold steamed tamales wrapped in corn husks and stuffed with shredded beef lathered in *mole*. He had a steady line, swaying rhythmically, as a CD player placed on a box crate busted out bass-heavy *cumbias* all night long. Fried *empanadas*, stuffed so full with potato stew it dribbled out into the hot oil. I almost cried every time we walked by, held my breath as long as I could. I could hear my mama's stomach over the music.

She made figurines out of scraps of driftwood collected by the riverbank to sell to tourists who were known to pay too much for too little, but they looked at Mama's figurines like they were trash. No hope, but for the dull red fog of brothels, under the furtive glances of *gringos* who thought everything was for sale, everything was negotiable.

Conjure a cold so sharp, it penetrates your bones, freezes them so the sun cannot thaw them out before another cold night descends. A cold so heavy it takes the breath right out of you, pounds your lungs into mush. Makes you wish for death. That is what living out in the streets was like, before my mother decided she would do what she must.

She never sold a single figurine, but she kept us sheltered.

Now, picture her weak in bed, hiding the blood she coughed up in rolled napkins, her stomach knotted so she clawed at her own flesh. See her in bed, pale faced, a slick sheen of sweat on her forehead, when Rafa came for me at last.

He stood on the doorway. By then, I knew who he was. He had collected other children. I cried at my mother's bedside while she held my head in both her hands.

This weak, she could not make me look at her any longer. She tried, whispering to me, her eyes rolling feverishly in her head. It must have taken all the energy she had left to call to me as Rafa pushed me out the door.

On the way out of town, Rafa made me wait outside a shack as he collected another boy, Damacio, who had been living alone for months surviving on a diet of drowned rats and malaria ridden river water. He looked dead already. On our way to *La Coronita* my mother's last words rang out over, and over again. They would for the rest of my life.

"I am not abandoning you, Tomas," she called.

In the end, she did.

"COME," IGNACIO SAYS and disappears, skittering on all fours like an insect into a hole.

I pull my flashlight from my belt, turn it on and point it in the direction Ignacio went and move, crawling forward. The stone presses down upon me like the teeth of a giant, waiting to chew me up and swallow me.

"Ignacio?" I call, hating the fear in my voice. Hating the echo. Hating what the tunnels do to it, carrying it down into the recesses. I imagine something waking down deep, heavy eyelids snapping open, yellow eyeballs, an enormous mouth full of sharp, grinding teeth. Hungry.

I pull forward again, towards a bend in the tunnel, my elbows scraping on the floor. The outline of Ignacio's head pokes out from around the corner, a grinning skull in the darkness, until I train my flashlight's beam on him, then the gaunt face of a small child replaces it.

Ignacio's lasted longer than the others. The others lasted about a week, and then they retracted. Their little eyes still watch us, and their damp, small soles slap the stone floor a few paces behind. Sometimes they whisper horrible things. Call me names they'd dare not say to my face when they were alive. I've learned to ignore them.

We move forward like this for an hour, Ignacio running ahead and disappearing for minutes that felt like hours at a time, then returning to tell me we are going the right way. Sometimes he stays with me to talk, to ask his questions.

He asks me how it is up at the surface. Mundane things like what the weather is like, the time of year. He always circles back to ask of his family. Sometimes I think that is the only thing he cares about, why he helps me in my endeavor at all.

"Have you seen them?" he asks me now. "Do they ask of me?"

"I haven't seen them," I say. It is the truth, but his silence makes me add, "But I hear they had a beautiful funeral for you."

Talk about it makes me remember Anna's. I think of the small empty casket they lowered into her grave. How when I close my eyes to sleep now all I can see is her small, frail body, down here, on a bed of cold, hard coal. How in the first waking moments I believe she's there, next to me, and I'm frozen, unable to turn, to see her.

I was the only one in attendance who knew her at the funeral, and one or two other men who might've been workers—I don't remember their faces. They showed up in their best clothes. They nodded down at my feet, never holding eye contact, mumbling *lo siento* in unison, clutching their small worn rosaries in sweaty palms.

I couldn't stop crying, thinking about how my wife was two states away in our small apartment, unaware her daughter was dead. She always sent two letters, one for me and another for Anna. Anna's was always written in violet ink—her favorite color—and was placed in a small envelope inside of mine. It was my wife's way of reminding me that Anna was always in my heart, a piece of me that would never go away.

A pile of the letters go unanswered in the drawer next to my bed, the messages within getting ever more anxious. *Where is my daughter? Why won't you answer? Is something wrong?*

In the last one I read, she said she would come look for me but never showed up. I think she is afraid of what she'd find. If I could only find Anna's body, I'd answer her, as hard as that would be.

I clench my fists and fight the budding tears.

"Did my mother lay white gladiolus on my grave?" Ignacio asks.

"Yes," I lie, choking back my grief to accommodate Ignacio's.

"Those were her favorites." I can hear the smile on the boy's lips.

"Mine too," I say.

A MONTH INTO it, we had our first collapse.

Upon arrival at *La Coronita*, Damacio and I received little training.

"Follow Jose," Rafa said, looking over paperwork and pointing at a group of men standing by the lip of the shaft. I remember thinking that they looked nothing like a team of workers. They wore no uniforms, no hardhats, no masks or gloves. Some had no shoes. "Today you are ghosts. You will not be seen. You will not be heard. You will watch, you will learn. Tomorrow you start work."

They sent us into tunnels too narrow for the men to enter, with ceilings too brittle to risk equipment. Rat holes, they called them. Some of them were so narrow we had to suck in our stomachs and hold our breaths. Sometimes, only Damacio could slide through. I passed the pickaxe to him. Ran back the coal he passed back to me.

The humidity was unbearable. We were always coughing. I tried not to breathe in the coal dust. The walls bled toxins, and with little ventilation we could suffocate. Our hands bled most of the first week, and at night we slept little before beginning anew in the morning, our arms and legs never quite recovering.

On the third week Damacio and I worked a rat hole that had proven to be highly productive. We worked from dawn to dusk. I picked at the far wall while Damacio ran back the coal back and forth to the miners waiting on the other end. We were to clear the area quickly.

I must have fallen asleep as I relieved myself onto the wall because the next thing I remember, Damacio was squealing and the wall sliced open my hand as it rolled away, floor and ceiling seemingly moving in opposite directions, throwing me like a rag across the floor, tearing me up and grinding us down. Damacio's arms appeared from the Rat hole and I grabbed them and pulled. He was almost through when the ceiling bit down, hard on his waist.

In my pocket the flashlight's beam faded as the bulb cracked. The filament glowed an angry orange before dimming. Damacio was silent.

"No, no," Ignacio says as I turn right towards the light. Amusement is in his voice, like he's watching a rat in a maze heading towards a dead end. "Not that way. Cave tunnel is broken that way. Many dead. It is this way. She is here."

He points to a narrow slit in the wall to my left that in my hurry I completely missed. The sound of dripping water and the smell of fresh, wet soil. I train my light at it and am relieved to see the ceiling rises so I can finally stop crawling. I pull myself the last remaining feet and Ignacio offers his hand to me so I can stand.

His cold fingers tug at my own, much like Anna's little hands tugged me along through the carnival last spring, to some other ride, some other amusement. *Daddy. C'mon Daddy, just a little more.* She had brown curls, big almond eyes, and thin little eyebrows that told the world how she felt about it at any given moment.

Thinking about her, I wonder how old Ignacio was when he died in the shaft. I know more about the boy now that he is dead than when he was alive, and yet I've never asked his age, though he seems to be about the same age as my Anna—nine.

His body was never recovered. To be honest, we never really looked.

In this line of work, you don't stay optimistic for long. That's another pearl of wisdom from Rafa. There are lots of ways to die down here. If you were *really* unlucky, you might live weeks before you suffocated. Sometimes the rats got at you before you fully passed out, but *after* you'd gotten so weak you couldn't stop them from gnawing on your face. We've found the remains after, when we blow open the rock again and find a hundred rats covering the remains like a wooly blanket, quivering in bliss.

Only once did I send a crew to search for a missing worker, but the dip in production alerted my bosses. I know there's more than one because it's someone different each time they call. Different accent. They use different words to compel me to push the coal harder, faster; find reasons to skimp on machinery, safety measures, uniforms, training, whatever.

The one who called that first time spoke quickly, with a jangling twang in his accent, speaking about numbers and revenue. Quotas. *Big* quotas.

My English was still not very good then. "Se murio un niño, señor."

"Have this *niño's* people come looking for him?"

"Well..." I trailed off.

My boss on the other end of the line hissed, taking my silence as an answer. "Well, fuck. Then there ain't no emergency."

"*Jefe*," Ignacio says. We have stopped. Or, rather, I've stopped. He looks up at me, his cadaverous hands tugging at my own.

"How did you die?" I whisper, before I am able to stop myself. Suddenly, the urge to know is overwhelming. My heart thunders, ringing in my ears, filling the tunnel.

Ignacio turns quiet, and for a brief moment his hand loosens its grip on my own and I know I've startled him.

"I died here like the others," he says, his voice dropping to a whisper, secretive. "I died alone. Lost and hungry."

Ignacio turns to me and smiles. "Eventually the emptiness in my stomach was too much to bear."

I shine my light on him to see him more clearly. Wiry arms and legs, head large and bulbous as though it were draining the life from the rest of him. His cheeks were sunken, bags under his eyes like the bruised skin of a rotting peach. Around his mouth a black slurry dribbles from the corners of his mouth.

"So I filled it," he continues, reaching out and touching the wall, tracing his finger up and down as if remembering, "I filled it with the only thing there was plenty of. I filled it with coal. And when my stomach was good and full I...I slept."

"My God..."

"God? What *God*?" the boy laughs. "The only God I know lives deep, deep. He eats to his fill and spits out the bones of children. Some of the other boys say you know of him. Do you, *jefe*?"

"I...do not," I say, my face flushing red. I try to recount the turns we've made. Suddenly the stones all around me are sharp hungry teeth pushing in. The other dead boys watch us, slipping out from the walls like blood. I didn't have much time.

"Anna. Take me to her, please."

After a moment, Ignacio shrugs and, without a word, continues on.

I DID NOT know true darkness until I was trapped a mile inside the earth, in a hole just large enough to cup my body. And half of Damacio's. I could not see my hand an inch in front of me, and every so often the rocks groaned under the weight, and dust rained down on me. I was afraid to cough for fear it'd all come crashing down.

The concept of time was the first to go. I could have spent only hours down in the hole, maybe a few days, a week, a whole godforsaken month. The point is I lost my grasp on time as soon as the light went out. I was floating in the abyss.

My canteen of water was the only thing that mattered. I pulled it from my belt, shook it. Judged I had about half left. Instantly my mouth felt dry, and I started crying into my hands.

"Water," Damacio whispered, to my left. Smacking lips, ragged breath. His hacking cough shook the walls. "Please. Tomas. Water."

"Shh. Hear that?" I said. Scratching, though I could not pinpoint the direction. "Hear that, Damacio? I think they are coming for us!"

"Water," Damacio said. "Water."

I dragged myself over to the sound of his voice.

When I reached him I felt with my hands to find his mouth, picked him up from the back of his head, pressed his lips to my canteen. Just a few drops.

The back of his head was wet and sticky, a gaping hole in his skull where his head was bashed against a stone.

"Water," he repeated.

"We must save," I said. I listened for the scratching. Nothing. I checked him for supplies. If he had had water, the tunnels had swallowed it when they ate his legs.

It was the last drink of water I would give him. Even when he begged, crying for a few drops, anything.

"I see you," Damacio said. Then he went silent. They were the last words he said.

I wasn't as lucky. I stayed in the tunnel twenty-one endless days. Until my ribs poked through my skin and the smell of Damacio's rotting body began to smell like the overripe flesh of a papaya. My stomach turned. From hunger or disgust, I didn't know which.

I began passing out from the hunger. I woke disoriented, sweaty, a rat nibbling on my toe, bouncing away when I jerked awake. They were on Damacio, eating. Loud little eaters, rats. They hissed and snapped as I scooted close, squeaked as I grabbed for them frantically, my mouth watering. I was weak and slow.

I passed my fingers over Damacio's extended belly, feeling the boy's bellybutton. I lifted his head, light, hollowed out by the rats. The flesh had rotted to the point that it was easy to dig in with my fingers.

I don't know how long I had been asleep when they dragged me out of the shaft. What I knew, what I came to realize when the warm sunlight touched my skin again and I had regained my mind, was that I would do anything, anything to not enter the mine again. I'd fill the mines with all the children Rafa needed in my stead to make it so.

And I did.

THE TEXTURE OF the walls change. I touch them with my free hand, letting my fingers run along the smooth contours. Even the air tastes cleaner. Fresher.

I picture Anna running through this very same tunnel, wearing her white summer dress, the jade earrings her mother bought her in a shop in Mazatlan last spring sparkling in my flashlight's beam. I picture her face, innocent with pale gray eyes.

"We're not in the coal shaft anymore, are we?" I ask, my voice small, hoarse, and raw.

"No," Ignacio says, after a few moments. His mind pulls away from me. Leaving me behind as he finds his brothers who crowd tightly around us, their wretched sour breaths on my face, their open, broken maws, slick with coal juice.

Their thoughts are hideous, loud in my head.

Leave him. Break his light. Leave him down here. Die.

Ignacio laughs, a high-pitched gleeful cruel laugh of a child pulling the wings and legs off a fly and watching it squirm as the ants tear it into pieces.

Let him hurt like us. Let him feel what we feel.

Others chime in.

Liar. Murderer. Feed him coal.

"There is a cave system close to mine shaft. We passed into it not long ago—wait here."

He lets go of my hand before I'm able to say anything, and I stumble in the dark.

"Come back!" I scream. "Don't leave me here!"

He scampers away, shuffling in the dark. My breathing is jagged and hoarse from inhaling the fumes and soot from the mine. I step after the sound of his footfalls and strike a rock. My foot is trapped as I fall forward. My leg cracks like a dry branch. There's pain, hot and sharp. The bulb from my flashlight cracks against the wall in a shower of sparks. Pure darkness.

"I'm sorry," I say, the tears spilling from my eyes. I'm afraid to reach down and touch my leg. I try to move and scream, vomiting from the pain. "I'm so sorry."

"Shhhhhhhhhhhhh…" Ignacio's voice comes from about ten feet away, obstructed by something, as though he is around a corner. "She's afraid. She not come if you make noise."

"She. She's...?" I struggle to talk, to ask. Afraid of the answer. Afraid of un-knowing what I thought I knew. What I was ready for. "She's alive?"

And I hear her. Her breathing. Quick breathing, like she's frightened. The soles of the white shoes she was wearing on that last day click towards me in the dark. Her feet inside squelch, like wet soggy cardboard, her breath hoarse and raw like mine. Shambling, she approaches me, her steps awkward.

"I was so worried about you, sweetheart," I hear myself say, my voice cracking. The dead boys spill out from the shadows, smelling blood.

Liar. Filth.

"I love you so much," I pull myself towards her, dragging my leg on the floor and I nearly bite my tongue. Blood floods my mouth. Frantically, I paw with my free hand to reach her.

She takes my hand in hers, her skin loose and wet over small birdlike bones rolling just beneath the flesh. Immediately the shadows are quieted. It's just our breathing and the silence that thrums through the cave walls, like the lifeblood through the veins of a god that is always hungry.

"Daddy," Anna says and she pulls me along, her feet squelching. I howl in pain as I get to my feet, forcing myself to follow, my injured leg dragging behind. Tears fall to my cheeks but her touch is reassuring, and I follow her. I'd always follow her.

"My *pequenita*, my little one," I say, sobbing. So happy, the pain flaring. "I love you so much. I'm so sorry."

"C'mon, Daddy," she says, her fingers interlocking in mine as she pulls me further into the cave, into the wet, sweet inviting earth.

"Just a little more."

Crow Woman

April Steenburgh

She was not beautiful, not by any typical aesthetic. Too often there were twigs and tangles in her hair. Too common were scratches and scars across her skin. Her voice was rough as a cat's tongue, coarse as a jay's shout. Her limbs were long and spindly, sun-toned skin and exuberance-toned muscles stretched taut over bone. All too often she forgot simple things like shoes or a shirt, seeming content to lay on dewy grass and sigh as the sun rose to warm her.

No, she was not beautiful, not to anyone who did not know her. But I knew her. I knew the way she tilted her head when she was listening, even if her eyes were flitting about, looking anywhere but at me. I knew the way she leaned in, just a bit, when she wanted company and contact, and the way she went still and straight when she would rather be left alone. I knew the way her dark eyes glittered when she smiled.

And she smiled at me often.

I found her, or she found me honestly. It was cold, it was rainy, and I was trying desperately to get a key to turn in a stubborn lock to let myself into the house that had been mine for less than four hours. It had worked effortlessly for the realtor, a smiling young man who was so very earnest.

The key had turned and he had gestured me in to where it smelled slightly of old potpourri, of cinnamon.

I bought the tiny house to answer a need. It was so different from what I was used to with its bare, shoe-worn wood floors and peeling floral wallpaper. I bought it as a retreat, a place to hide, to provide a piece of the world that was small enough for me to fully comprehend. Instead it provided the incomprehensible as I tried to coax the door to open.

She slipped past me as I stood on the stoop, hair dripping water onto my nose. She jiggled and jostled the lock and it yielded instantly, as if sorry for its previous behavior. She let me enter before squelching in after, leaving toe prints on the old wood as she stalked forward on the balls of her feet.

My world consisted of a tiny house in the woods outside of a small town in upstate New York and a wet, skinny woman who had yet to say a word but who looked at me expectantly.

"Thank you." I had no towels; they were packed away somewhere still. So I offered what I had on hand—thick curtains that smelled somewhat like old smoke and mildew. I held them out to her as I stood by the window, smiling awkwardly—what else does one do in this sort of situation?

It would never occur to me to strip down in front of a stranger, exposing every inch of flesh without a care. But she did, sliding out of a dress that was more a courtesy covering than proper clothing anyway. She wriggled about in the curtain, huffing quietly and happily. I could smell the musty damp odor that accompanied her, the smell of something that has not been dry for quite some time. I wondered if her fingers and toes had gotten all pruney. I was jostled from my rather strange train of thought by fingers plucking at my shirt.

"Hey, wait a second…"

"Shhhhh." Her voice was the dry rattle of wind through dead leaves as she batted my defensive hands down. "Shhhhh." It was a gentle susurration, as she pulled my wet shirt over my head, coaxed me out of my pants, and wrapped me into the dry panel of the curtain.

I looked at her, all lean, uncooperative, naked angles. I looked down at myself, stripped to my skivvies and wrapped in a curtain that smelled old and misused. And I laughed. I laughed until I warmed up, until my sides hurt and my stomach tightened around the hole where dinner should be. I laughed and she smiled along with me, mouth cracked open and eyes glittering with a strange brand of humor I would learn to recognize as solely her own. She was intent and amused, dark and deliberate, and reminded me of young crows I had enjoyed watching as they explored and entertained themselves. If crows had a monarch, I imagine she would be their queen.

I laughed and my world pulled together—my little house, my musty curtains, and my crow woman with the rough voice, dark hair, and darker eyes.

SHE WAS NOT beautiful in any normal way, but most definitely somehow insidiously so. She settled into my little house like she belonged there, helping me unpack boxes the next morning until we found the coffee pot, and then the coffee. Sugar was discovered lurking in the very bottom of the box of pantry items and two mugs had been scavenged from the slightly dilapidated box of dishes. The look on her face as she watched the coffee brew was amusingly endearing, the expression as she slurped in her first mouthful divine. She was beautiful in that everything seemed new and magnificent to her, from the curtains I purchased that first afternoon to the welcome mat I rolled out in front of the door.

Bit by bit she helped me make my little house into something wonderful—unpacking and organizing and being present to the point that I never questioned her right to be there. She was the unplanned element in the middle of my attempt towards control. Somehow, I did not mind. She was never invasive, intrusive—she seemed more interested in the game of making house than making a nuisance of herself.

She liked to putter. I was not at all used to being puttered around—was not used to having people around me. Not anymore. But she slid casually into and through my personal space with a quiet rustle, moving things from here to there, adjusting and designing as I moved in. I could not tell to whose preferences she was arranging knickknacks on a shelf, bowls in the cupboard. Either our tastes were so similar as to not matter or she was a rather quick study in partialities I did not realize I exhibited. My favorite mug was always clean, always waiting by the pot first thing in the morning (regardless of where I left it the night before). My shoes always made their way to the mat I had placed to the left of the front door (even if I had managed to kick them off across the house somewhere).

She pressed close in the evening when I turned on the television to start turning off my overactive brain. It wasn't a cuddle, but it was definitely a plea for contact, and it was not long before I reflexively adjusted my position upon sitting down to accommodate her angles rather than readjusting as she moved in.

I soon learned to take an attitude of wry indulgence when it came to her half-feral nature in regard to clothes. She was predictable in her negligence towards things like pants, sometimes getting half there in attending to one sock, but not the other. She would shimmy and scratch if she stayed in clothing too long, or would wriggle if she found something too confining. And those were the times she remembered clothing at all. My unplanned housemate was not at all suited to going out, heading to a restaurant or club. But that suited us both just fine. I was more inclined to paint than to plan an outing anyway.

Her disregard for social expectations extended to sleeping arrangements.

To say I was surprised the first time I woke to bony arms wrapping around me would be quite the understatement. I fumbled out of dreams and almost out of the bed before I recognized her particular chuffing laugh. "What? What are you doing?"

"Shhhhh," came the familiar response, as she reached out for me. Her dark eyes glittering in the bit of light sneaking in from outside, asking what she could not seem to find words for.

I will admit, I was as lonely as she, and I curled back up in the bed and learned to go to sleep soothed by the sound of her regular heartbeat, her light breathing with its slight whistle of a snore. Her arms and legs on and around me. And if she always made sure a window was open, letting in the sound of insect and amphibian and owl, I did not mind. It was infinitely more comforting than the noisemaker I had purchased ages ago at some store or another to make thunderstorms for me while I slept.

SHE STARTED A garden out front, a garden of forest flowers and creeping vines that were as wild and beautiful as she was. I planted tomatoes and peas beside them, the juxtaposition making me smile. She liked to sit out there, beside flowers that were small and purple, humming quietly with her toes in the dirt and her eyes towards the sky. I could never make out words in her voice, but the melody was calming.

Even if I did eternally worry that someone would come by and catch sight of more skin than was socially acceptable. We were outside the town proper, in the hills where houses were too small, too old to be attractive to tourists. But the hustle and bustle of the seasonal wave of visitors was close enough that I worried, occasionally, that someone would wander our way. Even if just accidentally.

I learned to have my mail delivered to a post office box rather than the house, as she was fickle around strangers. Often she did not like them getting too close to the house itself, while other times she was inappropriately affectionate and open. Either way, it was just asking for trouble and explanations I had no way of giving.

That first time the mail had been delivered, after I had changed my address and convinced weeds and vines to relinquish their grip on the old post box at the end of the drive, my crow woman had gone still as a pointer with a scent. Her eyes had narrowed and she had started to stalk forward, movements predatory. The flowers she had been tending forgotten, her grace slipping into something a bit more threatening, her elegance alien and monstrous. I stumbled to my feet and rushed to the end of the drive, knowing I needed to get there before her, to be handed the mail, to demonstrate there was no harm in it. At least, right then, she was wearing a sort of sundress so that was one less thing I had to distract a smiling civil servant from. Life and limb were preserved that time, but my heart took a long time to stop its stuttering, to calm. I was terrified to think of what would happen should the mail come when I was out. Or asleep. Or doing any of the myriad of other things that kept a person from sitting and watching for their mail. There being no market for "Beware of Crow Woman" signs, a post office box it was to be. I did not think too long on why I was so sure things would go so very wrong. I was good with body language, and there had been a definite threat in her eyes.

I never stopped to think on why she never frightened me.

It occurred to me it was probably unhealthy, this isolated relationship I had with my crow woman, but I was content. I was happy. Which was more than I had had previously, before my little house in the woods. Before my crow woman. The warm smell of her was soothing, the thin but not at all fragile feel of her around me was comforting. Something quiet had been coaxed to life deep in me, and she nurtured it with every casual embrace, with every harsh, happy laugh. I tended it with every mug of tea I handed her, with every evening I pulled her close before she had a chance to shift as close as she dared.

She kissed me for the first time as we sat in our garden, watching fireflies in June. Her lips were dry, her tongue darting aggressively even as her eyes were tentative. I reached around and rested my hand on the back of her head, gently holding her in place. Gently accepting. Wanting. Loving.

HER EYES WERE on my back when I left for town—groceries did not get delivered in a place such as this and I wanted a better liner for the shower. Comfortable enough in my own skin for the first time in so long I did not realize I was a stranger in my own town. The weird woman who lived on the hill. I did not feel eyes on me as I filled my car with gas. Never sensed how they sized me up, judging, assessing. My mind was already home, making adjustments, nesting. Curled around my crow woman.

I started drawing again for the first time in ages shortly after I learned my crow woman tasted like berries and a hint of old tea, wanting to capture the quirk of her smile, the sharpness of her laugh. I wanted her angles to slant across my paper, soft in charcoal, blended and caressed into shape with my own fingers. There, in my own little pocket at the edge of civilization, I pulled myself together on paper, reshaping myself even as I gave shape to her.

I had been an artist, once, loving nothing more than that feeling that there was nothing apart from what was unfolding on the paper in front of me. There was no awareness of self, of tools—just creation. I missed that. It was some of what had prompted me to purchase a tiny house in the middle of nowhere. I had lost something previously when my life went sour. Somewhere my ability to create had frayed. I limped along, but I was still too aware…

"Shhhh…" she whispered, wrapping her arms around me the first time I grew frustrated with the limits of pencil and paper and tore a sheet from my sketchbook. "Shhhhhh…" she soothed, pressing kisses into my hair until I calmed down, allowing myself to be frustrated without getting violent against my tools, against myself.

When she unfolded from around me, taking with her the slightly musty smell that reminded me of fall and forests and birds and her, I started a new drawing. I drew her as she stretched and lounged amidst black-eyed susans and bee balm, naked and comfortable in her skin as I never seemed to be.

Unless her skin was pressed to mine, her breath rasping in my ear. She was like putting on another set of clothes, rolling into a favorite T-shirt that had been worn to extreme comfort, perfect fit, and always smelled just ever so slightly of things loved.

I smiled, this time, as I drew. And she smiled as I worked, as she watched a bee alight on her knee for just a moment before moving on. It was idyllic, this moving in and settling in, this discovery of my little house and all the little pieces that seemed to fit so effortlessly.

IDYLLS ARE ALWAYS broken. Mine was disturbed by a knock at the door. I looked up and around. My crow woman had brushed past on her way outside to play in the wind that came before the rain that had been threatening since we woke. I was less of a wet creature, preferring to stay indoors when thunder rumbled nearby. Alone and anxious as I had not been since I had driven my hatchback out to this place in the woods, I moved through the little house to answer the door.

"Hello. I hope I'm not bothering you. My car died, down the road. I just need a phone…"

He seemed awkward where I am pretty sure I looked terrified. "No. No bother." My voice was as rough as my crow woman's, harsh from disuse. We communicated in smiles and looks around here, touches and weighty glances. He was almost familiar, in that way some people from the town were familiar—faces I saw when I picked up mail and milk, part of the scenery but not part of my life. I never sought eye contact, much less social interaction. "Would you like to come in?" The words slow and deliberate.

That is what one offered in these situations.

"Thanks, I appreciate it."

I was too comfortable in my little house, in the safety of isolation. I had never paused to consider the danger. The danger was in hands far stronger than my own that pushed me aside as soon as the door was shut, in a body that was frighteningly concerned with intimidation. I was breathing too fast, too shallow to scream. I was too terrified to do anything but freeze up as he pulled a gun. I pressed myself back against a wall (recently repainted, I remembered laughing at a dollop of pale yellow on my crow woman's cheek), trying to be as small as possible. I don't know what he could possibly want in my tiny, isolated house. I had so little of value to someone who was not myself or my crow woman. He scared me with his abrupt motions and the weapon he handled like he was familiar with it. He terrified me as he started to rifle around the living room, seeming increasingly irritated to find nothing important, expensive, special.

I was anxious, always anxious. Terrified of people, of the unknowns they carried around with them, the unknowns they represented. It had driven me away from my big apartment with the expensive furniture and my art on the walls. Away into the woods where my crow woman found me. This intruder was the embodiment of late night fears, the stair or the hall making a noise when all should be silent. He was the embodiment of a fear of crowds and being crowded as he rounded on me, gun raised, wanting to know where my valuables were.

The sound of breaking glass was accompanied by the screaming of crows. A whirlwind of fury funneled into the living room from the kitchen, black wings slashing through my panic, cutting the silence.

A murder of crows—all furious shouts, jabbing beaks and scratching claws. They filled my little living room, pulled at the hair, the skin, the clothes of the man from the town. His blood splattered on my pale yellow walls as he desperately tried to protect his eyes—his interest in me, my things, forgotten as he stumbled away.

Even predators can turn prey. I watched as they scratched and jabbed at him, pecked and tore. I smelled urine and fear as he tried to find the door in the tangle of wings and anger that wove confusion through such a small space. I cowered there, against the wall where he had left me, and watched dark feathers snap through the air, listened to the shouts and screams of the crows and was comforted. They sounded so much like my crow woman, her presence expanded to encompass an entire flock, to fill the entire space.

And in stalked my crow woman, dressed only in her long dark hair, her face painted with an anger I had never seen before. The crows quieted when she entered the room, but did not release the man, keeping flesh and clothing clutched in claw and beak. He stood still, dripping a humiliating mix of bodily fluids onto my carpet (I remembered my crow woman wiggling her toes in it in delight when it was first installed) and he stared at her in horror.

She was not beautiful, my crow woman, not to anyone but me. Her angles were harsh, her voice was rough, and her eyes at this instant contained nothing even remotely kind or human. But I had never loved her more. She brushed a hand along my arm as she passed, comforting, consoling, and promising. She tilted her head to the side, eying the man from cold, cold eyes—analyzing, assessing, terrorizing. This was a side of my crow woman I had never seen—a darkness and vicious edge that threatened that which had intruded into her territory, had intended harm to what was hers. Who was hers. If crows had a god, she was here standing before me, defending me.

"Make him go away." I whispered in a voice that was now rough from fear and embarrassment. I pressed myself against the wall, to try and smother the shaking.

She opened her mouth and blinked once, slowly, at the crows, then pointed at the intruder with a finger that was sharper than I remembered. The crows erupted in chatter and my crow woman added her voice to theirs, slipping a vicious hiss and rattle into their shouting. Wings flapping, beaks snapping, they drove the man out my door and soon their voices faded until it was myself, the musty and musky smells of conflict, and my crow woman alone in the living room.

Her expression beckoned, eyes warming even if her face did not soften, not really, as she opened her arms.

I pushed away from the wall, stumbling the few feet that divided us and fumbling into her. I could still feel his hands, smell his breath as he shouted. I shook as she embraced me, nails like talons as she gripped me close. "Shhhh…." She huffed against my hair, nuzzling ever so slightly.

My beautiful, impossible crow woman. She was a thing of forests and sketchbooks. She was a thing of dreams and myths. She was holding me close, holding me together.

The skin on her palms was rough from working, from gardening, from being outdoors as much as she was, but her hands soothed the shakes from my body. Her harsh voice sang calm into my ears.

Dark, sharp eyes appraised me the next morning after I showered. I breathed deep and met her gaze, water dripping from my hair to my nose. I had made a decision, standing beneath hot water, the smell of soap strong in the steam, the memory of her strength and ferocity vivid in my mind.

"I need to go to town."

A smile broke over her face, mouth gaping open as a single approving laugh shot free.

I needed to learn people. My crow woman, with the dark core that seethed beneath her laughter, made me safe. Now I would be strong. I would pack my purse, gather my coat, and drive in to town in my battered hatchback and file a report. I would spend some time in the café, in the library, and learn the people in the town, how they looked at me. How they looked at each other. My crow woman had taught me the trick of casual glances, subtle touches. Of learning a person so that I could taste their personality.

Maybe I would even stop by the local gallery and see if they might be willing to carry my art.

Now, I was willing to be pulled close, to breathe in the warm, musty smell of my crow woman, to feel the peck of a kiss against my hair. Now I would tangle limbs with my impossible, perfect crow woman and remember how to be something other than afraid.

The Dandelion Disorder

Charles Wilkinson

———◆———

THE ARRIVAL OF the swifts a week early that year, their shrill cries circling above the house, should've accompanied a promise of fine weather, sunlight with the strength to warm the cold corners of the house, drive the morning frost-ghosts from the garden. Instead they bring only the memory of the last summer with her husband, who over the years had announced himself to be on the brink of becoming a superlative composer and subsequently a great artist. After these careers had come to nothing, he proclaimed he was on the verge of producing the finest poetry of the century. He is the man who asked her to murder their child, her son, now a pale boy of nine wearing a blue hat with a broad brim and reclining on a divan just inside the sitting room.

The French windows, which lead onto a wild front lawn littered with clumps of daisies and daffodils, are open. Lawrence is leafing listlessly through a book on dinosaurs. This morning his habitual curiosity seems to have abandoned him. He's in no mood for what is after all a tale of a grand extinction, but the energy to swap fact for fiction, or even turn on the television, is lacking. She must interest him in the world.

"Do you hear the swifts?" Although she's seated a few feet away from him on the veranda, she's angled her chair so she has a clear view of the interior.

"Yes, I think so. A kind of screaming, although I don't think they're in pain."

"Yes, they're perfectly happy, darling. Although they've come a long way."

"Where from?"

"Africa."

"They must be tired."

"Perhaps. But they can take a nap on the wing."

He smiles, wistful. "I should like to be able to fly while I'm asleep. When I'm at boarding school, I'll flap out of the window at night and not come back. Nobody could blame me, not even Matron, because I wouldn't really mean it."

"You're not going back to boarding school, Lawrence. Remember?"

"Yes, that's one good thing about…what's happened."

She doesn't want to talk about it now. The busy prattle of the house sparrows and sudden low swoop of a swallow across the lawn contrasts with her lassitude, the stillness of her son, his forehead grey in the shade of his blue hat, holding the dinosaur book in his thin white hands. She moves a short way across the lawn. It would be a discourtesy not to mow it before the lease on the property runs out, but there is no machine in the shed and she's yet to put an advertisement in the newsagent's window. As if to counter this thought, she bends down and picks the largest dandelion, its solar yellow suffused with the deepest radiance.

As she walks back towards Lawrence, he lets the book slide off his lap, all pretense of looking at it, let alone reading it, having been abandoned.

"Did my father know about me?" he asks.

"Yes."

"Is he still alive?"

"I only saw him once after you were born."

"Where?"

"It was a long time ago." She will not tell him about the court case.

Lawrence peers up at her, narrowing his eyes as he tilts his head. His forehead whitens as the shadow retreats under his hat. "Was he rich?" he persists.

"No, he was not."

Gently she tucks the head of the dandelion under his delicate chin; of course, there's no gleam of gold on his soft white skin.

TEN YEARS EARLIER, at the start of what had promised to be a summer of hope—for herself and her husband Theo, the father of her unborn child—she laid three places at the kitchen table for lunch. Not one room in their tiny, cluttered cottage had resisted the advance of Theo's current project, a series of paintings with the provisional title *The Legends of the Plants*. Preparatory sketches have had to be removed from the table; jars filled with brushes and bottles of turpentine taken out of the sink and draining boards; a primed canvas banished from the top of the stove. After twenty minutes, she reclaimed the kitchen for cooking. Fortunately Theo's oldest friend, a fellow artist whom he's reviled since their schooldays, was late. She hadn't told Theo about their child, not yet showing beneath her billowing skirts, barely visible even when she was naked. This was, she told herself, because their poverty would make its arrival inopportune. Her teaching job was poorly paid; Theo disdained practically all attempts to market his art. He talked of building a body of work that would provide unassailable evidence of his genius; then he'd command any price he asked.

"Harold is here at last," said Theo, his huge rock of a head, uncombed arabesques and corkscrews of dark hair, angled round the door. "Bring in a few bottles of beer when you've a moment."

Once the vegetables were set to boil, she went through. Although an argument about aesthetics was raging, Harold found time to acknowledge her with a nod and a soundless movement of his lips that suggested he had once again forgotten her name.

"Lunch is ready when you're ready," she said, opening the bottles and pouring out the beer. But already they were moving in the direction of three pictures leaning against the wall, a triptych that was to form the centerpiece of *The Legends of the Plants*.

Again, she was struck by how short Theo looked, in spite of his large head and powerful upper body, when standing next to the tall and spindly Harold, whose height was accentuated by the lines of his striped blazer.

"Well, they have your customary reverence for vegetation and text book exactitude," said Harold.

The foreground of every painting was dominated by enormous plants, precisely painted but with any sense they might be growing eliminated. In the background, a few tiny mythological figures were frozen in antique attitudes. Although she had never ceased to praise her husband's formidable skill, she wondered whether his paintings, in a style close to photo-realism, had so far failed to attract the attention of the top galleries she'd taken them to because they'd no sense of either the uncanny or the transcendent.

Pudding had just been served when Harold made his pronouncement. She had already sensed he was holding something back. Never knowingly a modest man, Harold had been even more superior and condescending than was his custom.

"I've had some rather good fortune recently," he said.

"Oh," said Theo, holding his fork suspended in mid-air.

"Yes, I've had two paintings accepted for the Summer Exhibition."

A tremor ran across Theo's forehead; something was crumbling on the rock-face. Any second now, trails of scree would fall down his checks. He put down his fork and attempted to compose himself. "Only two?"

"Well, it's a start," said Harold, beaming delightedly. "I think you'll agree."

"Congratulations, Harold," she said.

When she went through with the plates a few minutes later she found him up to his forearms in foam-castles, the knives rattling furiously beneath the water. He had never been known to assist with domestic duties before. If she spoke to him there would be no acknowledgement. His canvases had been rejected by the Royal Academy. It was her fault he'd suffered this humiliation. He'd argued that his work could only be hung to advantage if he was accorded a gallery to himself, a privilege reserved for the most senior academicians. She'd said it was important to build a reputation. In the end, he reluctantly assented to submit, on the condition she parceled up the paintings and took them down to the capital herself. How could Harold's pallid flower paintings, weak imitations of Winifred Nicholson, have been accepted when his work had been returned without comment?

To deflect attention from Theo, crabby and petulant in the kitchen, she showed Harold round the garden. There was little to see. The cries of swifts overhead were just audible, although the house martins had yet to return to their shell-like nests under the eaves. She put her hand to her stomach: a faint stirring deep within.

TODAY SHE TAKES the short cut to the post office, down a narrow rutted track lined with grassy verges. Overnight, the yellow fire of dandelions has gone to be replaced by soft grey globes, the stalks still upright, the seeds not yet dispersed; the daisies and buttercups are still visible alongside delicate webs of cow parsley. Once she's close to the village, the track turns into a path with the vestigial remains of tarmac. Her route will bring her by the Bowls Club, which is on the edge of the village. Although the round trip will take her no more than three quarters of an hour, she worries about leaving Lawrence alone. Once again, he's had little for breakfast and lunch; if she had some bathroom scales, she could confirm her impression that he has lost weight.

As she walks down towards the village, she sees a match in progress on the bowling green. From a distance, the white clad figures are ethereal yet stately; one after another, they genuflect, ghosts at an Elizabethan court. The sky above them is high, only a few sail-shaped clouds suspended in the blue. The hedge surrounding the green has been trimmed so low that there's a clear view of the club. As she comes closer, she realizes the game must be important, for it is being played in silence; no sound except for a snatch of subdued birdsong. A man wearing a flat white cap takes a few paces and bowls. His movements are deliberate, a hint of arthritic stiffness contrasting with the fluency of the bowl whispering over the grass. The click as the jack is struck sounds unexpectedly loud in the surrounding quiet. The bowl sidles and comes to rest, black and winking in the sun. Then she sees him: Theo is seated on the veranda of the Club House. Although he's lost all his hair and his face is grey as pumice, the hard cast of his features is unmistakable. What looks like a hospital blanket is draped round his shoulders, arms, and below the upper half of his body. The men watching the game are sitting well apart from him on the bench. It's a second before she realizes that his trousers are rolled up and his feet are soaking in a large porcelain bowl. He's looking in her direction, but there's no hint of recognition in his small, sunken eyes. With a shiver, she turns away and hurries on. Once she's finished she will have to take the long route home.

It's when she's in the post office that she starts to fear for Lawrence. There can be only one reason why Theo is here. He wants to harm her son, the boy whose birth ended their marriage. If he has found out where she's living, he can easily be at the cottage in a matter of minutes. Although she's locked the doors, breaking in would be a simple matter. On the other hand, he appeared shockingly ill. And why was he watching a game of bowls? She can't remember him showing an interest in any sport or recreational activity. Something is amiss. Is he dying? Does he wish to confront her one final time with all his old accusations? Despite her misgivings, she must take the shortcut. Without stopping to chat to the postmistress, she withdraws her money and hurries back up the road.

As soon as she reaches the entrance to the Bowling Club, she's aware of a change. The sense of witnessing an ordinary event that is simultaneously veiled in ritual has vanished. Groups of women in pleated skirts are chatting normally. Although the game is still in session, the members in the Club House are leaning towards one another, possibly conferring or commenting on the performance of individual players. There is no sign of Theo. Is he on his way to the cottage? He appeared very weak. If she hurries now, she will surely have a chance of overtaking him.

The path leading back home is steeper than she remembered. The verges are flecked with the foam of high cow parsley. The dandelion clocks become large grey eyes peering through long grass. Although conscious of hurrying, it's as if she is moving slowly, pushing forward against an unknown source of resistance, soundless and invisible, a power channelled towards her that has nothing to do with the faint wind in the treetops.

Through a gap in the hedge, she catches a glimpse of the cottage; for a second, it is tantalizingly close, but when she next sees it, it is further off. Absurdly she wonders if it knows she's moving nearer and is retreating up the hillside. She's not out of breath, but her legs are heavy, as if she's been struggling for hours against an incoming tide. Then whatever force she's been fighting absents itself; she's moving freely at last. Within minutes, she reaches the top of the path. The cottage still stands in its unkempt grounds, the garden a confusion of grasses, wild flowers, and weeds, but now every window is wide open. Has some mad thing been rushing from room to room, screaming at the world outside? The front door's unlocked. She dashes through the downstairs rooms and up to the top floor. No sign of her son. She's in his room when she spots him. He's in the garden, crouched down in a corner by a hedge. From the window above, it looks as if he's trying to make himself as small as possible under his broad-brimmed blue hat. She stops to catch her breath and then goes outside.

He doesn't look up until she's within a few feet of him. His mouth and eyes appear even tinier, as if fear has driven them deeper into his face.

"What's happened?" she asks. "Why is everything open?"

"I had to let it out."

"What? A man?"

"No, not a man."

"Are you sure? A rather…unpleasant man…has been seen not far from here."

"It wasn't a man."

"Then what was it…precisely?"

He looks down, trying to disappear under his blue hat. "I can't explain. It would sound silly, and it wasn't silly…at all."

That night, after she's put Lawrence to bed and checked twice that every door and window is shut tight, she goes into the room that serves as her study, where there are several cardboard boxes containing the data and detritus of her past life. Amongst the old bank statements, yellowing photographs, exam certificates and diplomas is the address book that she used when she was married to Theo. It has a telephone number she needs.

AFTER HAROLD'S VISIT Theo stopped painting. Sometime she found him in the sitting-room, his hand on his chin, as he stared down at his incomplete canvasses. At nights he would leaf through the notebooks containing his preliminary drawings for *The Legends of the Plants*. Then one morning, after she'd been shopping, she came back to find his oil paints, sketch pads, water colors, all the impediments of his life as an artist, had been cleared away.

"I've decided my vision can best be expressed through the medium of poetry," he said.

"Oh? And your painting?"

"Will no longer be my primary concern; in fact, you may take it that I have stopped. For the moment. Of course, it's not inconceivable I might produce a drawing or an engraving to complement my work. Once it has found a reputable publisher."

She crouched down and started to unpack the cans of tinned soup with quick, irritable movements; then she placed the cheapest cuts from the butcher's into the fridge along with the milk and vegetables.

"A change of direction which was long overdue," he announced, ignoring her hostile silence.

"And so what are we going to live on?"

"What do you mean by that?"

"It's perfectly obvious, I should have I thought. We have my pittance from a part-time job and an occasional income from your paintings. Not much admittedly, but it was something. And you were beginning to make contacts."

"Mine is an artistic decision, my dear; one you'll just have to accept."

"I can't think of a way you could impoverish us even further. Anyway, you may recall that the original plan was for me to be the poet. You were going to write your first symphony and a concerto for organ and orchestra and then I was—"

He turned away from her and stalked out, slamming the front door. She finished putting the yoghurts in the fridge and then went over to the window. As she expected, he was walking, swiftly and coatless, in the direction of the village inn. It was not his first tantrum that week. She decided to prepare an evening meal instead of lunch.

In the early evening, he returned. They did not speak until she had served supper. Then once he'd sunk into the most comfortable chair, she was treated to a speech replete with alcohol-induced wisdom. She'd been aware when they were married that he had the highest possible artistic ambitions; the road to distinction let alone greatness was not an easy one; a man of vision must not allow the thought of mere pecuniary advantage to deflect him from the path of true creative fulfillment; with recognition, came the possibility of riches, but the building of a reputation was not the work of a moment; the way was arduous, but the two of them…

"Three!" she put in.

He sat up at once. "Three?" For the first time in months, she could feel his eyes wandering over her body, weighing up its width. "I thought you'd put on…but we agreed. Remember?"

"It wasn't planned."

"How could you do this to me? It's not simply the money. Although, as you have pointed out, our circumstances are straightened at the moment. What appalls me is the sheer lack of consideration. You know I need absolute silence, complete calm, if I am to have the slightest chance of producing my best work."

"I'm sure we'll adapt."

"You must get rid of it."

She knew how much he distrusted any display of emotion in her, but in spite of herself there were tears in her eyes. While expecting his shocked reaction, she must have hoped that at some level he would be pleased, even if only by the evidence of his potency.

For a week, they hardly spoke to each other except on practical matters. Once, when he reminded her to put out the rubbish, he stared hard at her stomach. Then there was a note in his black copperplate, which he left on her bed: "Don't forget how I suffered in my childhood." But it wasn't until the day the dandelions turned to seed that she decided to leave him.

He was lying in a deckchair on the lawn, his eyes closed, his feet stretched out. The exercise book, in which he had been writing since his rejection of painting, had fallen onto the grass. As she was bringing him a tray with his lunchtime sandwich and bottle of beer, she wondered why she continued to cater for him. He was wearing a slouch hat and summer shorts. The bottle rattled as she approached, but he made no attempt to take the tray from her.

"I hate to think of it growing inside you," he said, still with his eyes shut.

"It will be your child too."

With unexpected speed, he sat up and plucked a dandelion from the lawn. For a second he sat there contemplating the downy clock, rotating the stem between his finger and thumb, studying the complexity, the constellations and wisps of star fluff. Then he opened his mouth wider and blew. "Your child's head," he announced, holding the stem of the dandelion out to her. At the end there was a small white cap, bald with the tiny black indentations from which the ghostly remnants of every seed had flown.

A FORTNIGHT SINCE the afternoon the house was invaded, her efforts to understand what frightened Lawrence have progressed no further. Every attempt to broach the subject brings another of his headaches, which have worsened considerably since the incident. There is a letter on the table in front of her. With a sick child to care for, she has been forced to relinquish the full-time job she took after leaving Theo. Fortunately her father has consented to pay the rent on the house now that he no longer has the burden of boarding school fees.

"You must eat something," she says through the open door to the sitting-room.

Lawrence levers himself out of an armchair. As he sits down at the kitchen table, he takes off his blue hat. Since the treatment intensified, he has lost his hair. His white skull has a vulnerable, porcelain gloss, like something precious and easily broken.

"Are you feeling sick?"

"A little."

She has been to the Bowling Club to make enquiries about Theo. They listened to her open-mouthed and askance. No one recollects seeing a man wearing a blanket anywhere near their premises. The Club does not have a strict dress code but everyone is respectably turned out. There is no plan, a humorist in a striped blazer adds, to admit Mexican members.

It is five years since she took out an injunction and his threats stopped. Yet her instinct is always to flee, to move from property to property, to find a remote corner of the country, a place she'd never mentioned to him, where she'd no contacts, somewhere he'd never think of searching. One problem is that since the court case she's no idea where Theo is living. She must not risk revealing her whereabouts to his elderly parents, who have always taken their son's side. But now she has Harold's number. She's tried to contact him on three occasions with no result, but at least she's been able to leave a message on the answerphone. Surely he is every bit Theo's longest-serving enemy as well as his oldest friend?

"Do we have to go to the hospital today?" says Lawrence.

"I'm afraid so. We have to speak to the consultant about the X-rays. Remember?"

"Will I be allowed back?"

"Of course. You're only going for a…"

The phone rings. She picks it up at once and takes it into the next room.

"It's Harold here. I received your messages. Sorry to take so long to get back to you. Now you want to talk about Theo…"

"Yes, but please don't let him know I've been in touch."

"There's no chance of that. I'm afraid he's dead."

"When? I'd no idea."

"Only about a month ago. I went to his funeral. Although to be frank, we'd not seen all that much of each other in recent years. He was writing his epic poem about plants and he always wanted me to read and comment on whatever he'd done. A frightful bore as he was offended by any criticism I gave. Even when it was mildly favorable. When he became very ill I did visit. Once or twice. He was very bitter."

"How did he die?"

"A brain tumor. Inoperable. And oh yes…there is one thing he asked me to send you. A section of his long plant poem; it's called 'Dent-de-lion', if I remember rightly."

"Is it about…is it…any good?"

"That depends on whether you think visceral hatred is a suitable subject for poetry."

Later that morning she sets out with Lawrence to the hospital. Although the sun has burnt away most of the early morning mist, there's a haze in the distant blue, a sense of driving towards another and more ethereal landscape.

"Mummy?"

"Yes."

"You remember the day when you went out and I was scared?"

"Of course."

"Well, I never told you what happened…not really. It would have sounded stupid. But now I only want to worry about real things. Not things that might not be here."

"That's very sensible. You must tell me what's troubling you."

"I was in the sitting room when I thought I caught a glimpse of a very round, grey-white head. It had one brown eye right in the centre surrounded by wisps and tiny stars. It was only there for a moment and so I went outside to see what it was. I looked right round the house and couldn't find it. But then there it was inside the house, staring at me through the window. This time it was huge, a kind of furry head on a green stem. I know this is silly and you won't believe me, but it was like a big dandelion clock all gone wrong. I opened everything inside to let it out."

It would be another hour before they reached the outskirts of the town. They were driving through bare empty hills with no hedges, only a dribble of stone, the faintest of mists still lingering in the hollows.

"I don't think that's silly at all. It's terrifying to think of something so ordinary turning against you."

"Yes, but was it…real?"

"Perhaps it's because of the medicine you've been taking. We'll ask the doctor. But what you've got to remember about dandelions is that they'll be dead by the end of May."

"So only a few more days to go then?"

"Yes, and then you don't have to worry until next year."

Whether the prognosis proved to be good or bad, when she gets home she will begin a poem, a blessing to counter the lion's teeth curse, a celebration of how the blown seeds are used to tell of love and bring grief to the gardener but joy to all who prize what's indomitable and wild; and how her son's head will grow hair again, and the dandelions will defy the black earth, raising the blaze of bright petals to the sunlit day.

Of Marble and Mud

Farah Rose Smith

———◆———

"Good sister, wrong me not nor wrong yourself."
The Taming of the Shrew

The windows will be the first to go. Then the walls, the bones of the walls, the ashes. Rotting skin touched by pale violet light, the scents, the birth of flowers from toxic soil. A great curtain from the sky will fall down, draping over the memory of the black tree. Instinct rises, the heat of the world, in mansions, in men. Today will be grey-dark, marble, and mud.

The place where the house stands was chosen with particular care, to avoid prior habitations and the potential for eerie nonsense, as Helen attracted such happenings wherever she went. At times, Vanessa questioned the strain in her relationship with her sister. The volatility. Then she remembered that blood would always be, and carried on with her preferred state of living.

The storm. With no television, no radio, no means of measurement, she can't know what time it will arrive. Only by the creeping darkness of the western sky can she imagine that it will be later tonight.

The great "Palace" Parsis, under the black globe. Not a palace at all, but her home, glowing faintly as a spectre of what was once a spectacle of libertine living. Imagine, the happenings in this strange town! In those days she would have found the neighboring haunts unmanageable but in *this* age there is reason. In *this* age, there is rest!

The stairwell. Both doors, top and bottom, have been locked. A single candle lights the space, illuminating only her marsh-soaked shoes, and the occasional passing tail of her sister's mouse. That hideous creature, Mendelbaum. A dwarf shrew, flitting in filth about the house as though it were welcome.

All that remains in the house of Helen is her scent, though it is masked by the pungent gloss, newly-painted on the staircase.

Disquieted by the moan of gusts, she sits, she breathes.

A THEATRE OF pain it is, to dream without sleep. Images. Constant, assaulting images! Her fragile sister, now swamp wraith, hovering over the muck in eternal indecision over her predicament. She assumes this, caught in the tendency to assume when one has inflicted circumstance upon another in bad faith. She watches and listens, warmed by the ever-cooling rays. Vanessa sits in contemplation of Helen's body. She calls her sister, not Helen, fearing some supernatural stirring should her name ring out into the distant night.

HELEN'S EYES WERE bright and full of waiting. Her mythic glamour disgusted Vanessa. Her beauty, a shimmer of honesty in a house built by fiends. Helen too often took to reckless wandering, getting lost in the tedium of the marshes, accompanied by an invisible court of creatures.

Engrossed in a singular reluctance, the labyrinth of the night, disbelief sets in. Met with supernatural claims alone, Vanessa listens, and misunderstands.

She didn't want to take care of Helen anymore. Her nightly jaunts into the wilderness had grown exceedingly tiresome. In the company of wolves, Helen was without weeping. So Vanessa allowed her to continue. But what of allowance, in sisterhood? Is it not obligation to watch over a younger sibling with the delicacy and attention of one's own child? Or is it duty to only warn, to nudge, to temper? Should one temper beasts, spirits, or wistful women?

After reasonable hours, the heaviness of walking through dense muck becomes a tiresome chore. At the moment of indifference and a swift turn back towards the house, a delicate globe of pale light lingered by Vanessa's left cheek, grazing slightly before shooting off into some uncharted distance.

The looming magnificence, painted by nature in black, sent pain through her heart. A raw, metallic scent disturbed her nostrils, as did a peppery haze that gathered on the surface of dense, bluish mud. She stood before the great, black tree for the first time.

The orb circled overhead in a mockery of revelation. Exhaustion, the discharge of the evening, snaked through her, filling the empty space with deep aggravation. Still, she could not find Helen. The world disappeared in the omnipresence of the black tree.

Doubt filled her, wondering how she may find the area again. That doubt would soon be a distant memory. One look to the skies would reveal another natural abhorrence. All winged creatures, birds and bugs alike, would sway outward over a single patch of dense forest in the north, meeting again after traversing a semi-ellipse of strategic avoidance. All save for a single, coal-black owl that appeared out of the strained aether, shooting straight down into the mist with the age-old security of an expected familiar.

Are there witches in these wetlands? The spoils of their dark methods? Vanessa slid a cold hand over an enormous root, protruding from the muck. How can it live? In wetlands like this, it should have drowned. The roots are exposed, though they must run deep. Logic cannot accommodate the existence of such a thing, but it lives, and ages beyond the comings and goings of the landscape.

I feel my life when I love, more so than when I'm loved
But this is not to say that the latter is not needed
It is a gift of excess
Rarely expected, cherished on high
As something I may not deserve
But wait for with the patience of the soul.
—H

In one instance of decorative chatter that left Vanessa humiliated in important company, Helen expounded upon wisps of light, lanterns of the supernatural lurking in bogs and swamps and all such soaked earth. A fire grew in her as she spoke of them, a rarity when she found herself among others. Each wave of exhaustion dipped Vanessa further into cynicism.

"Fireflies." She spat, tired of the esoteric nonsense.

Helen sat upright.

Vanessa shook her head.

"You'd be wiser to fear water snakes, my dear."

"I don't fear *them*."

Annoyed, Vanessa gathered herself and approached the old oak bookcase beside the great window overlooking the marsh. She continued listening, as Helen mentioned the orbs as being young boys doomed to haunt the marsh, or spirits of stillborns, or unbaptized children caught between heaven and hell.

"In Ipswich? Please." Vanessa spat. A dark look flashed across her sister's eyes as she continued. "I believe we have, at least, avoided the stain of sorcery."

Helen smiled faintly as a dim glow pulsed in the distant marsh, visible from the polished window.

"Have we?"

THE FAERIES OF nature know no lesser landscape than this. They crave the rainbow soil, rearing o'er the moonbeams. Not this muck, this gloom.

Without wings, they strut with a measure of grief, the Eternity worm gauging their anguish, weaving frenzied fortunes through mortal horns.

They will have their ending, and I will have my peace.
This is the way of things in the dark world.
Blackness crowds failing eyes, and I
See myself a memory
Holding hands with the girl who shares my name
Whistling in the darkness
Sighing as I die
And am born again, as water, through the hollow hills
All is still in memories of wickedness
I built myself there, in the well of shame
Tasting life, as poison, to remember
How good it will be to be
Myself again.
—H

VANESSA CAN'T PUT the dream out of her mind. It is living alongside her now, undeterred by reality. A sorceress of decrepitude, sinking inch by inch in the shadow of the black moon. She watches her, an elemental agony sinking into her long-dead bones, stirring up a new, virulent death. One that recognizes the conditions of her first expiration with an absence of earthly reason. She is not the sole wraith doused in the muck. A wind turns north and stirs a corpse of a different age. No—dozens of them. Fragmented. Dear lord…children. Infants! Mangled bones suggest deformity in every case. Long-dead bodies. Long- dead souls.

Dark deeds made porridge of sapphires and buried them here. Darker even are these deeds of menace and mayhem, a grotesquery of animals rising from the farthest untold reaches of the marsh. A heathen porridge of snakes, insects, and vague, writhing creatures, amassing on the surface of the wetlands, a menagerie of warning…How can she see them? Sense them? These are not true senses! Vanessa is still in the stairwell. The pungent odor of the wood gloss makes her head ache. Mendelbaum continues to scurry past her feet.

> *I once stood as a beggar before the might of Autumn.*
> *I walked into death's garden with the tenderness of the age.*
> *Delirium struck—gold, purple, orange yellow, blue!*
> *Heaven hid from all when shown my teeth,*
> *With ages sealed in red dust.*
> —H

TINY CARVED HOLLOWS in the railing. The cascade of the steps—a delicate, wistful drop—a cryptic elegance that stood apart from the rest of the house. Nothing else, the wood, the marble, the furniture—nothing else was that black. Not even the dense darkness during a night of storms. The ornamental detail in the wood was immaculate. The golden fixtures at the top and bottom, striking, eerie, familiar…

Helen was distressed.

"Oh no, you couldn't, you shouldn't!" Angst soaked into her bones as her hand lifted from the black rail, a gesture seen only when one dips their hands unconsciously into the remains of the unjustly deceased. The tree now existed solely as the immaculate ornamental staircase in Parsis, a pretentious construction that didn't even fit in with the décor of the house.

"It's already been done, Helen." Practical reassurances. Helen's light dancer's body leapt unconsciously to escape the psychic odor of the tree's remains.

"All that is left is the gloss, and then, we will not speak of it again."

Her eyes grew wild with despair. Helen slowly stood upright and lifted her eyes to the space above Vanessa's head.

Overcome by uncomfortable air, Vanessa succumbed to the bowels of her fury.

"You stupid girl, come to your senses! Your *true* senses!"

"This is evil!"

"I should tie your hand to the rail and whip you for saying such a thing!"

Tears of fury slipped down Helen's cheeks. Tread a worm on her tail, and she would turn again. Vanessa's fear of her sister was alive in her. Helen lifted her hand so strangely that Vanessa lost herself in that very fear. Her hands latched onto Helen's shoulders and thrust her down the staircase.

She didn't make a sound beyond a sharp inhale at the start of the fall.

Her body, with grace, plummeted down the steps. From Vanessa's vantage point overhead, her body seemed to float, a mangled heap of pale flesh and scarlet lace.

A luminous festivity it is, to die without attention. Without circumstance.

To float off into an immediate darkness, the bells of a familiar street becoming warbled mumbles in the distance. If such dreams are to erode a hole in Vanessa, in the stomach, or farther down into the gut, she would not be offended. Such a retribution would be easier than all this waiting. Helen's scarlet dressing gown was removed carefully, burned without care. The silk ribbons in her wildly curled tresses, snipped away and cast off onto open flame.

With supernatural strength, Vanessa carried her sister deep into the tangled mess of the marsh. A dull, pressing instinct in her ribcage compelled her onward, towards the jagged remnants of the black tree.

Tired eyes wandered over the faces of punishment. Corpses, unobserved, over the fragile passage of time. The bliss of heaven glowed in some invisible high ground, beyond the sheath of screams in the quickening place. Weightless, invisible flesh crowds behind her. The Palace Parsis in the murky distance. The splendor of eternal night growing cold-cold in the depths of her bones. She placed her there, as quietly as in her crib. Rocking her gently, quiet-sick sister. Her figure, dimly lit and clothed in a billowing white gauze befitting the most delicate of angels, sank down into the murky depths of the marsh. Bodies, crisp and icy-blue, stirred. Their frozen, mummified remains intertwined in some heathen embrace that knows no sound or memory but those of death.

THE WAKING DREAM comes to Vanessa again.

The black tree stands still, in a desert of sound. A heathen wetness ebbs, feeding roots. The swamp wraiths gather, sprinkling dust over the blue muck. It begins to rise more rapidly.

An unfamiliar woman, in a long-forgotten kind of gown. Figures in black, holding books. Torches. Herbs. The tears, the helplessness! She is forced to swallow the yellow powder and pushed into the muck. Her face scrapes past one of the tree roots jutting out from the water. Blood pours down her neck, each gush of fluid timed perfectly with the croaking of hidden toads.

Bundles of cloth are unfolded to reveal deceased infants. A dozen other women are dragged to the muck at the base of the tree. The gouging of eyes, slashing of throats, disposing of all accursed flesh! Bodies, one by one, fall to the great, dense slop. There the world trembles. There, the horror of the marsh becomes magnified. The great tree, once of an innocent color, grows blacker and blacker, fed by the flesh of the accused. The burden of history takes possession of Vanessa, in the stairwell, dream-awake.

Helen slips back into the accursed half-water and presses tired feet to the nothingness below. This is she—divinity marked by softness, and elemental whispers from the deep. Her mouth slightly open, tongue to terror, she trembles. The muck has come to her lips.

Stillborns, deformed children, mutated animals—a tree that was not black upon birth. A tree that changed course, as it soaked in the dense darkness of betrayal rooted beneath.

There have been witches here.

Might their very footsteps have passed over the land before the house was erected?

Half-swallowed by the scene at hand in Vanessa's waking dream, Helen grows earth-tired. Desperate and alone, she descends into the cosmic recklessness of hope. Her mouth pulls back, against the wind. Vomit dribbles lightly down her chin. A blind eye sweeps over the dagger of eternity. Contained almost entirely in the depths of the muck, her head still hovers slightly above.

I am great and I am nothing.
The disease of eternity lives inside of me.
Blinding time, the dagger of intention
Wills me to move forward and move on
There is a seat to take above all movement
Seeing, breathing life as life again
I think of these brief moments at the end
When all has spun to spirit threads above me.
  —H

She rips her face from the glistening lips of fiends and sees the dead world's dawn. This is the waiting place of fallen dreamers. The place of dismal recompense. Of slights. Vanessa fights. She will not succumb to the haunt of waking dreams. A solemn phosphorescence breaks out from the dying house. The storm grows. Helen, far from her, dissolves—a dream of meditation in alien light.

In the height of dreams, I want what is not meant to be. I have come again to the place of pure perception.

I forget the meaning of all things and bask in the eternity of not knowing.

I assign nothing with the vanity of consciousness I possess, only by some cosmic misstep.

With human eyes, I see nothing, know nothing. With the eyes of eternity, I no longer have to know.
  —H

It is guilt! If not a pure and unquenchable masochism that led Vanessa's hands to hurt her own flesh and blood. She will beg Helen for forgiveness.
She will hear me!
She will forgive me!
She is mine and I am hers, and blood will be! Blood will always be!
The storm has not yet reached full malice.
That isn't wind! That is her gentle knocking on the door.
Here, Helen! I'm coming! I am opening the door!

The door opens.
Her body is torn to shreds by the swirling remnants of the decimated house, awash with broken wood and a sea of blood, strewn upward by a peculiar wind, decorating the grand staircase with the scarlet remnants of human life, bloody flesh, and bone splinters and dust, lit by the single fading candle at the center step, the delicate patter of Mendelbaum felt by her unending consciousness for as long as the stairs may stand.

No one will tear them down.

For a moment, the faint sounds of a tired owl echo past the window. A flash of darkness speeds by and leaves with equal swiftness, off into the gloom of night and the great dark marrow of the marsh.

All Is There Already, Just Not Seen Yet

Armel Dagorn

———◆———

AURÉLIE SAJID'S FAME came with its share of rumors, so I wasn't too surprised at first by her quirks. Like the requirement that I come in from the start for instance, and work not only on the editing, but attend the shooting as a PA of sorts, a handywoman. She wanted the whole team involved in everything. I didn't mind—it was worth it for a shot at working with the cult filmmaker.

My first task was to manage transportation. Sajid had insisted on casting on location, so we bused some eighty pre-selected people to Brocéliande for tests. Sajid divided the crew in four teams, giving each a small camera, and reminded us of the phones she'd given us for the duration of the shooting. She encouraged us to take photos and films if we found anything of interest, and the phones would automatically upload everything into the database. She didn't say if the whole project would be in found-footage mode, but it would definitely play a role.

Each team was given a handful of actors and made to roam off into the night woods. We fed them lines, filmed them close up.

"What's that?"

"I heard something."

"Stop!" a tiny cry would reach us from the darkness, where another team was shooting.

I'd been skeptical, and as Sajid's informal assistant, anxious at the hole this weird test dug in the budget—Sajid insisted on paying the actors for the casting, even though not one of them would have missed the opportunity to work with her.

"It'll be worth it, you'll see," she told me. "They'll write the film for us."

I must say I saw what she meant. I knew just as much as the rest of the crew about the script, which is to say next to nothing. All we had was a couple running away, scared, through the woods. Not even names—Sajid was waiting until she'd cast the roles, so her characters would simply bear the actors' names. She joked that it was less work, that this way she didn't have to come up with them, and it was easier to remember people's names.

The tests did make the project more concrete for me. The actors seemed disoriented, looked around, jerky, when another team's spotlight danced on trees in the distance. Their faces showed worry even before we started rolling, and their lines, when they said them, came naturally, and I felt that they were maybe not talking to the camera but to me.

SAJID HAD DECIDED to shoot in Brocéliande, despite the fact that we could easily have found a similar setting closer to Paris and not have to get everyone all the way to Brittany. It was her thing, though. Just like she'd done for *Littoral*—she wanted to jam together stories and places that had nothing to do with each other. Let the viewer pick up or not on such nods. She was borderline mystical about it, about how a setting, with its historico-mythical baggage, could influence, weave tapestries in the unconscious. So of course the current, as-yet unnamed project, despite being set exclusively in Brocéliande, would have nothing to do with Brocéliande, with Arthurian legends.

"Except if people want it to," she told me, smiling.

IN THE EARLY morning the actors' faces looked empty, as if a little of them, of their substance, had made off in the night, sucked by a thousand midges, as if each scripted cry they'd let out had carried a little of them. The forest changed hues, and though the dark persisted under the canopy we could feel the sky brighten, like a light coming on in the next room. We drove back to the outskirts of Rennes, spent.

I looked a little baggy too as I caught a glimpse of myself in the mirror, reversing the van in the dirt tracks, joining the caravan back to civilization. Driver, that's another hat I wore then. A hat many of us had, as the cheapest option had been to rent a fleet of vans.

As we reached the main road I looked back and saw Marius, the sound editor, in the mirror. He'd been conscripted to drive a van too. I wondered if he could see me, lit by the feeble glow of the dashboard. If he looked.

We got to the hotel in twenty minutes. We'd pretty much booked out the whole cheap Formule 1. The vans released their passengers on the lot, puzzled zombies who fumbled for their room keys, trying to compute where they came from with this ugly neon-lit morning.

I looked for Sajid, or Marius, but only saw the shuffling crowd of tired actors. I gave up and walked to my room. A couple of men in suits came against the flow, from the few rooms we weren't occupying, on their way to the breakfast buffet.

After sleeping for most of the day, I started going through the rushes. I did it right there in my cheap, soulless room. Sajid wanted us to stay put and go back out again filming as soon as possible.

I sent her the rushes sorted by actors, along with a few comments on each performance. I found it difficult—it wasn't my job, after all. And looking at these mad people shouting in the forest, it was hard to remain level-headed, to judge value, to comment in meaningful ways. In ways that would impress Sajid, if I'm honest. Of course I was trying to impress her. Even though I hardly knew what she wanted me to do.

I guess it didn't help that by the time I was starting, night was falling outside, creeping into the room through the shitty curtains. I was just finishing when I heard cars drive into the parking lot, their lights flashing onto my bedroom's walls. Aurélie Sajid was returning from the woods with the scouting crew she'd recruited to get some atmosphere shots.

I sent her an email before going to bed, and I fell asleep like a stone in a pond.

I WAS AWAKENED by the ping of my phone. It was two in the afternoon. The room was bathed in light, and I frowned like some disturbed bear after her long winter sleep.

It was Sajid. She had watched the rushes. I rubbed my face hard, trying to knead wakefulness into it. Had she slept at all? *All good*, she texted. She had a list of names, *and that young woman. You know the one, dark hair, petite, great presence.*

I tried to review in my head the young women we'd cast, to bring up faces from the crowd, the faces lit in the forest, the lost walkers in the parking lot. When that didn't yield any results, I opened my laptop and looked through the head shots. One of the names Sajid had given me came close enough to the description, and I wondered if she had got mixed up, thought there was another actress.

"No, damn it," she said when I told her. "It's not her."

"Well, there's no one else like that. I've gone through the pictures three times," I said, worried Sajid might lash out at me.

"Really? All right. Must be me, then. Never mind."

I WONDERED LATER if Sajid had just been messing with me, trying to shake me. I'd heard of course of her methods, of the way she immersed not only actors in the filming, but the whole crew. There's that line from an interview that had made the rounds at the time. Before the shooting, I looked it up again—watched loads of interviews, in fact, like an overeager student.

"Do you try so," Sajid had been asked, "to allow viewers to insert their own ideas, their own bits into your stories?"

"No I don't. Or rather they don't. All is there already. Just not seen yet. And what one person may see, another might not perceive. You see what you want to see, I guess. So really, you're out making a film that might well be about something you don't even know about."

THE SHOOTING, WHEN it started, was almost normal. We drove again to the forest, and once we set up for the first scene—Tom and Gwen arriving in the woods, ramming their car off the dirt track—Sajid was much more hands on. The two actors got out of the car visibly shaken. Tom was livid, his fists tight as he got out, holding the shocked memory of the wheel. Gwen recovered before him.

"Come, we don't have time!"

He followed her as she ran into the dark. We went after them in pursuit. Sajid had only given broad directions, so it felt like it was some messy instinct that carried us after them. Sajid jogged along the Steadicam guy, guiding him with a hand on his shoulder. Gilles, who would play a cop the following night, had been given a small camera, and he was running to my right, his gaze switching awkwardly from the cold bright screen to the dark shapes scurrying ahead. I followed with the rest of the crew a little behind. I felt a strange frenzy, the weightlessness of bounds broken.

We heard "Cut," a breathless yap, and the whole troop, Tom and Gwen, the cameramen, stopped in long, slowing steps. We came to a rest together, some leaning hands on knees, others lying down in the cool crumpling mattress of the forest floor. For a minute all I could hear was the heavy breathing of a dozen people over the rustle of leaves.

"Why are we running?" someone said, and we all broke out laughing. That's when I spotted the mike hanging down over us. I was lying down, and I followed the pole up into the branches, saw the dark shape of Marius, the glint of his glasses. The white of his teeth as he smiled at me.

THAT'S WHAT TOM had said when Sajid briefed them on their first scene. "Why are we running?" He'd had trouble swallowing that he had to potentially wreck someone's car, and he wanted to know at least what he was supposed to act.

"You'll know in time," Sajid had answered. She wanted the actors in the dark, only fed them pieces of their characters' stories just before a scene. She said she didn't want them to pollute it with their preconceptions, their medium-like knowledge of what was to come.

"This is real, Tom, or at least we want it to be. If I told you you were going to die in there," she said, pointing her outstretched hand at the dark she wanted him to plough the car into, "would you do it? If I told you you're going to run in there and someone, not right away, not a hundred meters in, is going to come out of the dark, and kill you, would you still go in? No. That's why I'm not going to tell you anything. Let me worry about the mood, all right? Let me worry about you being in the right frame of mind."

Tom looked away from her into the forest. Sajid had told me the next part of the story, as I had a few things to organize for the next shoot, but I might have been the only one who knew. That Tom and Gwen were running away from cops, a real, tangible threat, rather than the hazy menace of the forest. She'd made me source a gun, with blanks, and I prayed she'd tell them before it was fired.

"COME ON," SAJID called out on the parking lot when we got back to the hotel that morning. "It's included!"

She looked happy with how the night's shooting had gone, and we all caught her cheerfulness. We stormed the breakfast buffet with the same exhausted giddiness a hangover day with friends brings. We scared a few suits into gulping down their coffees, I think. Those nervous extras.

Sajid maneuvered me toward a small table Marius was already sitting at.

"You two'll have to work together, my children."

I wasn't used yet to Sajid's shifts in tones, but it somehow made sense. Here she was with her kind smile, the lines of light in her otherwise pitch-black hair. She had smoothly orchestrated for us three to sit there alone, as if she were setting us up, and I realized the messy, let-whatever-be attitude she seemed at times to have was in no way lack of control. I wasn't complaining, though. I'd been hoping I'd get to work with Marius. He'd attracted a lot of attention for his work on Sajid's previous project.

"Marius will do his own thing, mostly, while the rest of us shoot, but I think it'd be good if you kept track of whatever it is he's doing. You'll need to work with his material, and with him, when we've wrapped up the prod. I don't want you to get a shock when you see what crazy things he'll bring to the editing room."

"Not like your actors then?" I tried, jokingly.

"Oh, don't be jealous, love, you're my little actress too. You might get your surprise as well. If you're good."

She patted the back of my hand. "Get some sleep, angels," she said as she rose to leave, and I felt like an awkward twelve-year old. Marius hadn't said a thing yet, just nodded along to Aurélie Sajid, and now he looked at me, smiling mouth closed as he chewed on a croissant.

"I…I loved your work on *Littoral*," I said. He just nodded, and I told myself that if he didn't say thank you it was to spare me a projection of croissant particles, and a view of dough-speckled teeth.

On *Littoral*, he'd created a richness in the soundtrack beyond anything I'd ever heard. I'd seen it in the cinema, and it had left a deep impression on me I hadn't been able to explain. I'd marveled at how that seaside romance had given me the weird impression of being a foggy allegory for the afterlife. I watched it again and again, and when I understood that much of the unease I felt came from the soundtrack, I took to listening to it in the dark, with headphones on. I got a little obsessed with it, and it took a few hours of sleep from me every night. I explored the soundscape like a strange yet familiar place. Under the traffic sounds of a street scene, I'd make out neighs, or in a sea-side scene, a distant, dull hammering as the kids played ball on the beach.

"Are you planning something similar for this?"

He wiped his mouth with a paper napkin, took a sip of coffee. He brought his hand to a small recorder then, a pocketknife-sized rectangle I hadn't spotted on the table, by his cup of coffee. He pressed stop.

"Yeah, pretty much. Not really revolutionary, right? But I think there are still things for me there to dig out. Plus *Littoral* was tentative—now I know what I'm doing."

"And this?" I said, raising my eyebrows at the recorder.

"Ah, yeah. I hate hearing myself. Plus this is not about me. Step back, erase yourself. Let the work speak."

"But me?"

"Well, you know. Everything is part of it."

"*All is there already…*"

Marius laughed. "Yeah. Yeah. All right. A bit dickish, maybe. A bit like a cult, and I've bought into it."

"Some hipster's cult."

"Yeah, with a rite of passage in highfalutin."

We laughed. It was a relief that talking to Marius came easy. The boy-genius aura I'd draped him with didn't get in the way.

"So, what's your big plan for tonight?"

"Ah. We'll just listen to Mother Forest, hear what she thinks," he said, giggling.

THAT NIGHT I shadowed Marius. We sneaked out into the forest, away from the crew, as they got ready to shoot their scene. When we got to where we could only see the crew's lights flicker on trees, he stopped and turned around, brought a finger to his lips. We stood there intently, listening. His mike up in the air, like some levitating roadkill.

I heard "Action!" and the plainclothes villains rushing through the leaves. When the hubbub quietened down and Marius relaxed, pressed something in his satchel, we started off again, further into the dark.

"What was that for?" I asked him. There was a boom operator with the crew who'd get clean sound for the scene.

"Who knows?" Marius said, and laughed.

I followed him until we lost track of the dim presence of the others in the distance. I lit the ground where I stepped with my phone, but Marius seemed not to worry where his feet fell and progressed easily, a few meters from me, pointing his mike like a prospector with his metal detector at the nooks roots embraced in the dark, at the whispering leaves overhead.

It was a little spooky, venturing that way deeper and deeper, farther from the crew and the vans, but I didn't say anything. He seemed so concentrated when the weak blue of my phone landed on his face, made half of it appear in the night when he'd turned a little my way, lured by a noise. Sometimes a sound rose from the non-silence of the night, the wave-like hush woven of a hundred imperceptible things, and we'd both stop, prick our ear to the forest. Once a heavy hum grew and sustained itself for a dozen seconds, like an invisible murmuring cloud overhead. When it stopped, we both exhaled audibly.

"Weird, eh?" Marius said.

I knew it was our brains teasing weirdness out of the dark, that the hum might have been just traffic—that for all we knew the N24 cut through the forest not a hundred meters away. I tried to remind myself that this was only a pretend wilderness, that it was the tamed wild that had been allowed to remain, and that the fright I got was adult make-believe.

After that I put my phone away in my pocket, tried to navigate the forest as confidently as Marius did. For a few seconds, everything went dark.

Then I felt the shake, saw the dim light through my jeans pocket. It was a text from Sajid. *Come back here, I'll need you for the next scene.* It seemed I wouldn't be allowed to go unseeing. Unseen.

I called Marius, who was already a dozen meters ahead, crouched, bringing his upturned palm into the blanket of decomposing leaves and lifting them, letting them fall to the ground in a soft rain.

"I need to get back to the shoot," I said low, afraid to disturb him, or maybe to disturb the sound of the woods, like a clueless tourist. Marius didn't move, and I turned towards where I felt we'd come from. I thought I might get lost, childhood frights rushing back, but after what seemed like only a few steps, I noticed the halo of the crew. They were coming to the rotting cabin that Sajid had somehow found, or conjured, maybe, where the climax was to take place.

FOR THE REST of the shoot I alternated between working with the crew and roaming the woods with Marius. He seemed really to go around at random, recording lengthy tracks of nothing much, and at times I worried about the hell post-prod was going to be. I hardly knew what was going on with the plot, and the hours spent in dark, silent contemplation colored my vision of the project. I came back from jaunts with Marius to find some new twist had been revealed to the crew and actors.

I once came to the group and learned no crime had been committed. Yet.

"I'm a hitman—woman," Gwen told me, giggling, between two shots. She'd been contracted to kill Tom, when his big-shot industrialist father had refused to pay off a blackmail threat.

"But I've fallen for him, you know. I won't go through with it."

"Does he know?"

"Tom? No."

"No, I mean, Tom Tom, real-life Tom."

"Tom doesn't know," she said, "and he doesn't know *I* knew all along about his little cabin in the woods."

I guess Sajid had succeeded in her little plan—I worried about Tom as if I didn't know it was all an act. That night, I'd noticed the gun was missing from the props trunk in my van. I'd asked Sajid about it, and she'd told me not to worry about it.

Often at the breakfast buffet, in the reality-check machine of the Formule 1, I chided myself for thinking I had a grip on the film, when all I'd done was let myself muse about someone else's half-remembered dream. I saw myself at the computer, editing bits of empty forest, letting the hum of the night tell a tale of nothingness. Or rather of things lurking, huge, just out of sight. Unseen highways and highwaymen, mechanical diggers and shovel-wielding killers.

I'd voiced my worries to Sajid a few days before the shooting was to end, as we walked to the van, telling her it might be better if I stayed with the crew for the night, to get closer to the film, the actual film she was shooting, and not the lonely fantasy of it that was growing in my mind, but she'd interrupted me.

"Why do you think I told you to go away? To follow Marius? I don't need another me, I need a you. A you from the forest. A mean little sprite with a chip on her shoulder."

THE LAST COUPLE of nights of shooting, Sajid told me and Marius to stay at the hotel, and start work on the post-prod. I thought I would be excited to work with Marius, after all the time we'd spent together in the forest, but it turned out that the first few hours were very awkward.

Of course I was attracted to Marius. The few smiles he'd granted me, these ghostly alms caught in corners of my phone's halo, had made me giddy with yearning. There'd been a few breakfasts when I'd kept silent over coffee and toast, working up the nerves to invite him back to my room, only to chicken out when we rose and I wished him sweet dreams instead.

The twist was that Marius seemed to be as attracted to me as I was to him. I felt like I was back at school and we were teenagers struggling with enormous emotions we weren't equipped to deal with. I hadn't had a remotely serious relationship in forever.

We worked in a clone of our own rooms, the two of us on shitty chairs, playing back rushes and tracks to each other. It was all part of Sajid's plan, to have us do all the work in the same atmosphere the film had be shot in. Now and then she'd pop in, rustle us up into coats and drive us out to the forest so we wouldn't forget what it felt like.

We got over the weirdness quickly enough. We laughed at some tracks Marius had recorded, actors caught unaware, or the shitty videos some in the crew had earnestly shot, hoping it would be useful in the final edit.

Marius took the uncomfortable "Why are we running?" Tom had said when trying to work out what he was being made to do, and slipped it into an early scene, when Gwen and him were in town by day, behind the white noise of traffic, the chatter of passersby. It was inaudible, really, if you didn't know it was there.

It made me look at the clumsy videos more intently. Between goofy glimpses of the crew, I found some unnerving shots of the forest, spinning trees, that I used as if filmed by the characters' phones.

One evening, as the sun was setting, Sajid came into the room, two bottles of Merlot under her arms, two glasses hooked on her fingers.

"Here kids. You deserve it. I'm heading off to the forest with the guys, I got to think a couple of things through. You keep up the good work."

She went out again, and Marius and I looked at each other, raising our eyebrows until we giggled. I looted my bag for the Swiss army knife that never left its clutter, that I forgot about for months on end and that always made heroic reappearances. I fished it out with a "Ta-daa!"

"Nice one, MacGyver," Marius said, presenting the bottle to me. I opened it, and I took a picture as we clinked glasses. We had a sip and got back to work.

That night, we finally reached the final scenes. We hadn't had a chance to talk with the cast, and we watched the mixed-up rushes glued to the screen, as Tom and Gwen ran towards the cabin, then entered its black inside. They sat shivering in the blue light of their phones, listening to the rustling night. Their phones caught the rundown interior in wild swoops, and their faces, wrinkled in worry.

The swish of the forest grew in the room, as if a dozen animals were rushing through the leaves, and on screen Gwen's hand slipped in between the cushions, and to Tom's shock, came out with a heavy handful of darkness.

Bang.

It happened that night, of course. Halfway through the second bottle, after the wine had made us more and more expansively enthusiastic about each other's ideas and finds. Pats on the back lingered, became static, then moved to caress. Cue silence, stare, kiss.

We had sex on the bed after pushing the bags and gear off it. The sex was good, but I couldn't help feel a strange discomfort. I don't know if it would have been any better elsewhere in the hotel, in my room, or his. Maybe the Formule 1 atmosphere would have ruined anything, but it felt worse here, in this room rented for work, this room Sajid had set up. Even as we were having sex, as I was losing myself in it, in Marius, letting myself give in, I felt the glare of the monitors behind us. The dark glow of the forest still on the screen casting itself into the room, the dead eye of the computer.

We lay down for a while afterwards, in each other's arms. It was three when Marius said we should get up in case Sajid came back early. We got dressed, glanced at the computers.

"Hum," Marius said.

"Yeah. Call it a night?" I said. I had meant it invitingly, imagined him coming back to my room, or me to his, but it came out wrong. Standing there, fully clothed, I found myself unwittingly closing a door on that chapter.

"I guess, yeah. We've worked well." He'd meant it seriously, and he was right, we'd made some progress, but he got the double-entendre in his own words, and he blushed.

We turned off the computers, then said good night without a kiss or a touch.

So I felt it was my fault when the next day our relationship resumed on its pre-coitus basis. After an awkward start, we were soon back to our chummy usual. We had a few days' work left, and I thought it better to leave things as they were. I have this thing, this ability to find reasons to take the easy way out.

I didn't want to give up on Marius, though. We got on really well, and I thought something might come of it, of us. I told myself I'd text him when we were done, gone home. Meet him out in the real world. Outside of Sajid's fantasy. We'd have a drink. Do the whole date thing.

In the meantime, we were professional. Although we were doing good work, something I knew I'd be proud to have on my CV, I looked forward to being done with it. I felt the strange confinement of these few weeks, the closed-circuit world of the night forest, the breakfast buffet, the sad rooms we slept and worked in, were getting to me.

I found myself always returning to the same pictures, the same paths between the same trees, except—could I ever be sure they were the same? We had so many different rushes, taken by different cameras and phones, from slightly different angles. Sometimes I found myself looking at rushes I didn't recognize at all, shots I felt had been sneaked into the file behind my back. I often came up with a new rush, a couple of seconds of phone-lit forest floor, that I showed Marius to transition between two scenes.

"You've already used that one," he'd say.

"I have?"

He'd bring me back to a spot we'd edited a couple of days before, show me the transition again.

"Put it in again."

I raised my eyebrows at him.

"Put it in, in the background. Very light."

Marius did the same on his side, layering different tracks instead of the simple presence the boom operator had recorded at each shooting, as the whole crew stood mournfully silent not to taint the forest's ambient sound. Marius let whispers and distant shuffling feet be the normal background voice of the forest.

ONE DAY MARIUS was gone. I got up in the early afternoon and went to the editing room. He usually got up before me, but after working on my own for a couple of hours he still hadn't arrived. We were done, really, except for a few finicky things and double-checks. I texted him (*Did you die of existential dread in thy Formule 1 room?*), but he didn't answer. I forced myself, with varying degrees of success, to keep working and not check my phone every couple of minutes.

Sajid came in later, and I showed her a few scenes. She nodded, satisfied. I asked her if she knew where Marius was.

"Oh, he's gone home," she said, as if I should have known. "He told me he was done, and he's right, the brilliant little sound wizard. I viewed his final version with him this morning. It's perfect."

I raised a few points with Sajid, things I wasn't sure of, little nagging doubts I'd thought I'd have time to work on with Marius before she saw anything resembling a finished film, but it seemed this, like everything else, was to work on Sajid's time frame. She reassured me that she'd look at it, that if need be she'd get back to Marius for any tweaks the film might need.

I left the hotel that night. Sajid told me I could stay, that it was booked until the next morning, but most of the crew was already packing.

"And I'd fear for your safety, leaving you behind on your own, with those feral salesmen bent on revenge. They're bound to be vicious, now they see they can reclaim the breakfast buffet watering hole."

THE TIME BETWEEN leaving the Formule 1 and the film coming out was a blur. I couldn't say what I did, what I filled my time with. I sure didn't work.

The day the film came out, I rushed to the cinema. A little arthouse place. It wasn't distributed in any of the Gaumonts or Pathés. I tried texting Marius, as had been my original plan, but he never answered. I left a couple of voicemails before giving up.

It was brilliant. Of course it was. It had that textured sound, a real heavy sonic atmosphere, like *Littoral* had. At times it was like I could see the sound, and once a scene finished I couldn't tell what had been there on screen, and what I'd heard, at the very bottom of my ear, the murmur of something hidden behind the trees. The sing-song of moss, the grating of mushrooms growing. The flow of the blood of foxes and boars drawn by a million gorging ticks.

It was brilliant, of course. Although I'm not sure I saw it. The first pictures, the sounds, sent me right back to that forest, that Formule 1 room. I guess the experience of shooting and editing the film had been so intense that the finished film ended up completely enmeshed with it. I saw things, as I sat there in the cinema, that shouldn't, couldn't have been there.

I spent two hours in a fog, replaying these weeks in my mind. I heard our breathing after we lay panting on the forest floor, breathing as we lay in bed, after love. I heard a gun loaded and fired, the cry of "Police!" and a door broken open, the cries for someone shot who shouldn't have been.

When the credits fell on the dark forest background, and I saw all of our names, Tom's, Gwen's, mine, Marius's, it reminded me it was true, that this time had happened. We had made something, and it was now out in the world.

Reviews were overwhelmingly positive. I sought them out, like a lifeline. Not two reviewers had the same thing to say, and at times I wondered if they had seen the same film I had, the film I'd made, or helped make. There were comments on the wolves, theories on forest fairies, questions about the clinking of swords that could be heard here or there…

I NEVER SAW Marius again. I have spent the years—five, six?—since intermittently watching the film, pursuing it wherever it is shown in retrospectives, in back-alley cinemas. I always try to spot something new, and I always do. The problem is I never see again what I saw the previous time. I wonder if Sajid kept tinkering after I'd gone, adding scenes, superimposing landscapes onto landscapes, sounds within sounds. Or were the shots always so textured, misty, even before we started playing with them? Sometimes I feel like I'm still watching rushes looking for this woman Sajid wants to cast. Sometimes I feel I've just seen her, if I could just remember where.

What I want to see is something that makes sense, that answers more questions than it asks. Something that makes me say I was right to think that the film was the last valuable thing that happened to me, and my routine existence, the boring subsistence jobs I'd taken since, aren't even worth talking about. As if time stood still and I was left with my memories, my remorse, my yearning. Always coming back to the screen. All is there, really. Every time I feel like I've just missed it, a shape behind a far-off tree, a tiny voice lost in the crackle of fallen leaves. And sometimes, I get the feeling that the theatre isn't so empty, that Sajid, Tom, Gwen are there, and in the seat next to me, if I turn around, Marius will be there facing me, leaning in for a kiss, his maw the forest's, wide and dark and ready to engulf me as the credits roll down, as all of our names fall through the dark like dead leaves.

HALF-GIRLS

Cate Gardner

THE GRUB-URCHIN crushed the shell beneath her sandal. Brown curls hung in her eyes as she laughed and dug her feet deep into the soil, anchoring her sister to the earth. Cordelia, the mermaid-sister, responded with a tantrum. Their mother, wearing a ladybird-printed apron and dripping soapsuds, rushed from the kitchen. She picked up her babies, who were long past toddling and mother-smothering. In tandem, they kicked against their mother's shins. She didn't let go. She carried them to safety.

Under the pretense of needing the toilet, Cordelia dragged Heather, her grub-urchin sister, up the stairs. Much to Heather's protestations, Cordelia filled the bath. When they needed to toilet, both sisters wished they could unpick their stitches and separate their bodies rather than being united at the side by ugly black thread. The bath filled to almost overflowing, Cordelia pulled her half of their dress over her head and stepped into the water. Heather had no choice but to disrobe and climb in. Cordelia pressed her lips to hers and they lay beneath the water until Heather's skin puckered.

Heather's eyes stung and she cried until their mother wrapped a beach towel around their shoulders and rubbed the wet from their skin.

"Be careful with your sister," Mother said. "You'll drown her."

Heather became so mortally afraid of the bath, of water, that if she hadn't been conjoined to her sister, she may never have washed again.

On their fourteenth birthday, their father died. Their mother wanted him buried at sea, a Viking funeral. The council refused. Sometimes, Heather thought her parents hated the land, and in her peculiar way, determined this meant they favored her sister. That night, she asked Cordelia, "Do you think they have ruined our lives?"

Cordelia thought about it for a minute or so and returned, "It depends what lives we would have otherwise lived."

"Do you miss your real family?"

"Do you?"

"They are my family?"

"So you say, little grub-urchin. I think you were born of worms and tree-roots."

Outside their room a floorboard creaked.

On their eighteenth birthday, their mother fell from a rowing boat in the old harbor. They watched her sink and sink and sink. Heather kept her sister weighted to the boat. Cordelia's kisses wouldn't be able to save them both.

HOME-SCHOOLED, THE sisters' knowledge of the world outside their seaside cottage was the acceptance of their small-town neighbors and the ridicule, amusement, or pity of tourists. The local seamstress made their clothes, having measured them fully dressed, and the local doctor was their uncle. They were not equipped for university or overseas travel, and while one wanted to be either a gardener or gravedigger, the other wanted to work with dolphins and sharks or study marine biology. Because they couldn't settle to give up their dream for the other, they settled at nothing.

Nothing leads to sharp words and sharpened things. Guilt and want proved sword...or scissors.

Heather's side ached. She murmured in half-sleep and nudged at Cordelia's neighboring arm, only to find her own pushed forward.

"Let me sleep, Cor."

The green-illuminated hands of the wall clock offered just past midnight. Again, a jab in her side. At first, she dismissed it as indigestion (onion never agreed with her) or Cordelia's sharp elbow, until it grew to an intensity of raw pain, burning, blinding, agonizing. Beside her Cordelia grunted.

"What is it?" Heather asked, touching her side, fingers coming away slick, wet.

Faint with growing pain, Heather reached for the bedside light switch, fingers fumbling, slipping. Dim light illuminated a hand wet with blood.

"Cor."

Grim determination ruined her sister's face. Scissors glinted in the half-dark. They were semi-parted, scissors slicing through stitches, through skin.

Heather couldn't form more than a cry. This was a nightmare. Cordelia wasn't snipping at their sisterhood. Her original thought of indigestion had to be the cause. And yet, the dream did not vary, did not spin off in tangents. It only worsened. Scissors nicked inflamed skin. Heather tried to push her sister away—not so easy when you remain joined even if it is now only at the hip.

"What? Why?" At last, she formed words. "Please, don't."

The please-don't redundant for it was already done. The final stitches. The final inches of skin. Trying to grab the scissors, they cut her fingertips. Slices sharp as paper cuts. A moment's stillness, eyes locked, a sorrow to them both. Did this have to happen? An inevitability time had rolled towards. They were no longer children. Their parents were dead and their wants no longer of any consequence. Eventually, they had to find themselves. Still, a conversation, daylight, their uncle's scalpel would be preferable, safer.

"You could have...asked."

As the last stitches unhitched, Heather fell back with the emptiness of freedom, hitting her head on the sharp edge of the bedside table.

THEY WERE SEVEN-YEARS-OLD. An assortment of safety scissors that cut waves and curls and jagged edges covered the kitchen table. They were making greeting cards for their uncle's birthday. Cordelia cut waves. Heather cut jagged rocks. Boredom struck Cordelia first, so she pushed her half-finished card aside and tried to leave. Heather wound her calves around the kitchen chair and held onto the edge of the table. She wasn't finished. In retaliation, Cordelia grabbed the wave-scissors. She began cutting at their conjoined dress with little success.

A scream of NO cut across the kitchen. A metal bowl clattered to the floor, cake mixture splashed, the dog, a Bedlington terrier named Barney, almost tripped up their mother in his rush to get to the spoils. Their mother tore the scissors from Cordelia's hands. In a mess of panic, all three of them landed on the floor with a thump.

"You don't do that," Mother said, wrapping her arms about them. She kissed Heather's forehead. "The earth will suck at your toes until you lie six feet beneath." She turned to Cordelia, kissed her knee. "You'll drown."

YOU CAN DROWN without water. They slept naked in the summer. Thus, Cordelia lay bare on the cold bathroom tiles, wiping her wounds with antiseptic and covering them with gauze pads. She winced against the harsh sting, eyes watering. *You could have...asked.* Why hadn't she? Because she feared a no. Heather had always seemed more comfortable in their attachment. Now, she had gone too far. Breath hitched. Harder to breathe above water without Heather.

Heather lying cold and still, breath ragged, blood. If she hadn't meant to hurt her sister, then how to explain cutting into her skin. *You did not think this through.* She wiped tears from her cheeks. From the washing basket, Cordelia removed her rainbow-knit mermaid tail. Shivering into it, she secured it to her body with a rope of silk scarves. Not easy to plan escape when your captor spies every waking move. Well, this was one that dear Heather, little grub-urchin, hadn't seen.

She wasn't certain how to move without her sister at her side, never mind the disability of a mermaid's tail on land. A seashell pressed to her ear blotted out the silence from the bedroom. If she hadn't meant to hurt her sister, then why the scissors? The first step was to stop lying to herself. The sea roared in her ears. It called her home.

Shuffling along tiles and then wood flooring, into and through the bedroom where Heather only showed signs of minimal life, the stairs appeared stories high and treacherous. She navigated them one bump at a time.

As the house creaked about her, the seashell's magic abandoned on the bathroom floor, she awaited the ghostly cries of her parents, of Heather, of a life stolen. Their shared childhood haunted each drop, accompanied her descent. Here they tumbled, here they scraped their knees. Beneath here they hid from their parents, who must have known where they were all the time, their patent-leather shoes poking from the stair cupboard door. Barney waiting behind the front door for them. Precious dog. They'd buried him at sea. Perhaps she would find his doggy bones, his ghost, waiting for her.

Blood bloomed beneath gauze. The wounds, however, remained contained, did not pull or split further.

She'd left the front door unlocked. That sleight of hand had slipped by Heather. So strange to be unseen, no longer weighted in favor of her right. A cold breeze slipped into the hallway. She left the door open.

The garden at the front of the house: a weight of grass peppered with buttercups, a narrow path of loose paving stones about the edge, leading onto the coastal path and down to the beach, to the eternal sea. Cordelia looked up at the cottage, at their bedroom. Heather did not look down and only the dim light of the lamp shone behind the net curtain. Of course, if Heather were fine, she wouldn't wave or look from the window; she would chase after her sister. She would sew them together again. Cordelia didn't want that. She wouldn't allow that.

Sorry. A word weighty enough to drop her to the ocean bed.

The knitted tail proved a laborious weight over sand. Pebbles and broken shells cut into her palms, tore already damaged skin. Although to have dressed in her mermaid costume once she was at the sea front would have been a wiser idea, despite her mermaid-ancestry, she hadn't wanted to run butt-naked across the beach. Living on land had turned her prudish. Heather's blood had tainted her. Still, here was the sea and here was forever. She couldn't think on missing anyone.

Water filled her knitted tail, sweeping her and it along its waves, tossing her like driftwood, but not fully accepting her. For a moment, it was as if she'd forgotten to swim, but then the fake tail slipped off and she became fish-like in her maneuvers. She swam and swam until the shore reduced to far off lights with no identifying markers. Now colors moved beneath the water. A shimmer that circled her legs. There was something here with her. Something intelligent, manipulative, biting. A hand shot from the water, clasped her mouth and dragged her down and down and down.

When they were sixteen, their father long dead and their mother struggling, they set out to sea on a moonlit night to drop their old dog Barney into the ocean. At thirteen dog years, they should have expected his end. That is, if anyone can ever expect the death of the much-loved. Having long-favored Heather, Barney spent his last breaths curled on the sofa with his head in her lap, and her tears on his nose. Even in the rock of the boat, he remained swaddled on her lap. They had to fight her for his wasted corpse.

Their mother dropped Barney's remains over the side. Barney loved the ocean, the sea spray, he loved digging up shells and chasing seagulls, he ate daisies and rocks, anything really. For a time he floated beside their boat. They should have weighted his remains with something more substantial than love. Just when it seemed he'd not leave them, that they'd have to fish him out and bury him in their garden, he dropped. The descent so sudden, their mother gasped.

Barney hadn't begun to sink, something dragged him into the depths. Something with turquoise eyes and sharp teeth, something that knew Cordelia saw it.

Heather knew only pain. Everything swollen, even her thoughts. She hung half-out the bed, shoulder blade resting on the bedside table, fingers trailing the floor. Considering her mermaid-twin, the position should be impossible. Only, she didn't have a twin anymore. Memory stung sharper than wounds.

Unable to pull herself onto the bed, Heather dropped to the floor, lying on the cold floorboards, hearing no hint of Cordelia with the house. This would require some apology. Although it hurt to raise her head, Heather pulled herself up with aid of the mattress and the bedside table. The bed contained blood-stained rumpled sheets, no Cordelia. Had she left? She wouldn't have left.

Heather dropped onto the edge of the bed. The room spun, her side throbbed, and she wasn't certain how to maneuver without her mermaid-sister. Baby steps. Baby steps that left her lopsided, that caused her to grab onto the bed and wall to make it into the bathroom. Cordelia had used up the antiseptic wipes and gauze. The mess littered the bathroom floor. She needed to get downstairs. She needed to phone Uncle David. Despite Cordelia's actions, the thought seemed betrayal.

He'd sew them together again.

He'll lock us up, an imaginary Cordelia warned.

Her hand hovered over the phone. As much as she needed medical attention, she didn't want to harm her sister. Instead of phoning, she shuffled into the kitchen and swallowed two painkillers. A clean dishtowel proved bandage for her seeping side wounds. If she didn't find Cordelia on the beach, then she'd phone their uncle. Maybe. Definitely. She'd have no choice.

CORDELIA DIDN'T BELIEVE *Uncle* David was related to their parents. He certainly wasn't related to her, and she saw no resemblance between him and the grub-urchin and their parents. They were an experiment, and at thirteen-years-old, she didn't want to be the focus of someone's games. She refused to disrobe in his presence, despite the shouts and screams of her mother and the tuts of her father.

At night, she whispered her fears to Heather. Sometimes, her sister pressed her fingers in her ears. She wanted to trust her current family. There was less fairy tale to Heather's origins.

It can be lonely when you're the only one to see the conspiracy.

Uncle David with his lollipops and pinching of cheeks as if they were four-years-old, pocket money comprising of coppers, and most people going to the next town to visit their general practitioner. No doubt, Uncle David had been struck off years ago.

Footsteps on the stairs, then floorboards creaked outside their room. Cordelia switched on the bedside lamp. The door, which had started to open, clicked shut. Beside her Heather snored, but Cordelia wouldn't sleep. She wouldn't allow them to take her blood or check to see if they had fully fused or begun to rip part, whether she had started to scale or Heather to root.

A BRISK WIND cut across the garden from the beach. Heather shivered into an old coat that belonged to her mum, tying the loose ends of their dress around her waist. An old umbrella with a duck head proved walking stick. Soil sucked at her shoes, dragging her into the earth inch by inch. Without Cordelia, the ground wanted to claim her. She belonged to it. Without

Cordelia, she'd be trapped within their cottage or become tree, taking root in their garden waiting for the return of her mermaid-sister.

She needed to quicken her step. She'd forgotten how to—the disability borne from being alone rather than conjoined. By the time Heather reached the sands, she was buried to the knee in grass and soil. She grabbed onto the seawall, pulling herself up until she could sit on it. The earth squelched in regret.

Despite the emptiness of the beach, no human or mermaid, she called to Cordelia. The wind threw her words back, slapping at and drying her tears. Cordelia wouldn't have gone anywhere other than the sea, and the beach was closer to their cottage than the old harbor. Why had their parents planted them here? Better in a concrete city with no earth to bury Heather, no sea to drown Cordelia.

"Cordelia," a final sad cry, as the first dog walkers hit the sands.

If she made too much fuss they would drag the sea for her sister's body. No, there wouldn't be a body. She would swim and swim into forever. That was Cordelia's world out there, where she'd always belonged.

To just leave…she wouldn't have wanted to risk Uncle David sewing them back together. Perhaps this time, he would remove a limb or two, ensuring neither would escape the other. Mrs. Smith, who ran the greengrocers, waved across the beach at Heather, then stopped. Mrs. Smith-the-gossip. Mrs Smith-the-not-very-bright, trying to work out what was different about the girl from the cottages. Once she worked it out she'd race into town to tell their uncle.

Cordelia would be long out to sea now. She may never see her sister again.

THE DESCENT INTO the depths of the ocean was a whirlwind that twirled her round and round, threatening to break back or neck. The sea spun in a myriad of colors. Faces zoomed in and out, checking out the girl who fell and fell and fell.

At the bottom of the ocean, amidst a rainbow of fish, she landed on a rock. The sands shifted about her. A merman loomed, his muscles taut, face trapped in permanent snarl. He had no human speech, offering garbled and obscene screams. Sharp fingernails poked at and scratched her arms, her legs. The merman's hair was short, stubble as sharp as nettles.

A group of mermaids and mermen gathered. They howled and they cackled, upper teeth cracking against lower teeth. These were not sounds to draw sailors. They jabbed at her with spears, pushing her back. As her eyes adjusted to the gloom, she noted they pushed her towards a system of caves, their walls glistening an onyx black. She'd not the strength to escape, to swim however many fathoms to the surface.

She tried to speak, to explain of her relationship to them, but her words proved as garbled at theirs. They backed her into a corner, then dropped the walls of a cage formed from shark teeth and bones. Settled into a corner of the cage, salt water again stung her wounds, the adrenaline of the fall over. This was supposed to be home. These monsters her family. If her legs fused, if she grew a tail, would they accept her?

An elderly mermaid approached the cage, cracks to both face and tail and her left breast bitten off. She tipped her head to the left, then to the right, examining Cordelia. Cordelia drew her knees to her chest. Floating in front of the cage, the elderly mermaid shooed the others away. Though her fingernails were as tapered as the others, her hair as bristled, there was less sharpness to her.

Cordelia tried to mouth the word *please*. Neither of them understood the message in the bubbles that erupted from her throat. Eventually, the elderly mermaid swam away, and Cordelia alone remained within this cave. She wound her arms and legs around the bars. They did not move. She pushed at them to no further success. Light dazzled, borne of the smooth glittering surface of the stone walls. There was no more freedom here than on the surface.

BY THE TIME the paramedics roared onto the sands, Heather had slipped into a coma. The air ambulance hovered above the beach, dropping a basket to stretcher her into the helicopter. Across the town, word spread about the missing twin. Only Uncle David knew the full truth of the tale, and he was busy packing up his belongings and driving out of town.

It took three days for Heather to wake. Her first word, "Cordelia." By then, the newspapers had vilified her parents. Her cries of they were trying to save not destroy the children were dismissed. Fact was, they were destroyed all the same. The media, police and doctors blamed Uncle David for their separation surgery. Heather didn't inform them otherwise.

No belief in mermaids or grub-urchins here.

Far from the sea and surrounded by the concrete of the city, Heather knew she did not belong. Despite the improvement of her wounds, the removal of her stitches and a course of antibiotics, the hospital was reluctant to discharge her. There was also the question of her missing sister and the fact there was no record of either birth. Something she had long known, without Cordelia she was no one.

THERE WERE NO days or nights in this dark and glistening place. Food consisted of raw fish that swam into her cage. She saved their bones, using them to work at her prison. It would take a lifetime. The elderly mermaid proved a regular visitor. She'd rip fish apart and pass it through the bars. Unlike the others, she never scratched or bit. Unlike the others, she reached through the bars to rub an algae on Cordelia's wounds. An almost-communication rose between them. One that Cordelia feared to trust.

Sawing through the bars proving a no-go, she took to shaking them, to digging at the sand at the bottom of the cage, but each time she achieved a gap, the mermen kicked her back. Her anger grew to match theirs. Now she spat at them. Now she swore.

She was one of them.

She would not be a captive.

At night, the elderly mermaid sang to her, her voice coarse and sour, and yet it soothed Cordelia. Her legs remained persistently legs; not even any scales to them. She picked at the skin, dry and wrinkled in the weight of sea water. She missed the air, the sky, her sister. For all her companionship, even this mermaid wouldn't allow her to dig for freedom.

Screams filled the caves. A wounded, animal cry. On the seafloor, a merman flopped, a metal hook torn through his side. At the other end of the hook, tethered to the length of the line, a human man, red-faced, bloated, dead. While her elderly companion tended to the wounded merman, snapping at his wails with her sharpened teeth, Cordelia began to paw at the sand. This may be her only opportunity. She slid from beneath the bars, scraping her heel to the bone.

For a moment, she thought the old mermaid turned and saw her escape. If she had done, she didn't say anything. The others remained preoccupied. Despite the cramped quarters and the not-quite-healed wounds to her side, she swam faster than she ever had with Heather.

The cave system proved difficult to navigate. Each led onto another cave, none offering the freedom of the open sea. A screech behind her. At last, Cordelia found an exit. She could only hope she swam towards the surface. Fish lunged towards her, battering rams and inquisitive. Tiredness weighted her limbs until it became a struggle to do anything but float to the sea bed. Then arms caught around her waist. They'd drag her into the caves, into that cage, and she'd never escape. With her remaining energy she fought against her attacker until she realized they weren't dragging her down, but pulling her towards the surface, towards air and the sky and the world she'd been so eager to leave.

Only once they were on the surface did she recognize the mermaid's song. It was the elderly one with the missing breast, the one who had protected and now freed.

As air filled Cordelia's lungs, she found her words, "Thank you."

In the distance a boat bobbed on the clear-blue sea, but Cordelia headed towards the shore, to a sister she would sew herself to if it meant she never lost her.

SURROUNDED BY CONCRETE tower blocks and tarmacked roads, the grub-urchin couldn't breathe. Heather discharged herself. She was physically fit, had learned to navigate the world without her twin, and knew they searched the wrong places for Cordelia.

At the old harbor, she rented a rowing boat from Pete, who kept his eyes downcast, trying not to look at the empty space beside her. By now, everyone in town knew the story, or half-a-story at least. There would be many versions, most of them more fanciful than the truth, which was pretty fantastical itself. As she climbed into the boat, the trees at the harbor bowed their branches, their twigs reaching for her. If they could uproot themselves, they would chase their daughter away from the ocean.

She did not belong here.

Leaves drifted from the trees, landing in her lap like a talisman. They would bury her feet in soil and have her stand amongst them. She set out, an audience gathering at the harbor to watch the half-girl chase a ghost.

When far enough from the shore she called out to her sister. Perhaps Cordelia would hear her in the depths. Perhaps she'd come back to the sister she missed. There seemed no hope of it in the expanse of ocean. She could have swum across the world by now, found her family. Heather, their cottage, become distant, ugly memories.

Heather rowed until she heard the faint lilt of a song; an ugly and yet enchanting melody. *Cordelia*. The sea shimmered, a myriad of colors pulsing beneath the surface. She turned the boat towards the voice, rowing until her arms ached, until she saw an arm wave from the water. If Cordelia's, it was bonier, but then there were no chocolate or cakes to eat under the sea, only fish and seaweed.

Almost upon them, the call sounded strange, repellent, not like Cordelia at all. Despite this, she could not stop.

Rather than lifting and dropping into the boat, sharp fingers clasped Heather's left wrist, dragging her into the sea. Had Cordelia forgotten she could not breathe underwater without her kiss? In the thrash, she took in bits and pieces of her attacker, for that's how they seemed now. A ravaged chest, thin-bristles for hair, broken skin, housing Cordelia's turquoise eyes, but older, much older. Despite the endless blue, this wasn't her sister. This was a monster.

The monster pressed its lips to hers, offering her lungs breath, holding onto her until they dropped to the sea bed. Lying amongst rocks and fish, the ancient mermaid pulled away, and Heather began to drown.

Cordelia stumbled through a wave of tourists, towards their little cottage. Police tape strung across the doorway barred the entrance. Had they found Heather's body? She dropped to her knees in the buttercup garden. Fingers raked through soil as tears drowned what the sea could not. She should have called an ambulance.

She plain shouldn't have done it.

"Heather," she cried, hoping the door would open.

It didn't.

Her knees sunk into the earth, the grass parting. Trees bent forward to create a canopy. The ground began to drag her into its bed of soil and worms and roots. She dug her fingers into the grass, attempting to drag herself towards the path, towards the threshold of the house. Like quicksand, the soil used her struggle to drag her deeper into the earth.

The garden took her for its own and Cordelia began to suffocate.

A Different Sunlight

Jackson Kuhl

———◆———

IF YOU LIVE a long-enough life you will frequently encounter clever and talented persons possessing such poor judgment that it is a wonder they can cross a road without being struck by a mule wagon.

Randall's father was such a man. He was also a brilliant engineer. When the N&CR began work on its final leg into central Newcastle, Randall's father, employed by the company, scribbled his sums and carried his ones as they drove the spikes across the moors. The finished project was so successful at not collapsing that he received a promotion and went to work on the Borders County Railway, which ran up into the mountains of Northumberland to the junction at Riccarton. One of those mountains was the same upon which Randall's father also built a house in the belief that one day the rough outpost would be an exclusive satellite for Hexham, eighteen miles away, which he predicted would become an important city. Yet that was just another of his bad ideas.

There was a morning Randall had a fever. His mother came up to his bedroom, put her palm against his forehead, pulled the covers up to his chin. She knew, with Casey wagging his tail on the braided rug, that even if Randall wouldn't be cared for he would at least be safe. She left to catch the train to town.

Randall said he remembered the day distinctly. Sleep seized him and by the time he awoke, the fever had broken. He shuffled around his bedroom, listless, and for a quarter of an hour carefully arranged a charging line of lead soldiers on the rug. Yet the faux Culloden or Waterloo, which usually never failed to entertain him, soon grew tiresome.

He sat in bed staring out the window at the frozen pine needles on the ground. His perch offered a view of the whole yard and down upon the back ell, which lay perpendicular to the main house, and through the ell windows into the rooms beyond. There came a moment in the late winter morning when the sky curdled rose and purple, reflected in the panes, and Randall happened to look down at the ell, through the wine-colored glass. Within he saw a brightly lit room inhabited by limping figures. There were three of them, two taller and one shorter, but malformed and twisted, hobbling about, a family of hunchbacks and gimps. Then the light changed and the glass became opaque. When it cleared, the boy saw only empty chambers and bare grates.

Just before noon, boy and dog went downstairs to find something to eat. The house was silent save for the ticking of the kitchen wall clock. Then the bell chimed twelve, the pocket doors to the study banged open, and Randall's father walked straight to the liquor cabinet to pour himself a tumbler. He was still an engineer, still as precise as a slide rule.

Between gulps of whisky the father mumbled nonsense Randall couldn't fathom, gibberish about an Antichthonic sun and Phaetonic rays, until some clink of Casey's collar or tap of a fork on the dish provoked him to swivel his head and regard his son. He had no idea Randall had been sitting there.

Randall told him his mom said he could stay home sick. Afraid and not wanting to add too much.

The father nodded.

Randall asked, *Are you thinking of new ways to make houses?*

Yes.

There was a moment of quiet that seemed to need filling so Randall said, *With concrete?*

No. Not with concrete, said the father. He said he would use a new process, a process nobody's thought of yet. *Something they can't take away from me*, he said. *I will grow houses with light.*

A large part of his old job at the Newcastle and Carlisle, as Randall's father told it at the supper table, was overseeing the supersession of the railroad ties. The company had determined the old wooden ties, which rotted and demanded frequent replacement, were inferior to a new concrete design out of the Continent which lasted indefinitely and kept the rails from spreading under weightier loads. To perform this task, the company, under the supervision of Randall's father, built a gargantuan machine. He took Randall and Casey out to see it once. It steamed along the track, its cranes and pedipalps extracting the spikes, pulling the rails apart, uprooting the old ties, and planting the new ones before reassembling the railroad behind it. A goliath of smoke and vapor, it shambled with the sound of fifteen brass bands playing different pages of German sheet music, a slow-moving mechanical landslide, altering the geography it passed over. Casey strained on his leash barking at it.

Randall's father was proud of a particular innovation he developed. The new concrete ties were not prefabricated but rather poured into place by the machine using rebar and quick-drying cement. The possibilities of these materials soon seized the father's imagination; he became distant and preoccupied at meals, given to odd remarks about what seemed to Randall as random news events or statements of fact: the Great Fire of Newcastle in '54, or the lack of housing for the country's exploding population, or of the cheapness and abundance of concrete itself. Then, after weeks of midnights spent at his drawing table surrounded by reams of tea-ringed paper, he emerged with plans for a machine even greater than the company's steel snail chugging over the mountains.

Think of it, Randall, he said as he stabbed at various lines and shapes on the whiteprints, a *machine that can build a house.*

I do not pretend to apprehend all the details; having seen the plans, I can only think of an enormous spider-like gantry mounted on massive caterpillar treads. The gist was that it would roll onto a site, excavate the cellar, and then methodically *pour* a house into existence. Periodic stoppages were necessary for plumbers to install valves and fixtures, and glaziers and painters and wallpaper men would swarm the structure afterward for the finishing touches. But unlike rusticated concrete blocks, then very much in fashion, the machine formed the house as a solid whole, and by utilizing numerous molds and dies, did so with a precision so exact a fingernail couldn't be run between the cedar shakes it mimicked in calcium and silicon. Fire resistant yet affordable, pleasant to the architectural eye yet available to the Everyman, the products of Randall's father's machine would have been an advancement upon their creaking house of wood and plaster as four walls and a ceiling were to a teepee or a yurt.

Randall's parents were very excited about the machine. His father filed the patent with the office, and through his railroad connections attracted the enthusiasm of politicians and the capital of industrialists. Everyone told him he would be rich, and so he quit his job at the railroad, hired an attorney, and busied himself with starting a company he imagined would one day compare with Great Western Railway.

Then the letter arrived from London: the Patent Office had rejected the patent. It seemed that some tinkerer in Oxfordshire, who subscribed to the same trade journals as Randall's father and shared a likewise appreciation for the wonders of malleable stone, had developed a similar machine and registered it more than a year beforehand. There were inevitable differences between the two mechanisms but not enough for any of the father's designs to be considered novel. The Oxfordshire inventor puttering in his barn had, due to his lack of finances and contacts, never progressed beyond a simple tabletop model, and so his idea had languished in obscurity. Learning his name, the same investors who promised the inceptive funds to Randall's father immediately deserted him and instead threw their pound sterling at the tinkerer, who found himself suddenly elevated to a universe of Havana cigars and leather club chairs. And yet I understand the tinkerer's machine never worked properly and he died impoverished.

Any other man, after the elementary shock and disappointment, would have returned to the railroad company and asked for his old job back, and there's no reason to think they wouldn't have given it to him. But Randall's father could not accept the Patent Office's decision. He ranted against them at the table, dashed off counter-arguments and appeals, filed new patents for derivative machines differing only slightly from his original proposal. All the responses returned negatively. His wife urged him to abandon the idea, told him that another would take its place, that inventiveness was not a lightning strike occurring once a lifetime but a spigot that gushed no matter how many cups were spilled. Randall became aware—as aware as a child may be—that money dwindled, signified by the shrinking cuts of meat on his plate and the absence of those things he never before considered luxuries. The father left off shaving and slept in his study, forever busy at something, leaving only to grab some scraps from the kitchen or to argue with his wife. She soon found employment at a shop in Hexham, which at least kept her out of the house and away from him.

It was cold that winter, so cold Randall was not unhappy to escape weekdays to the heated one-room schoolhouse. With his father doing whatever he did in his study, it was Randall's responsibility upon arrival at home to go into the basement and shovel coal into the furnace, then spark a fire in the front foyer. Casey, having spent his day shivering in the kitchen, would curl up there close to the grate. It couldn't have been very comfortable in the foyer; the tiles of the fireplace had begun to pop and the floorboards curved like chicken ribs. Randall's mother attributed the distortion to the extremes of temperature the house had never before experienced: icy while the sun crossed the sky, then a roar of heat in the evenings to warm the air as much as possible before bedtime. The wood of the floor moaned and snapped all night long, and presumably when everyone was absent too.

Randall came home one day to discover his father in the foyer scrutinizing the floorboards. There was a noticeable rise in the boards to the right of the fireplace, and he squatted beside them, deep in contemplation. *These floors make such a racket*, he said.

Mother says they're warping from the hot and cold. Randall stood there, not knowing if he should light the fire or if it would make his father angry.

No, his father said but without confidence. *There's something under them, pushing up.*

A commandment was given to run and collect the toolbox, after which Randall's father proceeded to tear up the boards with pry bar and chisel, Randall handing him the necessary instruments as a nurse presents scalpels and forceps to a doctor.

Here's the trouble, said his father, and from the gap he pulled a length of wood, then another. Some kind of subflooring lay between the floor and the joists but only in that specific spot of the room. *That's what's causing the swelling*, he said, *These old pipes—*

His face darkened with confusion as a new mystery presented itself.

Randall peered into the hole. He saw joists and a beam and plumbing and, far below, the dirt floor of the low basement. *What's wrong?*

The pipes. They don't go anywhere. Randall looked and saw: the lengths and elbows of cast iron meandered in avenues of dead ends and cul-de-sacs.

His father surmised the pipes remained from some plumber's intent that had been abandoned during construction and then covered up and forgotten. Father and son spent the rest of the afternoon extricating them before reassembling the floor, and by sunset the wood lay flat and level.

Randall went to bed that night elated. The afternoon had been a glimpse of his old father, the man he knew before the shade of the Patent Office had fallen across the family. Often he felt like his father had receded into the blackness of a railway tunnel, his voice audible but just beyond the edge of vision. For the few moments as they worked together on the foyer floor, his father had stepped blinking from the dark.

An iron law in the house was the prohibition regarding the father's office. No one was allowed admittance, and even approaching the chamber's doors demanded a reverence unseen outside Westminster Abbey; when his father was wanted for mealtime, Randall's mother approached the doors almost on tiptoe, her two knuckles barely brushing the wood. Sometimes they witnessed blinding flashes from under the doors, brightnesses that afterwards could never be described with certainty as white or blue or red or any other color that appeared on an artist's palette but which regardless served as deterrents from inquiry. The study was like a haunted forest, its obvious terribleness its own safeguard against intrusion.

Yet after that afternoon in the foyer, Randall felt himself drawn to the study, magnetically swept toward it by the pole of his old father. In those moments when he and Casey found themselves alone in the house, Randall would cautiously crack the study doors and slip within to explore. Casey would never follow, choosing instead to stand at the threshold, ears flat against his skull.

The contents of his father's study often defied Randall's comprehension—or at least defied that of the weekly cleaning woman, who spied these visitations on more than one occasion. There were books and instruments and gently whirring machinery, but it was inhabited by stranger items as well: a length of braided steel, for instance, kept vertical under glass as if it was a rare orchid, and lamps that hummed with sound and warmth but no light. Strangest were the piles of boards and planks that covered every flat inch of the room, boards that possessed three ends or had misshapen growths curling perpendicularly from their knots and fibers.

January is a chill, wet month in Northumberland, and colder still in the higher elevations along the Borders County line. There happened a particular evening when the furnace itself seemed to shudder, the flame in its belly too insufficient, and the fires in their grates gave no heat. Meanwhile, Randall's mother jumped at every squeak and shadow. It was the same evening that Casey the dog began inexplicably scratching at the dining-room wall. Soon the scratching turned to whining, and the whining to barking and snarling. Randall's father stormed in, the noise interrupting his work, and demanded Randall tie him outside.

Randall protested. It was too cold; Casey would freeze. Casey barked and barked.

Take that damn dog out.

No.

The father grabbed Casey's collar, dragged him toward the kitchen door.

No, no, no.

Randall looked to his mother, pleaded with her. But even the fulcrum of this scene of minor violence wasn't great enough for her to land upon her child's side. The dog was pulled to the yard.

In the morning Casey was solid as a stone.

The ground was too hard to dig; Randall would have to wait until spring to bury him, so he and his mother left the body in the basement. Randall's father only grunted when they informed him of the news. He was, at that moment, too preoccupied in his examination of the dining-room wall; overnight it had sprouted pipes and boards like spruce branches.

This phenomenon worsened in the following days, so much so that the father hired workmen to saw and cut the plumbing and carpentry that ran like ivy throughout the house. That's how they described it, afterwards: pipework vines across the wallpaper and plaster, jumping like stairwell runners over step and riser; planks and boards emerging from the floors, their iron nails brandished like thorns. The men hacked and hammered then went home at night, only to return the next morning to find the strange foliage doubled.

And that is all I can really tell you about the house before it collapsed.

The villagers described being shaken out of their beds that final morning, when the roof split to pieces and the walls vibrated into splinters; that morning when the façade of the new house, ripped from inside the old, loomed over their heads. It shivered; it would stand only for a moment before gravity and earthly physics tore it apart and Randall, or somebody much like him, would be pulled from the wreckage. As they watched, cracks wound through its clapboard and its tower bent appreciably, an edifice never meant to abide under *our* sun. Behind the sidelights of the front door lurked blurry lumps. Witnesses said they counted three—parent, parent, and child—and heard the deep growl of the dog, but when it was over, searchers found only a single body.

Today Randall is to all appearances a well-formed young man. The scars from his several surgeries are not disfiguring and his limp is slight. Even so, the nurses have told me his mental condition negates any hope of a normal life. He has no cause to worry financially; these events I was able to reconstruct through interviews and documents and train-ticket stubs, and I could find nothing to void the insurance policies on either parent or property—my employers in London disbursed in full and the money is held by the trust to pay for the boy's care. At least his father had one good idea.

Or should I specify *Randall's* father? The boy I met in the hospital was wholly inarticulate, answering my questions with silence or hisses and howls. When I showed him the lead figurine I discovered intact among the ruins—the military officer with three hands and two mouths—the boy's eyes suddenly leapt with flame and he swiped it from my grip. I think it belonged to him.

Cinnamon to Taste

Christi Nogle

———◆———

MARNIE IS DOING the babka today, which means her aunt Cindy will do donuts. Babka starts with a dense egg-rich dough scented with vanilla. Marnie rolls it out into a rectangle, but then she doesn't put down pats of butter the way Cindy does. Instead, she melts the butter, mixes it with a generous scoop of cinnamon but also cardamom, ginger, clove, and nutmeg. When Cindy does it, she uses just the cinnamon and too much white sugar. Marnie spreads her cinnamon paste, crushes pecans in her hands, sprinkles them over the top and adds just as little brown sugar as she can get away with. She tucks the dough into a tight spiral, twists the roll, and places it in the pan in an S-shape. After an hour of rising, she brushes on an egg wash and carefully balances a double recipe of crumb topping on it.

The crumb topping is the best part: two parts flour, two parts butter, one part white sugar, one part brown sugar, pinches of the spices used in the filling, more hand-crushed pecans.

She places the babka in a cold oven and turns the temperature to two hundred. She'll turn it up in increments. This is the part Cindy cannot fathom; she thinks ovens must always be preheated. Twenty or thirty minutes into the cooking, the odor will be intense. Five or ten minutes after that, the babka will be done. Some of the pecans will be on the edge of overdone.

Fresh out of the oven, almost the entirety of the babka has a soft texture, with the crispy exception of the topping pecans. It will burn the mouth of anyone who eats it fresh from the oven, though they'll want to eat it anyway.

Ten minutes out of the oven is the ideal time. The crumb topping is butter-crunchy, the side and bottom crusts dry and crisp. The interior bread is steamy, soft. The interior filling bubbles, hot with spice, almost liquid, the interior pecans velvety. The spillage at the edges of the pan makes a most luscious spiced caramel.

When she brings the warm babka out front, five people are already waiting for their slices, which will be perfect if and only if she hurries. The cutting is delicate work—she has to gently pinch the crust to keep each slice from collapsing—and Marnie concentrates.

"They asked if they could have some of whatever smelled so good," Cindy says as she rings up a customer, sweet old Miss Helms who gets to bring her dog inside in a purse. The Wendells are here, and Luke, and more customers make their way from across the street.

Luke eats his slice and nurses his coffee so incredibly slowly that he outlasts the first morning rush and makes small talk as he finishes. It is only the three of them for now. Luke's beautiful face is set off by the yellow walls, the blue-and-white checked floor.

Marnie can't imagine a backdrop that would not set him off.

Marnie tries not to stare at him as she wipes the yellow counter, as she refills the napkins, as she rearranges the remaining coffee cakes in the display case. She can't help catching his eye. She knows that Cindy admires his looks, but she does not expect there is anything deeper between them.

Cindy stands with hands on hips, glaring at the donuts. She's made too many of them again. It seems that one day they'll sell out and then the next day they'll linger here to be collected by the man who takes them to the homeless shelter, or if he doesn't come, they'll turn dry and Cindy will have to take them out to the dumpster.

She hasn't quite admitted to herself that the days when Marnie makes them are the days when they do sell out.

CINDY AND MARNIE, almost the same age, were thrown together at every family event. Narnie and Ninny, they called each other. Until recently they've never spent much time together except at these gatherings, but they've thought of each other often all through their separate lives, and it seems right that they work and live together now.

They never looked like relatives. Cindy was always the pretty child, and she *has* aged well. There is a certain squareness to her upper body now, and her skin is a bit flushed and chapped, but otherwise she is still the same sunny, pretty woman she's always been. It's only that Marnie has aged into sultry, angular beauty. This, and her sweet, shy demeanor would be enough, apart from the magic she does in the kitchen, apart from her extensive travels. Cindy is so jealous of her that she can barely swallow.

After her husband passed, when she'd done her grieving and looked around for a way to take up something like the life she'd had, Cindy had thought of rootless Marnie, who'd said she would never marry, never settle—and whose life appeared to have suffered by that choice. They'd help each other, Cindy thought. And it has worked out, hasn't it? Business has been so much better ever since Marnie came.

Cindy keeps swallowing the jealousy until one evening when she goes out for a bottle of something to help her sleep. She comes down the stairs from the apartment and catches rosy-gold light far back in the storefront. The bakery has been closed for hours. The lights are still turned off except for one little stained-glass accent lamp in a corner, which silhouettes the figures of a beautiful man and an angular woman in a shy embrace.

There are some days between this and the fight, not many days, and then Cindy is following along behind Marnie as she packs her things, hurling bitter words at her. Marnie barely answers Cindy's attacks and never returns them, but it seems each comment she makes—something as little as a "yes" or a "sorry"—enrages Cindy. Her skin burns so red it seems she might not live.

Finally it is done. Marnie steps out the residence's front door, right beside the bakery's front door, and Cindy locks it behind her.

When Cindy locks the door, Marnie turns right onto the sidewalk, thinking to turn the corner and go into the alley where her car is parked—thinking this all will blow over soon and that she must get the bags into her car and spend a night or two at a motel to allow Cindy cooling time—and she does walk down the sidewalk a few steps before things begin to go dark.

There is a lady in a plum print dress walking in sunlight towards her, and Marnie intends to smile at her when she comes a little closer. These things are difficult for her, shy as she is. She doesn't want to leer at the poor woman from paces away, nor does she want to seem to snub her, and just when she feels it is the perfect time to turn her face up for the smile, the woman is gone. The sunlight is gone. Her visual field holds nothing but a many-colored static degenerating to brown-gray and rapidly falling to black. The memory of the sky still plays in her eyes, the afterimage of the woman's dress now a yellow-greenish rectangle.

"Oh my," she says, and with that, the sounds are gone as well. It had not been loud on the street, just light traffic and perhaps a shush of breeze in the trees, but the breeze is gone now. The traffic is gone.

"Cindy?" she says. She turns back towards the door. Nothing is there, not even an echo.

Marnie sets down her bags and crouches beside them. She is afraid that if she stops touching them they will disappear along with everything else. Some time passes with her crouched there holding them, sobbing, calling for help. No one comes to her. Her first thought is that her senses have been taken, but it can't be. She hears her own calls and her breath, after all. She hears the sound of her hands on the bags, the sound of the bags' fabric sliding together.

She stands. Making sure her legs stay in contact with the bags, she reaches out to where the buildings ought to be, just a foot or two feet to her right, but there is nothing. She is not close enough. She puts the bags back on her shoulders and grasps her suitcase, moves a few paces to the right. Nothing. She is too terrified to move again. She thinks the traffic could still be moving just a few paces from where she stands.

Relief floods over her as she remembers her phone and takes in her hand, but its light is incredibly dim. The photograph of her in front of a waterfall, which should be the screensaver, is just a brown-gray rectangle. There is no hope of seeing words on the screen. She tries the voice feature, but it does not seem to work, or perhaps it too is muted, like the screen.

Marnie thinks it's possible that if she sits here longer, her eyes will adjust. She puts the phone in its place in her purse and holds the purse close.

She sits cross-legged with her hands on the bags. Eventually she begins to feel the ground. It is not rough concrete. She crawls along feeling it, dragging her bags with her. There is no texture to it at all. It is smooth as marble or glass but not cold.

She grows quite hungry. It was after closing time when she came out the door, and she can't remember her last meal. She imagines she smells warm babka and donuts, frying eggs, fresh white bread with butter, sausage drenched in maple syrup, coffee with peppermint. She drifts off to sleep without knowing it's happening and comes awake to the darkness. She fumbles for a lamp before remembering where she is.

She turns on the phone. It is still a dim rectangle, but with real excitement she remembers the flashlight feature. It is difficult to make the gestures. When finally it does turn on, she can barely tell it has. The light should be intense, but it is so dim it will not reveal more than the rough outline of her fingers from half an inch away. She holds it to the floor and sees nothing. The floor is so black that it can't be lit.

She spends more time trying to make a call, trying to do anything, but there is nothing she can do with the phone. She expects that someone will call and she will be able to press the correct place on the screen to answer. She places the phone back inside its pocket on the side of her purse and hugs the purse close.

There comes a time when she has to use the bathroom. She is terrified to move away from her bags, so she carries them twenty paces in the direction of the buildings. She holds her bags up off the ground while she pees. She feels vulnerable—unsure if maybe she has gone blind and deaf and is doing this in reality, in the middle of a lawn perhaps—and also thinking something may attack her while she's in this position. It could be that there are other beings here—beings who can see, who will stalk her and take her.

Nothing comes for her, and when her bladder is empty, she stands and paces back to where she was before. She does not know if the traffic still moves somewhere off to the left of where she was originally, or if she has now walked into the area where the buildings stand—and the buildings could come back, of course they could, and then she will be trapped in a wall or in a tree that stands in this place where she sits. There is no way to know, but it is some comfort to think that she's come back not too far from where she started.

She laughs at herself for thinking there were beings able to see in this dark. They would be using echolocation, wouldn't they? She would not know they were present until they took her in their mouths. There is no point in thinking of them.

She takes her clothes out of the suitcase and makes a bed from them. She brushes her teeth with a tiny dot of toothpaste, carefully combs her hair and braids it. She places the other bags around her body and opens the empty suitcase above her head. It feels safe, like a tent. Her breath soon warms the space and scents it with spearmint. She is able to fall asleep.

The most terrifying part of her time in this place is the moment waking up from the first long sleep, disoriented, sure it has all been a dream. She wails, bargains with God, cries for help again, and all the rest. Finally, she moves her hands over her pile of belongings. She selects her heaviest sweater, rolls it tight in the purse. She takes a pair of pajamas, a couple of pairs of underwear. She takes the toothpaste, the toothbrush, the phone, her car keys. She searches the bags again for anything to eat, but there is nothing. She puts on a clean pair of jeans and a clean T-shirt, and, still unsure if this is the right thing to do, she walks away from the rest of her things.

It feels good to be free to walk, even if her steps are halting. She walks slowly for about half an hour and nothing changes. It is still black. The floor is still slick and tepid when she drops to check from time to time. She turns back.

There is some hope that she might step into the pile of things, but that does not happen. She walks for about an hour, turns back. She feels she will keep walking for the rest of her life. She checks the phone again. Dim as the screen is, once she turns it off, an afterimage lingers before her eyes. A brown-gray rectangle in front, a dim rectangle behind her if she turns. But there is something now, before her face, a larger rectangle. She is trotting towards it.

It is before her, the window of the bakery! All of the colors are terribly muted, but they are colors, the first she's seen in—what?—two days? As through a sepia-tinted screen, she sees the checkerboard blue-and-white floor, the yellow countertop. This is all the detail she sees at first, but as she comes closer, she can see blue cake boxes stacked on a shelf. She can see the cash register, rows of dark brown donuts. She looks behind her, and there is only blackness and a haunting violet and orange afterimage.

The storefront is empty, no customers, but the sign just behind the glass says it's open. The tinkle-click of her fingernail against the glass is enchantingly real.

Cindy comes into the room with a white cake. She just stands frowning towards the window.

"Let me in!" Marnie calls. "Please!" She gropes for a door that is not there.

Cindy sets the cake in the glass case, pushes it forward.

Marnie is banging on the glass now, and Cindy finally trudges over to the window. The shape of her mouth is so ugly! Marnie almost can't look at her, but she does. She stares into Cindy's eyes and mouths "Let Me In."

When the door opens, does it cut into darkness? It must, but Marnie does not see. Her eyes are full of tears now, stinging from the bright light. She is incoherent. She is grasping onto Cindy, and Cindy accepts the embrace for the first instant, then struggles away saying "What's wrong? What happened?" and "What?" and "Calm down."

Sitting at the bistro table, trying to drink a coffee and eat a cocoa cake donut, Marnie can't seem to calm down. It strikes her that Cindy is not Cindy and this place is not the bakery. She squints and holds her hand at her brow to cut the light at first. Her eyes are badly swollen from crying. Everything hurts—her limbs, her stomach, her skin—and the light hurts most of all.

She does not take in everything at once, but the donut is so bad, so bad! It is dry as a mound of potting soil, and then she sees the Cindy sitting across from her is so red in the face, her pores so large and black, her teeth so yellowed. There are dark hairs at her lipline, at her chin, dark hairs coming in below her eyebrows. The tabletop is lurid yellow, skimmed with something Marnie believes must be sweat.

The coffee reeks of piss. She can touch it to her lips, but that is all.

Marnie's heart is pounding, but she's trying to make her face calm. Thinking Cindy might try to force her out the door again any moment, she makes cringing smiles.

When she can speak, she says, "I think I just need to lie down. Can I? For just a little while?"

Cindy says, "I didn't think it was you at the window at first. There was a tapping but no one was there, and then you seemed to push forward out of the background. It was so strange."

Marnie says, "Could I just lie down? Would that be all right?"

Cindy says, "What happened to you? Did someone attack you?"

"I can tell you later. Can I?"

"Did you get in a car accident?"

"Of course not."

"Did *you* do something?"

"I don't think so. May I? On the couch?"

"You can go get in your bed, I suppose."

Upstairs, the bed has been stripped. Cindy brings a stack of folded linens and says she needs to get back. The bakery will be open for another hour or two.

The sheets look filthy and smell of sweat. The mattress pad is balled with rough, scratchy lint and hair, but Marnie curls up on it. The room smells bad. It does not feel like home, but she is still so terrified of going back out in the darkness, all she can do is lie still thinking of what she can tell Cindy to let her stay, what she can do so that she'll never have to go outside again. Her mind runs this way until she falls asleep.

When she wakes, she looks out the window. People move out on the sidewalk. There are trees, cars, streetlights, dogs. She imagines that her suitcase and her clothes must be out near the corner, but they are not to be seen from the window. Did someone take them or did they never appear?

The picture of herself standing in front of a waterfall, she stares at it for a long time. There is no angular beauty in this picture, just a skeletal, leathery woman with horse teeth and downcast eyes. She deletes the photo and all of the other lying photos she finds on her phone.

Marnie can eat her own cooking. She tries making the babka in the night and waits ten minutes for it to cool, all the time shaking with hunger and dread. It tastes good. She eats half of it feeling nothing but gratitude. In the morning she tries making an egg over medium. It does not taste like it should, but it tastes like food. She tries again, this time with more butter, more pepper, less salt. She watches it closely and eats it at the ideal time. She recognizes the taste of an egg this time, and it is excellent.

She cannot eat anything Cindy makes; she tries over the next few days but can't bring these things into her mouth.

All Marnie needs to do to keep her place is cringe and flinch, promise to do better. She apologizes for not being able to go out; she apologizes for anything she ever did in the past. She tries to stay in the back during the bakery hours, but the customers call to her.

Luke comes in, happy to see her back. She recognizes him only by his distinctive hairline, the set of his shoulders. His head is oversized now, the jaw monstrously overlong. The eyes she remembered being so beautiful barely look like human eyes. The brows jut out over them, hanging them in shadow. She evades him as best she can.

It is not just the outward things that have been transformed: her thoughts, too, have become monstrous. Where once she thought "I will never marry" with a whimsical air, maybe thinking of it as a challenge to the right man, she now sees that line as a grim certainty built up from horrible things she learned about marriage as a child. All of her childhood comes back to her in terrible detail, so much pain and so much boredom, and insecurity, and shame. Her travels as a young woman come back to her as a series of desperate, wasteful flailings. The past plays out in intricate detail.

Marnie scrubs the bakery floors and walls. She asks Cindy to bring in stronger lightbulbs. These efforts help the place to look something like it did before. There are more customers every day, and when they enter, they take in the surroundings with appreciative sighs. The expanded breakfast menu is a success, the bread and donut smells heightened by the addition of eggs and meat.

Marnie likes to watch television so much more than she ever did before. The dramas, the talk shows—especially the romantic comedies—they remind her of real life. Everyone is clean and vital, all the colors pure. Almost everyone on television looks human. She works as hard as she can all day, and in the evening she settles in her corner of the couch to escape into the these images until Cindy wakes her for bed.

"What's wrong?" Cindy asks from time to time. She's reconciled herself to the fact that Marnie is not going to go, and really, the business has never been better. And she feels guilty. It seems to her that she and Marnie will be partners now in a bond deeper than sisterhood, deeper than marriage. Marnie will stay, and it will always be the same. She thinks she needs to reassure Marnie of this and tries to do so over and over. It never quite translates.

One night, Cindy asks what's wrong and Marnie sits with her hand close to her mouth. Her eyes do not meet Cindy's.

Marnie says, "I was wondering if I might be able to get a TV for my room. I lost my laptop when I went out, you remember. I don't need another laptop, but a TV, maybe a couple hundred dollars. I don't have money of my own, but you say business has been good. I hope that if I haven't made enough money for us yet, maybe in a few weeks."

"Of course you've made enough money," Cindy says, sitting down on the sofa.

"Thank you, I so appreciate it." She slides closer to Cindy and directs her attention to a flier on the coffee table. "I saw this one on sale, and I don't think it would be too far away. If it won't fit in your car, you could put it in mine." The car. She hasn't thought of it, but it has been parked for weeks now. Could the battery have run down, or what else could happen to an abandoned vehicle? Has it been stolen, vandalized?

"I can go get your TV, not tomorrow though. Only—why *can't* you go out?" Cindy says. Her voice lowers. "Is it agoraphobia?"

Marnie brightens. "Yes, that's what it is, in fact."

But how could that be, when she's traveled so far and seen so much? She makes the effort to look straight at Cindy and smiles. Marnie can't speak of the nightmares she still has.

Cindy never gets the television for her, thinking that it will not turn out to be a healthy thing, thinking that if she had it, she would not ever come out to the living room.

Cindy starts watching movies with her instead. They sit close together, turn off all the lights. Marnie makes popcorn drenched in butter. They both begin to grow plump. It helps. Cindy does not go out as often. She grows paler, less ruddy. More and more, in the light from the television, she looks the way Marnie remembers her.

Marnie dreams she is back in the dark. There are many other windows; she only has to find them. All of them look in on Cindy: crying to herself in her bedroom, going about her sad process of getting showered and dressed, Cindy in her upstairs kitchen eating soup out of a can, in her bakery fumbling about with ingredients she doesn't understand. In the dreams, Marnie desperately pounds on the windows. When she recalls the dreams, she wonders at how her dream-self wants too much to be back inside Cindy's dreary life.

Cindy is dating Luke now, but it's such a low-key arrangement that Marnie often forgets about it. Cindy will come in at ten or midnight once in a while, and she'll send Marnie off to bed same as always. Marnie doesn't go to bed at all unless Cindy wakes her.

One night when Cindy lays her hand on Marnie's shoulder to send her off to bed, Marnie shrieks. Her face is all terror, and when Cindy sits to hold her, she pushes away

"What's wrong?" Cindy says.

Marnie, still almost sleeping, says, "I was watching a cartoon."

Cindy has no response. She tries again to hold her niece, and this time Marnie lets her. Up close, Cindy's breath is rancid. The oil from her face touches Marnie's cheek. It feels thick as honey.

"My life was like a cartoon compared to this," Marnie says. "Everything's gritty here. Everything's brown. And there are all these complicated histories behind the things we say. I want to go back." She pulls away from Cindy, wipes her face with her own sleeve.

"Back where?" says Cindy. She has no idea what this is about but thinks maybe Marnie means to travel back to a place she visited long ago, or maybe back home, but there are no parents for her there—and of course Cindy's parents passed over years ago—and there is no one for her really, back in her hometown.

"Where? Good question," says Marnie. She stands and trudges towards her room, turns back. She says, "Sometimes I think the black place was all just a metaphor about my trips. You know, you get scared traveling, you get excited, maybe scared of what's out there. You pack and you repack a smaller bag."

"The black place?" says Cindy. She comes close to Marnie. She strokes Marnie's hair back from her face and Marnie lets her. Marnie's eyes keep traveling over Cindy's face.

"Maybe that's where I was all the time when I thought I was seeing waterfalls," Marnie says.

"Do you want to go away again?" Cindy says. She knows Marnie doesn't have the money to travel. What good does it do Marnie to want to go somewhere?

"Is it Luke? I'll tell him it's over. I will. I don't want you to leave," Cindy says to help her niece back into this view of things. She reaches for Marnie's hand, doesn't notice her wanting to flinch back. "You know how much this place means to me. Before you, I was about to lose it. I was going to be alone with nothing, and so were you. We have a good life now, don't we?" Cindy is almost ready to cry.

"See what I mean?" Marnie says, her fingers writhing around her face to show the complexity of it all. "There's all this *history* behind what you say. It wasn't like this before."

FOR A LONG time, Marnie occupies herself cleaning and arranging the bakery and getting the food just as close to the real as she can. All of this delights the customers. They see it as someplace hyperreal, like a theme park, like being inside a movie. They come in droves, keep asking when the bakery might be expanding.

Cindy doesn't touch anything but the cash register now, but that keeps her busy.

Marnie is so busy she never dreams, almost never sleeps. There is cooking and cleaning, and every day she tries to find, within the building, a door leading back to where she was before. How many places there are to go! The storefront and cafe area, the bakery kitchen, which has two rooms, the downstairs storage areas and the public restroom. Upstairs, the two bedrooms and the living room, the kitchen, the bathroom, the odd little study. Many, many doors to open, linger at, check. If there is nothing new behind a door one day, who's to say there might not be something the next? Each door must be opened at least once a day, even the doors of the cupboards.

The bakery door and the front door of the residence, the door leading out to the alley: all of these can be opened and checked. She can't bring herself to send her whole body out of them, but she can step out with a leg. She can angle out her head, her shoulder.

Her restlessness has risen to a sufficient pitch, by now, that she stands in the open front door while the regulars eat their breakfasts. She has one foot on a blue tile, one foot on the sidewalk.

"You're going out?" calls Cindy from the cash register. Marnie looks back and sees Luke standing next to Cindy, his hand resting limp and grotesquely purple on her shoulder.

The Wendells are closest to the door, with their plates of babka, perfectly scrambled eggs, and pepper bacon cooked crisp in butter.

"There's nothing out there like this," says the smiley Mrs. Wendell.

It doesn't look like there is. The street is there, and the traffic, people walking, but all is dim and brown with a fine-grained texture. It's like looking at the world through a maple syrup—no, crystallized old honey—it's magnified, distorted, tinted amber. The people out there are no more real-looking than the ones inside.

Cindy is approaching. She takes Marnie's shoulders gently from behind. She is saying something. The revulsion nearly sends Marnie out to the sidewalk, but she wills her foot to stick to the blue tile. She pulls her errant foot back inside.

Marnie spins around. Before she knows what she is doing, her hands are grasping Cindy's arms ungently right above their elbows, and she is moving Cindy by force. She is holding the door open with her back and swiveling Cindy towards the outside.

"What?" says Cindy, pulling back.

"Help me," says Marnie. She turns her eyes to the regulars. "*Please* help me."

Mr. and Mrs. Wendell both stand up. Luke takes two more steps towards her, too. The others seem like they would help, if there were more time and if they understood, but their help isn't needed. Marnie moves Cindy outside all on her own and pulls the glass door closed, locks it.

Cindy is right up against the glass at first. She stands close for a moment, confusion coming over her face. She squints, and rubs her eyes. She takes just one step back, but it's enough. Everyone in the bakery watches as she pushes behind the background of moving cars and storefronts.

The Strigoaica

Ross Smeltzer

———◆———

"The worms had made a kingdom in the dead man's skull," the girl said. Her voice was cracked and broken. Her eyes were wild, like the eyes of a fox caught in the toothed maw of a sprung trap, its brittle leg snapped and weeping hot blood. She was afraid.

"His throat had been cut, turned to ragged strips, and frozen blood, clotted and rust-red, had pooled around him," she added, speaking slowly, without feeling, her voice not much more than an aching whisper. "I knew I courted death by staying there, near him. But I could not look away. I could not look away from the blood. His eyes were expressionless. The life had been drained from them."

"Perhaps he was an unlucky woodsman killed by wolves?" I ventured, unconvinced by such a prosaic hypothesis. "They grow bold in winter, when the deer are few. Men's meat is sweet to them."

The girl did not reply. She turned and looked into the nearby hearth, where the fire burned low. She shook her head slowly and her faraway eyes locked on the orange fire.

Flames danced in the pools of her dark eyes.

"No, boyarina, I do not think wolves could do such a thing. Only monsters could," she murmured.

Though we were safe in an inn at the edge of the forest, sheltered by stout walls and surrounded by strong woodsman and hunters, the girl was afraid. No harm could come possibly to us in this place. And yet, she shook like one who is feverish. She trembled.

Outside, the wind roared like a caged beast and an owl screeched, heralding murder. Reveling in the taste of hot blood. It gloried in the frenzied writhings of a thing—a living thing—not yet dead but nearly so. Nature is cruel. The cosmos is merciless to its playthings.

She was a sad little thing, this mysterious girl, cast up from the depths of the snowy forest. She had staggered into the inn a little earlier, pushing her way through the oaken door and falling to the floor, just as the moon—shaped like a peasant's sickle or like the perfect crescent of a Turkish standard—rose full into the starry blue sky. Her wails had rent the stillness of the winter night. She had howled like a wolf.

When she had first come, she was frenzied, with eyes mad and frothing mouth. She'd been incoherent, like one possessed, one whose skin beetles and seethes with skittering demons. I have seen such things. Do not scoff, you who are young and think yourself wise. You, who have seen so little of life. Life is a mystery to you yet. Learn from one who knows its secrets.

It had taken a long time to calm the girl. She had slept a while. She had resisted the strong spirits offered to her, pushed them away, as if they were poison. I had watched over her as she slept, prayed for her. That is the duty of old women, to be firm and strong when others are not. I had stroked her dark hair, glossy as a bolt of black silk.

I had touched her cold skin. It was white as alabaster. Her eyelids twitched and fluttered in her skull when she slept. As if she were in the throes of a nightmare. Her skin was clammy, fish-like.

This girl was an enigma. She had not been seen in this village before. I resolved to know what misfortune had befallen her, this poor little one who could not have been much older than my daughter Zaleska when she had sickened and died. When the life had gone out of her dark and beautiful eyes. That was a long time ago now, during the plague years, when the pest oozed down from the mountains and pooled in the plains and valleys. When these lands were scoured of life and laughter. My own daughter is little more than a dim glimmer of a memory for me, a distorted specter in the periphery of my failing sight. I cannot count the years since her death. I could, once. But that was long ago.

"Boyarina, it was by that discovery—the dead man in the wood—that we knew our danger," the girl said, wrenching me from my melancholic recollections. I appreciated her recognition of my title, worthless as it is.

"Tell me more, little one," I urged.

She stared at me with vacant, lustrous eyes. Doll eyes. Black and glossy as buttons. She mouthed words but said nothing. The danger of which she'd spoken only obliquely had passed. She was secure now, for the thick walls of this inn had repelled Tatar arrows and Saxon handguns alike. And yet her fear had not gone with the danger that had birthed it. It was like the doomed *gheist* of the person who cannot leave its dwelling. The poor wraith remains clinging to that place, desperate and stubborn, reluctant to be judged by its maker, though the mortal clay has crumbled to dust. Alas for her, the fear was deep in her yet, like a parasite—a worm of the gut—or a disease. Hatching. Growing.

"What did you find in the forest, little one?" I asked. "Tell me. Speaking of it would drive it away and purge you of it. Cast it from you like you would a bit of spoiled meat. Expel it."

The wind howled in the high, craggy hills and echoed in the black forests beyond the inn. Snow was falling now, lightly. It glittered in the blue moon-glow, like stardust, and danced in the air.

I thought that she would fail me. That she would begin to sob and wail like a newborn babe. But no, she was stronger than I supposed. She did not halt her tale, fearful and frail as she was. I was sure she would be overcome by tears and sorrow. She was more tenacious than I expected. She said more, unprovoked by me. Perhaps the strong Tokaji wine had loosened her tongue—though her glass was still full. Perhaps the walls of the inn made her brave. No matter. Her mood changed—with a peculiar swiftness, as if she simply cast aside her fear like it were a cloak. "In the cavity where one of the man's eyes had been—the place from whence he'd gazed tenderly upon his children and delighted in the nakedness of his woman—a wine-red snake lay coiled." She gazed at the glowing embers in the nearby hearth and whispered: "It hissed at me as I neared the dead man's body. It chilled me to see such a sight, boyarina. It chilled me more than the sparkling sugar-white frost that hung in the air or the steely wind that swept like a hawk through the forest. It was a mark of the devil. A familiar. Demon-hatched. And yet, chilled as I was by this thing, I yearned to know what misfortune had befallen the man."

"You are prone to morbid fancies, little one," I murmured gently. "And you are brave. It is a rare thing to find one so young and yet so heedless of death."

She spoke again, in a low whisper. But now, she was coy, kittenish. Playful, even, with a light and lilting laugh. I thought this strange.

"Thank you, boyarina. You are kind. The man looked so alone there, boyarina, lying shadowed under an old oak, his puckered face dark under the forest's thick canopy. His thin and wasted hands were clasped tight atop his silenced heart. I wished to see him up close. To utter a prayer for him. To comfort him on his long journey. And to give him the coins he would need to appease the gatekeepers."

She smiled shyly—though her eyes stared yet, unblinking—and said: "You will, perhaps, think me superstitious and unrefined, countess. Perhaps a trifle foolish, also. We who are noble born are taught that it is only among the heathenish peasant folk that such a thing is done. You must forgive me, for it is the way I was taught. My family is an old one, and our customs are...*singular*." She chuckled a little and brought her wine glass to her lips. I was perhaps mistaken, but I did not think she drank from it.

I did not think this very strange, for I, myself, was not thirsty. I did not drink from the wine that had been placed before me. It smelled sour, turned.

"No, little one, I do not think you foolish. In this land, superstitions are rarely without some basis—or some use. I, too, am of the boyar blood, learned and knowledgeable of the world beyond the borders of the Vlach land. I even traveled to Buda and Prague and other distant courts many years ago. I am no fool. But I, like any sensible person, buried my father face-down in his grave when he died. Did I think he might wake and come for me in my sleep? No! But I did it anyway. In this way, I meant to confound him, if he should wake, thirsting for the blood of his kin. There is, as I am sure you know, something wrong in the soil here, some poison in the loam," I added. She nodded her agreement.

"You are superstitious, boyarina. I would have thought you above such medieval worries."

"Nothing ill can come of precautions," I said.

She smiled. It was good to see her smile. Her teeth gleamed white, the color of fine porcelain.

"The path you took is perilous, little one," I said. "Bandits shelter in the midnight-hued shadows and masked highwaymen crouch in the caves that soar above that sorrowful track. Many go missing in that forest. Those who have made the journey safely say the only way one can spot the highwaymen in the forest is by their eyes, for they are like twinkling amber, wolf eyes lit by the fires they light in their hideouts in the caves.

"Forgive me for chiding you, but you were unwise to go that way, little one. Most unwise," I said, my voice stern, like a parent addressing a reckless child. Upbraiding her in this way reminded me of my happy years, when I washed the skinned knees of my little Zaleska or mended her torn dresses, or warned her to stay away from the forests and the churchyards—most especially the churchyards.

But that was many years ago now. Too many to count.

She was silent and still, cowed by my hectoring. Her eyes—wide and wondering yet—fell to the floor; she was ashamed of her childish folly.

It was then that I began to wonder at her age. She was young, not more than sixteen, with white, fresh skin. With plump cheeks. A full bosom. And skin—such lovely skin!—the color of fresh cream. She'd never worked in the fields. She was a pretty thing.

And her lips were red. The red of overripe berries, wet, then fallen and spattered in the dead leaves. The red of rage and battles. The red of longing.

She had not lived a life of toil; that was certain. She was draped in an ermine cloak, like those worn by the richest Germans. She was, I thought, the daughter of a Saxon merchant, come from the north to conclude some transaction or arrange a contract in her father's stead. Such women are not an uncommon sight in these parts.

They rarely come this way in winter, however.

Rarer still do they come by night.

It was then that I noticed her hands. They were white, yes, but an unhealthy shade—the color of bleached bone. Thin as swamp reeds, and they were tipped with long nails. Hooked and warped. The sharpened scimitar-blade hooks of the vulture. The claws of a killer. Made for grasping. For tearing.

She was not as innocent as she appeared.

I shivered, though I wore a heavy black cloak and thick fur gloves. I felt insecure, for my cloak is dirty and torn and caked with dried mud. Not like the fine ermine mantle my companion wore. My cloak is old and out-of-date. I am too poor to afford another. I, who am highborn, who once commanded esteem, must go about in rags, reduced to beggary. We live in strange and sorrowful times.

The girl's fingers glittered with jewels of all colors. They were dusty and dull, though, false finery. Her golden trinkets were mildewed and rimed with green-black mold. And the green dress she wore was of obsolete cut and had been mended by inexpert hands. Gold threads, dry and frayed like hay, hung from her bodice. Rose-pink ribbons that might once have fluttered in the wind now hung limp from her chest, still as fading butterflies. They were stained. She wore a lace ruff around her neck. It was very old, unfashionable even when I was young.

I felt less insecure now, as I cataloged these things. The girl was not as noble as she seemed.

She must have noticed that I was studying her, most especially her hands, for she swiftly drew them under the ermine cloak in which she was cocooned. It hung heavily from her slight body. She giggled like a wicked, knowing child. Like she had a secret.

I said nothing of this, but smiled, not showing my rotten teeth.

The fire was flickering low now, casting fidgety, angular shadows about the interior of the inn. The silk-clad Saxon merchants and the bearded Vlach huntsmen murmured to each other softly. Though I could not be sure, I was certain they spoke of the girl in their midst, the wild-eyed maiden just come from the forest. Their tones were furtive, conspiratorial. They thought her strange. Dangerous. I resolved to guard her against them.

One must fear the men in these lands. They are like wolves, cowardly, but ever slinking, probing for softness.

"There are many tales told of that forest," I said quietly, ignoring the sinister whispers of the menfolk in the inn. "The peasants of this village still tell tales of the Magus of Gorgota, a tinkerer in magicks, and a necromancer; one who stitched fairies with wasp wings just to see them squirm; who made a goat's gristle-caked skull cackle and speak with the voice of a man; and who summoned all the wickedest hags in the land to his spiraling tower and, there, bade them dance with the fauns, the not-men who lay with them and seeded them."

She laughed, snorting with delight.

"Surely, that is nothing more than a tale old women tell to frighten the young and suggestible," she replied, tittering. Her cheeks were flushed, blooming. "A tale to frighten helpless young maidens. I assure you, boyarina, I am not like that. Not at all."

"Perhaps," I said. "Perhaps not."

"What did you learn of the dead man in the forest, little one?" I prodded, hoping she might return to her tale. I must confess it diverted me a little. And in this place—at my age—diversions are rare.

She grew grave again and the smile that had played on her young face fell away.

"My guides inspected his body and found, as I told you, that his neck had been torn apart. He had been drained of blood. His eyes were open and staring."

The gathering wind battered the inn. I heard rats scurrying in the wormy wood of the old building. Its timbers groaned.

"Curious," I said. "Most curious. Wolves perhaps. They grow hungry in winter, when there are no beasts but men for them to feed on."

"Yes, that is what you said earlier, boyarina," she reminded me politely.

"Forgive me," I said. "You must excuse me, for I am an old woman, and my memory is not what it once was. It has become cluttered. Too many memories."

"Yes, of course, boyarina. In any case, my guides did not think wolves could have done such a thing." She smiled and said, "My guides, rough men from all lands, cutthroats and crooks, all draped in furs and smelling of old leather and gunpowder and strong liquor, gathered around the unfortunate man and began muttering to one another. Though I could not penetrate the murk of their many tongues, I gathered that they all thought the man a victim of some kind of predator, the prey of a blood drinker. There were as many names for this beast as there were men in my party: the Serbs stroked their curled mustaches and called it the *vukodlak*; the Hungarians said the work was the handiwork of the *izcacus*; the Croats said the man had fallen prey to a *vampir*; and the fur-clad Vlach cowmen called it the *strigoi*. These men were all alike in their fear of this beast, boyarina, and all began to unpack their muskets and crossbows and strap their swords about their waists. They lit torches and scanned the trees. Every man looked to the woods. They searched for movement in the voids between the white birches. They studied every shadow, hoping it would not move strangely. Praying they would not see what lurked in the darkness. In their mess of babbling tongues they insisted we go back the way we'd come. They said I'd be a great fool to press on and enter the hunting grounds of a beast. They had become cowards.

"But I am of noble birth and know what it is to command men. I told them that I would not permit such weakness. I'd been sent by my father to conclude business for him, and would not be delayed by the timidity of my subordinates. I would have none of it. I remounted my horse and rode on into the woods. I told them they needn't follow me, but reminded them that the beast in the woods—if such a thing did exist and was about—was not certain to slay them. It might let them pass in peace. Had it not recently slaked its thirst for blood, after all? Might it not be like a snake and digesting awhile in its lair? Then, I reminded them, that if they were to go back without me, my father would most certainly kill them all."

"Rough men such as those must be kept on a tight leash, young one," I said, chuckling. "You were deft in your handling of them. They respect violence, nothing else. The men of these lands, they are like dogs, brutes."

"No, boyarina, I should have listened to those men, for though they were rough and boorish and superstitious, they were far wiser than I."

"Oh?"

"Yes, boyarina." The girl gazed into the dying fire and continued her tale: "I did not heed their warnings, did not turn back the way we'd come. I pushed on, as the twilight descended and the half-light of dusk turned to night. We rode, into the black heart of the forest, where the path is all but swallowed by the tall pines and the old oaks; where vines, studded with dagger-sharp barbs, hang low from crags and snare the careless. The road eventually died away, becoming first a rutted, broken path before disappearing completely into the tangle of briars and thorns. Very soon, we found ourselves wandering in the depths of the forest, with only the moon to guide us.

"As you know, boyarina, the moon is a fickle guide, and is indifferent to the sufferings of the small things that must make their way by its weak light."

"Yes, little one. I shudder for you."

"We prayed for the coming of the dawn, boyarina. For, in the stillness of the wood, my men and I had heard sounds. Twigs breaking. Dried leaves crunching. Ragged breathing. Whispers carried on the wind. Ghost-speak and hexen-tongue. Hissed words. Old words. The velvet tongue of the viper, the language of the devil, the *Ordog*."

"My men swung their lanterns wildly, casting beams of golden light into the inky dark, hoping to catch sight of whatever shadowed us. But the darkness defied them. It kept its secrets."

The girl pretended to sip her wine.

"Boyarina, snow started to fall. The glittering flakes drifted down slowly, like unspooling spider's silk. The moon was high, uncovered by clouds, and blazing bright as a madman's eye. The trees swayed and moaned. Wolves howled in the mountains.

"We walked in the woods for a long time. A thin grey mist coiled around our ankles; black clouds thickened and grew fat in the mountains, their nursery. Fat as gravid women, these then descended, bringing cold that stung the skin, making knuckles bleed and eyes well with tears. Snow began to fall. Our horses became obstinate; they panicked at every sound, even the furtive movements of small things in the undergrowth. They cried out when they heard wolves, far off, in the foothills of the mountains.

"My men were silent. Seasoned killers all, none was a dunce with a blade. All had seen death. And yet they said not a word. They clutched their weapons tight. They huddled close, orbiting me like still-suckling children drawn to their mother. They submitted to infantile instinct. They yielded to their fear.

"At last we came to a clearing in the trees. In that place, the birches and pines had given way to tangled mounds of grass and weeds. In the center of the clearing, there was a dead tree, black as coal, its skin blasted by lightning. It had big ropey boughs that gave way to thickly-sprouted, spindly branches: a skeleton's fingers. They grasped. They clutched. They were desirous—an old man's unwelcome hands. Wanting. Wanton.

"The tree was surrounded by crumbling headstones: all askew, some broken apart, some tumbled-down. They were old. The inscriptions that had once marked them all had been scoured by the seasons, leaving them blank, annulled.

"Snow was falling more heavily then, boyarina, glazing the meadow grass with a silvery witch-glow. The wind was slight, yet it stirred the frail limbs of the dead tree, making it appear as if it beckoned us. It commanded we come near.

"I, alone among my companions, complied. I was driven by an instinct I could not contradict. I felt drawn to the tree. I walked towards it, slowly, feeling for the pistol I'd stashed in the folds of my cloak. Finding it there made me feel braver. My companions mouthed hushed warnings as I left the seeming safety of the group and entered the orbit of the tree. As I neared the tree, I heard an owl scream—far away. Its cry echoed in the silence of the clearing."

"You were brave, little one," I said. "And very foolish."

"Yes, boyarina. That is true. And as I entered the shadow of the dead tree, a figure appeared from behind it. It materialized, as if from a dream, a child of oblivion and ether. I thought it was unreal. An ambassador of the invisible sphere, come to greet me and guide me from that place. But, I soon realized that this was no wraith standing guard over its tomb. It was not a ghost. It had heft, dimension. It existed in our own plane. It breathed, though its breaths came unevenly. It gulped down air as we do, boyarina. The figure was small. Child-like. Its head was bowed, so I could not see its face. It was stooped as an old crow, and swaddled in a hooded black cloak that dragged in the grass.

"I halted before this strange figure. It simply stood before me, in the shadow of the dead tree, swaying a little; it grasped a headstone in one of its hands, using it as a support. Whoever this stranger was, I knew it was weak—sickly, I thought. I resolved not to get too close. Its skin shone blue-grey in the moonlight. The color of graveyard earth.

"'We are lost,' I told the stranger. 'We were taking the path to Brasov, but lost it in the trees. Do you know how we might find it again?'

"The stranger said not a word, boyarina. Its head remained bowed, as if it were praying. I nearly repeated my question before it spoke. Its voice was strangled, wet, and weak. A woman's voice. 'You are very far from the road you seek, child. You were mistaken in coming this way. Do not phantoms breed in the forest? Are not your grandmother's childish tales filled with monsters that live in the deepest part of the woods? Have they found you yet, child? Or did you stumble upon their nest, ignorant as you are? You who are so young and are so very foolish.'"

"Please help us find the path to Brasov," I said, frustrated, angered by the stranger's condescension.

"The figure raised its head with a sudden, snake-like jerk. Though I could not make out her face beneath her tattered cowl, I knew she stared, unblinking, with bright, reflective eyes. Red eyes. Hungry eyes. She was studying me, waiting for my reaction. Around her, a glittering mist swirled, forming helixes and spirals and whorls in the air. The strange woman's eyes bore into mine. I saw wolves in the trees just beyond the graveyard, black shapes, darker than the night air, circling phantoms.

"Then, just as suddenly as the figure raised her head, she came near. She moved without a sound. She slid close, seeming not to touch the earth. She glided on shadow. Her face, still hooded and invisible, pressed close to my own, and she said: 'Do not fear me, child. The danger is behind you.' It motioned to my men. 'Them,' it hissed. Its breath was rank—hot and metallic.

"Without thinking, I turned to look at my men, all shouting and pleading for me to turn away from the robed stranger. One of them, a Hungarian—Gustav, I think he was called—left the group and rushed towards me, drawing his curved sword and raising it for a killing strike. He was fierce-eyed, Tatar-blooded, with a grave expression. He made for the stranger, intending to slay her. But as he rushed towards her, the figure darted away. I saw her vanish, dematerialize into the snow and shadows that surrounded her. She moved with an uncanny, impossible swiftness, like a taut bow loosed. Gustav was left slashing at the air with his sword, hacking impotently at snowflakes."

"Men are foolish, child. They think nothing of their horses and blades and guns." I cackled a little, then let the girl continue her strange tale.

"The next thing I knew, I saw Gustav in the dirt, his head upturned and facing the sky, blood bubbling from his lips, lips that opened and closed and uttered silent cries. His eyes were wide with surprise and welling with tears. He gulped air and twitched like a gutted fish…he tried to scream but the words were drowned in blood…black blood that gurgled from his mouth like a fountain."

The girl's words died away and she looked away from me into a far corner of the inn. Her face was frozen, mask-like. I let her rest for a moment.

When she spoke again, her voice was a mix of fear and wonder. "Boyarina, that great strong man had been torn in half below the waist. And that robed figure had stood over him; blood dripped from her long fingers."

"And did you run, little one?" I asked, my voice high and quaking. I was growing weak. I had been with the girl for a long time. Dawn was drawing near and I had greatly exerted myself during the night.

"Yes, boyarina, I ran from that place! I made for the woods and slipped into the trees. I heard men and horses screaming, alike in their animal terror. I heard guns blazing, branches breaking and falling to earth, wolves yelping and barking, and swords being torn from their sheaths. And then I heard men crashing through the undergrowth, running hard, falling—and then I heard screaming—and then I heard silence.

"I ran and ran, boyarina, until I sighted an abandoned church atop a mound in the wood. Its roof had collapsed and its windows were broken, but it promised shelter. I did not think the devil's children could come near a holy place, and so I darted inside, intending to hide there until dawn, when the light would drive the devil away."

"That was prudent of you, little one," I said. "You were very wise. But the devil and his offspring are strong. Very strong."

"Yes, boyarina. They are. I know that now." She then turned and looked outside the windows of the inn and murmured to herself, as if she thought I could not hear: "it will soon be dawn."

"Yes, little one, it will," I said. She looked at me, surprised that I had heard her. "Though I am an old woman, I have excellent hearing, little one. You will keep no secrets from me." I smiled. "Finish your tale. But we must rest soon."

"Yes, boyarina. You are right. I ran into the church, forcing my way through the snow that filled the nave of the building. I reached the altar and, by chance, fell against it. It tumbled into the snow and debris, exposing a darkened tunnel into the church's crypt. I could see nothing below, in the pitch-black abyss of the crypt. But by the light of the moon, I saw the uncertain outline of narrow, irregularly-shaped steps, leading downward, ever-downward. Into the domain of the dead. Spider webs glimmered like hanging strands of silver and diamonds. They shuddered and fell away, disintegrating at the touch of the cold wind.

"The crypt exhaled poisoned air. It smelled of things dead and forgotten, of tomb-soil and scarab beetles. I did not want to go into such a place, boyarina, but I wanted to hide myself away. I heard the wolves howling, not far off. Coming close."

"So brave, little one," I said, my voice getting weak.

"I descended the stair leading to the crypt, boyarina, shuddering with every step. I could see nothing in the darkness below me, and I felt certain a host of spirits—the cursed and vengeful dead—would feast upon me in the dark. The passage was dank and cold, and the steps were slippery stones, worn down by generations of priests—all long dead. And boyarina, as I descended, I was filled with a horrible certainty that some abyssal thing waited for me, crouched at the base of the stair.

"But, as you can plainly see, nothing was waiting for me, boyarina. There was no monster at the base of the stair. I reached the crypt in safety and hid myself among the piled-up coffins and the old, crumbling sarcophagi. Bones littered the floor. I stepped on them accidentally and listened to them snap and crunch beneath my feet. As my eyes adjusted to the darkness, I saw that the whitewashed walls of the crypt were inscribed with fading black ink."

"That is an old practice," I said, not thinking. "Holy men once painted magical names and mysterious signs in places where the dead were buried. It was meant to safeguard the dead, warding them from wicked spirits during the dangerous time between their death and their appearance before the throne of God. It was a practice reserved only for the noble dead. Such a thing is rarely done anymore. One could never be sure of its effect." I laughed at my joke, though the girl remained grave. "Go on," I insisted.

"Boyarina, as I explored, I came upon a sarcophagus in a furthest corner of the crypt, all alone and away from the others. It was small and very old and roughly-hewn. No care had gone into it. No art. I felt drawn to it, though. Its lid had been split in two and, feeling its icy surface, I found letters and symbols had been scrawled into it. Swirls and crosses and diamonds. All gouged deep into the ancient stone. I had no light and could not make them out, however. They seemed to have been crudely done, as if by a trembling, fearful hand.

"Some part of me wished to look into this strange sarcophagus, but another part commanded I turn away and fly from that place. I felt revulsion, acid welling in my gut and burning its way up my throat. I felt the bile roiling in me. It was very cold in the crypt, dismally cold, and it reeked strongly of rat feces and spoiled ground, of dankness and mold. Rot. Corruption. The thick air in that little chamber smelled sour. My skin prickled and sweat beaded my brow. I felt sick to be so near that sarcophagus and wanted nothing more than to flee from that place. I would brave the wolves and the hag and all the monsters of the deep woods, if I could only be gone from that crypt.

"Boyarina, I staggered away from the sarcophagus, and felt along the walls of the crypt until I found the stairway to the church above. The sky was still black above, but I could make out the stars through the holes in the church roof. Stooped and bent low, I began to mount the narrow, pitch-dark stairway. Suddenly, as I scrambled up the little steps, big grey rats began crawling over my feet. They were dashing up the stairs, all chittering madly and bent on escape. They gnawed at the leather of my riding boots, hungering for the soft flesh inside, before dashing up the steps ahead of me. They squeaked and squealed. Something had frightened them…something in the crypt below. It was then, boyarina, that I did the most foolish thing of all. I turned and looked behind me. Back in the blackness of the crypt."

"And what did you see?" I asked, unable to contain my excitement, shuddering a little, forgetting to consider the traumas the girl had suffered. "What did you see, crouched in the darkness?"

"I turned and looked behind me, but I was paralyzed. Listening. My senses were heightened, like a cornered animal. A hunted thing. I gazed into the deeper dark of the crypt for what felt like an eternity. I heard it before I saw it. A slopping, dragging sound. The sound of something flabby willing itself across the floor. Sliding, slug-like. Then, I glimpsed it true. It gazed out at me from the darkness of the crypt. It was a woman. Old and naked, with hanging, heavy breasts. Her white and flabby flesh materialized before me, the color of thick milk, shapeless and glistening, slick with a sour, pus-thick ooze. Long hair dangling before her face in thick ropes. A veil to hide her face. I saw a mouth through the tangle of her hair, though. A gaping mouth, black as pitch and glistening and welling with red blood. Her mouth was an uneven gash ringed with teeth. Needling yellow daggers made to pierce and tear.

"She reached out for me. Her arms were skeletal, wasted to nothing but bone and a wrapping of thin flesh. She grasped at me like a mother embracing a child long lost. Her hands were coated in blood, still wet and dripping on the stones of the crypt. The blood of my men. It steamed in the cold air. Her skin was pale, streaked with roping blue and purple veins.

"'You cannot run from me, little one,' she said. "'You cannot hide. Embrace me, as you would your mother. Melt into me. Give yourself to me. Feed me. Men's blood is bitter. I would have sweeter blood. Your blood.'"

"The *strigoaica*!" I said, my voice not much more than a whisper on the wind. "The blood drinker! I thought such things dwelled only in legends and bad dreams."

"No, boyarina. Alas, this night I have found that not all monsters are born in dreams and nightmares."

"And how is it you are here, little one?" I asked. "Surely your pistol could not have harmed a devil that has lived on for centuries, defying death and stealing life from who've chanced upon it? How could you have escaped that foul place? Why would the devil let you live?"

"How did you know I used my pistol to defend myself against the monster?" the girl asked. "I did not tell you that."

"You are quite right, little one. But I surmised that—as you are here with me—you escaped the *strigoaica*, somehow frightening it with the only weapon you had in your possession: your little pistol."

"You are very clever, boyarina," the girl said, eyeing me quizzically, as if she were suddenly fearful of me. She calmed quickly though, and said: "You are right: as the demon came close, I snatched the pistol from within the folds of my dress and discharged it into her screaming face. She screeched like an owl, then vanished into a burst of fire and sparks. Then, boyarina, I ran from that place and came here. I ran until my feet bled and I thought the cold might take me. I do not know how I escaped, boyarina. I do not know why the demon let me live. And I do not know how I came to this village. There is nothing more to my tale, I'm afraid. I know only that I was fortunate. God protected me, just as a shepherd protects his ewes from wolves."

"It is very curious that you are here with me," I said. I felt tired and weak and longed for sleep. "Very curious."

"Fortune smiled upon me," the girl said, weakly.

The sun was rising in the distance, transmuting the dawn sky from dusky blue to a sickly, sulfurous yellow. Most of the men in the inn had gone or were sleeping, surrounded by empty tankards and plates covered in stale crumbs and bloody pools of meat drippings. We were alone now, just the girl and I.

"You did not touch your wine, little one," I said. "You should drink it up. It will help you sleep."

"I do not like this wine, boyarina. It is too sweet for me."

"Very well," I said. "You are right. It is too sweet."

"I thought—though I do not wish to impose—that I might sleep with you, boyarina. You remind me of my own mother and the comforts of my home. I feel certain I will sleep if I can only share your bed." She smiled broadly, displaying her gleaming teeth. Those teeth that were so very white.

"Yes," I said. My voice was unsteady. "You were very fortunate this night..." I let my thoughts fade away, incomplete and unformed. I was too tired to rationalize the girl's escape, though it disturbed me. I said: "Let us go now, then, before the sun rises full and the village wakes."

I took the girl's little hand in mine and we ascended the narrow stairway of the inn that lead to the rooms above. Her hand was cold. I could feel the chill of her skin through my gloves. I felt uneasy as we mounted the final steps. I turned to look behind me, to get another glimpse of the girl. She was so very lovely. So very young. And her skin was succulent and ripe to the touch.

As we reached the landing of the stairway, I chanced to look down back the way we had come...and I shuddered.

Her eyes welling with panic, the girl instinctively did as I had just done. She turned and peered back down the darkened stairway. Seeing nothing, yet remaining paralyzed, like a frightened rabbit, she whispered: "Boyarina, what is it? What do you see? What has alarmed you so?"

"Have you learned nothing, little one? The danger is behind you." My voice was thick. The words oozed from my mouth slowly, faultily; they'd been warped by my teeming teeth, all bursting from my gums. Blood filled my mouth, and glazed my lips, and dripped to the floor in glistening strands.

Just as I thought: her ruff was thin and old. It offered no protection against my sharp teeth. A thousand whirring daggers all working in concert, burrowing into hot flesh, drilling, and drawing out the blood beneath. That musty antique ruff and the ugly dress beneath, churned in my mouth and stuck in my probing teeth. Her skin, though, was slick with sweat and musky with dried fear. I licked it with my questing tongue. Her muscles were rich and fatty. And her blood. Her blood was far sweeter than any wine.

    I drank deep. It tasted nearly as sweet at the blood of my dear daughter Zaleska, my beloved. Lost so many years ago. More than even I know.

Swim Failure

Jennifer Loring

———◆———

WINTER HAD SUBJUGATED all other seasons up here—eight months of cold darkness punctuated by the green pop of cool, brief summer. Factor in that the cabin was accessible only by ATV, and most people wouldn't consider it even as a summer getaway, let alone a place to spend a significant portion of their life. Nikki Wellington, however, was banking on exactly that. The more space between her and civilization, the better.

The cabin had been a steal at twenty-nine thousand, and she had socked away enough from sales of her paintings over the past twelve years to make her dreams—her necessity—of artistic solitude a reality at last. The place boasted solar power, wood stove heat, and hot and cold running water pumped in from a brook, plus two bedrooms and a bathroom with a shower. Her grocery order would arrive monthly by floatplane on the body of water a shade too small to be called a lake.

In theory, she loved the city—its vibrant energy, its commotion, its people. It inspired and nourished the creativity she translated into strokes and splashes of acrylic. In practice, she'd spent far too much time imagining what her perpetually stoned and drunken neighbors' blood would look like running down her latest canvas. Sensitive to both light and noise, what was the symphony of life to some became pure dissonance to her. Her neighbors had soon disappeared—moved out in the dead of night, according to the older woman across the hall, bedecked in garish costume jewelry even at eight AM—with a shocking level of stealth considering the source. Three days had passed before Nikki, in the midst of preparing a new show, realized the upstairs had gone quiet. Until.

Until.

She must have painted the damned thing in her sleep. And if she could no longer trust herself, no one could.

She fed more wood into the stove and brewed a cup of coffee in her Keurig. The smaller bedroom's coziness appealed to her enough to designate it as her sleeping quarters. She quickly filled the larger with several easels, canvases, and panels in various sizes, 200-ml tubes of paint, and brushes both round and flat, after putting down drop cloths to spare the hardwood floor her bursts of creative fury. Safer here, those eruptions. No one to feed them. Turn them bad.

Both bedrooms overlooked the pond scattered with a million stars she'd never seen from her old urban vantage point, though her bedroom had sported a Juliet balcony. Light pollution had blotted out nearly everything but the Big Dipper and Sirius. The dark of night here was so vast and deep it might have touched every corner of the Earth, and she the only thing not dead or sleeping. Though it was early October, a crust of ice had formed at the pond's edges and was creeping daily inward. Solid enough to skate on soon, and the cabin had come with an ancient pair of skates hanging from the coat hook just inside the door. Nikki wondered how many other exiles had found solace here. She'd grown up in a small northern town not unlike Harper—the nearest thing to a town up here—but after so many years away, you didn't realize how deeply the noise of human existence was knitted into the daily fabric of life until it disappeared. Nikki found sleep ironically impossible the first few nights, the silence as complete as deafness and driving her to put on music.

After a couple of weeks, the ice had thickened and coated the pond in a glittering white sheet reflecting the bleached sky, solid enough to support caribou. Just as Nikki had grown to appreciate the silence, the solitude struck her as it did sometimes, out of the blue, precisely when she thought she'd finally accepted it as her lot in life. The danger inherent in connecting with people nursed her misanthropy until the prospect of something like real friends, let alone a romantic relationship, seemed as cruel and remote as the frozen white disc hanging over the pond at night. Nikki crawled into bed and for a while gazed out the window, but even the animals had abandoned her. Her eyes slipped shut and fluttered back open, her mind thick with the greasy residue of remorse. None of it had been her fault, technically. But if she really believed that, she wouldn't be here. She'd continued to do it, even when she understood what was happening.

A shaft of moonlight illuminated the pond and something that assuredly did not belong on it, not in this cold. Nikki scrambled out of bed and jammed her feet into her slippers. You didn't live in a place this remote without a weapon; she grabbed her shotgun (one of the first and only things her father had taught her was how to shoot) beside the window. By the time she threw open the front door, the figure had vanished, presumably into the forest. The quiet closed in, stopping up her ears. Harper was twenty minutes away by ATV, on the other side of the pond.

Nikki double-checked all the locks and sat in her studio with the shotgun on her lap. Every time she dozed off, she jerked awake within seconds, certain the faceless paintings were watching her.

Nikki rode into Harper the next day, the morning bright and frigid despite her balaclava and several layers of clothing. As trapping had gone out of fashion, so too had the town until only the most stalwart residents, the ones who wanted to live off the land and away from other people, the ones with secrets, remained. It reminded her of her hometown—evacuated after the EPA detected toxic waste in the groundwater, runoff from the nearby mine. She'd been eleven when the government bought everyone out of their homes and declared the town a Superfund site. They'd razed it to the ground so no stubborn old-timers could squat there for nostalgia's sake as they had in Centralia. That had been her first lesson in impermanence. Maybe it was what had drawn her to art. Eventually, even the greatest masterpieces would flake apart like dead skin, leaving behind on those brittle canvases only ghostly traces as documents to prove they'd existed.

Snow sprayed away from her as the ATV carved a path through the snow, dark evergreens flashing past. Her Keurig sufficed most of the time, but nothing warmed her like a cup of rich coffee from Morana's Diner. Nikki parked her ATV alongside four others and trotted into the diner, trailing snow. She pulled off her mittens and balaclava and stuffed them into her coat pockets as she approached the counter. The aroma of French toast and real maple syrup hit hard and fast, as though she hadn't eaten in days. She was all but drooling as she ordered. The cook began frying two thick slices of egg-battered brioche, and Morana—sporting her usual red flannel shirt rolled to the elbows—filled Nikki's coffee cup. "How do you like it out there so far?"

Nikki mentally thanked her for breaking the ice, as it were, so she didn't have to. "It's nice. I mean…" She hunched forward. "Have you seen anyone hanging around? Like at night?"

Morana's brown eyes twinkled. Her sleek black hair was pulled into a ponytail; Nikki thought she was at least part indigenous. "No one hanging around at night in this cold, sweetie. People shouldn't even be here, if you want the truth. They just get…" Morana wrinkled her nose and shrugged. "Fixed here sometimes, you know?"

"But I saw…" *Didn't I?* She'd been half-asleep, after all. Tricks of light and shadow could easily convince untrained eyes that they'd seen something out there. Probably a damned caribou.

Or a ghost.

Nikki coughed into the crook of her elbow. The weather would only get worse, yet from the moment she'd arrived, the cold had crawled into her lungs with fingers made of knives. She caught Morana's gaze slide to one of the regulars, who met it with a look Nikki was glad she couldn't decipher.

"Why are you really here?"

"I don't…" She glanced around the diner. Everyone feigned preoccupation with their coffee or eggs; no one was speaking to one another.

"You don't figure that out, you'll be stuck here forever." Morana offered a faint but kind smile. "Trust me, you don't want that. I just try to help you and everyone else in here see the light." She delivered the French toast and, except for coffee refills, left her alone until she gave Nikki the bill.

Sure, most of the time Nikki would rather not engage in small talk, but only because she didn't want to end up liking the person. It was for their own protection. She gravitated instead to the ones she knew she'd despise, to the repeated, pretend conversations with strangers who'd forgotten you before you'd even told them your name. You attended your gallery shows and lingered at the edges, sipping champagne while collectors and critics disparaged every color choice, every placement of a stroke. The same people who, once your agent introduced you as The Artist, gushed that you were the next Mark Rothko (he'd slashed his arms with a razor blade and overdosed on anti-depressants, and part of you thought this was the real comparison they were making, that somehow they could see the dark thing that wore your face as a mask). By the end of the night, you'd collected more business cards and promises than money and, if you were lucky, an art student willing to fuck you for a few hours. The student hoped you'd paint them—*if they only knew*—but it was the collector or critic who had insulted you that ended up in the next piece. When they disappeared, people automatically assumed suicide. You know how it is with art people.

NIKKI STARTED THE wood stove before ridding herself of her winter gear. Her little home heated quickly, but she kept a blanket draped over the sofa anyway. She often painted the pond, which became two distinct places from day to night. The day: incandescent, harsh, all color except for tall swipes of pine washed away by snow. The night: indistinct, magical in shades of silver, white, and black, the frozen pond an invitation for wildlife to play.

You could survive thirty to sixty minutes under there, as long as your airway remained above water.

In the nighttime paintings, a pale and indistinct shape appeared between the trees, an argent mist floating above the ice, a frozen will-o'-the-wisp. It had invaded her subconscious. As winter deepened, more snow fell and the temperature with it. Consummating her isolation, trips to Morana's were too dangerous now. That was good, really; Nikki was sometimes too tempted to paint people she liked.

She worked despite the handprints on the outside of the windows and despite the unpredictable brownouts. Despite the thing that, on nights when the fingernail of moon was almost too weak to shine, stood on the pond with hollow eyes cast toward the cabin.

"I'm imagining you," she said, because she hadn't spoken to anyone in weeks. There was a dull edge to her voice, like a tool left to rust. The romantic notion of creative exile had succumbed to cabin fever. It would be another five months before the snow melted, and now a mist the consistency of cotton had rolled in between the trees it turned into hurried, vague sketches. The world lost all detail.

Nikki pretended the smudged, dirty-window face wasn't closer each night, that her loneliness hadn't contacted it through some otherworldly frequency. That she was imagining its silent insistence, the susurrus in her head urging her to paint the person she hated the most. She fought off another coughing fit that punctured her lungs with icy needles. There wasn't supposed to be time to think about it in the city, about regret, except you were surrounded by millions of strangers who found you as interesting as a greasy cheesesteak wrapper on the curb. You were a featureless part of the landscape. No one could forget you, because to them, you'd never been there at all. And it was, except for the people you loathed, all by design.

Middle of the city or middle of nowhere, it didn't matter. You were always alone in the end. And she'd seen that ghostly face dozens of times before coming up here, hadn't she; it was that face in the mirror which had driven her out of the city in the first place. That desolate, empty-eyed visage, devoid of hope.

She could have chosen differently. A different career. And what a heavy burden that was to carry, enough to—

—make your body struggle instinctively, but swim failure sets in within five minutes. Hypothermia slows your metabolism and reduces your need for

oxygen, but there's no point in drawing it out. If you're smart, you'll make sure your airway is submerged.

It had been one long swim failure, that imposed loneliness, robbing her of strength month by month and year by year. Freezing her slowly enough that neither her indifferent roommate nor her distant parents would detect anything wrong—no "sudden changes in mood or behavior," as the Big Pharma commercials went. You acclimated to gradual things by virtue of their being unremarkable. Her agent, with whom she communicated mainly by email or phone, commented only that Nikki appeared to be going through her "dark" period; all artists had one. Look at Goya's Black Paintings. Look at Cezanne's dark period. Art was emotion—otherwise, what was the point?

But her agent hadn't been there when Nikki discovered her "talent." Hadn't lost people she cared about to haunted acrylic facsimiles on canvas, been judged by their accusatory stares. When you were an artist, the people closest to you always wanted you to paint them, begged you to, and how did you say no? How did you explain what happened when you painted people?

You said no by shutting them out completely.

She could share her work with the cultural elite who offered blank gazes and false smiles, and who mostly showed up for the free champagne or to hook up with some young studio assistant. Nikki would return to her apartment alone, standard operating procedure, jaw clenched so tightly it throbbed and tears scorching her eyes. Needing the counterfeit company of a new painting.

"You're almost there," she heard Morana say in her ear, but Morana was in her head too, just another phantom. Another whisper at night, if gentler, beseeching her to admit why she'd come. To make peace with it.

She could not have lived with the endless internal recriminations, and yet here she was. Clinging to her pain as if it meant something, as if it meant more than the pain of those her work had left behind.

And so she closed her eyes, and in a flash of intense, nauseating light found herself home, to a place that no longer existed on maps, to the poisoned lake on which she'd learned to ice skate. In which she'd learned to swim. People weren't the only things that could haunt; places could too, lingering in and around you like secondhand smoke, their echoes distant voices beseeching you to come home one more time.

There were no guards anymore, not after twenty-three years. Even the power lines were gone, though Nikki could recall where each major building had stood, and the positions of her friends' houses—when she'd still had friends. Nothing but the cemetery and a few crumbled foundations now, the lots reclaimed by nature. There was also little chance anyone would find the painting. She'd gone home one more time after all, to create the first and only canvas she should have ever painted. A stark and sorrowful face crowned with waves of pallid blond hair, blue eyes staring out from dark caverns, her grave mouth set in a straight line. The details were essential; the details gave it life. *Don't forget the beauty marks, or the acne that persisted into your mid-thirties. The crow's feet lightly stamped at the corners of your eyes. The neck wrinkles. It must look exactly like the subject. People always said you had a gift—human faces are the hardest thing to draw (after hands and feet), but not for you. They were the* only *thing you wanted to draw.*

Nikki had brought only a canvas panel, a few brushes, and one tube each of ivory black and titanium white. Color didn't matter. Only the details. It was funny in painting the face you saw reflected back at you every day, the façade that to strangers conveyed everything you were, how much of the minutiae you forgot. She pulled out her phone several times to ensure she'd captured the angle of her nose (canted slightly to the left), the proportion of her (weak) chin to jaw, the precise shape of her eyes.

She looked out once at the lake, dead leaves floating atop it in ripples of golden autumn sunlight as the wind blew a kiss across the water's surface. Then back at the face, that mirror-face, sagging and aged before its time with afflictions no one could imagine. Numbness surged from her stomach into her limbs. Her vision flickered and with it her body, as if she were vanishing. That was what they did, wasn't it? Vanished, leaving their families and friends with that most futile particle of hope: *Maybe she's still out there somewhere.* Nikki gritted her teeth. She, the giver of that faith when, as capricious as any god, she'd removed them from their lives simply because she could. Because she had a *talent.*

The lines of her body, the texture of her clothes, undulated as if they were paint swirled beneath horsehair bristles, smearing her into the background of her extinct hometown. The canvas dropped to the ground, along with the brushes and paints, and a stronger wind propelled them as if by unseen hands toward the gilded waters of the lake.

Visions of the Autumn Country

Tim Jeffreys

———◆———

WHERE HAVE YOU BEEN? Her voice on the answerphone. *I've been trying to reach you for...where have you been?*

I can answer that. For the past few days, at least, I've been in limbo-land. Ha! Look at that. I've gone and created another of those paracosms my childhood psychologist used to talk about. Another of Dolan's imaginary worlds, or subjective universes, as the psychologist sometimes called them in the letters she wrote to my mother. I can picture her now. Susan, wasn't that her name? Doctor Susan something. *You can call me Soo if you like*, she'd said, that first time we met, though I never did. She was always Doctor Susan, because that's what my mother called her. *Did you have a nice chat with Doctor Susan today?*

I can picture Doctor Susan now with her loose smile and affable tilt of the head. I can imagine her saying, with that faux enthusiasm adults so often use with children, "So, Dolan, tell me all about Limbo-land."

What would I tell her? One glance out of the window and I can see it's springtime, and that seems appropriate. Isn't spring, after all, the season of waiting? Waiting for the weather to improve, waiting for those buds to grow, waiting for the lambs to be born. Waiting. A pale grey sky. A nothing sky.

And silence, broken only occasionally by the trill of the telephone which I don't answer. This is limbo-land.

I try to occupy the time with things I've been putting off for months—mending furniture, pulling weeds from the small flower garden at the back of the house, or clearing out my cupboards—but all I really want to do is paint. I can't paint of course because a few nights ago when the noises woke me I locked the door to my studio, and I can't open it again because there's something inside. Or someone. I'm not sure which. Whatever or whoever it is, I know it's still in there because whenever I go and put my ear close to the door, which I find myself doing more and more often, I sometimes hear shuffling on the other side. There are no other noises. No shouts or pleas or scratches or hammering. Just shuffling. I imagine what it must be like to be trapped in there surrounded by so many of my paintings, both finished and unfinished. How one might move around the room and try to decipher them, wondering what kind of lunatic you've gone and got yourself imprisoned by.

But something tells me that's not how it is.

I thought to try and speak through the door, to see if I could get a response, but something stops me. One time, without thinking, I almost said, "Gangel? Is that you?" But I couldn't get the words out, so I went and sat in the lounge, staring out of the window at that blank expanse of sky. That was when the phone rang. It must have been ringing for some time before I became aware of it, as just when I thought to pick it up I heard Beth's voice on the answerphone.

Dad…where have you been? I've been trying to reach you for…where have you been?

"WHO'S THIS BOY who keeps appearing in your drawings?" Doctor Susan asked me once.

I didn't want to tell her. I remember that. I didn't want her to know, but I worried she'd tell my mother I wasn't cooperating.

"Gangel."

"And who's Gangel? Is he your friend?"

"He is. Kind of my friend."

"Kind of?"

"He acts like he's my friend. But I don't trust him. Not really."

"I see. And is Gangel from The Autumn Country?"

"He is. But sometimes he's…here."

I CALLED IT The Autumn Country because everything I saw there looked dead or dying. It was a brown decaying world, a world moving towards winter. A place on the brink, eternally ending. I first started drawing scenes from The Autumn Country when I was eight years old. It was shortly after the death of my father, around the time my blackouts started. It didn't occur to me until much later in life that these three things might be linked.

Drawing and painting was in my blood. That's what the biographers always say. *Art was in his blood. His father was the great Irish-born abstract painter, Sheehan Foley, known for his bold emotionally-charged imagery, who sadly committed suicide in 1972 at the height of his success, aged just 46.*

In saying this, I often think these writers are trying to explain or even excuse my own paintings which are frequently described as weird, bleak, and disturbing. Or dark. How I hate that word, *dark*. But it's true that I started drawing almost as soon as I could hold a pencil. Like most children I drew grassy scenes of family outings, with big yellow suns, or colorful chaos straight from my imagination. But after my father died I would no longer draw rainbows or pirates ships or rockets headed for the moon. From then on it was stick figures trapped in empty landscapes or crowded together in odd sinister gatherings, crooked skeletal trees drawn in heavy black crayon, and barren landscapes littered with rocks and pebbles and broken bits of machinery.

"What's this?" my mother said once. I can still hear the ring of horror in her voice. "What is all this?"

That's when I told her, for some reason thinking she'd understand. "It's The Autumn Country."

Soon after, I paid my first visit to Doctor Susan's office.

NOW IT'S NOT the phone that's ringing but the doorbell. Someone's banging on the wood with their fist. I hear Beth's voice.

"Dad? Dad, are you in there? Dad?"

What's she doing here?

What time is it?

Clamoring out of bed, I put on my dressing gown and slippers. As I approach the front door, I can here Beth talking on the other side of it and I briefly wonder if she's brought more people with her. Thinking of the locked studio door, I start thinking about what I can say, how I can get rid of them. But then I realize it's a one-sided conversation. She must be talking on her mobile phone.

"Hang on," I hear her say, as I unlock the door. "Someone's coming."

When I open the door, she gives me the same low look of condemnation her mother used to use. She shrugs, glancing about as if waiting for an answer to some question she doesn't need to ask. She's looking more and more like her mother those days; thin and colorless. Washed-out, like the landscape at her back. Her hair is pulled into a tight bun, from which the wind teases strands loose, and she's wearing some kind of constricting outfit that makes me think of boardrooms.

"Beth?"

"Never mind, he's here," she says to whoever was on the other end of the telephone. Lowering the phone from her ear, she looks me over. I know she's seeing the unwashed hair, the week's worth of stubble, the ratty dressing gown.

"What's going on?" she says. "What is it? Are you working?"

"Working?"

"Painting. I know you like to shut the world out when you're in the middle of something."

"Not at the moment."

"Then why won't you answer the phone? I've been trying to contact you for a week or more. I was worried. You could have had a fall or…I don't know…got stuck in the bath or something. How would I know?"

"Now you're making me feel old."

"Well, you're no spring chicken." She moves forward so that I have to step back and open the door wider to allow her to enter. She starts taking off her jacket. I remain by the open door, looking out across the empty yard.

"Did you drive here, love?"

"Of course."

"Where's your car?"

"I parked it behind the barn where it'll be safer."

"Safer?"

"It's a Merc, Dad. I'm not just going to leave it stuck out front."

"Are you staying long?"

"How many times have I told you to sell this place and move to the city where I can keep an eye on you?"

"I told you, Beth, love. Don't like the city. Too many distractions."

"Is it fair that I have to drive all this way just to check on you? It keeps me awake at night thinking about you living all the way out here on your own."

"I'm fine. You can see I'm fine."

"It's so silent out here."

"I like the silence. It helps me think."

"I need a drink. Do you have coffee?"

"I'll look."

On my way to the kitchen, I pause for a few seconds to listen at the studio door. I hear no sounds from inside. *That's good*, I think, *maybe he's gone. He could have opened a window and climbed out. Fled.* I wonder why I'm thinking it's a he. Surely I don't still believe it's Gangel I trapped in there? Gangel, my imaginary childhood friend. Gangel, who I've drawn and painted so many times he seems real to me. Maybe Beth's right; maybe I am getting old, losing it, losing my mind.

Beth isn't surprised when I tell her I'm out of coffee. I make tea instead.

"There's no milk. Just the powdered stuff."

"That'll do," she says, not without a roll of the eyes.

I'm always surprised by her, surprised that someone so straight—isn't that the word, *straight?*—could be my daughter. When she was a girl I waited for that artistic blood to show, but Beth never had any interest in art. She was keener on making tallies of everything. *Six dolls. Seven cups. Eight dresses.* Marching around the house with a pencil and a clipboard, drawing up itineraries, bossing all her friends around, always making them play shop when they wanted to do other things. It was no great surprise that she became a banker. It was a relief of sorts, for what is this creative compulsion if not a curse? How many times have I heard that question: *Why do you paint this stuff?* I have no answer, other than that I'm compelled.

It's like that same question of my mother's all over again.

What is all this? Why not portraits or seascapes or colorful abstracts, paintings people might want to hang in their living rooms? Why all this dark, disturbing stuff?

It turns out some people like the dark disturbing stuff. The dark, disturbing stuff has made me a living for twenty-five years.

Beth makes small talk as we drink our tea. Eventually, she becomes annoyed that I keep asking how long she plans on staying.

"It's like you can't wait to get rid of me," she says. Then before I can say anything, she sets her cup down and stands. "Well, I'll just use the loo and then I'll be on my way. Will that make you happy?"

"Beth, love…"

With a huff, she's gone. I sit and finish my tea. When I realize Beth seems to have been gone a long time, I feel an inexplicable rush of panic, and I get up to look for her. Maybe I'd caught the smell of turpentine. In the hall I see the studio door standing open and it feels like my heart drops as far as my feet.

"Beth."

I start to run, but then I halt. She's standing at the far end of the studio. She has her arms folded and she's examining one of my paintings which stands propped against the wall. I enter the studio looking everywhere in the room at once. When she notices this, Beth knits her brow. I'm relieved to find that there's no one here but the two of us, at least physically. But all those figures in the paintings—they're here too, and it suddenly feels as if all those eyes are watching me as I cross the room to stand next to my daughter.

I can't help but look at her, marvel at her.

Beth's mother badly wanted a child. I understood that urge to create, but her urge seemed purer, less hollow than mine, so how could I refuse? It took six years of IVF treatment for her to fall pregnant. Maybe that's why we always treated Beth like she was doubly precious, and perhaps we spoilt her, or maybe that's how every parent treats their child. How would I know?

"Beth, what're you doing in here? The door was supposed to be locked."

"The key was in the door," she says, looking at me as if I need sectioning.

"Why? What's the big deal?"

"No big deal. Just that I thought I'd locked the door."

"Why lock it?" she says, throwing her arms out to indicate the surrounding paintings. "Are you worried some of these guys might make a run for it?"

I know it's supposed to be a joke, but for some reason it makes my blood go cold. I can see them in my mind's eyes, the figures from my paintings, trooping out over the fields, finding the road, leering at passengers in passing cars, causing the drivers to veer off the road, to crash into each other, descending on the occupants as they fall, bloodied, from their vehicles.

"Don't be daft, love."

She looks to my face. "I'm not intruding, am I?"

"Of course not."

"I like seeing what you're working on. You're still painting The Autumn Country, I notice."

"Yes." I know what's coming next.

"You never feel like painting something a bit cheerier?"

"This is just what comes out."

"They're always so..."—here it comes—"...*dark*. What's this one about?"

The painting she's been looking at shows a group of figures wearing hooded robes. Their faces, just visible inside the hoods, look like death masks. They crowd together around another figure knelt on the floor before them. This kneeling figure is only roughly sketched in, since I haven't yet completed the lower half of the painting.

"It's the Council," I say. "The Council of Eight."

Beth noticeably shivers. "And who's that down there?" She points at the figure outlined into the bottom half of the painting. "I wouldn't like to be that person."

When she looks at me, I shrug. Then after a moment, I say, "So? Shouldn't you be heading back?"

"You know I always thought of your paintings as...snapshots."

"Really?"

"Yes. It always seemed to me like this was a place you'd actually visited. You went there and saw these scenes and you brought back these snapshots. Does that make sense?"

"I suppose it does."

"Where's Gangel?"

Shocked, I cast my eyes about the studio. I think I see a shadow shift behind a large canvas set at a wide angle from the wall. *There you are*, I think.

"Well?"

I twist to face her. "Huh?"

"Where is he? I thought he always appeared in your paintings. He's like your—our—guide or something. Our guide through The Autumn Country."

"Oh, he'll be there somewhere. Hiding. You'll see when it's finished. So—what was it? Don't you have to be somewhere?"

Beth lets out a long sigh. "You know what—I don't feel like driving back today. Maybe I'll stay with you tonight." Perhaps seeing my expression change, she adds, "That's okay, isn't it? I mean, you're not doing anything. Are you?"

"No, love. Of course, love. I always enjoy seeing you. I'll make up the spare bedroom."

As she follows me out from the studio, I make sure to lock the door behind us, this time taking the key out from the hole and dropping it into my dressing gown pocket, before ushering Beth through to the lounge.

DOCTOR SUSAN IS holding up one on my drawings. It shows a figure squatting on a rock. Using a biro, I've given him big black eyes and a scribble of hair, but I've used a red crayon to draw dots all over his face. I've also scribbled his clothes in black, so that it looks as if he's wearing a suit jacket and a long ragged skirt. I've drawn his mouth in such a way that he appears pleased with himself. On the ground at his feet lies a litter of broken objects.

"Is this your friend Gangel?" she asks.

I nod.

"Why do you say you don't trust him?"

For a moment I can't speak. Then I say, "Because he's always stealing my things."

"Things?"

"Toys. Books. Anything. He takes them back there."

"Back? You mean back to The Autumn Country?"

I nod. "They don't have nice things there. Mum doesn't believe me. She thinks *I* lost them."

"Are these your things?" Doctor Susan asks, pointing at the various objects strewn about the ground in the picture: a teddy bear, a book, a model train, a jar of marbles.

I nod.

"He stole all these things from you?"

"Yes," I say. "He always takes something. Even Mum's things sometimes. He shows it to them and they decide what to do with it. Usually they just break them. They like destroying things."

"And who're they?" Doctor Susan asks.

Leaning forward, I scrabble through the sheets of paper set out on the low table between us. I select one sheet and hold it up for her to see.

"Them," I say.

Doctor Susan takes the paper from me and frowns at it. "Who are these scary-looking people, Dolan?"

"The Council of Eight," I say.

BETH AND I stay up late, drinking wine and talking. Beth likes to talk about her mother. She likes to remember her mother. Though I try to be attentive, my mind keeps returning to that locked studio door and I can't help listening for sounds: a footstep, a jar of brushes being knocked over, or a painting being overturned. I'm terrified Beth will hear something too, although it's unlikely anything happening in the studio could be heard from the lounge where we sit. A couple of times, when the TV is momentarily silent, I notice Beth glance towards the hallway as if something has caught her ear. But she says nothing; and I hear nothing myself.

"Mum never liked your paintings, did she?" Beth says.

"I think she hoped—like most people—that one day I'd paint something a bit jollier."

"Have you ever tried?"

"Not for a long time."

"Did you ever paint Mum's portrait?"

"No," I lie. There was that one painting, done after Jayne died. It was a crowd scene, full of blank-faced figures in hoods all shuffling forwards against a late evening sky. The light was low along the horizon. The impression the figures gave was of endless, silent suffering. And there amongst the crowd was one face I recognized. It surprised me to see her there. I hadn't intended to put her in the picture. But there she was.

I don't know why, but I painted over that picture with emulsion. I suppose I just couldn't bear to see my Jayne there amongst that crowd of damned figures.

As Beth goes on talking I feel a sudden sense of frustration with myself, a loathing. What could possibly have compelled me to paint my dear departed wife into such an ugly scene?

Maybe some kind of insanity.

At some point I must have fallen asleep. I dreamt of my own mother. I see her that sunny spring day when she was tending the flower bed which bordered our garden. She was there most days after my father died, yanking up weeds and coaxing chrysanthemums into bloom. Perhaps she had an urge to see things grow and live. That day, as I sat on the grass watching her, her hands found something buried in the dirt and pulled it out. I see her rising up onto her knees and turning to me, her face flushed with shock and anger.

"Dolan?" she says. "Why do you do it?"

WHEN I AWAKE it's daylight, and Beth is no longer in the room. I feel ravenously hungry, and my hands are black with dirt I don't remember touching which makes me think I've suffered another blackout. I'm not certain what day it is because I haven't been keeping track. Though I look, I can't find Beth anywhere in the house. The bed in the spare room is neatly made, as if no one slept there and I wonder if Beth was ever here at all or if I'd simply dreamt it. I hurry around the house, up and down the stairs, calling her name. If she had been here, why did she leave? Could I have done something, said something, to force Beth to hightail it out of here? Something I now can't remember? I'd been so keen for her to leave, but now that's she's gone I want her here. I need her here. All I can think about is a day long ago when I was woken by a grinning six-year old in green pajamas, who thrust a bundle at me and said, "Happy birthday, Daddy!"

Remembering that she wrote her mobile phone number down for me on a scrap of paper, I hunt it down and dial the number. There's no answer, just a few rings before the phone goes to voicemail.

"Beth," I say. "Call me back please. Let me know you're okay. I hope I didn't…you know I love you, right? I just wanted to say…you know…?"

A bleep signals that I'm out of time. I set the phone down and, after gazing at it for a few moments, head to the kitchen to wash my hands and prepare some breakfast. It's only now that I realize—to my horror—that the studio door is standing open. Sliding one hand into my dressing gown pocket, I find the key is still there. Could Beth have taken it whilst I slept, or had I opened the door myself during my blackout? I take a tentative step inside the studio and look around. But for the paintings, it's empty. Feeling braver, I cross the floor, tilting to look behind paintings, lifting some away from the wall. I find nothing, and no trace that anyone has been here. Of course, I tell myself, there never was anyone here. It was all in my imagination. Or perhaps I dreamt it too. Maybe I'm cracking up. Maybe all this dark stuff I keep painting is finally getting to me. Maybe I'll start painting bright things instead. Sunflowers perhaps. Okay, not sunflowers. Something happier, sunnier, like the stuff I used to draw as a child before the darkness set in, before my first visit to The Autumn Country. A seascape—yes! What a challenge that would be. And what a change. The sea has never featured in my paintings before, although there have been boats. Landlocked boats stranded on dry rock beds, occupied by bizarre, lost figures clutching oars and rowing fruitlessly at the ground in some impotent bid for freedom or escape.

I find myself standing in front of the half-finished painting Beth had admired. *Admired*—is that the right word? Perhaps not. I remember how she'd shivered as she looked at it. The Council of Eight cluster in judgement around the sketched-in figure knelt at their feet. Looking at the picture I feel a familiar itch—not a literal itch—something deeper, beneath the skin. My fingertips prickle. My heart picks up. The anticipation builds in me, as if someone's just placed a luxurious meal before me and I can't wait to tuck in. I tell myself there'll be plenty of time for seascapes. I'll finish this painting first.

Why?
Why do you paint this stuff?
What is all this?
Dolan? Why do you do it?

Most of my father's paintings are kept in the storerooms of galleries the world over. On occasion they are brought out for a retrospective. One, and only one, is owned by me and hangs on the wall above my staircase. My father named the painting Dun Sky IV. Though my father's paintings were meant to be abstract, I always saw them as landscapes, and this one is no different. He used a familiar pallet of brown, black, and orange with slashes of red and pink here and there like open wounds or mouths crying out in torment.

Though I've never admitted it to anyone, in my heart I've always thought that my father too was painting The Autumn Country. That muddle of angry lines and blotches of brown were my father's attempts, I believe, at rendering this place we both knew.

Or perhaps they are merely abstracts. Perhaps I'm merely projecting my own ideology onto his paintings.

Either way, I wish he'd stayed around. I wish I could have known him better. He would have understood, I think. He would not have been one of those asking *why*.

Doctor Susan thought my blackouts were caused by stress, possibly brought on by my father's death. It was I who had discovered him, after all, racing into the house ahead of my mother, eager to tell him all about my day at school. The smell of the PVA primer my father used is still associated in my mind with the image of a kitchen chair lying on its side and my father suspended silhouetted against the big window of his studio. That's why I've always primed my canvass' with rabbit skin glue.

My mother thought otherwise. She thought I lied about the blackouts. She thought they were a way I had of not taking responsibility for the destructive things I did.

I SET TO work the next day. I don my overalls and lay out my paints. Then I place the Council of Eight painting on the easel and study it for a while. I like to listen to classical music when I paint: Bach or Beethoven. There's something about the rise and fall, the swell and sweep, of the music that mirrors my emotions as I paint. I slide a CD into the little boombox I keep in one corner and then begin. Very quickly, something else takes over and I become lost in the process. Hours go by before I stumble out of the studio, smeared in paint and bleary eyed. It's dark outside. I'm hungry but too weary to prepare food. All I can do is slip off my overalls and collapse onto the sofa. The painting has taken all my energy. I feel drained, emptied out in a way that is not entirely unpleasant. The phone rings as I lie there, but as much as I want to answer it—hoping that it might be Beth—I'm too tired to get up. I let the answerphone take it. There is no voice, just odd sounds, a kind of distorted metallic warble as if someone's calling me from the bottom of the ocean. After it ends, I close my eyes and am soon asleep.

I DREAM OF my mother again. Of that spring day when she tended the flower beds and I paused in my lawn games to watch her. What is it about that day that makes it return so often to my subconscious mind? Doctor Susan would know.

My mother finds the sack buried in the dirt and with some effort she drags it out into the open. She seems surprised by how large it is, but equally at how easily it comes free from the earth. Loose dirt spills onto the grass. A flush rises in me as I watch my mother open the sack. After a pause she begins to take things from it: broken toys, torn up books, ripped T-shirts, and a few items of her own, jewelry and such, now damaged beyond repair.

My flush deepens when she turns to me.

"Dolan," she says. "Why do you do it?"

I START AWAKE remembering something Beth said, that day she arrived.

It's a Merc, Dad. I'm not just going to leave it stuck out front.

Why was that suddenly so important to me? Of course. She said she'd parked behind the barn, a spot that couldn't be seen from any of the windows in the house, and when I looked for her I hadn't thought to check if her car was still here.

Why would her car still be here? She's gone. She's gone.

Something compels me to get up and go outside. The day is a grey void. Land and sky seem equally ambiguous. As if in a trance I move around the side of the house. As soon as I turn the corner I see the car's bright red tail sticking out from behind the barn.

Still here. Still...

I run then, back to the house and into the studio. Something awful is forming in my mind. I stand in front of the newly finished painting and take it in. There they are, the Council of Eight. And that figure knelt at their feet wearing a tight grey suit with her blonde hair pulled back into a bun…

"Beth," I say, my hand instinctively reaching out to her. She's a small figure before the Council of Eight in their long dark robes, cowering, her head bowed. Beth was not the sort of woman to cower, but there she was, cowering before The Eight. I squint at the painting, noticing something else. There, peeping out from the robes of one of the standing figures is a pale face covered in red markings—they are *burns*—a face framed with badly cropped and unkempt black hair. He appears to be looking directly at me. And he is smiling in a way that I know well—an evil mocking little smile.

He always took the things that were most precious to me.

I think of Beth saying: *Where have you been? I've been trying to reach you for...where have you been?*

Stella Maris

Elana Gomel

IT IS EASY to be lonely in Venice.

The beauty of the city is composed of sly memories and dignified decay. Sinking into the tarnished mirror of the Laguna, La Serenissima accepts everything and is troubled by nothing. She has seen it all: plague, war, massacre, politics, art, greatness, and fall. She is an indifferent mother who has buried her children in the watery grave.

I walk down Calle del Magazen toward Canareggio. Tourist crowds are sparse and when I come to Ponte de Gesuiti they have melted away and I am alone with the peeling brick walls and the dazzling canal. Pigeons fly into my face, scattering dung.

When the last IVF cycle failed and Owen packed up and left I faced a well-trodden path. Depression, counseling, Xanax, and at the end, a life carefully glued together like a broken mug. Instead I sent a resignation email to my boss, emptied out our savings account, and bought a ticket to Venice.

I pass by an artless image of Madonna and child set into the chipped wall. It is a humble token of devotion, overshadowed by the magnificent paintings of Tintoretto and Bellini in every church and museum. But to me it is a sign that the old faith still survives in the city that is selling its past in order to have a future.

Why Venice? I don't really know. I had dreamed about visiting one day with Owen and our child. But I will never have a child. And Owen, practical and domestic, would be immune to the watery magic of La Serenissima. When we were together I tried to be practical and domestic too. But after the first week in Venice, the old Jennie sloughed away, as if dissolved by the opaque waters of the Laguna. What has emerged is raw and unfinished. I don't have a name for the new me yet.

I picked up a newspaper in the café where I had my evening espresso and *tramezzino* and now I sit on a bollard by the side of the canal, squinting into the dazzle, trying to read. My Italian is decent, acquired in the course of my studies in art history. My *useless* studies, as Owen had never failed to emphasize.

The roiling wavelets of the *rio*, which is the Venetian for "canal," are throwing handfuls of sharp reflections into my face and I am almost glad I can't read on because what I make out from the lead article is so shocking. The city is bankrupt. The rising water has destroyed too many historical sites, bred too many new infections, and cloyed the humid air with too much pollution. The tourist industry has hit the bottom. This much I know. But the new plan to bail out La Serenissima is to sell some of the contents of San Marco Basilica to an unnamed consortium. The article is vague about what those contents might be, and of course, the entire thing is wrapped up in thick layers of platitudes about "preservation" and "ensuring the viability" of something or other.

San Marco has been the patron saint of Venice for two thousand years, preserving the city from the devouring Laguna. Even if his protection has weakened, what will the city become when it is withdrawn? The saint's relics are in the Basilica; how will he react when his home is plundered?

I know these thoughts are childish but I let them run through my head defiantly, silencing Owen's taunting voice that has been lodged in my brain like an inflamed splinter. I am sure he could see the economic wisdom of this plan. What I see is sacrilege.

My sight is swimming with blue spots. I get up and water splashes over the lip of the embankment, soaking my sandals. I squint against the orange glow and see a dark shape pass sinuously between the narrow banks. No, this must be an illusion. There is no big fish living in the polluted urban canals. The only living things flourishing in the city are garbage eaters: pigeons and rats. The rotting body of the Queen of Adriatic breeds foul life. I imagine her body is like mine: lush and overripe, sliding into decay. "Fat and mad," as Owen called me.

I walk through a covered alley toward my rental ground-floor apartment whose peeling walls weep with condensation. There is no air-conditioning but I keep the shutters closed and the apartment feels cool by contrast with the boiling streets. Sometimes I think of the winter storms when *acqua alta*—high water—rushes through the narrow streets. Will I be flooded? Probably. But whatever happens, I will not leave Venice.

I slept for a while but now I am tossing and turning in my sweat-soaked bed, the ancient fan fighting a losing battle against the heat. I get up and open the window. Something ghostly flutters in the night. It is my neighbors' wash. Venice is festooned with laundry hung on lines strung across alleys. And because the air is so humid, the laundry takes forever to dry, sheets and baby clothes growing into the ropes like fruit on vine.

But this…this is something else. I squint, peer into the murk. Not much light in the alley but my eyes adjust and I can see that the flopping shape is too solid to be an ephemeral conglomerate of T-shirts and underpants. This is…what *is* it?

It is a bird. And it is too big for any bird in Venice. No, it is too big for any bird anywhere.

I lean out the window as I am trying to take in this impossible sight. The bird has gotten itself tangled in the laundry line but it is so heavy that the entire thing collapses with enough noise to wake the entire neighborhood. Nobody comes out and no lights turn on, which convinces me that it must be a dream. But how can I be dreaming when I am not asleep? This is too real, too tangible: the sweat on my face; the metallic taste in my mouth; the thrashing that fills the alley.

The bird struggles on the ground. I grab my iPhone, turn on the torch, and aim it at the floundering mass. The light picks out a round chest covered with dirty fuzz, a flapping wing, and a blood-red eye. A low cooing, as relentless as a dentist's drill, rattles my brain. The creature has now extricated itself from the pile of laundry and is advancing toward me. The circle of light wavers on its wicked beak, as long as my hand, and festooned with feathery clumps.

My paralysis over, I bang the shutters closed and collapse on the bed. The shutters vibrate as something slams into them. The rotten brickwork of the wall cracks. I jump off the bed and scuttle into the corner. Another thud, and the shutters fly off their hinges. A nodding head pokes into the room, its spidery vibrissae twitching. A wave of stench, like limestone and shit, makes my eyes water.

I run into the living room, unlock the front door, and rush out. In the damp darkness, I am running through the streets of Venice, clad only in panties and T-shirt, my bare feet slapping on the ancient cobblestones.

After a while, I slow down. My breasts wobble and I flash back to the time Owen had compared me to the Tintoretto painting of a lush nude I showed him. And another time, later, when he told me I look like a blancmange.

Well, never mind this now. My marriage is over. I am in Venice now. And La Serenissima, my adopted mother, has suddenly turned feral on me.

The stitch in my side makes me double over. I limp over to the wall and lower myself onto the ground. As my vision clears, I realize I know where I am. I am crouching in the lee of the brick church at Campo dei Santi Apostoli, dripping with sweat despite my state of virtual undress, my breath coming out in strangled gasps.

There is a *carabinieri* station nearby, I should go there…

And tell them what? That I have been chased out of my home by a giant bird? Yes, a bird. A pigeon, to be precise. As I am thinking back on the encounter, which is sharp and clear in my mind, with no hallucinatory blurring, I realize that, its size aside, the creature looked like one of those flying rats that foul Piazza San Marco, strafing timid tourists and snatching ice cream cones out of kids' hands. A pigeon the size of a condor.

I am trying to imagine the reaction of a bored Venetian policeman to this statement. And while weighing my options, I am becoming aware how unusually dark it is. Despite its financial woes, Venice still maintains decent services, pathetically hoping for an economic miracle. At night, the orange glare of sodium lamps floods every nook and cranny of its street-maze. But now the only light is coming from the full moon above the ruined steeple of the church.

Ruined? Chiesa dei Santi Apostoli, a 7th-century Romanesque building, is intact. Its rectangular tower always welcomes me home when I walk back to Canareggio.

I stare up. A jagged nub looms above my head.

And it is not only the church. As my sight clears, I am confronted with a scene of utter devastation. Not a single building around the square is intact. The small coffee shop where I drank my espresso is reduced to a heap of stonework. The well in the center of the campo is missing its cover and a whiff of rot comes out of its gaping maw. Glass slivers glisten on the cobblestones like hail. It looks like a scene from a World War 2 documentary: a city reduced to rubble by aerial bombardment. But even in that war Venice was spared; Allied bombers did not dare pound the art treasures of La Serenissima. Whatever has happened in the hours between my falling asleep and awakening has not been so considerate.

Something moves in the shadows. A small boat is gliding into the canal. Not a touristy gondola but a small serviceable boat like the ones used to make deliveries and pick up the plastic bags of trash left by homeowners outside their doors. Its presence is a whiff of normalcy in this madness, and I even have a second to grow embarrassed at my state of semi-nudity when

I see the boatman. My throat closes up once again. He has the face of a monstrous bird: chalky-white, with a curving beak and hollow eyes.

I would run away if I could but my legs refuse to obey. Another moment of blind panic…and then I grow so angry with myself that I miraculously regain my breath. What an idiot I am! I have seen this face in every souvenir shop in the city! He is wearing the mask of the Plague Doctor, modeled after the protective gear physicians put on during the numberless epidemics that bedeviled La Serenissima. The beak contained aromatic herbs to dispel the stench of corpses. The grimness of the story has been worn away by repetition, and the Plague Doctor today is no more than an amusing tidbit of Venetian lore.

But why is the boatman masked at all?

He stops paddling and stares at me through the shadowed eyeholes, the boat bobbing gently on the dark water.

"Who are you?" I ask in a wavering voice.

With one fluid movement he removes his mask and I see an ordinary face: youngish, dark-eyed, and thin. No, not thin. Gaunt. The man looks emaciated.

"I am Luca," he says. "But who are you? You don't belong in the *sestiere*."

Is he making fun of my Italian?

"I live here," I say angrily.

"I know everyone who lives here," he replies.

What nonsense! Sestiere Cannaregio houses thousands of people!

His eyes grow round as he takes in my disheveled state. But I sense no danger from him and no prurience as he studies me. He looks genuinely perplexed.

"The Seppia told me there might be a guide," he says, half to himself. "But a beautiful woman like you…"

I blink. Did he just call me beautiful?

And what is the Seppia?

"Where are you going?" I ask.

"San Marco," he says.

Piazza San Marco is the heart of the city. Whatever strangeness has engulfed the rest of it, it is reassuring to hear the heart is still beating.

"I'll come with you," I say impulsively.

He frowns.

"I am likely not coming back," he says. "The Wings will kill me and pick my bones. But if Signora wants to come with me, she is welcome. At least I won't die alone."

LUCA IS ROWING quietly, trying to mute the splashing of his oar. The thick water smells of sewage. It is covered by a scum of feathers, small bones and unnamable rubbish.

I am sitting in the stern, huddled into the large cloak he gave me. The night is not cold but I am shivering, trying to wrap my head around what he told me.

What is this world? The future? Some sideline of time? Venice is soaked in history, the past alive in every stone. But according to Luca, history has been lost. There is no collective memory anymore. He does not know how this nightmare came to be; nor does he know how it will end. He only knows how to survive in the dwindling present. And yet he survives by raiding the past.

Luca is a treasure-hunter, a scavenger, a looter. He robs churches and museums. He collects precious works of art, paintings, sculptures, jewelry, knick-knacks; anything he can find in the ruins. He trades these priceless treasures for…yes, for *fish*. Because without fish he, and his family, whatever is left of it, without fish, they would starve.

"Why don't you fish yourself?" I asked. "You have a boat."

He shook his head.

"The Seppia won't let us into the Laguna. And the Wings will attack any vessel on the canals. They have sunk most of our boats. I am lucky to have the *Carina*. I keep her in the basement."

So the city is divided between the Wings and the Seppia. The Wings are some sort of flying monsters…the Seppia…I am not sure what they are. He speaks of them without rancor, even with a kind of remote respect. They are his buyers.

They buy the art he scavenges. They feed his family. But they are not human.

Why do they need Venetian art, then? He just shrugged and I realized it was a dumb question. Art is art. Surely whoever can appreciate beauty has a soul.

The Wings, on the other hand…there is real hatred in his voice when he speaks of them. Malice. Stupidity. Foulness. These are the words he uses.

But where did they come from? And if the situation in Venice is so dire, why didn't the remaining humans try to escape to the mainland?

Luca's answer is staggering. There is no mainland. La Serenissima is a world unto itself now, a watery world beset by monsters. And humans are clinging with their fingertips to the existence that is spinning away from them, falling into some dim abyss of which they have no understanding.

I wanted not to believe him. But how can I? I stare at the ruined, deserted city. Venice—*this* Venice—is an eloquent testament to the truth of his words. No house is undamaged. Many buildings are reduced to heaps of brick. Broken windows gape like screaming mouths. Bridges sink into filthy canals.

But as the moon climbs higher into the sky, I am beginning to see stranger things. Something the size of a dog but with a long naked tail crosses an alley. A campo is filled with an enormous nest made of old clothes. Wooden pillars sticking out of the canal are topped with piles of twigs.

The rhythmic splash of water lulls me into a dreamy reverie. Drops falling off the oar glisten like black pearls. But I should not succumb to the pleasure of this ride. According to Luca, we are heading into danger.

Piazza San Marco has become a death trap. Nobody goes into the forbidden *sestiere*. Nobody but him, Luca. Because he is desperate. His family are starving. And a Seppia, one of the mysterious Lords of the Laguna, has promised him a daily shipment of fish if he brings him what lies on the altar of the Basilica.

I try to puzzle this out. I, an art major, having spent uncounted hours in the golden splendor of San Marco, cannot put my finger on what Luca's client wants. There is so much in the Basilica, with its Byzantine abandon of mosaics, statues, frescoes, paintings, sculptures…there is enough to satisfy a legion of art collectors.

But we shall see, I tell myself, as the gentle rocking of the boat slows down my agitated heartbeat. We shall see.

A SPLASH! I jerk awake. Something rises from the viscid water in front of us: a banded tentacle, as thick as a light pole, swaying and rippling in washes of cobalt and slate. A blue luminescence sets the canal aglow as a torpedo-shaped body hoists itself onto its lip. The delicate mantle shimmers in many-colored swirls like Murano glass, and eight long arms spread along the embankment, anchoring the creature in place. Its large round eyes stare at me dispassionately. The pupils are shaped like the letter W.

Stupidly I flail around looking for something to strike the monster with. Luca pats me on the shoulder and addresses the creature calmly, like an acquaintance in a coffee shop.

"Good evening, Signore!"

The mantle—it is not slimy but glassy like a jellyfish—ripples and a voice answers. The voice is slurred but its Italian is perfectly understandable. The beaky mouth remains closed, so the creature must generate sound by vibrating the fringe of its body.

"Are you going to San Marco?"

"Yes," Luca replies. "But my bargain was with a Signora, not you."

"…(an undecipherable sound) speaks for all of us. We will repay all humans if you bring us what we want."

Before I know I am about to speak, the words are leaving my mouth.

"What do you want from San Marco?"

The creature's W-shaped pupil stretches and distorts, spelling some incomprehensible thoughts in living hieroglyphs. A wave of purple washes over its body, darkening it to the color of a storm cloud.

"Stella Maris," it says and contracting its arms, slides off the embankment and disappears into the canal with a strangely minor splash.

Luca and I stare at each other. My brain is so scrambled that the first question that pops out is totally irrelevant.

"How did you know it was a he, not a she?"

"Males have eight arms," Luca answers equitably. "Females only six. The Seppia males use the two extra arms for lovemaking."

I simultaneously blush, curse myself for blushing, and feel grateful that Luca forbore a smarmy Owen-style comment. He resumes rowing, as I mull over the encounter. So this was a Seppia! Well, now I know Luca neither lied nor exaggerated when he described the situation in this drowned city.

But what did the creature mean by Stella Maris? This translates as Star of the Sea, one of the titles of the Virgin. But I can't think of any specific painting with this name.

Something floats on the tarry surface of the canal, something sparkling and lacy. I reach for it. Luca whispers furiously. I lift the feather, as long as my forearm, moonlight shining through its wispy barbs, as I imagine masked and bejeweled women lazily fanning themselves with peacock plumes…

Spidery legs skitter on my hand as a coin-sized tick sinks its proboscis into my bare skin. I scream and shake my hand frantically, trying to dislodge the giant arachnid. Luca slaps it off and covers my mouth. His bony fingers linger on my lips.

The boat rocks violently. A whiff of acrid stench, and more ticks patter over my neck and shoulder, land in my hair, crawl on my face. A rain of parasites! And the rain cloud is falling out of the sky, the boat seeming to shrink under its spreading wings. A thunderous cooing drills into my head. Luca dives under the seat, pulling me down. A ruby eye the size of a dinner plate hangs over the gunwale like a bloody moon.

"A Wing!" Luca cries.

The ginormous bird is trying to perch on the stern but the *Carina* is too small to bear its weight. The boat is listing, threatening to overturn and chuck us into the polluted water where we will be picked out by that gaping, vibrissae-festooned beak as easily as worms. Luca's hand snakes toward mine, grasping, our fingers intertwining.

"Stay under!" he whispers.

I understand. He wants us to stay under the hull if the boat overturns.

But what if this creature can crack the waterlogged bottom?

And then the feathery cyclone suddenly doubles in size. I am blinded by flying plumage, battered by surges of acid air, deafened by chirping and cackling. A webbed foot grazes the stern, big enough to stomp a man into a smear. A scimitar-shaped beak closes on the Wing's neck. Something the size of a small biplane is dunking the Wing's head into the water, impervious to its thrashing. The canal is churned up into a stinking foam, the boat is jerked around like a toy…but Luca somehow manages to steer it into a side cutting. When I look back, I see a gull dismembering a pigeon.

WE HAD TO abandon the *Carina*. It was leaking too badly. We are skulking through the garbage-choked alleys, ducking through splintered doorways, crawling over piles of masonry and bricks.

We have not met a single human being. We saw plenty of rats. They dragged their well-fed bodies through the ruins of La Serenissima with unhurried insolence. I remember the T-shirt I saw in a tourist shop: the picture of a rat and the Gothic letters spelling "Nightlife in Venice."

What surprises me is how thoroughly the city has been emptied of its treasures. When I first came to Venice, I would wander for hours, peeking into churches and galleries, gawping at the shop windows with displays of handmade paper goods, masks, glass, jewelry, silk, and paintings. And then I would realize I had walked just a couple of blocks. Each building held something worth seeing: an inset colorful icon; a bronze door with a guild design; a sculpted mask at the cornice; a tiny store selling handmade perfumes in Murano bottles. But now…The city has been denuded, ransacked; even the rubbish has been picked over. The buildings that still stand glare with the hollow stares of ravaged windows. Not just the panes but even the molded pilasters that gave them their traditional arched shape are gone.

But picking my way through the bare bones of La Serenissima, I suddenly realize that this is *my* city. Until now, I have been held back by Venice's opulence, as humble and unsure of myself as a poor country girl in service to a great lady. But now the lady has been brought low. And I almost choke with love for those splintered sidewalks, polluted canals, and ruined palazzos. Now she needs me as she had never needed me before.

Luca is walking at a fast clip but I am beginning to slow down. I ask for a break and flush with shame when he turns back and looks at me. I have taken off the cloak he gave me and my baggy breasts and doughy forearms are exposed. And then something shifts between us and suddenly I see myself through his eyes, the hollow eyes of a perpetually hungry man, and my spillover flesh becomes a vision of abundance.

He drops his gaze and the moment is over. We press on.

The sky is turning silky-gray. I can see plaques with street names set into the brick walls and I realize I know exactly where we are. We are coming to the commercial heart of La Serenissima that used to pump the lifeblood of credit throughout medieval Europe. Even in my own time, the warren of alleyways and *campi*, small squares, between San Marco and Rialto throbbed with crowds of tourists, shopping for fake—and occasionally real—antiques. The Rialto Bridge was encrusted with small shops.

My own time? It was only yesterday. History has collapsed in upon itself.

The steely water of the Grand Canal glistens in the gap between two collapsed palazzos as we come to the embankment. I knew what to expect but my breath still catches in my throat. The biggest waterway in Venice is crawling with rafts of rot. Shoals of garbage span the remaining girders of the Rialto Bridge. The dome of Santa Maria della Salute stands out against the lightening sky like a broken eggshell.

I glance in Luca's direction, wondering how the degradation of the city is affecting him. His face is impassive. He stares at the filthy water pullulating with nameless parasites. A whiff of a rotten-egg smell stings my eyes but he does not react.

"We can't go across," he says.

"There is no need," I say. "I know a way."

Indeed I do. Defiled as they are, the streets of Venice are still the same. Maps are useless in La Serenissima; one learns to navigate its dreamy maze by walking until the correct route is burnt into one's aching muscles, as it is burnt into mine.

Luca obediently follows my lead. Owen would have argued…but I realize that I can no longer recall the sound of his voice.

As the sodden sky lightens to the color of milky coffee, the sickly life infesting the alleys is becoming more noticeable. Instead of disappearing at dawn, rats are scuttling around as bold as cats. Something invisible is shaking a pile of bricks. And I don't need to follow Luca's troubled glances upward to know that the shadows flitting above our heads are not clouds.

We reach what I recognize as the square of *Teatro Le Fenice*. Only one column is left of what used to be one of the most beautiful theaters in Europe. It is streaked with dirty brown and rust-red.

Not far now. Even though my feet hurt, I am almost running now, impatient to reach San Marco, as if expecting that I will see, once again, the heart of Venice as it has been for a thousand years: the glorious herring-bone-patterned mosaic pavement; the glittering arcades; the soaring tower of the Campanile di San Marco; and dominating it all, the Byzantine splendor of the great Basilica. Surely, my journey with Luca has been nothing but a nightmare; surely, the only pigeons here will be the tame postcard doves. I will be back where I started: a stranger in a strange land, a homely woman, a failed wife, a childless mother...

I peer through an arched gateway, hearing Luca's labored breathing behind me.

One glance, and I know that the heart of the city has been eaten by the same cancer as the rest of her body. Pigeons remain and flourish; everything else is gone or hideously transformed.

The mosaic pavement is drowned under billows of crusted guano. The loggia and the arcades are trashed with dry branches, stinking fish skeletons, piles of feathers and rags—whether of clothes or bodies, impossible to tell. And the floors above the arcades have become monstrous roosts. Protruding from broken windows and clinging to befouled walls are giant untidy nests. Clouds of flies fill the air and the acrid stench is so strong that my eyes tear up, mercifully blurring my vision.

The Campanile di San Marco lies in pieces, and its ruins are covered by a thick shroud of spiderwebs. The Basilica is still standing but its golden domes are hidden under layers of guano, so it looks like a crude model of itself fashioned out of bird shit. One of the stone lions at the entrance is missing; the other's face is pocked by holes as if somebody had taken a drill to it. But the worst are the pigeons.

Should I even call them that? I have already realized that the Wings are no ordinary birds. They are too big, for one, and strangely misshapen. And the sight before me makes it clear that some malevolent magic is at work here, having degraded the city of the sea into the nest of pests of the air.

There are actually fewer creatures than I expected. Perhaps it is understandable: some of them are so big that a flock would pack the entire Piazza. How can they even fly? The largest of them look like obscenely blown-up pigeons, nodding idiotically as they mince around or brood in their nests. But others are something else: human-avian hybrids, their naked bodies festooned with mangy clumps of feathers, their eyes red and mindless. I see a creature strutting around on plump naked legs and flapping misshapen wings. His face is dominated by a yellow-lined beak. And here is a fleshly caricature of an angel: a winged manlike body with a dog's muzzle. White teeth flash in a chick's hungry mouth opened to its parent.

Luca gasps. Hasn't he seen it before? I remember that he referred to Sestiere San Marco as "forbidden." Forbidden by who? Never mind. We have to get inside the Basilica. *I* have to get inside the Basilica. Why? I don't know; I only know I will do it or die trying.

I turn to Luca.

"I know a way around," I say.

He is staring at the Basilica, shocked. I risk peering through the arch again and now I see that what I took for a shapeless mound of guano above the portal of San Marco is, in fact, an enormous nest. On the pediment, where the triumphant horses of San Marco once stood, squats a molting sack of flesh, brooding her eggs.

"We have to go," I say firmly.

Luca nods and follows me as I am creeping through the maze around the Piazza. The noise from the square recedes but I know that within a short distance is that avian hell, packed with mutated birds, fighting, eating, shitting, dying.

I spent a lot of time in the Doge's Palace Museum adjacent to the Piazza and I know there is an underground passage leading into the Basilica from there. When I last visited the passage was guarded by a uniformed attendant but I don't think museum rules apply anymore.

Amazingly, the Doge's Palace is still relatively intact, its distinctive pink-and-white marble façade standing. I duck into the arcade. Above me on the pediment is the familiar huddle of small stone figures, representing the four sons of Emperor Constantine.

As we pass under them, one of the figures detaches itself from the rest and leaps down, landing on Luca's shoulders.

"Run!" Luca yells, while the figure pummels him with its child-sized fists, grinning with bloody teeth. It is another Wing but its actual wings are two bony nubs sticking out from its shoulders.

I pivot and, grasping the creature's scrawny arm, drag it off Luca. It snarls. Its flesh is fever-hot, covered with unclean down. It is twisting in my hands, astonishingly strong. Its unfamiliar bones are grinding under its slick skin. Bubbles of blood pop from its mouth.

Luca jerks the creature away from me, hurls it on the ground, and lifts his foot. I turn away. A piercing shriek and wet plop, then silence.

We dive into a shadowy hall. I am concerned that the interior of the Palace would be infested as well, so I promptly turn to the familiar side corridor leading to the underground prisons. It is cool and dark. But I don't need light. I could navigate these corridors blindfolded. Even the flapping of wings and the high-pitched whistling somewhere above my head don't faze me. I am buoyed with absolute certainty of purpose. For the first time in my life I understand how it feels to run an Olympic record or win in BGT.

I hear Luca's ragged breathing behind me as he stumbles. I reach back, pat his hand in reassurance. There is a sliver of pale light ahead and I rush through, unmindful of danger.

Here we are. Inside the Basilica. And the leaden weight of disappointment drops on me.

It is not the lifeless light dribbling through a broken skylight in the dome.

It is not the hillocks of guano on the flagged floor. It is not the stealthy stirrings in the shadows of the side-chapels.

I expected all of this. What I did not expect was the absence of everything else.

No statues or paintings. No mosaics. What used to be the shimmering golden heaven above is now dirty pockmarked plaster. No Byzantine Christ, no majestic saints, no frowning apostles. Somebody has removed all of them, stone by stone, tile by tile. Somebody has ripped off frescoes, packed icons in bubble wrap, stowed virgins and martyrs in crates among plastic peanuts. And where are they now? In some rich man's collection in that other world that no longer has any need for La Serenissima? Ravaged of its treasures, she would be a reminder of the world's shame, as embarrassing as a homeless beggar at a stockholders' meeting. But she can still keep her pigeons, of course.

I walk toward the empty altar, dragging my feet like an old woman. I am old. And fat. And useless. As useless as this sodden, sinking city! My body blossoms with a bouquet of deferred pain as all the injuries that I have incurred in this fool's errand of a quest wake up. My knees are skinned, my arms lacerated, my legs are throbbing with fatigue.

I hear Luca's bewildered voice but it seems to be coming from very far away.

"Where is…where is Stella Maris?"

Poor Luca! The Seppia have played a cruel joke on him. There is a legend that the relics of San Marco in the Basilica have kept the waters of the Laguna away from the city, letting her rule the Adriatic. Now the relics are gone together with everything else. There is nothing to trade anymore.

Where the altar stood, all that remains now is a flat hollowed-out stone. There is stagnant water in the hollow. A fat pigeon is drinking from it, its stupid little head going up and down like a metronome, a burbling sound coming from its wheel-shaped chest.

This final desecration is too much to bear. I lunge at the altar-stone, grasp the pigeon, and wring its neck.

In its death-throes, the bird has lacerated my hands. Blood is dripping from my palms. More blood than a couple of scratches would account for. And more blood is gushing from my skinned knees, from the gashes on my back and my forearms. Strangely, I don't feel any pain.

I touch the worn surface. The thought that the patron of La Serenissima had lain here for thousands of years is a source of comfort. I kneel by the altar, put my head down. The stone does not feel hard; it gently cradles my bruised body. Even the intensified bleeding does not bother me. It is pleasant, a dreamy dissolution. With no surprise, I notice that my breasts

are also gushing blood—or is it water?
I lie on St. Mark's stone bed and it embraces me like a lover.

Luca stared reverently at the woman as she walked toward the altar. When she touched the stone, he knelt down.

In the dirty light falling from the dome, Jennie's white body glowed with an almost preternatural clarity. Her dark hair tumbled off the altar, falling down, lengthening…

No, it was not hair. Streams of clear water gushed from the altar, as if she were melting, a Snow White dissolving but not diminishing. Streams and jets of water, gurgling, joining, gaining strength, becoming a brook, a river, a flood…washing through the Basilica, dissolving carpets of filth, drowning skittering vermin…and as Luca lurched to his feet, trying to make his way toward the altar where Jennie lay as white and serene as a marble statue, he heard a roar from the outside.

He gave up fighting the pressure of the water and let the gathering wave carry him out. The Piazza was a maelstrom of rubble and drowning birds; the flapping cacophony of their shrill calls deafened him and their flailing threatened to toss him aside like a piece of garbage. But Luca fought off their assault and swam toward the open water of the Laguna. Still, he would not have made it had not the murky soup of the flood suddenly lit up with multicolored lights. Pink, blue, emerald, aquamarine…festooned with living jewels, a squadron of Seppia rode in on the rolling wave, snatching Wing stragglers with their tentacles and drowning them.

Luca trod water, barely keeping his head above the flood. He tried to find his client among the cephalopods but they all looked alike, decked out in triumphant lights and bright colors, asserting their dominion over the reborn Queen of the Adriatic. He would like to have been acknowledged as successful in his quest to find the Stella Maris but he realized it no longer mattered.

A wavelet slapped his face, cold water snaking up his nasal passages. He knew he would soon have to give up and plummet to the bottom where the new city was quickly taking shape, her sinuous alleys and green-roofed churches emerging from the ooze. He hoped he would be reborn as a quick, darting fish or an adventurous eel, exploring the drowned treasures of La Serenissima.

Rainheads

Mike Weitz

———◆———

TRAX CAUGHT A rat today.

Said he found it in the trenches, the liar. It wasn't soupy or scarred up at all. I bet he didn't even go out there. I bet those trenches are so deep now even a big bastard like Trax couldn't plod through one without it starting in on him. Probably just covered his legs with muck after he caught it in the tunnels to joke with me. To Trax, jokes and lies are one and the same. Dumb brute. Good thing I told him to change his wraps.

All that aside, I know he lied anyhow because he raised his bald eyebrow when he told me.

He's a real piss-on-a-rock liar, Trax is. Raises that eyebrow every time.

I love that son of a bitch. He might have the only perky face left in the entire melting pot of a world. That's just how he is. If Trax was marooned on an island of shit, he'd just plug his nose and start exploring.

Anyway, we're lucky he caught that squeaker. Ain't seen one in too long. It only made half a mouthful between us, but somehow it still lifted the mood. Who knew such a nasty little thing could ease your breathing like that.

"It sang when ya hehd it over the fie-ah." Trax said, after it was all bones charring between the embers. I make him throw the bones in there, otherwise I'll catch him gnawing on 'em in the middle of the night. I wouldn't mind, except the grinding noise is maddening, and then later when the moon is high he'll wake me up whining and writhing with a gut ache.

I looked at Trax across the flames. His eyes were black rocks surfing on the glow. His hair is all but gone now. Too much time outside. His pink scalp glistened like a wet exposed muscle. The places where it had melted slightly and scarred over looked wretchedly alien. When we first started drifting together, there was hardly any pink skin on him, let alone those scars. Now he only looks like half a man. Hells if I know what the other half is.

"Didnja hear it, Carn?" he asked. "It sang."

I told him off then. Dumb brute knows the difference between what's moving and what's melting in the muck. Sometimes I think a little too much rain might've trickled in his ears one of those times he got caught coming in late, during the front end of a torrent.

Probably not though. More likely he just says those stupid falsies to itch me on. Lugger knows good and well whenever he says 'em I'll tell him off or rip him up one hard—but he does it for me, see? He knows me ripping him up one always brings my mind out of the dark.

We're drifters, Trax and I. This time we're living underground. Normally we'd be on the move during the stretch of light, but because of my clumsy ass we're grounded down until I heal. Oh well. It's a decent post-up if you ask me, especially compared to some of the other scrap heaps we've been in. At least this one's dry.

Don't ask me how. If you did though, you wouldn't be the first. Trax does it every other bleating day. Most of his memory is no different than those muck trenches. Anyway, since I'm dragging it on, my guess is that maybe the old ancestors rerouted the system at some point and forgot to close this one in. Or maybe something's clogging it up.

I don't really believe that second theory though. I only mention it Trax now and then to lift him up. Deep down I know it's a crock uh shit. Trax has run the tunnels all over. Pretty sure he's got half the city all mapped out in his melty mind. If there was something that was withstanding the runoff of the torrents, he'd have found it by now. Strange, ain't it? Trax can't remember half of what I say, but he knows them tunnels better than his own instincts.

Who knows though, maybe it is clogged. Maybe I'm just speaking falsies. No matter. Speaking's all I've got anyways. All I can do is run my mouth until I heal. I order Trax around and tell him off when he's here, and when he's gone I tell off the spiders and roaches. And just for the extra book-keeping pages, if on one of his run-outs Trax ever did find something clogging up the sewers, I expect he'd run it back in a heartbeat.

That's no swing against him. If I was in his shoes and that happened to me, I'd just about do the same. Hells, I'd still be out there scavenging with him if I hadn't stepped in that rain hole.

Lucky Trax was with me when I did, or I might be out a whole leg, maybe to the hip. Some of them holes are deep as darkness. Lucky for me Trax jerked me out just as fast as I dipped in. Way things went, I just got some scarring and a little feeling damage, but it'll still work again eventually. And if it don't, hells with it. I'll just have Trax hack it off, and then we'll have ourselves another meal.

That was a joke by the way. We still know jokes. The burning rain might've melted its way through all the book-keepings of the old world, but as long as Trax and I exist, it ain't gonna eat through the funnies. Laughter might be as scarce as life itself these days, but we still get into it now and then, usually in the stretch of light between the torrents.

TRAX IS OUT again. Let's hope he finds something 'cause my guts are getting stormy. Feels like there's a small torrent raging around in there right now, laying waste to my insides. Must have been a bad rat we ate yesterday. No surprise there. Most of the rats are bad now, but we eat 'em anyway so we don't eat each other.

That there was another joke, just in case the word is all forgotten by the time someone reads this. I wouldn't be surprised.

For the pages, it ain't gonna come to us eating ourselves though. Not for a while at least. I haven't told Trax, but secretly I've still got five cans of old-world goodies in my sack. Saving those until we're really starving. Look, I don't like keeping secrets like this, I know that's what killed most of the colonies, secrets and trickery, but I can't tell Trax about those cans or he'll eat 'em all when I'm sleeping. Big mucker can't help himself. I gotta admit, I don't know how he does it. Here I am sitting in the hole all day while Trax is out there tromping around on half a rat. Gives me the feeling he's been catching and eating things out there on his own. Raw.

Best not to think about that. Best not to think about the reddish mud cracks I've seen forming on the back of his neck either. I don't know what's going on with Trax. All I know is that he's still with me when he's with me, somewhat. Like I said, his memory of things is piss-poor except for those tunnels. He's a downright scientist when it comes to those, but that's about the extent of it. Poor brute can't hardly speak right.

He ain't going mad though. He can't tell 'em himself for shit, but he still laughs at my jokes when I tell 'em, so who cares if his brain's half melted. He wasn't much for brains to begin with.

One other thing about Trax and me. I feel I have to say this because I want to make sure it's going in the book-keepings. My old name is Carl. That's the name my mom and pop gave me. It's my born-name, or however they used to say it. Anyway, since Trax has an issue with L's I guess I'm Carn now, until we meet someone else. That seems unlikely until we drift to a new town or city, which depends on when my foot heals. We ain't seen a living—*hells*, even a *solid* human body since Mackovick died.

THERE'S ANOTHER TORRENT coming in. I saw it riding in on the horizon this morning, just after Trax left. It's not wise to leave the hole, but damn it all, it's been about two torrents and three stretches of light since I breathed the open air, and being down there so long, I felt like I was changing into something gaunt and gangly. Man ain't meant to live in holes.

I guess that's part falsie though. It ain't a hole exactly. We got one grate in the middle where the rain comes in during the torrents and runs down the entry tunnel, and where the light shines in around midday and midnight, but that ain't hardly enough of a window. I had to get out, just once before my head turned inside out.

It was a long, shitty trek hobbling down the entry tunnel. To cope with my gimp leg, all I had to crutch on was a black metal pole Trax got for me. Took half the daylight to get there, but damn it all if it wasn't worth it.

When I finally climbed the ladder, pushed off the lid and felt the true light of day spill over me, it felt like bathing in heaven.

The sun sat like a crown on the head of the great green sky. The haze that normally hovers below it—radiation most say—was barely visible. Just a film. I smiled. It was a good day. A proud day. I'd actually accomplished something for once, rather than sitting in the gloom, throwing scrap wood and cement clods at the roaches and thinking myself to death.

All around me, the environment appeared the same as always. In one direction, the countryside looked like something chewed up and spit out. In the other, the remains of the city looked like the mouth that'd done the chewing.

At first the sight was gut-rotting, but then an easy wind crept across my back, and I felt better again when I noticed how dry everything'd become. It'd been quite some time since the last torrent. I thought about those muck trenches then, way out on the other edge of town where the earth dipped low and hoped they were drying up too.

Not sure if I would've had the nerve to go back down again if I hadn't seen that black train of clouds. It's gonna be a rough night.

I WAS WRONG. Somehow the torrent missed us. Lucky it did, because Trax didn't return until after the death of daylight.

And for good reason. He came back with a rabbit in his hands. It was a nasty, scrawny thing, but it was something. Better than a rat. Those are the two good parts of this book-keeping account. The torrent skipped us and Trax brought home a rabbit.

Now it's time for the two bad parts.

The first thing was the rabbit itself. Its fur was completely burned off. Its teeth were carnivorously overgrown, and the face above them was nothing but a pink skull with hideously tall ears. All in all, it looked like something from the old monster stories. Something vampiric. But that ain't even the worst of it. Its back and sides were covered in the same red-lined plates I've seen growing on the back of Trax's neck. I almost couldn't eat it. Almost.

The second thing was Trax. He came in like a horse, galloping down the entry tunnel, stirring up his own torrent of echoes. Once inside, he plopped it down on my lap like a giddy old dog, bragging that he killed it all on his own.

I believed him. The rabbit's throat was missing and Trax's jaw was dark red.

I told him off for it. I told him off bad. I could tell he took real offense this time. He cowered back, stumbling all over the remains of last night's fire, kicking ash and embers all over the hole, making muckery of everything and cringing under the sewer grate.

Night was already in by then, and the moon was high. It threw minced streaks of light down on him through the grate, and for a moment the lines of light and shadow showed me half of what he was and half of what he was becoming.

Had to tell myself off then. He ain't becoming nothing. He's just Trax. He just got a little savage, that's all. No real harm in it. In this world, you need to be a savage now and then, if you're looking to survive.

Then again, he didn't have to do it that way. He's got hands for shit's sake. He could've at least done it with his hands.

I CAUGHT TRAX eating bones in the night. Sneaky bastard must have stowed some of them away when I wasn't watching.

I woke up to the sound.

Not gnawing this time.

Munching.

Not gonna lie, I really went off on him. Not sure what happened then. Not sure what to make of it.

Trax cowered back like normal, but this time I kept coming on. I had the pole in one hand, and I clambered over to him, beating him with it, five times—ten, when all of a sudden I saw something like black water rippling in his eyes. On the last swing, he caught the pole with one hand and ripped it out of mine with a head-jutting snarl.

That was the end of it. I shambled back, spooked out of my wits. I hadn't ever noticed how massive Trax's teeth were. They made me think of that rabbit's teeth, too big for its ugly head. But the sight of him wasn't nearly as terrifying as the noise. It was guttural and primal, like nothing I'd ever heard before.

Trax broke down afterward. Big bastard bawled his fat pink head off, wallowing at my feet, blubbering like a baby, swearing he'd never eat the bones again. It might be hard to believe, but in that moment he was just as scared as I was.

After the shock wore off, I calmed him down with some stories about the days of the blue skies. I don't really remember much about it, to be honest. I mostly just make up falsies that sound nice, like rain that tickles instead of burns, lakes that you can actually swim in and hideouts that never collapse. Falsies like trees with green leaves on them and flowers of every shape and color; like whole houses filled with canned goodies that we could eat and eat and eat until our bellies burst.

MY FOOT'S GETTING better. Noticed it as I changed my wrap this morning. The scar tissue is ugly and thick as a hide, but I can finally manage to put a little weight on it.

Trax is out again, as usual. He tried to apologize about last night, but I wouldn't have it. I told him we all do bad things. That's the difference between us and the beasts. We know what's falsie and what ain't. We know what's bad and what's good. We have reason.

He didn't understand it all, but I think he got enough. I don't think we'll have another incident like that again. God help me if we do.

TRAX CAME BACK in a bit of a stupor tonight. He walked in with nothing but extra scrap wood and said he saw a woman today. That's right, a female, out by the trenches. I thought he was joking at first, but the big oaf held to it. Passionately.

"How do ya know it wasn't just beastie or a man?" I asked.

Instead of replying, he bent down, cupped his hands under his chest.

"All right, all right," I said. "Drop it now, I get you. You caught sight of some woman parts, eh? So were they all exposed then? What, was she naked as the day?"

Trax became uneasy. He didn't respond or even look at me directly.

"What? Damnit Trax, what? Why the forgotten hells can't you talk to me?"

"It huhts," he whined, pressing a hand up to his jaw. I guess Trax has an issue with R's now too.

"That's cause you've been eating too many bones, ya rat-brained bastard. Let me get this right, then. We ain't seen a man since we buried Mackovick months ago, and we ain't seen a woman in a lifetime of light, but now you expect me to believe you saw one just today out by the trenches, walking on her merry way, naked as the green bleating day?!"

Trax shook his head.

"What? Ain't that the truth of it? What's falsie about that?"

He looked down reluctantly and shifted away. From the new angle, I could see those red lined squares, those volcanic looking plates had started creeping their way in under his neck. Now they ended at the corners of his jaw, just below his earlobes. They looked reptilian, like the misplaced scales of some oversized snake.

"Out with it, Trax!" I commanded. "I don't care if it hurts your precious *wittle* mouth. Quit speaking falsies right now, quit circling the kill and spill the blood! I swear by all the for—"

"She wehwen't walkin'!" he burst. His face was real knotted up. Almost purple.

"What's that?"

Trax raised another hand to his jaw. Once again, his eyes were fixated on the fire, and in the reflection of his pupils, I saw the tongues of flame licking and licking.

"She wehwen't walking, Cahn," he repeated, his eyebrows set in place. "She went down on awe foahs. She was *crahwin'*."

THE SUN HAS sunk. The moon is hunching in the sky.

Trax is late. He's never this late.

Part of me wonders if he was attacked and killed, but most of me's against that. It'd take more than a handful of men or beasts to kill Trax. In all my time, I'm not sure I've ever seen a bigger man.

There's a torrent coming in. No doubt about it this time. It's already started. The winds are in a shift and the air is coming about. Already, the black clouds are starting to cry. I can hear it. The soft patter of the rain on the ground and the sizzle of steam where the drops are eating in.

I'm hunkered down in the furthest corner of the hideout, shivering and clinging to my wraps. I can only hope the old tunnel can withstand another torrent. There's no telling how far the prior rains have eaten into the cement, or how soon it's going to collapse.

The rain eats right through just about anything organic, save wood. That's why we got those trenches. The rain just keeps sizzling through the dirt, sinking deeper and deeper. But when it comes to rocks, cements, and metals, it depends. Mostly on the density, according to Mackovick. His father was one of the old-world scientists, so Mac knew all about the book-keepings on it. He said the destruction levels of a torrent depended on the potency of the rain, the acidity, so he called it, and the velocity of the wind. High enough

winds could turn the rain to razor blades. You get caught out in that, and *poof!* Before you know it, you're nothing but red mist.
Now I'll admit, I've never seen torrents like that, but I've heard more than a few stories.
Trax better get back quick.

HE NEVER CAME.
Torrent lasted all night, and he never showed up. He must have been too far off when it hit and had to take shelter somewhere else.
The hole's pretty much done for. The rains finally ate through the concrete around the grate and it clattered down sometime in the night. A short while later, the wall across from me caved in. I was struck with a little bit of rubble and rain, but I'm all right. I'm still breathing. It was just blind luck that it happened on Trax's side and not mine.
With no food in two days, I had to eat one of my goodie reserves. It was an old sweet food. Something called peaches.
It's light out now and I can finally walk. It still hurts a little, still tender, but I've found myself able to transfer enough weight on it so that I don't need to lean on that pole as much.
I don't have any idea where Trax might be. I'll wait for him a little longer, but if he doesn't show up by high sun I'm going to have to write him off dead and start drifting on my own. I can't afford to waste this stretch of light. I need to find a new hideout.

STILL NO SIGN of him.
Hate to say it, but I'm starting to really miss the big lug. High sun's long passed though, so I'm setting off.
Sorry Trax. I really will miss ya, ya old rainhead. And who knows. Maybe we'll meet somewhere else down the road. At the very least, I'll mark you down here in our own book-keeping. I'll mark you down well. I owe my life to you, scrounging up all them rats. We had our differences, sure. I'm small and you're big. I'm a genius and you're dumb. I tell truths and jokes and you laugh and tell falsies. You mucked up and I told ya off, and I told ya off so you mucked up. What a mess we were. A real renegade, as Mac used to say. Thanks for everything, Trax. Like I said, I owe you.

BEEN A LONG time now since I did a book-keeping. Two torrents and three stretches of light by my make of it.
Foot's completely healed now, and I'm getting on ok. Things looked pretty skimpy there for a while. I went through all my goodie cans before I was fit enough to hunt and kill again. I dug up a few more a while later in

the ruins of some collapsed market store. Beans they were called. I tried to eat 'em but I irked 'em up. Something about 'em didn't sit right in me. Probably just too old.

Anyway, I'm getting along fine on rats and rabbits. Even killed something once that was bigger than a rabbit. It was a hairless little monster no higher than my shins, with jutting yellow teeth and plated on its back and sides with the same red-lined scales I know too well.

I still managed to recognize it though. If my knowledge of the old world is right, I'd say it used to be a cat.

It came at me heels over head so I struck it with my pole and killed it. I'm still carrying the same black pole Trax gave me. Don't know why I still have it. There's better poles out there. I could fashion myself a deadlier weapon if I really wanted to, but for some reason I can't bring myself to pitch it aside. I guess you could call it a keepsake.

I'M DRIFTING NORTH, I think. That's where I'm trying to go, anyways. Back in the old colonies, there was always talk about going north. Folk used to say the more north you go, the less torrents there are. It's cold up north they'd say. Too cold for rain, only snow, and according to them the snow ain't nearly as acidic.

Now I know that's all just theories. I know good and well it could be falsies, but if there's a chance of less torrents, I say that's worth walking towards. Besides, where else would I go?

Anyway, the other day I was hiking up a hill on a highway road. There were no black clouds on the horizon, and to the west, the sun was dying. Beneath it, that all-present haze that's normally so cloudy and bogs the eyes to look at reversed its effect and intensified the light.

I'd been walking all day, and my legs burned white on the incline. I thought about stopping for a rest, but somehow, seeing all the colors in the sky gave me the strength to push on until I finally reached the summit. On top, I perched for a moment, leaning on my pole, and looked out upon the harrowed land before me.

Sometimes, late into the stretch of moonlight, after Trax had gone to sleep, Mackovic used to talk science to me. He'd take on this low voice and give me his whole smartsy speech on the goings of the world. One thing I remembered then, standing atop that hill, was when Mac used to say the torrents were breaking down the earth, same as how our stomachs broke down whatever rat or vermin we'd eaten that night. He'd say the torrents were working the world like a digestive tract, and that eventually everything would be reduced back to the same primordial soup it started from. And then, according to Mac, after millions of torrents and stretches of light, the earth would adapt and parts would harden up again, and life would crawl right back out of that soup.

He was a real mucker, Mac was. Full of falsies.

Hells, I miss him.

I sat up on that hill a long time before I got the nerve to stand and start off again. By then, the sun was long dead. It had bled out all over an orange moon on the rise.

I took a few steps forward, when my eyes caught a rustle in the dark. I stopped and stooped, looking far into the bank where the road bottomed out.

That's where I saw Trax.

I couldn't see his face. I didn't have to. I knew who it was just by the massive shape of him. He was on all fours, creeping across the road towards a steaming set of muck trenches on the other side.

And he wasn't alone.

Next to him was another, smaller shape, black and dimly glowing from the red lines between the scales that covered it from head to foot—same as he.

Each of them crept with freakish speed, so low to the ground their bellies might've dragged.

I couldn't breathe. I was scared pissless, all weak and wobbly in the knees. It felt like my face had turned white, like I too was glowing.

But for the moment, I was lucky. The two of them had their sights set on those trenches. Trax in front, they spidered their way across the road. I watched in horror as he slid into the hot, bubbling mud, and out of his disturbance, a cloud of rising steam blurred him from my sight.

But not the other one. The other one halted at the edge, rearing around as if sniffing for something.

Then it stood up and looked right at me.

My knees crippled. I lost my breath and fell right on my ass.

Then it took off. It made after me on all fours, as rampant as that ugly cat had, heels-over-head.

I cried out and scrambled back, panicking like a blind rabbit, dropping my keepsack and clutching the pole in two shaking hands. For some reason, I couldn't catch my stance. I couldn't just get up and face the mucker.

It kept coming. *She kept coming!* I could see it as she now, her woman parts bouncing uselessly while the rest of her plundered up the road, bent on ripping right through me.

I choked out a breath and prepared to meet the forgotten hells. She was at the base of the hill—the middle—then *right on me!*

When out of the gloom rose a deep feral call. It carried through my ears as a sound without reason, a sound without name.

I gasped again, and opened my eyes. Go on and mark me down as a rat-piss fighter, but I couldn't see it through. I just couldn't.

The woman-thing was crouching right in front of me, an arm's length away. Without moving, I sized her up.

It was sort of like Mac always said. She was a monster born straight out of the torrents. She stunk like seared flesh and mud. And she was hot. I could feel the heat beating out of her in waves, as if a fire was raging inside. The red between her scales glowed in wires. Her jaw bulged. It was as big as an old world beastie's. The teeth inside, too massive for her lips to cover, were gnashed and spread in a horrid shit-eating grin. In the hellish moonlight, they looked more like two rows of bones, almost as long as my fingers. Her slant, watching eyes might've been the only humanly thing about her, but as soon as I looked into 'em, I saw nothing but savagery.

Another call cut through the air.

It was Trax. He was at the base of the hill, howling.

The woman-thing hissed and glanced back, then scampered off to him.

I stood up. I understood.

Trax told her off. It was the same as how I used to do it to him, only with sounds instead of words. He saved my life again.

I looked down at him. As she crawled past and slunk into the trenches, he stayed and stared back, standing on his hind legs. Tails of steam whispered up from the muck that was still dripping off him.

I was split. Half of me wanted to walk down there, and half of me wanted to run off. Instead, I did nothing. We just stared at each other for a long, long while, as the red moon rose and glared. Eventually, the wind picked up and covered him with a sheet of trench steam. By the time it settled, Trax was gone again.

THE LAST OF my hair fell out today. That's what happens when you get exposed to too many torrents. I got caught in the front of one yesterday. Lucky I'm even alive. I took shelter in the undercroft of some half-decimated building and had to dodge leaks and collapses all night long.

Later this morning while I was taking a piss, I felt an itch on the back of my head. I reached around to scratch it and off came all the hair. Where it had been was a big leathery scab. That last torrent must have burned into me worse than I thought. Oh well. The scab will heal and scar.

I'm going out to scavenge now. For some reason, I can't stop thinking about bones.

My House Is Out Where the Lights End

Kirsty Logan

———◆———

JAY APPROACHES THE old farmhouse with her sunglasses and the radio off. She wants to see it and hear it clearly. In her memory it looms so huge, so loud and technicolor, that she's sure she'll be overwhelmed by it.

But it's been abandoned for years now, and the bright painted boards are faded and rain-dragged, and the tin roof is rusted through in places, and the driveway is overgrown with weeds. She pulls the car to a jolting stop and sits there, watching the empty house as if waiting for someone to come out and greet her.

EVERYONE SAID THAT sunflowers couldn't grow here and they were right, they couldn't and wouldn't until finally, one day, they did. Pop always said it was because of his Secret Method. He said it in capital letters like that to make it sound scientific and complicated, but Jay and Yara watched him in secret from Jay's bedroom window and knew exactly what his method was, and it was this: he sang to the sunflowers. Big Pop, terror of the town, half the teeth smacked out of his head, body more scars than skin, faster with his fists than a kung-fu star. He sang to flowers.

Jay thinks now that she should have found that sweet. Her father, a surprise like a wrapped present, hard as nails but soft as trifle—it was sweet, right? But at the time she found it frightening: that Pop was so unpredictable, that he could be two opposite things at once, that there was no way to know whether he would respond with fists or song.

JAY GETS OUT of the car and walks round to the back of the house, where in her memory miles of sunflowers gleam brighter than the sun. She finds a field of withered grey stalks, bent under the weight of their dead heads. The ground is heaving with black seeds, piled thick, gleaming like insect shells. She kicks at them and hears them sift and tumble, an uncomfortably sensual sound. For many seasons the field must have grown wild, alone all summer, then sank back on itself through autumn, only to repeat the whole thing again next year. A ghost harvest.

She shoulders aside a dead sunflower to go further into the field and jerks back with a shriek when a smatter of small black somethings land on her shoulder. She stands on open ground, shuddering, brushing off her bare shoulder long after she's seen that it was just sunflower seeds, withered black carapaces now scattered in the dirt around her feet. She knows they just fell from the head when she knocked it, but she can't stop thinking of the word spat, that the sunflower spat the seeds at her on purpose.

JAY GOES TO the back door of the house, faltering on the steps when she feels the lack of a key in her hand. Then she shakes her head, laughing at herself: *city girl*. All through her childhood this door was never locked, and she and Yara clattered in and out all summer, the door banging in its frame, the checked curtain whipping in the breeze. Now that she looks at the door, it doesn't even have a keyhole; it's just a brass housing and a handle, like on an internal door. And anyway, everything is rotted to hell now; the wood is soft and yielding under her hand, and the door creaks open easily. The floor is more dirt than lino. Everything has been ripped out: the sink, the oven, the cabinets.

ON SPRING DAYS Jay and Yara went exploring, eating blackberries straight from the bush, even though Mam said they were covered in fox piss. They'd stay out collecting berries so late that the sun went down and the light dropped blue and the owls swooped over their heads, making them run shrieking with laughter through the bramble-choked lanes. When they got home their arms were all scratches and their bellies ached from eating too many berries. Mam said they were sick because of the fox piss, and didn't that just show them that it wasn't safe for girls out there, and that the world was a sickening place, and they were to be home before dark from now on. Jay and Yara laughed—quietly, under the covers where Mam couldn't hear— oooh, the dangers of the owl were terrible and oooh, the brambles were deadlier than the devil, and oooh, fox piss was coming to get the softest girls in the night.

YEARS LATER, JAY was in a bar, cigarette in hand and onto her fifth beer, and she mentioned to some pretty bit of rough the name of her hometown. Where all those folk went missing, said the pretty bit, and Jay laughed and waved her beer bottle like she was stirring cake mix and said nah, it's a boring old town, nothing ever happened there but scarecrows and fox piss. The pretty bit laughed in that way you do when you're not sure if something is a joke, but Jay stubbed out her cigarette and turned away because yes, people had gone missing, she remembered that now, at the time it had been in the papers and on people's lips but she hadn't cared.

She and Yara had been so busy in those days, preoccupied with hating their mother and trying to get their hair to do things it wouldn't and pretending they were from a big city and wanting their periods to come and then wanting their periods to go away. She'd always had a thought that her tiny shitty town might someday be known for her, that she'd do something amazing and when anyone heard the name of the town they'd say yeah, isn't that where Jay Kelly grew up? And instead it's known for nothing at all, just some people whose names she can't even remember, if she ever knew them at all.

JAY GOES INTO the living room. It's thick with shadows and she rips a sheet of newspaper off the window and lets in beams of dusty light. She's not the first one in here; there's a bucket with the remains of a fire in the middle of the room, and empty beer cans are snowpiled in the corners.

SOME DARK NIGHTS Pop would tell them ghost stories. There was a fire and hot chocolate and pajamas. It was *Little House on the Prairie*, though Jay had never read that book and didn't actually know what a prairie was—some kind of prayer?

Pop liked to tell the stories best on rainy nights. He told them all the classics: the hook, the rat, the babysitter, the licked hand, the phantom hitchhiker. Mam would be annoyed that he was winding up the girls before bed because she'd be the one who'd have to deal with the nightmares, but in the end she settled down to listen too. In the gaps between Pop's words and the rain, Jay was sure she could hear the sunflowers growing, the slow creak of their stalks like someone calling out to her.

JAY OPENS THE door to the cellar, but she doesn't go down the steps because she's not a fucking moron. It's dark and there's no electricity and the steps are probably rotted through. Even from up here she can smell the stink of it: wet earth, old blood, secret rot.

FOR A WHILE Pop turned the cellar into a mushroom farm. That sounds like it was a well-considered plan but it wasn't; one day he found a crop of mushrooms sprouting in the corner of the cellar's dirt floor, and he figured if they were already growing then he could make them grow more. He spent a whole season encouraging them, fertilising the earth under the house with bone meal and glass jars of frothing blood. He hadn't checked before he grew them which were the edible kind and which were the poisonous kind; he just grew what was already there. Every dinnertime Jay would fear mushroom soup, mushroom pie, mushrooms chopped and blended in secret into everything she ate.

But instead of being afraid she decided to laugh, and she and Yara would wind each other up that Pop was growing magic mushrooms, and they'd egg each other on to go and steal some so they could take them together, lean back on the soft pillows of Jay's bed and hallucinate freely, see new worlds blossom and flower around them as outside the sunflowers nodded and the scarecrows crept closer and their father sang, sang, all through the night.

So in the autumn dark Jay and Yara crept down the creaking cellar steps, ready for dares, ready to open new worlds—and found nothing but bare earth, the mushroom harvest gone. Pop had sold them, or given them away, or eaten them all himself.

JAY'S FIRST JOB out of school was at a mushroom farm, a proper industrial one with flickering fluorescent lights and the choking smell of dried pigs' blood and the dirt sucking at her boots as she tried to pick enough mushrooms to fill her container to the top so that she would have enough money for her rent. When she finished her shift and shucked off the heavy white boots and the thick white suit in the staffroom, replaced them with her cheap ballet pumps and her black skinny jeans and cotton vest, she felt so light and so dark, insubstantial, like she could slip into the shadows and no one would notice.

She remembers those times as being always night, always sitting gritty-eyed on the night bus with city lights swooping yolky past the window, always that place between waking and sleeping. She didn't sleep much then. Partly this was because she took on as many shifts as she could at the mushroom farm, but also because even when she got back to her tiny studio flat and fell into bed, she had such awful dreams. The dreams seemed to come before she'd fallen asleep, and they were always of the sunflowers, their heavy heads like hoods on drooping necks, their leaves twitching like hands.

JAY GOES UP the stairs carefully, catching her breath at every creak, but the old treads hold. The landing window is spiderweb-cracked and she can't see the dead field she knows is out there. She remembers now that it wasn't the sunflowers that bothered her, but the scarecrows. Every time she looked she was sure that there were more than before, though when she slowed down and counted them one by one it always came up the same. Now the sunflowers are withered and so are the scarecrows, all their clothes and flesh gone to leave the bare wooden crucifixes.

ONE NIGHT YARA was going out with her friends to see a film so she ran a bath, and at the very end of the water there was a splutter-splat and into the tub plopped a mess of tiny white bones, scraps of black velvet, and two rows of teeny-tiny razor teeth. Yara came screeching out of the bathroom and Mam smacked her hard on the bare thigh and told her to stop being such a princess and that there was no more hot water in the tank so she'd just have to wash in the water as it was. Jay can't remember now whether Mam scooped out the rotted bits of bat or not. She does remember that she made fun of Yara for weeks about her bat-bath.

Though now she realizes what she hadn't at the time: that bat was down to the bones, so couldn't have died in the water tank that day, so they'd all been having bat-baths for weeks.

JAY GOES INTO the bathroom. Or rather her head and upper body go in; she keeps her feet on the threshold because the floor of the bathroom is rotted, the boards smashed right through in places, the kitchen downstairs visible through the splinter-edged holes. Everything here has been ripped out too: the sink, the tub, even the toilet. The walls are gouged with holes and she figures maybe that was to get at the pipes, for copper or something.

She laughs then, out loud, standing there on the threshold, remembering the scrap metal dealer in town whose sign was always getting the 's' stolen off it, and how much she and Yara used to laugh at that, even though they had to spell out the word c-r-a-p as they didn't dare say it even when they didn't think Mam was listening.

ONE WINTER IT got so cold and the wind blew through the gaps in the walls and everyone complained about it, even Mam. Pop didn't put in heating or anything poncey like that—instead he built a thin inner wall of wooden matchboard, about a foot from the outside walls. It was warmer, after, though the rooms were much smaller and they had to push all the furniture closer to the middle. There was no space to walk around it so you had to climb over everything all the time like you were playing The Floor is Lava.

But Jay didn't mind that: what she did mind was sitting with her back to the walls, because she knew how big the space between the walls was, and she knew that it was big enough for a person. She taped squares of newspaper over all the knotholes in her bedroom walls so that no one could put their eye to it and watch her sleep.

JAY GOES INTO her bedroom. It's utterly empty: no bed, no chest of drawers, no posters pinned up, no line of trainers along the wall. She walks around the edge of the room, counting her steps for some reason. She thinks maybe she wants to check if the room is bigger than she remembers. When she was a child this house felt huge and tiny. It enclosed her whole world, everything she knew, everything she'd ever loved or hated; but also she felt trapped in it, held tight, her limbs stretching too wide for the walls. She reaches the empty space where the window used to be and looks out to the field of rotted sunflowers and straight away she's thrown back into the past.

The scratch of the straw against her skin as she hoisted them up, the straw hands stroking the nape of her neck, the footless legs bumping against her calves and trying to wrap around her ankles, the warmth of them. Pop telling her higher, lift higher, and she strained her arms as much as she could because they were heavy, much heavier than she thought they could be, and finally Pop got them tied to the crossbar and Jay could go inside.

AT NIGHT JAY would wait for Pop to come and tuck her in, which she desired and feared in equal parts, but she shouldn't have bothered because since he planted the sunflowers he was rarely ever in the house at all. When the moon came up and licked the world silver, Jay opened her window and anchored her feet against the bedstead and rested her belly on the splintery sill and closed her eyes and leaned right out so that she could hear Pop singing to the flowers and imagine that he was singing to her.

ONE NIGHT, DRIVING home with Pop, rain lashing and his breath steaming the windows and the smell of hops and fart filling the car, and Jay didn't know whether to make a joke about that or just keep quiet, and the country lanes were winding hairpins and the hills left her tummy behind like a rollercoaster. The trees seemed closer to the road than usual, like they were raising their arms to scoop her in and whisper secrets. Branches blatted along the roof of the car and wet leaves stroked Jay's window, and she wanted to roll it down and she turned her eyes front to ask Pop if she could and a big black shape loomed up fast and *smack* against the car's front bumper and *thuck* over the hood and Jay screwed up her eyes so she wouldn't accidentally see in the rearview mirror. The next second she snapped her eyes open and turned around in her seat but the road had dog-legged and she couldn't see behind them.

A deer, Pop said, hands tight on the wheel.

But, Jay said.

A fucking deer, Jay, he said, it shouldn't have been on the road.

And perhaps that should have changed everything; perhaps she should have felt differently about her father then. Scared of him, or suddenly sure that he was a monster; or reassured, even, more trusting that she was a kid and he was a grown-up and he knew what was and was not a deer. But it didn't change anything. Why would it? They lived in the country, and it's all nature there. In nature, things die.

JAY GOES BACK downstairs and through the kitchen and out of the house. She ducks her head and covers the back of her neck with her linked hands to protect them from skittering seeds and she goes into the sunflower field.

There are four crucifixes in the field but she only checks one. She digs a little way into the dry earth, feeling it stick under her nails and settle on her tongue. Her nail catches on something hard and she pulls it out. A tooth. It's big, a molar maybe. No filling. It could be hers, or Yara's; sacrificed to the Tooth Fairy and buried out here for some reason. She keeps digging. Her fingers close around a hank of hair and she tugs it from the earth, thinking it could be hers, it could be Mam's, remnants from a hairbrush or—the hair comes free and there's scalp attached, a rough square the size of a teabag.

Everything is spinning and she hears the dead seeds clacking and the sunflowers creaking and the empty crucifixes leaning down towards her and she digs, she digs, and all the way down it's teeth and hair and bones and teeth and hair and bones.

ABOUT THE CONTRIBUTORS

V.H. LESLIE's short stories have appeared in a range of publications and reprinted in a number of "Year's Best" anthologies. She is the author of a short story collection, *Skein and Bone*, and a novel, *Bodies of Water*, and her fiction has accrued a number of awards and nominations. She has been awarded fellowships for her writing at Hawthornden in Scotland and the Saari Institute in Finland and her non-fiction has appeared in *History Today*, *The Victorianist* and *Gramarye*.

J. T. GLOVER has published short fiction in *Best New Horror*, *The Children of Old Leech*, and *Pseudopod*, among other venues. His nonfiction has appeared in *Postscripts to Darkness*, *The Silent Garden*, and *Thinking Horror*. By day he is an academic librarian specializing in the humanities, and he studies literary horror, writers' research practices, and related topics. He lives in Virginia and can be found online at www.jtglover.com.

JOANNA PARYPINSKI is a college English instructor by day and a writer of the dark and strange by night. Her work has appeared in *Nightmare Magazine*, *Haunted Nights* (ed. Ellen Datlow and Lisa Morton), *The Beauty of Death 2: Death by Water* (Independent Legions), and *Vastarien*. Her forthcoming novel, *Dark Carnival*, will be released by Independent Legions in 2019. Living in the shadow of an old church that sits atop a hilly cemetery north of Los Angeles, she writes, grades essays, and plays her cello surrounded by the sounds of screaming neighbor children. Visit her website at www.joannaparypinski.com.

STEVE RASNIC TEM is a past winner of the Bram Stoker, World Fantasy, and British Fantasy Awards. His novels include the Stoker-winning *Blood Kin*, *UBO*, *Deadfall Hotel*, *The Book of Days*, and with his late wife Melanie, *Daughters* and *The Man on the Ceiling*. A writing handbook, *Yours To Tell: Dialogues on the Art & Practice of Writing*, also written with Melanie, appeared last year from Apex. His young adult Halloween novel *The Mask Shop of Doctor Blaack* will appear in October from HEX publishers. This winter will see his YA (& older) collection *Everything is Fine Now* from Omnium Gatherum. He has published over 430 short stories. The best of these are in *Figures Unseen: Selected Stories* from Valancourt Books.

L.S. JOHNSON lives in Northern California, where she feeds her cats by writing book indexes. She is the author of the gothic novellas *Harkworth*

Hall and *Leviathan*. Her first collection, *Vacui Magia*, was a finalist for the World Fantasy Award. Her novel remains vexedly in progress. Find her online at www.traversingz.com.

DANIEL BRAUM is the author of *The Night Marchers & Other Strange Tales* (Cemetery Dance/Grey Matter Press, 2016) and *The Wish Mechanics: Stories of the Strange and Fantastic* (Independent Legions Publishing, 2017). One of his strange stories is forthcoming in the anthology *Shivers 8* from Cemetery Dance. He can be found at bloodandstardust.wordpress.com.

M. LOPES DA SILVA is an author and artist from Los Angeles. Her fiction has appeared or is forthcoming in *Electric Literature, Glass and Gardens: Solarpunk Summers, Year's Best Transhuman SF 2017 Anthology*, and *Bikes in Space Vol. VI*. She has also written for *Blumhouse, The California Literary Review*, and *Queen Mob's Teahouse*. Her work frequently explores themes of obsession and anatomy, and boldly celebrates the fantastic and strange. She tends roses and cats alongside her partner, a film critic.

MATHEW ALLAN GARCIA lives in the Pacific Northwest with his family. His fiction has appeared in *Cicada, Fitting In: Historical Accounts of Paranormal Subcultures*, among others.

APRIL STEENBURGH is an author, freelance editor, and eBook formatter living in the Finger Lakes Region of New York. They share their small homestead with an overabundance of chickens and a very understanding husband. Their stories appear in *The Modern Fae's Guide to Surviving Humanity* (DAW), *Were-* (ZNB), and *Fell Beasts and Fair* (Spring Song Press). When not writing, they can be found working as a librarian and teaching at a local community college. Online, you can find April at www.aprilsteenburgh.com.

CHARLES WILKINSON's publications include *The Pain Tree and Other Stories* (London Magazine Editions, 2000). His stories have appeared in *Best Short Stories 1990* (Heinemann), *Best English Short Stories 2* (W.W. Norton, USA), *Best British Short Stories 2015* (Salt), and in genre magazines/anthologies such as *Black Static, The Dark Lane Anthology, Supernatural Tales, Theaker's Quarterly Fiction, Phantom Drift* (USA), *Bourbon Penn* (USA), *Shadows & Tall Trees* (Canada), *Nightscript* (USA), *Vastarien* (USA) and *Best Weird Fiction 2015* (Undertow Books, Canada). His anthology of strange tales and weird fiction, *A Twist in the Eye*, appeared from Egaeus Press; his second collection with the same publisher is due out soon. A full-length collection of his poetry is forthcoming from Eyewear. He lives in Wales.

FARAH ROSE SMITH is a writer, musician, and photographer whose work often focuses on the Gothic, Decadent, and Surreal. She authored *The Almanac of Dust*, *Eviscerator*, numerous short stories in horror and speculative anthologies, and is the founder and editor of *Mantid*, an anthology series promoting women and diverse writers in Weird Fiction. Her experimental film work has received festival accolades, including Best Short Screenplay (Rapture, 2016) at the Massachusetts Independent Film Festival and Best Experimental Film (The Atrocity Shoppe, 2015) at the Shawna Shea Film Festival. She lives in Queens, NY with her partner.

ARMEL DAGORN lives in Nantes, France with his partner and young son. He is the author of the short story collection *The Proverb Zoo*, and his fiction has appeared and is forthcoming in *Liminal Stories*, *The Shadow Booth*, *Tin House* online, and *Nightscript III*.

CATE GARDNER is a British horror author who lives in the concrete wilds of The Wirral with her husband, horror author Simon Bestwick. Her work has appeared in *The Dark*, *Black Static*, *Shimmer*, and *Postscripts*. Forthcoming for 2018 are stories in Stephen Jones' *The Mammoth Book of Halloween Stories*, Paul Finch's *Terror Tales of the North West*, and Johnny Mains' *Best British Horror*.

JACKSON KUHL writes and talks American history, pirates, privateers, and utopias. His fiction has appeared in *Black Static*, *Weirdbook*, and numerous anthologies. His e-book collection, *The Dead Ride Fast*, includes six stories of existential dread on the haunted frontier. www.jacksonkuhl.com.

CHRISTI NOGLE teaches writing and lives in Boise, Idaho with her partner Jim and their dogs and cats. Her short stories have appeared in *Pseudopod*, *Escape Pod*, *Lady Churchill's Rosebud Wristlet*, and *Nightscript III*. You can find Christi on Twitter @christinogle.

ROSS SMELTZER is a teacher in Dallas, Texas and writes as a hobby. His written work has been featured in several online publications, including *Sanitarium Magazine* and *Body Parts Magazine*. In addition, his horror short fiction has appeared in anthologies by Egaeus Press, Dragon's Roost Press, and Hic Dragones. In the coming year, his fiction will appear in *Deadsteam*, an anthology by Grimmer & Grimmer Books. He has also published a collection of three linked novellas in 2016. He is currently working on a novel.

JENNIFER LORING's short fiction has been published widely both online and in print, including the anthologies *Tales from the Lake*, vol. 1 and vol. 4. Longer work includes the novel *Those of My Kind*, published by Omnium Gatherum, and the novella *Conduits* from Lycan Valley Press. Jenn is a member of the International Thriller Writers (ITW) and the Horror Writers Association (HWA). She holds an MFA in Writing Popular Fiction from Seton Hill University with a concentration in horror fiction and teaches online in SNHU's College of Continuing Education. Jenn lives with her husband in Philadelphia, PA, where they are owned by a turtle and two basset hounds. Find her online at www.jennifertloring.com.

TIM JEFFREYS escaped the north of England more than a decade ago, and now lives in the greener surrounds of Bristol. Despite valiant efforts including studying Graphic Arts and Design at University, his original career plans went completely wrong and he ended up working in a tiny office in a Dental Hospital. The screams he sometimes hears from the clinics occasionally make it into the strange stories he writes when no one's looking. His short fiction has appeared in *Weirdbook*, *Not One of Us*, and *Turn to Ash*, among other publications, and his latest collection *The Real Rachel Winterbourne and Other Stories* is available now. Follow his progress at www.timjeffreys.blogspot.co.uk.

ELANA GOMEL teaches at the Department of English and American Studies at Tel-Aviv University. She is the author of six non-fiction books and numerous articles. As a fiction writer, she has published more than 40 fantasy and science fiction stories in *The Singularity*, *New Realms*, *Mythic*, and many other magazines; and in several anthologies, including *People of the Book* and *Apex Book of World Science Fiction*. Her fantasy novel *A Tale of Three Cities* came out in 2013 and her novella *Dreaming the Dark* in 2017. Two more novels are scheduled to be published this year.

MIKE WEITZ lives in Kansas City, Missouri with his wife and three children. In addition to horror, he delights in writing science fiction and adult thrillers. Mainly influenced by Stephen King, H.P. Lovecraft, and Robert Bloch, Weitz spends every evening in a darkened corner of his basement, dreaming up terrors and grim tales that have yet to be told. "Rainheads" is his first published work.

KIRSTY LOGAN is the author of the novels *The Gloaming* and *The Gracekeepers*, short story collections *A Portable Shelter* and *The Rental Heart & Other Fairytales*, flash fiction chapbook *The Psychology of Animals Swallowed Alive*, and short memoir *The Old Asylum in the Woods at the Edge of the*

Town Where I Grew Up. Her books have won the Lambda Literary Award, Polari Prize, Saboteur Award, Scott Prize and Gavin Wallace Fellowship. Her work has been translated into Japanese and Spanish, recorded for radio and podcasts, exhibited in galleries and distributed from a vintage Wurlitzer cigarette machine. She lives in Glasgow with her wife. Her next book is a collection of horror stories, *The Night Tender*.

C.M. MULLER lives in St. Paul, Minnesota with his wife and two sons—and, of course, all those quaint and curious volumes of forgotten lore. He is related to the Norwegian writer Jonas Lie and draws much inspiration from that scrivener of old. His tales have appeared in *Shadows & Tall Trees*, *Supernatural Tales*, *Weirdbook*, and a host of other venues. *Hidden Folk*, his debut story collection, is due to be released in late 2018. He hopes you have enjoyed the twenty-one tales collected herein.

———◆———

For more information about NIGHTSCRIPT, please visit:

www.chthonicmatter.wordpress.com/nightscript